DEATH ON THE BURNT OCEAN

BOOK ONE OF THE TALES OF THE TERRITORIES

PETER WACHT

Death on the Burnt Ocean
By Peter Wacht

Book 1 of The Tales of the Territories

This book is a work of fiction. Names, characters, places, and incidents are the product of the author's imagination or are used fictitiously. Any resemblance to actual events, locales, or persons, living or dead, is coincidental.

Cover design by Ebooklaunch.com

Published in the United States by Kestrel Media Group LLC.

ISBN: 978-1-950236-32-9

eBook ISBN: 978-1-950236-33-6

Library of Congress Control Number: 2022923775

❃ Created with Vellum

ALSO BY PETER WACHT

THE REALMS OF THE TALENT AND THE CURSE

THE TALES OF CALEDONIA

Blood on the White Sand (short story)*

The Diamond Thief (short story)*

The Protector

The Protector's Quest

The Protector's Vengeance

The Protector's Sacrifice

The Protector's Reckoning

The Protector's Resolve

The Protector's Victory

THE TALES OF THE TERRITORIES

Stalking the Blood Ruby (short story)*

A Fate Worse Than Death (short story)*

Death on the Burnt Ocean

Monsters in the Mist (Forthcoming 2023)

The Dance of the Daggers (Forthcoming 2023)

Bloody Hunt for Freedom (Forthcoming 2024)

THE SYLVAN CHRONICLES

(Complete 9-Book Series available at Amazon)

The Legend of the Kestrel

The Call of the Sylvana

The Raptor of the Highlands

The Makings of a Warrior

The Lord of the Highlands

The Lost Kestrel Found

The Claiming of the Highlands

The Fight Against the Dark

The Defender of the Light

THE RISE OF THE SYLVAN WARRIORS

*Through the Knife's Edge (short story)**

* Free short stories can be downloaded from my author website at PeterWachtBooks.com.

YOUR FREE SHORT STORY IS WAITING

THE DIAMOND THIEF

This short story is a prelude to the events in my series *The Tales of Caledonia* and is free to readers who receive my newsletter.

Join Peter's newsletter and get your FREE short story.
PeterWachtBooks.com

SETTING THE STAGE

The Tales of the Territories continue the adventures of Bryen Keldragan and Aislinn Winborne as they travel across the Burnt Ocean to the Territories, what will eventually become the Kingdoms of *The Sylvan Chronicles*.

The events occur more than one thousand years before the happenings in *The Sylvan Chronicles* and take place in the lands far to the west of Caledonia that have been opened for colonization thanks to territorial grants sold by the deceased King Corinthus Beleron.

There Bryen and Aislinn will take on new challenges, make new friends and enemies, and continue to battle those who have turned to the Curse.

In the Territories, sometimes called New Caledonia, as in the other realms, the ability to use the Talent sets apart the person gifted with this unique skill. But being able to use the Talent is only part of the dynamic. For if a Magus chooses to follow a darker path, the Talent becomes the Curse.

Both *The Sylvan Chronicles* and *The Tales of Caledonia* are a part of the larger world of *The Realms of the Talent and the Curse*.

1

A DISAPPOINTING HUNT

"Can't you run faster than that, soldier!" The man standing guard at the entrance to the tower, a very large blacksmith's hammer held in his hand, had to bend down to fit through the doorway without banging his head. He was glad to be free of the confining space as he stepped out onto the grass. He didn't like being locked away from the outside and the fresh air. It made him edgy. "You need to lay off the ale, Bertie. It's all going to your gut."

Bertie huffed and puffed his way up the slope. The once musclebound figure, now going a bit soft around the edges, was no more than a shadow in the descending grey mist.

For just a second, the man by the door, the hilt of his sword peeking out above his shoulder, thought that Bertie was carrying three large sacks across his broad shoulders. It wasn't until the soldier turned farmer was less than a dozen yards away that the large figure in the doorway grinned, finally able to pick out what Bertie was hauling.

"You try carrying three children up that wretched slope, Duff," muttered Bertie. He struggled to catch his breath as he let down the two daughters who had been slipping from their perches as he sprinted up the hill. He kept the youngest, a boy no more than two years old with his hands twisted tightly in his father's hair, on his shoulders as he ducked inside. "Is Winnie here?"

"She is," Duff replied, giving Bertie a friendly slap across his back for his effort as the man passed by him, glad that he had made it. "Almost everyone else from the village is here as well."

"Not all?" asked Bertie. He turned back through the entryway, the son on his shoulders pulling with greater vigor on his hair, obviously frightened as the thin wisps of white began to darken to a thicker grey. Bertie carefully extricated what few strands he had left on his head from his son's tight grasp. It wouldn't be long now, so they would need to be quick. "Do we need to go back out?"

Duff smiled, nodding his thanks for Bertie's generous, likely suicidal, offer. Bertie was a brave man. Duff had seen it with his own eyes more times than he could count. The soldier in Bertie had never really left, just as had been the case for him and so many others in the village. But there was a key difference between them now.

Bertie had a young family. Duff didn't. If anyone went back out into the encroaching fog, it would be him. Only him.

"We should be all right," replied Duff, giving Bertie a gentle nudge so that he would follow his children into the tower. "Why don't you go find Winnie and see what kind of trouble those twins of yours have already gotten into."

Bertie snorted at that. "You've got that right. Nothing but headaches from sunup to sundown. That's why I spend so much time in the fields."

Duff chuckled, hearing the love in his former corporal's voice. With Bertie and his family now safely within the stone broch, Duff turned his gaze back to the valley that stretched out below him. The valley that was disappearing slowly before his eyes beneath a smothering blanket of thick fog.

It wouldn't be long now, Duff mused. He chafed at the circumstances he and the other Highlanders had to deal with, yet they had no choice. Another night hiding in the fortified tower. An occurrence that was becoming all too frequent. How long they would be locked away was anyone's guess.

Just the thought of it was making him itch. This was no way to live. He had journeyed across the Burnt Ocean from Caledonia for the freedom and opportunity that could be found in the Territories. Not to be shut away cowering in fear whenever the fog descended.

He studied the encroaching grey mist as he had done so many times before. It looked no different than the fog he had played hide and seek in as a child while growing up near Roo's Nest. But it was.

Because this fog didn't come off the ocean. Although the Sea of Mist was just a few leagues to the east, this gloom drifted down from the north, no doubt having started out in the Wyld. It then tracked the coast through the Northern Peaks, all the way across the Northern Steppes, finally settling here deep in the northeastern Highlands.

It was an unnatural gloom. Heavy, deadening, and with a much too light touch of dewy moisture compared to what you would expect from a mist coming off the sea. The sun couldn't brighten the haze once it fixed in place, and with that suffocating fog came a sense of palpable evil lurking within, an evil with very sharp claws.

Duff wasn't a superstitious man by nature, not after all that he had seen fighting in Caledonia and beyond his Kingdom's borders. There was little that frightened him, and almost nothing that could take him by surprise, because he had seen it all before.

At first he had scoffed at the stories that he had heard from farther north when the fog had first appeared more than a year before. More like nightmares, actually, likely told by those knee deep in their cups.

He began to believe when that fog made its way into the Highlands with a startling regularity. The fog that some had begun to call the Murk, claiming that it was actually an extension of the terrifying gloom that covered the wild land far to the northeast.

He knew for certain that the tales were true when he glimpsed the hazy figures for himself, those nightmares becoming flesh and blood. Tall and lanky, the monsters in the mist were no more than vague shapes.

No one in the Highlands had ever gotten a good look at one. And if they had, it had been right before they had become one of the creatures' many victims, and they certainly weren't in a position to reveal their attackers' secrets.

Although not well seen, these monsters were well known. These beasts radiated a sense of menace. A sense that they cared little for life. That they cared only for taking it.

The Wraiths.

So named by a trader who had made the long journey from the Wyld and explained that's what those poor souls living in the coastal cities just south of the Murk called them.

The monsters that hunted in the fog. The monsters that couldn't be seen unless they wanted to be seen. The monsters that couldn't be heard. The monsters that couldn't be killed.

They were silent assassins, the remains of their bloody work visible once the gloom drifted back to the north. No one caught out in the open when the fog settled over the land had yet survived. The only way to avoid a gruesome and terrifying end was to find a strong, defensible shelter before the thick grey tendrils blinded you.

A shelter like the broch that Duff stood in front of.

When the Murk had first appeared, a delegation of Highlanders led by Duff had gone to see the Governor of the Territory. Appointed through a grant given by then King Corinthus Beleron, Torstan Sharperson, a younger brother of the Duke of Sharston, had listened to their entreaties with a smile on his face. He had spoken the appropriate words of support. He had offered his condolences for the people murdered by the creatures that came with the fog.

The callow lord had assured the people for whom he was responsible, and from whom he collected taxes, that he would study the threat and do what was needed to protect against this new, unforeseen danger. That study apparently was still ongoing, as Duff and the others had seen or heard nothing more from their supposed lord since, or at least that's what the tax collectors said.

The Highland Guard was nowhere to be found and those greedy bastards who picked every coin out of your pocket appeared with greater frequency than the Murk. When they did, they sought more than just a pound of flesh.

It had been a wasted effort, Duff knew. Governor Sharperson was little more than a thief in a lord's clothing.

Duff stopped himself, his mind always going down a road better left untraveled when he considered how badly the Governor had failed his people. Besides, he was giving thieves a bad name. Most of the thieves he knew at least had some sense of honor, a set of rules they played by.

Torstan Sharperson made up his own rules as he went along, changing them whenever the whim or necessity took him. In reality, he was no different than any of the other nobles granted Territories by Corinthus Beleron.

These lords and ladies who played as Governors in New Caledonia operated by one simple rule. What's mine is mine, and what's yours should be mine.

Just thinking about the Highland Governor's response, or rather the lack thereof, made Duff's blood boil. Several dozen people murdered in just the past year by these Wraiths and nothing done about it. Not a single thing.

"Are they here yet?"

Duff turned toward the worried, crinkled face of Martin, the blacksmith who lived at the edge of the village and served the surrounding region. He had gathered his family and gotten to the fortified tower at the first signs of the fog, the bell atop the broch ringing loudly and echoing off the surrounding peaks to warn those living in the valley of the rapidly approaching threat.

Martin was worried. He had yet to see any sign of his sister or her family. They lived farther up the slopes to the northeast, their goats and sheep enjoying the grass at the higher elevation.

"No, not yet. But I'm sure they'll be here soon. They always make it."

Martin nodded, taking a deep breath to calm himself. He, too, was a former soldier in the Royal Guard. The idea of a fight never fazed him. He would take on any man or beast without a thought to protect his family. Even though he knew just as Duff did that you couldn't fight the monsters that stalked the fog. Not with any hope of surviving.

In the Murk, for all intents and purposes you were blind, unable to see more than a few feet in any direction in the billowing grey. The Wraiths could hear you. The Wraiths could see you. But you couldn't see them and often you didn't hear them until their steel or claws slid into your flesh. Because the Wraiths moved as if they were a part of the fog while you stumbled about.

The Wraiths were meant to be there. The Highlanders weren't.

If Martin had to enter the fog to look for his sister and her family, he would without a second thought. But he wouldn't be marching toward a combat. He would be going to his death.

There was no good way to defend yourself if you couldn't see what you were fighting.

The Highlanders had learned that quickly, and they had taken what action they could to protect themselves even faster. Not caring to wait for help from a Governor who seemed to have little interest in helping them if he couldn't help himself at the same time, they modeled their defense on a series of small fortresses that Duff had visited while serving near the Trench. They built more than a dozen brochs in the northeastern Highlands, each roundhouse tower situated in the center of the larger Highland communities.

Each broch had a single entrance with a three-foot-thick oak door wrapped in steel, hinges on the inside with slots for three steel bars to be set in place once the door was locked. The antechamber narrowed to half the size of the doorway the farther you walked in so that a broad man had to turn to the side to walk through, an essential modification to ensure the safety of those taking refuge in the tower.

If somehow the creatures of the Murk broke through the door, one soldier could easily hold the narrow gap. To make the passage even more lethal, slits in the wall on each side allowed for spears and pikes to be thrust through, making the entryway a death trap.

Once past the entrance, a spiral staircase wound its way between the inner and outer walls, connecting the galleries on each level that served as temporary shelters and storerooms. Each broch was eighty feet in diameter and one hundred feet in height, the walls always ten feet thick. Halfway up the towers there were narrow slits for archers, the spaces so small that not even a child could climb through them.

On top of the tower was a large pyre, the fire used to signal other brochs before the Murk consumed the flames. More important was the massive bell that could be heard for leagues around and was the first warning that the creatures lurking in the mist approached.

There was also space for archers to fire and a pile of large rocks that could be dropped from the parapet. Useful defenses against more conventional foes. Not so the Wraiths.

Few Highlanders remained atop the parapet when the fog came in, the creatures having an unnatural ability to scale the stone with their clawed feet and hands. When the bell sounded the inhabitants of the broch usually closed the thick shutters and ensured that the door that let out onto the roof, designed just like the main entrance below, was bolted and guarded.

Then they waited. For however long it took. The main entrance wouldn't be opened again until the fog cleared.

"Sally!" yelled Martin. "Hurry!"

The blacksmith had caught the faint movement in the thickening fog, his sister appearing out of the grey. She ran up the slope as fast as she could while holding onto the hands of two of her children, almost dragging them behind her across the large green that surrounded the tower because they were struggling to keep up with their mother. Martin ran out and picked up both children, hustling them through the door.

Benyen, her husband, came right behind her, a small child under each arm like he was carrying sacks of wheat. The boy and girl were laughing and giggling, obviously enjoying the ride, not seeing their father's ashen face and the spark of fear behind his eyes.

"They're already out there," he whispered.

"How could you tell?" asked Duff. Because of their ability to move without being seen and without making a sound, the Wraiths usually couldn't be identified in the Murk unless they wanted to be. When they wanted you to know that they were watching. That they were waiting to kill you.

"I could feel them," Benyen replied.

Duff nodded, not questioning his friend's explanation. He

was a former tracker in the Royal Guard. He had explained to Duff once while they shared an ale in the only tavern in this small village that much of what he did as a tracker wasn't based on what he saw or heard, but rather on what he felt.

Admittedly, they were both quite sloshed at the time, but Duff had never been a tracker, so he was in no position to dispute his friend's answer. And he had yet to come up against an instance when Benyen's feeling hadn't been right on target, both in Caledonia and here in the Highlands.

"Where's Mari?" asked Sally, standing in the doorway, fear and desperation for her oldest daughter coloring her voice.

"I thought she was here with you," said Benyen. "You didn't bring her from the house?"

"I thought she was with you," countered Sally, a look of terror spreading across her face.

"Where was she before the bell rang?" asked Duff.

"She was tending to the goats along the ridge to the northeast," said Benyen.

A sick feeling settled in the pit of Duff's stomach. That was the direction from which the fog had come. From the direction it always came. The retired sergeant cursed silently.

"You all get inside. I'll get her."

"I'll go with you," said Benyen. "I can ..."

"You can move faster than I can and more quietly," continued Duff, taking in his friend's slim frame that seemed to allow him to move with a speed and grace that he had only seen one other time, several years before.

Duff hadn't wanted to attend the gladiatorial games in Tintagel. If truth be told, he had seen enough blood and gore for a lifetime and had no desire to see any more.

Even so, he didn't want to explain that to his friends. They were quite intent on taking in the spectacle, so in the end he acquiesced to their demand.

Strangely, when it was over, he had valued the experience.

Not for the unnecessary violence and slaughter. No, that had sickened him.

Rather it had given him the chance to watch the Volkun fight. The Wolf. The greatest gladiator in the land, and much to his surprise a young man at least a decade and a half younger than he was who exhibited the seasoning and savvy of a hardened soldier.

It was an experience that he would never forget, and it had confirmed for him that it was time for him to move on, to leave Caledonia and the army and make a new life for himself. Someplace where he could avoid the fighting that, although he excelled at it, he had come to dread. The fighting that unfortunately seemed to have followed him across the Burnt Ocean to his new home in the Highlands.

"But I don't have a family," Duff finished with a strong hand on Benyen's shoulder. "You do."

"She's my oldest daughter, Duff. I can't leave her out there."

Duff gripped Benyen's shoulder a bit more strongly, hoping that his bruising grip infused a sense of confidence within his friend, making sure that he caught Benyen's eyes and kept them on his own. "You're not leaving her. I'm going to get her."

Benyen stared at his former sergeant for several seconds. He had known Duff ever since he had joined the Royal Guard. Usually his sergeant had a smile on his face. When there wasn't, then you knew that there was going to be trouble. And you never wanted to get into trouble with Duff.

Duff wasn't smiling now. His hard expression just made the man more frightening than he already was, inadvertently aided by the wound that he had taken across his scalp that extended from the back of his head around the left side to just beneath his jaw. The hair had never grown back where he had been sliced open, so Duff kept his head shaved.

Thanks to the Magus who healed him, the wound was just a very thin, white scar rather than a jagged patch of flesh.

It still proved to be unsettling to look at, however, Benyen always wondering how his friend had survived such an injury.

Duff had told him once that it was because he had such a hard head. After getting to know Duff, Benyen had believed him.

It was because of that wound that Benyen finally nodded, then stepped back. Duff was the toughest man he knew. He would bring Mari safely to the broch or he would die trying.

Duff returned the nod, then stepped out into the billowing fog.

"Tommie!"

"Yes, Sergeant!" replied a slim woman wearing spectacles. She, too, had served in the Royal Guard with Duff along with many of the other men and women in this Highland settlement. Archer by trade, some said that she could hit an ant at one hundred yards. After watching her in a skirmish against a band of brigands, no one was willing to challenge that assumption.

"Is that the last?"

Tommie looked at the paper she carried, running through the list of the families quickly. "Yes, Sergeant. That's the last."

Duff nodded, then started walking down the slope toward the northeast, calling over his shoulder, "Lock it up."

"But Sergeant ..."

Tommie never had a chance to complete her protest, the fog swallowing Duff after he had taken only a dozen steps. Growling in irritation, Tommie stepped back and then called to Benyen and Martin for help. Together, the three of them pushed the heavy door in place, locking it, then settling the three bars in the brackets across the oak and steel.

Turning away and heading up the spiral staircase that led toward the balustrade, Tommie wanted to check the door that led to the roof to make sure that it was just as tightly sealed. As she did so, she wished Duff well and hoped that she would see her sergeant again.

Even so, Tommie was a practical woman. She refused to allow her hopes to get too high. Few ever survived the Murk, especially on their own. To be caught in the fog was a death sentence.

Likely even for Duff. A man who should have been dead, but apparently couldn't be killed.

WHY DIDN'T I follow my brother when I had the chance, Duff wondered as he slowly, ever so slowly, navigated down a steep, narrow path that led to the long grass along the cliffs that Benyen's goats preferred. He could barely see where he was walking, moving more by memory and touch than sight as the grey mist swirled around him.

His brother had received a grant from the King to settle the Western Isle, which was just off the coast of the Ferranagh Territory and on the other side of the continent. Maybe that's why he hadn't made it out there yet.

It had been a long trip across the Burnt Ocean. Duff had gotten tired of the storms that seemed to strike every other day, sending the merchant vessel dipping into the troughs and then surging over powerful crests, much to his displeasure his stomach mimicking the motion of the ship.

That and those massive wakes that he had spied from the crow's nest. Thankfully those creatures swimming through the sea were not interested in his ship, because if they had been he knew the likely result.

Because of all that, when he landed in Ballinasloe, he had no desire to get back on the water. Instead, he had decided to visit with several of his former soldiers who had settled in the northeastern Highlands. He had thought that he would only be in this rugged, beautiful land for a few weeks at most, the urge to leave Caledonia, the desire to see more of the Territories, pushing him farther west.

Yet in just a few days that desire to move on had gone quiet. He had been in the Highlands for almost five years now.

He liked it here. He liked being with his friends. And he couldn't bring himself to leave in part because of the Murk.

When that cursed fog rolled in, and with it the terrors that it hid, he couldn't make himself go even though it was the smart thing to do. Of course, Duff had never been accused of being too smart.

He had been accused of being too stubborn, of failing to give his superiors the respect that they believed they deserved, of offering unwanted opinions, of refusing to accept orders from fools ... and of several other faults that he tended to ignore or forget when doing so was convenient. But he had never been accused of being too smart.

And he had never been accused of running from a fight. In consequence, he was still here with his friends, making a good living as a hunter and trapper, and helping out whenever they needed it, whether with the flocks or the crops.

Or wayward children caught out in the fog.

He stopped again, just as he stopped every few steps, spending more time listening than moving, seeking any sign, no matter how small, that a Wraith might be near. Because the Wraiths were always near when the Murk came.

About to begin his downward journey again, Duff heard a scrape maybe ten feet to his left. The noise sent a shiver down his spine. He kept one foot above the ground, not wanting to give himself away. Not wanting to cede the advantage of surprise just yet.

He had his sword strapped to his back and several large knives on each thigh. He liked to be prepared for anything. But his weapon of choice was the large hammer that the fingers of his right hand gripped almost delicately.

The thick wooden handle tapered to the steel head, a weapon and implement that many a blacksmith could barely lift much less swing with any effectiveness. In his hands, however, the steel felt right. As if it was meant to be there and was simply an extension of his arm.

A faint shadow coming down the gentle slope drifted toward him. He could see nothing from the knees up. He pulled back his arm, ready to strike, his focus solely on the threat that approached.

His shallow breaths thundered in his ears. A cold sweat ran down his back. Then a soft bleat released the tension that had been building up within him, and he had to fight not to laugh with relief.

A goat trod carefully down the rocks, rubbing against his leg in welcome as he passed. Duff closed his eyes in thanks for just a second. At least he knew that he was close.

With this fog, in addition to worrying about the Wraiths, he feared that he might walk right off a ledge. Wanting to avoid that possibility, he allowed the goat to precede him, showing him the way, and hoping that the animal's movement would mask his own approach.

Duff continued along the trail. Slowly. Carefully. Vigilant with each step. Doing all that he could to ensure that he didn't make a sound.

Once, he thought he saw a large shape coming toward him from his right side. That froze him in place. But he couldn't even be sure that he had seen what he had thought he had seen, the figure passing through the fog so swiftly.

Then another shadow appeared, this one feeling more substantial. The tall silhouette remained there above him on the crest of the hill. Not moving. Not making a sound.

Watching.

Waiting.

Hunting.

Duff wasn't certain that the shadow was a Wraith. Nevertheless, he couldn't be certain that it wasn't, and he had no desire to find out.

He remained where he was even when his knees began to ache, then throb, the wear and tear of decades of military service catching up to him at the absolute worst time. He ignored the pain, knowing that it was nothing compared to what it would feel like to have a Wraith's knife slice across his throat.

Now he knew what it felt like to be hunted, and he would be the first to admit that he hated the feeling. He wasn't afraid to fight a Wraith. It's just that if he was going to combat one of these monsters, he wanted to be able to see the creature so that he could have at least some possibility of success.

In the Murk, all the advantages played to the Wraiths. If he were found, he was nothing more than a sitting duck to be slaughtered at a Wraith's convenience.

With those negative thoughts taking up residence in his mind, he stayed perfectly still, barely breathing, his eyes fixated on the shadow in the mist that was no more than a dozen feet away. As the minutes passed agonizingly slowly, he realized that he'd have little chance of getting a blow in with his hammer.

If the shape in the fog was indeed a creature of the Murk, then the Wraith would be on him before he could even take a step with his rickety knees. His best chance was to grab a dagger from a sheath on his thigh and hope that the Wraith slipped coming down the slope and fell on him. That certainly wasn't a good way to win a combat, but it might be the only way in his current circumstances.

Several minutes more passed before his patience was finally

rewarded. The figure in the fog either moved away, disappeared, or was never there to begin with.

Duff didn't care. The only reason he had been able to see the shape in the first place was because he was near the coast and a strong breeze off the Sea of Mist had thinned out the usually dense grey. Still, he waited several more minutes before finally pushing himself forward, his aching knees screaming in protest.

He ignored the pain, working out the stiffness as he continued farther down the trail, step by slow step. Every so often another soft bleat sounded to either side, confirming that Duff was moving in the right direction.

As he stopped every few feet, the mist caressing him as he listened for anything that might suggest that a Wraith was near, his thoughts turned to how to find Mari in the fog. He should have given that a great deal more thought before he left the safety of the broch.

Her father had been an excellent soldier. A good fighter. Smart. Creative. Disciplined. Always prepared. The last suggested to Duff that Benyen probably had taught all his children what to do if they were ever caught out in the fog.

Bringing to mind a mental map of Benyen's property along the cliffs, Duff thought of the most likely place where he would have taught his children to go. Somewhere Benyen would have a camouflaged shelter or a place to hide.

Then he had it. Benyen had shown him just a few months before while they were clearing a patch of ground so that he could expand his garden. There was a cut along the cliff that led down to a small cave. If you didn't know what you were looking for, you would walk right past the trail to get there.

Duff continued down the path in that direction, moving no faster than his grandmother, who had two bad hips, would have, stopping and listening for a minute or more after taking only two or three steps. It was a slow process, nerve-wracking, but so far, so good. No more menacing shapes appeared in the fog, and in just a few minutes the cut between two large boulders, one resting right in front of the other, appeared in front of him.

He waited several more minutes before disappearing between the rocks, worried that a Wraith might be watching him.

The monsters in the mist were smart. They were also cunning. He didn't want to lead one of the creatures toward Mari if she was hiding here.

Yet, it seemed that his caution was unnecessary. No sound. No movement. There was nothing to suggest that he had anything to worry about.

Duff continued down the narrow trail, walking very carefully, not wanting to make a noise with all of the loose rock beneath his feet. When he finally reached the end of the path, the dark mouth of the cave opening before him, he stopped sooner than he wanted to.

Something wasn't right. He could feel it immediately. There was a presence ahead of him that shouldn't be there.

An unexpected though welcome flash of sunlight that broke through the fog and lit the first few feet of the entrance to the cave confirmed it for him.

For just the blink of an eye, before the fog blocked the sun once again, Duff caught sight of a tall figure standing just a few feet inside the grotto. The incredibly brief glimpse still gave him a good look at the creatures who were terrorizing the Highlands when the Murk came in from the north, or at least as good as he was going to get with the Wraith's back turned.

Unnaturally tall and thin, the Wraith wore what Duff took to be a whitish grey leather armor, its unprotected flesh shifting between shades of white and grey. He understood now how the creatures hid so well in the fog. Their natural coloring allowed them to blend in perfectly.

What really drew his eye were the weapons that the Wraith held between his exceedingly long clawed fingers. He had never seen anything like them before. Three-foot-long rods with a grip in the center, half-crescent blades on each end curling in opposite directions. It was as if two long daggers had been melded together at the handle.

Nasty pieces of work and certainly to be avoided. Then Duff realized that he wouldn't be able to. The Wraith had taken another step deeper into the cave.

Thankfully, the Wraith hadn't sensed that Duff was only a few feet behind him, the creature's attention focused on the back of the hollow. That could mean only one thing.

When the Wraith took another silent step deeper into the darkness, Duff struck.

On silent feet of his own, he rushed toward the Wraith, swinging his hammer with destructive accuracy, the metal head crushing the creature's right knee. The debilitating injury did nothing more than elicit a hiss of pain from the Wraith, the creature tottering because of the blow though not falling to the ground. At the same time the injured Wraith swung his twin-bladed weapon behind him, hoping to catch Duff unprepared.

The Sergeant suspected that the Wraith would make such a move. It's what he would have done in his place. That's why he was able to avoid the steel.

Because he was ready, he knocked the blind swing away with his hammer. Before the Wraith could turn fully, Duff pulled a dagger from the sheath on his thigh and drove it into the back of the creature's other knee.

He had thought about trying for the Wraith's lower back, then decided against it, not knowing if such a strike would kill the creature because of his armor. In his opinion it was better to go with the sure stab and disable the Wraith, who finally collapsed to his knees on the rocky ground.

Duff swung one more time with his hammer, not wanting to

miss such a good opportunity. The metal struck true, slamming into the Wraith's head and sending him to the dirt.

"Mari!" Duff hissed as quietly as he could.

In just a heartbeat, she was there right in front of him, Benyen's oldest daughter, all of ten years old, ready to defend herself with a dagger in her hand.

"Are you all right?" Duff whispered, kneeling down and hugging the young girl to him.

"Yes, Uncle Duff," she mumbled into his shoulder, her voice calm. She appeared to be less upset about being out in the fog than he was.

"Good. Then let's go."

Duff pushed himself to his feet, his knees protesting the entire time. He was about to head back outside the cave, Mari's hand in his own, when a tall, strangely thin figure that was barely more than a shadow coalesced out of the grey haze.

THE WRAITH STOOD in the entrance to the cave, Duff having a hard time picking out the creature. The fog had thickened during the fight with his now wounded, hopefully dead, adversary. He did see the Wraith blocking their way turn his head to his left, taking in the crumpled form of his brethren.

"Mari, get behind me," Duff ordered gently.

Mari complied quickly, her eyes widening in terror as the Wraith took a few more steps into the cave, stopping no more than a spear's length away from Duff.

Duff crouched, one foot in front of the other, hammer raised above his shoulder. He wasn't a fool. He couldn't be a fool to have survived for so long as a soldier.

He was a realist. He knew just how fast and deadly a Wraith could be. Therefore, he had no illusions as to how this combat would end. He could only hope that he could create an opening so that Mari might be able to slip away.

"You will die here."

Duff stared at the Wraith, stunned. Though some of the words were difficult to understand because of the peculiar accent, Duff was able to comprehend the monster.

"Yes, that's a very strong possibility," Duff replied as calmly as he could, although his heart was beating so fast that he thought he was going to pass out.

"You do not fear death," said the Wraith, nodding as if he had just made a great discovery, still having made no move to come forward farther into the cave.

Apparently, the creature wanted to have a conversation. Duff was more than happy to accommodate him, enjoying whatever time he had left in this world while he searched for a solution to his dilemma.

"I don't," replied Duff, who then clarified. "I don't want to die, but I don't fear it."

The Wraith nodded again, although Duff couldn't tell for sure with the fog swirling around the figure. "The other humans I have killed have always begged before I cut their throats."

"I won't beg."

"Do you really want to try your hand against me? You took my comrade through deception. You will not do the same with me. Better just to accept your fate."

"Looks like I don't have much choice," Duff responded with a shrug. "Better to fight than to surrender. You might kill me, but it will be on my terms, not yours."

In the silence that followed, the Wraith appeared to consider what Duff had said, then shook his head as if he had reached an important decision. "Then I will kill you quickly. You have courage. You deserve a swift death."

Duff didn't know what to make of that comment. Should he

be flattered? Should he thank the monster? He didn't have the chance to contemplate it further.

The Wraith burst forward, his movement so fast that Duff could barely track it. Still, he got his hammer square to his body, blocking the Wraith's slash. Duff thought that he was doing well until the blade in the Wraith's other hand sliced across his shoulder.

Gritting his teeth against the pain, Duff pivoted away from the bloody steel, swinging his hammer toward the Wraith's unprotected side. The creature leapt over the hammer with a remarkable dexterity and immediately rushed forward again, Duff having some difficulty keeping up with the Wraith's attacks. The retired sergeant survived the onslaught by blocking or avoiding the most dangerous strikes and ignoring the dozen bloody slices that welled up with a deep red on his arms and across his chest.

The wounds were shallow. He would live. For now.

"You will die, human," said the Wraith, stepping back, making sure that he continued to block the entrance to the cave, not wanting either of his prey to have the chance to bolt like a hare.

"You're probably right," said Duff, seemingly unconcerned by the possibility.

Before he could get out the rest of what he wanted to say, a streak of steel shot right by his head. Mari's throw wasn't perfect, but it was good enough, the dagger spinning through the air and slicing across the side of the Wraith's throat.

Not enough to kill the beast, the cut no worse than what Duff might do if he were trying to shave without a mirror. Even so, it was enough to distract the creature, and it was the unanticipated though very much appreciated chance that he couldn't afford to lose.

Duff jumped forward, smashing his hammer into the Wraith's hip, hearing the bones crack as he did so. For good measure, he drove his dagger in between the creature's lower ribs, just to give the collapsing Wraith something else to worry about.

Then he reached behind him, grasped Mari's hand, and ran out into the fog, hoping that there weren't any more Wraiths waiting for them along the cliffs.

DUFF AND MARI ran as fast as they could, which wasn't very fast, more like a trot, the fog thick and threatening, slowing them down, Duff's bad knees not helping. Duff didn't mind.

They needed to be careful. Putting some distance between them and the two Wraiths was good. Silence and another place to hole up even better.

Duff was trying to recall every aspect of Benyen's property, having visited more times than he could remember. The house was too large and had too many windows for it to be of any use. It was also in the direction they had come from. The barn had too many entrances. He couldn't defend them all. The pens were too open.

Mari started pulling him toward the east. "Where are we going?"

"Just follow me."

Duff had little choice as no good solution came to mind. Besides, she was the one who had gotten them past the second Wraith. As they made their way through the fog, he convinced her to slow down.

Mari, anxious, wanted to move as fast as she could, desperate to get out of the open. Duff stopped her every few steps, worrying about what might be around them, what they might miss or give away if they moved too swiftly.

It made for slower going. But better slow than to be taken by another of the creatures in the fog.

It wasn't long before they walked through a copse, Mari leading them with her unerring sense of direction to a small cottage built into a cliff that was really no more than a shed, the structure falling in on itself. That didn't bother Duff in the least.

The roof still appeared to be solid, not thatch but wood beams packed tightly together and filled with dirt, thick grass growing on top of it. The stone walls were still strong. Best of all, there were no windows and much of the doorway was blocked by a large pile of rubble.

"How did you find this place?" asked Duff as they scrambled over the stones that rose to his chest.

"I like to explore," Mari replied, sitting against the back wall, leaning her head against the cold stone as if this was nothing more than a regular day for her.

"Were you exploring today? Is that why you missed the bell?"

"Maybe," Mari replied reluctantly.

Duff nodded. "We'll keep that between us. How does that sound?"

"Thanks."

Duff peered out from the doorway, looking for any hint of movement in the fog. Nothing. What he wouldn't give for a storm right about now. It would drive out the fog and the Wraiths with it.

"Your father teach you how to throw a dagger?"

Mari nodded, then grinned. "Said I was a natural."

"He was right. If you weren't, we'd both be dead."

Duff glanced to the left. Of course, there was still a good chance that they both still could die.

Four shapes had appeared, positioning themselves in a semicircle around the cottage, the figures drifting in and out of the swirling fog. As one, the four stepped forward, or rather two stepped forward. The two in the center hobbled.

Duff shook his head in amazement. The two Wraiths he had encountered in the cave already were back on their feet. Clearly, their injuries were severe.

The first Wraith he had taken down with blows to both knees could barely stand. The second leaned to the left side, trying to keep his weight off his shattered right hip, one clawed hand pressing against the wound in his side. Yet there he was.

He couldn't see the Wraiths' faces, but he didn't need to. He could feel the hate radiating from them.

The Wraiths wanted another chance at him and Mari. So be it. This time, however, the Wraiths would have to come for them while they were in a more defensible position, and that would give him an advantage that he hadn't enjoyed before.

Duff prepared himself for the charge. It didn't come from the direction that he had expected.

The Wraith to his far left glided through the fog, blades in each hand. Duff acted without even thinking, swinging his hammer and hitting a rock that was on top of the pile that blocked the doorway.

The stone shot through the air, batted with a shocking accuracy and striking the Wraith in the forehead. The creature crumpled to the ground, not moving for several seconds before it slowly tried to push itself up, then slumped back to the dirt, groaning, unable to get his bearings.

"Did you plan on doing that?" whispered Mari, who peeked around the pile of rocks, a broad grin splitting her usually serious countenance.

"Would you believe me if I said yes?"

"No, I wouldn't."

"Good for you," said Duff. "Just as sharp as the blade with which you're so skilled."

Duff shifted his attention to the right. The Wraith who had been standing there was gone. The heavy thumps on the roof and the dirt that sifted down between the beams revealed the creature's location.

For almost a minute, the Wraith walked and jumped above them, seeking a way in. Then he appeared in front of the cottage again, having jumped down without making a sound. Despite the age of the cabin, the roof was still in excellent shape. Lucky for them, thought Duff.

With no other options, Duff assumed that the Wraiths would attack through the doorway. He might kill one of them. Maybe two of the monsters if he was lucky. But not all three who still stood. And not if the one who was struggling to regain his feet rejoined the fight.

"You have any more throwing knives, Mari?" Duff asked.

"I just had the one," she replied. "My dad said I was too dangerous with them. Better I just have one at a time."

Duff nodded. After seeing her accuracy, that made good sense. Although if they survived this combat he planned on talking with Benyen about that. This young lady should be carrying as many knives as she could.

Desperate times called for desperate measures. He pulled two daggers from the sheaths on his thigh. They were the smallest he carried and a bit longer than what Mari probably was used to.

Even so, he was certain that she would make good use of them. She was a natural after all. He handed them to her without taking his eyes off the Wraiths.

"You have earned yourself the right to live, human," said the Wraith Duff had spoken with before he had injured the creature's hip. Imagining the pain that he must be experiencing, Duff didn't know how the Wraith could still be on his clawed feet.

"That's very kind of you," he replied from behind the pile of rubble. "Thank you."

Mari looked at him as if he were playing the fool. Duff

shrugged. The Wraiths might be trying to kill them, but there was no reason to be impolite.

"Enjoy the time that you have left, human. We will be back for you. We will not forget you. Count on it."

Silence fell over the small clearing then, the fog billowing as if it were being stirred by a giant hand. Duff stared out into the mist, hoping to glimpse any movement. Yet there was nothing to be seen. The Wraiths had disappeared into the grey.

Even so, Duff didn't sleep that night, staying back within the doorframe, his eyes seeking to pierce both the darkness and the fog, drawn to the slightest sound, the slightest movement. He didn't breathe easy until the sun began to rise, the warm reddish glow revealing that the fog was moving back toward the north.

Even then, he and Mari remained within the cottage until every wisp of greyish white had drifted away.

They were lucky to be alive.

He smiled when the warmth of the rising sun hit him. A saying from his former Sergeant in the Royal Guard ran through his mind: "You make your own luck, because no one else is going to make it for you."

Declan had so many sayings that Duff could never remember them all. But there was always some truth to them.

For a brief moment, he wondered how that crabby bastard who was difficult to like but impossible not to love was doing. The man had made it his mission in life to ensure that every one of the soldiers he commanded did exactly as he instructed exactly how he wanted it done. Duff wouldn't be alive now if not for the discipline and precision Declan demanded.

And once again, Declan had been right. He and Mari had made their own luck against the Wraiths, and they were still alive because of it.

2

A NEW START

"Was there ever a time when you thought that this would be possible?" asked Aislinn Winborne.

She rode on the back of Astuta. The Griffon had befriended her after rescuing her from the collapsing Temple of the Ghoules, the link between the two growing during the last few months thanks to their many flights together.

Although the Caledonians had decimated the Ghoule Legions in the Winter Pass, there were still a large number of the creatures to be dealt with in the Shattered Peaks, and she much preferred that work to what was required of her as the Lady of the Southern Marches.

"What do you mean?" Bryen Keldragan asked.

Aislinn's eyes narrowed, one eyebrow rising. Her Protector seemed to have an almost uncontrollable desire and ability to make the simplest things more difficult than they needed to be, just like this conversation.

"You know exactly what I mean," she countered, her eyes gleaming.

"I don't know that I do. Do you mean with respect to Caledonia? The Ghoules? The Weir?"

"Bryen ..."

There was a touch of friendly menace in Aislinn's voice, which meant that he was beginning to aggravate her. A skill at which he excelled, though one that he had learned should be used judiciously and at the right time. And clearly, based on the look that Aislinn was giving him, now was not the right time.

"Sorry, force of habit." He smiled at Aislinn, then turned his gaze back to the Weir, one hand gripping tightly to Banshee's feathers, the other stroking her golden neck as they glided along the boundary of the magical barrier. He was using the Talent and the Seventh Stone to check the Weir's structure, making sure that the weave was just as strong as it had been when he had put it in place a few months before.

"Maybe you should come up with a less irritating habit."

"As you command, my Lady."

Aislinn couldn't stop herself from smiling, although she chose not to return the playful banter. They had spent the last few weeks preparing for their journey with little time to talk of anything else.

"So was there a time when you thought that this would be possible?" she repeated.

Bryen continued to examine his creation -- well, not his entirely, the Ten Magii assisting him of course -- checking the weave, looking for any hitch that would suggest a weakness. He had spoken with Viktor Keldragan, the spirit of his uncle, only the night before, who assured him that he had nothing to fear.

Still, he had wanted to inspect it for himself. Just to be certain.

"You mean that we'd be able to do what we're about to do?" he responded, clearly distracted.

"Yes," Aislinn replied. "Even after all that you and I had a hand in during the last few months, that we'd be able to make a fresh start."

The list of meaningful events really was quite extensive as it ran through her mind. Ending the reign of Marden Beleron and freeing the gladiators. Reaching the Sanctuary and reconstructing the Weir. Entering the Lost Land, killing the Ghoule Overlord, and gaining control over the Curse. Stopping the Ghoules' second invasion before the beasts could reach the Breakwater Plateau and then flood the Kingdom.

"I was hopeful," Bryen admitted as he continued to examine the Weir. "But not confident, not if I'm being completely honest. I thought the odds would catch up to us eventually. They still might."

Bryen had a lingering fear that he'd made a mistake when working with the Ten Magii to rebuild the Weir. That the magical construction was all going to unravel and allow the Ghoules remaining in the Lost Land to invade, which was why they were here now, flying above the Shattered Peaks to the west. He needed to be confident in his work.

But he realized that it was wasted effort and wasted worry. Viktor was correct.

The Weir was exactly what the Magus said it was. A new creation. Stronger than the last. Never to weaken. Never to fail.

"You have nothing to worry about. What you did, it will never be undone. The power will never fade thanks to the Seventh Stone."

"How did you know that I was worried about that?" asked Bryen, Aislinn seeming to have read his mind.

"Just a feeling."

"You think you know me pretty well," he said with a smile that also mixed in a gentle challenge.

"I do know you pretty well. Sometimes better than you know yourself."

"Because of the collar?" he asked, touching the silver metal that he still wore around his neck.

"At first, yes. But not now. Now I know you because I know you."

Her smile said everything that needed to be said as they turned away from the shimmering, almost translucent barrier that flashed when the sunlight struck it, Banshee heading to the south, Astuta right on her wing, having almost reached their destination.

A few more minutes passed before dozens of flattened stone peaks sticking out of a billowing fog came into view. Only a quarter of each sandstone pillar was visible, and for some not even that much, the stacks rising out of the floor of the Trench, the canyon a mile wide and just as deep.

Banshee and Astuta glided halfway into the Trench, then landed atop the stone pillar from which a blazing energy shot up into the air, down into the fog, and to the east and west for as far as the eye could see. Both Griffons shrieked a challenge. They sensed the black dragons that lurked far below them, living in nests dug out of the sides of the canyon and the stone pillars.

Despite their deadly nature, those creatures were of little concern to the Griffons, the black dragons rarely leaving their lairs. Rather, the Griffons kept watch for the Wyverns.

Smaller versions of the black dragons, these animals were known to fly through the fog and then shoot back down. Careful to never risk getting too close to the Griffons, although more than happy to taunt them from afar, perhaps even tempt them to come closer to where the larger number of Wyverns might have a better chance of earning a kill.

This was the first time that either Bryen or Aislinn had returned to the Sanctuary since that fateful day when Bryen had crushed the dreams of the Ghoule Overlord. Of course, he would be the first to admit that he could never have accomplished that task without the help of so many others.

After sliding off the backs of the Griffons, both he and

Aislinn used the Talent to search for any threats that might be nearby. That done, neither moved for several minutes. They simply stood there, taking in the quiet. A strange serenity draped over the summit upon which the most important battle in the last thousand years of Caledonian history had taken place.

They then walked slowly across the stone surface that gleamed in the sunlight just like the stone used to construct the Aeyrie. The almost clear white rock was marred in more places than they could count by a large scattering of stains, many a reddish brown that had dried over time. Just as many if not more were a deep black, the dried blood mixing closest to the ten columns that surrounded the depression cut into the center of the sandstone pillar, the color reminiscent of the rust-colored pools of acid common in the Lost Land.

Neither felt the desire to rush as they did their best to step around the reminders of that deadly fight. Their thoughts inevitably drifted back to all that they had needed to do to get Bryen to this summit so that he could rebuild the Weir and stop the Ghoule Overlord. The many clashes with the Ghoules, the Elders, and the black dragons. And, of course, all the people they had lost along the way, the friends who had sacrificed themselves for the greater good.

Walking through the entrance to the Sanctuary, Bryen's eyes flickered over the columns closest to the steps, reading the names of the Magii carved into the stone. Oraan Kvo. Clarissa Dumay. Mikayla Benewyn. Viktor Keldragan.

They and the other Ten Magii had given their lives after crafting the first Weir, and their spirits had aided Bryen in making the second. They were still with him thanks to the Seventh Stone.

Walking down the steps into the excavated oval, Bryen and Aislinn stopped for a few seconds, taking in the six pedestals upon which six of the Seven Stones rested, held in place by barely visible threads of gold wire. The center pedestal, reserved for the Seventh Stone, was empty, just as it should be.

The stream of energy that erupted from the Stones blasted into the sky at a steady, unbreakable flow. The incredible power, which also permeated the hollow, made the hairs on their arms and the backs of their necks stand on end.

Bryen walked over to the center pedestal, taking the same position he had when he had worked with the Ten Magii to craft the Weir. Then he waited, Aislinn watching him from the base of the steps.

The power for the Weir continued to flow at a constant, unstoppable rate, the barrier itself remaining strong, glassy in appearance although solid, the shimmering whitish grey never fading, never flickering.

Finally, Bryen nodded, the tension that had been troubling him draining away. Both Viktor and Aislinn were correct.

When he had last entered the Sanctuary, he had disrupted the flow because the Seventh Stone had joined with him. Now, his presence had no impact whatsoever.

He smiled. One less thing for him to worry about. He could leave Caledonia knowing that he had done all that he could to ensure the safety of the Kingdom against the Ghoules. Knowing as well that he could leave his past here and begin anew in the Territories.

"You know, he was proud of you," said Aislinn. "He might not have told you, knowing him he probably didn't, but he was."

"I know," said Bryen ambiguously. He still wasn't sure how he felt about the Magus because of their complicated past, still trying to come to grips with who Sirius truly was and the role that he had played in Bryen's life during the short time that he had known him. "I think that more than anything he was just pleased that we succeeded in stopping the Ghoules. That was his primary goal as soon as he assumed his position as Master of the Magii. In the end, he achieved it."

"You're right," Aislinn agreed, who walked up to him and took one of his hands in her own. "He did care about you, though. He didn't always show it, in fact he probably didn't know how, but he did."

"I know." Bryen couldn't bring himself to admit that he had cared about Sirius as well, not really having any desire to delve deeper into those emotions. At least not now.

He was willing to admit to himself that he missed the old Magus, wishing he was still here with them. He had never really taken the time to process Sirius' death, always moving on to the next challenge until finally reaching the point where he now had the opportunity to contemplate the impact that Sirius had on him, both the good and the bad.

The Magus had done a lot for him. He had expected even more from Bryen. Demanded it, in fact.

Sirius had stood ready to kill him if he had made the single mistake that would have allowed the Curse to corrupt him.

And when it proved necessary, when Bryen's life hung in the balance, the Ghoules pressing the Blood Company and Bryen struggling to craft the Weir, Sirius had stood against the Ghoule Overlord even though he knew that he was going to die, giving Bryen the extra minutes that he needed, sacrificing himself for his grandson.

"He was the hardest tutor I ever had," said Aislinn. "He was the cranky, irascible uncle I never had. He pushed me. Every day."

"I know, I was there for a part of it."

"There were times when I hated him." She could sense that Bryen was experiencing many of the same emotions that she was, and she hoped that talking about it would help him.

"Me too," Bryen replied in a soft voice.

"I loved him too."

"I don't know if I would go that far," murmured Bryen with a shy grin.

"Everything he did, he did for a reason."

"I can't dispute that."

"I know, you don't have to say it. He pushed me because of my skill as a Magus. He did the same to you because of what happened with the Seventh Stone. He wanted us both to succeed. For us."

"I know. But it wasn't just for us."

Aislinn nodded, unable to disagree. "For him as well. Sirius always had a larger goal. A larger purpose. Our success was his success. But there's nothing wrong with that."

"You're right. I just wish he had been more honest with us from the beginning. It would have made things easier."

"True," nodded Aislinn, her fingers gently rubbing Bryen's hand. "That would have been asking quite a lot from him, though. He was who he was."

"You're using my own words against me again," Bryen said with a smile.

"I am," Aislinn admitted. "Do you hate him?"

"No, I just feel sorry for him. For me as well. A part of me kind of wanted to spend more time with him once all this was done. There were some things that we needed to talk about. It would have helped both of us if we had. Now it's too late."

"I don't know that he'd be able to teach you much more about the Talent."

"Not with respect to the Talent." Sirius had been his grandfather. Bryen would have liked to know the answers to dozens of questions he had about his family and himself. Viktor had provided those few details that he could during their conversations, but there was a thousand year gap that the dead Magus now tied to the Seventh Stone couldn't fill. Not wanting to dampen what had been a good day so far, Bryen shifted to a different topic, remembering too late that this issue had been a thorn in Aislinn's side since she had first told her father her decision. "Did your father try to convince you to stay again?"

"It was a very muted attempt this time," admitted Aislinn. She had been thankful for that, not wanting to get into another argument with him. She had grown tired of her father's efforts to change her mind, subdued though they were most of the time, a few episodes more animated. "It would have been a much more difficult conversation if not for Noorsin's gentle guidance."

Her father had been badgering her ever since she had told him that she'd be accompanying Bryen, raising repeatedly her duties as the Lady of the Southern Marches, the responsibilities she needed to fulfill to her people and her Duchy. Then, inevitably, his argument for her staying shifted to how much he needed her in the Southern Marches followed by a host of other excuses to keep her in Caledonia.

She knew that he did it not only because of his sense of duty, but also because of his love for her. His fear for her safety. She had humored him as much as she could, at the same time deflecting each argument with a stronger argument of her own for why she needed to go to the Territories.

That hadn't stopped him from trying, though the energy of each attempt he made faded as her father began to understand why she had to do this. Why she couldn't not do this.

He didn't want to hold her back. He was just afraid for her. Even more so, he was afraid for himself. Of what life would be like with her gone, if only for a time.

"You expected him to keep trying to keep me here, didn't you," said Aislinn, raising her sparkling eyes to his, the cold grey sending a delightful shiver through her.

"I did. I thought that his willingness to commission a ship that would take the Blood Company to the Territories was the fastest way for him to get me out of his hair."

"My father is sorry for what happened," Aislinn said, though she wasn't trying to defend her father.

Everything had worked out in the end, better than she could have imagined, all because of her father's decision to make Bryen her Protector. That still didn't excuse what he had done, however. That rash decision could never be forgotten and Bryen would never forgive him for that.

"I remember the apology."

"You could be right," said Aislinn, having thought much the same herself, which was why she hadn't told her father that she would be going to the Territories until construction of the ship was well underway. "Or he could be trying to make amends."

"Do you really think so?" Bryen's tone suggested that he was quite skeptical.

Aislinn smiled. "I don't know. I do know that you still make him uncomfortable."

"That's his problem, not mine."

"I'm not suggesting otherwise."

"Are you sure you want to go?" Bryen asked, afraid to do so but needing to know, his worries, some real, some imagined, gaining too much traction in his head. They had not spoken about it since she had told him that she had accepted his offer, and that had been months past. "You know what you're leaving behind."

"I do know what I'm leaving behind," responded Aislinn, her voice hard now, challenging. Contained within that tone was the Magus who was almost as strong as Bryen in the Talent, the Vedra of the Pit.

"I do know what I'm leaving behind," she repeated, taking her hands from Bryen's and pulling on the shoulder straps of his leather armor so that they were nose to nose. "I also know what I'm gaining by going with you."

She then leaned forward, her lips brushing against Bryen's.

Tentatively at first, then with more ardor, neither able to control the passion between them that was never far from the surface.

BRYEN AND AISLINN didn't talk much as they flew back through the Shattered Peaks and then south to Battersea, the capital of the Southern Marches on the Silent Sea. They didn't feel the need to, simply enjoying one another's company as Banshee and Astuta soared through the sky, the Griffons shrieking in pleasure as they reveled in the strong gusts that pushed them to the east and then across the Northern Spine toward the coast.

As the land rushed by beneath them, Aislinn and Bryen both used the Talent to search through the snow-capped mountains. It had only been a few months since the Caledonian Army had defeated the Ghoule Legions, forcing the surviving beasts back north up the Winter Pass and then into the mountains right before the winter returned after its brief hiatus and buried the rugged cut in a hundred feet of snow.

In that short time, the Order of the Magii had been quite thorough in its work, helping the soldiers charged with rooting out the beasts do so with a brutal efficiency. Aislinn and Bryen could sense just a few Ghoule packs remaining deep within the spires in places that with the worsening storms would make it exceedingly difficult to reach.

Bryen smiled as he thought about that. It was no longer his problem. The Ghoules posed a threat, though certainly not on the level that they once had.

He had done what was demanded of him. Defeating the Elders and the Ghoules had required his use of the Seventh Stone. Eliminating the beasts entirely from Caledonia could be accomplished through more conventional means.

Not having that burden on his shoulders gave him a sense of freedom that he was still trying to get used to. So much had been expected of him for so long that he still wasn't comfortable with the fact that his decisions were now his own. He was no longer constrained by larger issues or concerns, or at least not entirely.

He could do as he wanted, which might be why he was so unsettled. It was the first time that his life was his own since he had been forced into the Pit. While enslaved in the Colosseum, he had thought about what he would do when he was free of the white sand, yet never had he thought that he could turn his dream into reality.

Circling the harbor, they looked down at the dock that extended out toward the breakwater, the massive merchant ship commissioned by Aislinn's father tied up to the pier, the hundreds of people scrambling around it appearing to be no larger than ants. The vessel truly was a marvel, built according to the Duke's specifications with several improvements incorporated that were suggested by Duchess Stelekel in consultation with Bryen and Declan.

Named the *Freedom*, the ship was one of the largest ever built in Caledonia, measuring three hundred yards long and fifty yards wide. Four masts, the tallest reaching one hundred and fifty feet into the air, soared into the sky, a crow's nest on each one. Along the stern were five large platforms, each having a retractable shelter for bad weather, that extended out over the water.

Right in front of those additional decks and to each side was a schooner, each one fifty feet long with two demountable masts. They were actually built as part of the larger ship, the railings and hulls connected cleverly, but the smaller vessels could be detached and sailed on their own in just a matter of minutes.

When Captain Gregson had first come aboard to assume command of the *Freedom*, he had stared at the two small cutters for quite a long time, not saying a word. They increased substantially the large ship's sailcloth, which meant an extra few knots of speed.

He had never seen anything like it before. Large rowboats fitted for small sails along the side to escape a sinking ship, yes, those were common on the large vessels used to cross the Burnt Ocean, a trip that he had made dozens of times. Never two small ships that were a part of the larger whole, however.

Then his usually sour expression had broken into a salty grin, his sharp mind already working through the many possible ways that he could make use of ships like that.

Banshee and Astuta landed on the platforms extending off the ship's stern with a graceful touch. The sailors who scurried about the deck preparing it for the tide watched the animals with a wonder mixed with trepidation. They had heard of the Griffons the Protector had befriended and how they had aided in the defeat of the Ghoule Legions.

Still, they kept their distance, not entirely comfortable with the animals that were several times larger than draft horses, their bodies, tails, and legs that of a lion, their heads and wings those of an eagle. In addition to Banshee and Astuta, three more Griffons were already waiting on their own platforms, napping under the awnings that were designed to protect them from the sun and rain.

Aislinn and Bryen slid off the Griffons' backs, rubbing down their feathers, scratching the skin beneath and earning several purrs of pleasure before they turned their attention toward the ship that stretched out before them. They watched as the Blood Company began to come aboard, carrying their packs and weapons up the ramp. As expected, Declan was in the lead, Davin and Lycia right next to him as they worked with Captain Gregson to get the gladiators situated in their quarters belowdecks.

Bryen and Aislinn smiled and stepped down from the platform onto the stern deck when they saw the familiar figure walking toward them. He hadn't spoken with the Magus in more than a month and hadn't expected to before he left the Kingdom.

"Rafia, I thought you were still in the Shattered Peaks."

"I was. Our efforts are proceeding better than we thought they would be."

"I'd have to agree," said Aislinn. "We flew over the mountains just now. You have the Ghoules penned in with nowhere to go. The Order should be able to finish the job faster than we thought possible once you can get to the beasts."

"That's the hope," confirmed Rafia, her eyes tightening, a hand reaching up to put a stray lock of curly black hair streaked with grey back behind her ear. "You went to the Sanctuary."

"We did."

"You're satisfied?" asked Rafia, setting her piercing gaze on Bryen.

"I am."

"Good. I didn't think you needed to worry, though I can understand why you would. Now you know that you don't have to."

"What are you doing here?" asked Declan, who had come up to join them once the Blood Company had gone in search of their lodgings.

"I'm going with you," said Rafia with a smile, though her eyes didn't join in. There was a sadness lurking there and had been ever since Sirius fell to the Ghoule Overlord.

"To the Territories?"

"Yes, to the Territories. Where else would I be going?" Her natural testiness, however, remained.

"But you're the Keeper of Haven," said Aislinn. "You're the Master of the Magii. You can't leave Caledonia."

"Why ever not?" said Rafia in a very tired voice, as if she'd already engaged in this exact conversation too many times already. "Haven will survive without me for a time. Irelda and Benjin will lead the Order in my absence, so no worries there. And as you and Bryen confirmed today, we have nothing to worry about with respect to the Weir. Once the remaining Ghoules are eliminated, there will be little to fear. With Noorsin and your father leading, Caledonia will be in good hands."

"It sounds like you've been thinking about this for quite some time," said Bryen, understanding why she might want to get away from the Kingdom at least for a little while.

"I have," Rafia shrugged, as if the Master of the Magii leaving the Kingdom for the first time in millennia was a matter of little concern. "Besides, I've always wanted to see the Territories."

"Rafia, I thought we discussed this. I thought we came to an understanding that ..."

"You can't escape me anymore, Declan. So stop trying so hard to do just that. I've made up my mind. You'll just have to deal with it."

Declan stared at the Magus for quite a few breaths, his hard expression actually appearing to soften, something that Bryen had only seen under the rarest of circumstances. The Magus stared right back at the Sergeant of the Blood Company, not blinking, not flinching. As always, there was a spark of challenge in her eyes.

"Are you sure about this?" he asked finally.

For the first time in months, she smiled genuinely, from a place of pleasure rather than one of expectation.

"I am. This is what I want to do. This is what I need to do."

Declan stared at Rafia for a little while longer, reminding Bryen of when the Master of the Gladiators used to evaluate the new fighters consigned to the Pit. Declan had never been wrong with his assessments. He had known in an instant who had a chance of surviving more than a few combats on the white sand and who would be dragged out of the Pit and buried in a potter's field within just a few weeks of arriving, if not sooner.

Finally, Declan nodded.

"I'm glad that's settled," said Rafia, "although I should note that I don't need anyone's permission to go where I want to go, even yours Sergeant of the Blood Company."

"No one ever suggested as much," replied Declan.

"Good," nodded Rafia. "Now if you wouldn't mind, perhaps you could take me to the Captain so that I can find a suitable cabin?"

Rafia looped her arm in Declan's and steered him back toward the bow.

"I wasn't trying to escape you," Bryen heard Declan say as the two walked away among the controlled chaos of the ship.

"What do you mean?" asked Rafia.

"I wasn't trying to escape you."

"I know, Declan, I just wanted to put you on edge. A habit I'm still struggling to control."

That last comment made Rafia pull Declan closer to her, Bryen's friend and mentor not pulling away, actually seeming to enjoy the closeness that he was experiencing with the Magus. An interesting development, though not unexpected. However, the person who was striding toward them, offering his greetings to Declan and Rafia first before joining them on the stern deck, was quite unanticipated.

"Captain Klines," said Bryen with a nod of respect.

"Captain Keldragan," Klines replied with a similar nod of respect.

Bryen chuckled, remembering the last time that they had engaged in a similar pattern of engagement. "You enjoy addressing me that way just to see how I react."

"I do," Klines admitted.

"Who knew the famed Blademaster, silent and deadly, also has a sense of humor."

"Very few people," replied Klines, "so please keep it to yourself."

"I'll do my best," replied Bryen, then sensing that the conversation to come did not require him, he excused himself. "If you'll pardon me, I need to check on the Griffons."

"I knew you were visiting Battersea, Blademaster. I didn't know you were here for this purpose," Aislinn said, motioning with her hand toward the two large rucksacks he carried, one over each shoulder.

"I must admit that when I came here, I wasn't certain that I would be doing this," noted Klines, his sharp green eyes flashing brightly.

"How did you come to this decision then?"

"I had been thinking about it on the journey here from Tintagel, though my thoughts had not yet solidified. Then I talked with Declan late last night. We were reminiscing about our time in the capital."

"But not for long," prompted Aislinn.

The Blademaster preferred not to dwell on the past. It held too many memories of what could have been. Wisely, he focused more on the future.

"No, not for long. Our conversation shifted to more serious matters, though I won't bore you with those. The catalyst for my decision actually was the Volkun."

"What did Bryen do?" asked Aislinn, her concern growing.

"Nothing for you to worry about, Lady Winborne," replied Klines. "I ran into him this morning before you went off on the Griffons."

"What did Bryen say, Blademaster?" Aislinn's smile had shifted into a frown. She worried about how much influence her Protector had exercised on the man who had befriended her when she was subject to the will of Marden Beleron, former King of Caledonia, once her betrothed and now dead.

"Very little," chuckled Klines. "That's his way, isn't it? After I spoke with him, I saw a large part of him in me. Please don't take that comment as arrogant, it's just that my situation is much like that of the Protector. He's finished his business in Caledonia, as have I. When I was talking with him, he said that he was in need of a fresh start. I realized that I was in need of one as well. That my coming here now was just the first step in that longer journey."

"There was more to it than that, I'm assuming," said Aislinn, arms now crossed.

"There was," the Blademaster admitted.

"What else did Bryen say to you?" she asked suspiciously. "He can be quite convincing when he wants to be."

"The Protector said that it would be a shame for me to stay here when there was so much for me to do in the Territories."

"Did he say what it was that you needed to do in the Territories, Blademaster?"

"The Protector wasn't specific, Lady Winborne. He did seem to think that you might have a few things in mind for me in which I could prove useful."

"That was a bit presumptuous on his part, don't you think, Blademaster?"

For a few heartbeats, Aislinn wondered if Bryen was trying to provide her with additional protection. The Blademaster had made his loyalties plain during the insurrection. Looking into the Blademaster's eyes, however, she understood that had nothing to do with it, or at least if it did it was a very small part.

She could see the pain still lurking there, and she understood in that moment that his decision had more to do with the closure he finally gained upon killing Killen Sourban, the soldier who murdered his daughter, and his desire to put to rest the shades that had followed him for so long.

"Perhaps," said Klines. "Of course, there is some truth to it, is there not? Based on our experience together in Tintagel, you always seem to have some schemes in play."

"Strategies, Blademaster. I do not engage in schemes."

"My apologies, Lady Winborne," replied Klines with a smile. "Strategies."

Aislinn smiled as well, knowing that she was trapped and not minding it in the least. She would need good people with her in the Territories if she was to achieve her goal. "I hope that you'll train with me during the crossing."

"I would like nothing better," replied the Blademaster with a nod and a slight bow.

"That's good to hear. I'll leave you to find Captain Gregson so that you can stow your gear."

The Blademaster nodded and then headed back across the busy deck. She was thrilled that the Blademaster was coming. Still, she needed to have a conversation with Bryen, just to make sure that there was no ulterior motive. She turned to do just that, wanting to get a better sense of what he had in mind when he spoke with the Blademaster, then thought better of it, as Bryen was already occupied.

"Are you sure you don't want to come with me? We have accomplished quite a lot together. Think of the damage we could cause on the other side of the Burnt Ocean."

"A kind offer, Protector," said Tarin Tentillin. "Although I am reluctant to admit it, I will miss having you around, as well as the regular back and forth between us, the veiled barbs and jokes and minor irritations. But Jerad and I must stay here. The Duke is assuming greater responsibility in Caledonia, and we must do the same in the Southern Marches."

"I'd actually love to go with you," interjected Jerad. "I just have a small issue that I can't evade."

"You mean the fact that you're engaged and that Dani would skin you alive if you tried to leave her behind," said Bryen, enjoying his friend's discomfort.

"Yes, that's probably the best way to put it," Jerad admitted resignedly, though his eyes said differently.

Bryen looked more intently at the Sergeant who had been the first to befriend him when Aislinn's father brought him to the Southern Marches to serve as her Protector. He could tell that it was an act.

His friend, though he talked a brave game about wanting to go to the Territories, would do nothing without Dani. And not just because she would, in fact, gut him if he ever considered leaving her. No, his heart and soul belonged to Dani, and the Sergeant was glad for it.

"That I can understand," acknowledged Bryen, deciding for old times sake to turn his attention toward Tarin and have a little bit of fun before his friends returned to the Broken Citadel. "So tell me about Cerillia."

"Cerillia?" asked Tarin, attempting to maintain his composure, though his eyes flashed with a hint of wildness.

Both Jerad and Bryen caught the slip by the Captain of the Battersea Guard, the slight change in tone a clear giveaway.

"Yes, Cerillia," confirmed Bryen, enjoying how the usually collected Captain was showing some chinks in his armor. "I understand that you've been spending more time with the Magus."

"How did you know ..." Tarin grimaced, stopping himself before he said anything incriminating. He should have realized that Bryen didn't really know. He had been guessing and Tarin had confirmed it for him.

"Who's Cerillia?" asked Jerad.

Bryen grinned at Tarin as if he'd just beaten him in a sparring match, which was an all too frequent occurrence in Tarin's opinion. He had yet to get the better of the Protector in the practice ring, and he feared that he was about to face the same result now as Bryen dug a little deeper into what Tarin viewed as a private matter.

"You had to do this?" asked Tarin. "You couldn't just leave it be?"

"I did have to do this," Bryen replied with a grin. "I couldn't let it go. It would have been wrong of me to do so."

"Wait," Jerad said, finally catching up to the conversation. "The Magus who fought with us in the Winter Pass? That Cerillia?"

Tarin had no choice but to nod, choosing not to offer any more than that, knowing how Bryen could use anything else he said against him.

"Captain, she is truly quite an impressive Magus. She was a whirlwind of a fighter against the Ghoules."

"Sergeant ..."

"And she is quite beautiful as well."

"Sergeant ..."

"And I must say, I can understand why ..."

"Sergeant," Tarin said in a commanding tone, finally catching Jerad's attention.

"What?" Jerad stopped himself, finally seeing his Captain's less than pleased expression. He offered a smile of contrition, finally catching on to Tentillin's unease. "Right, sorry. I won't say another word."

Tarin turned to Bryen now that he had Jerad back under control. "I blame you for this."

"I would expect nothing less. I just wanted to leave you with something to remember me by."

"Trust me, I will never forget you, Protector. It is impossible to forget you."

"That's very kind of you to say."

"Don't take it as a compliment," countered Tarin, although he couldn't stop a smile from breaking through his usually stern countenance.

"Don't worry, I won't." Bryen nodded, then smiled himself. "The honor has been mine, Captain Tentillin."

"It has been mine as well, Protector," replied Tarin, extending a hand that Bryen gladly shook. "Do you remember what I said when you left Battersea with Sirius before all the madness began?"

"Don't trust anyone."

"That piece of advice still stands."

Bryen nodded, Tarin releasing his hand, the Captain and Jerad heading for the ramp.

"Tarin." The Captain turned back, a wistful smile on his face. "I'll see you on the other side."

Tarin stared at Bryen, his hard expression softening. Then he pulled his sword from his sheath. He brought the steel to his forehead and nodded, the ultimate sign of respect from one warrior to another.

"I'll see you on the other side, Protector."

3

A NEW THREAT

"It was just like all the other attacks?"

"It was, Governor Winborne," replied Argenta Rensom, Captain of the Northern Guard. She was direct. To the point. Never wasting words. "Virtually the same."

"Then there were more of those creatures in it? There had to be."

"We have to assume that there were, Governor Winborne, even though no one saw them. It's the only explanation."

"How many?"

"Three farmsteads."

"How many?" Winborne asked again, wanting more specific details than just the number of granges attacked.

"Eleven people killed," Argenta replied, the touch of sadness in her voice mixing with her mounting frustration. She felt the weight of each death on her shoulders. She believed that the safety of the people in the Northern Territory was her responsibility. Since the fog had first covered the province more than a year before, she had yet to find or even kill any of the monsters in the mist, while the creatures who lurked within had slaughtered more than three hundred people. "Two children got away. They hid beneath a haystack until the fog cleared."

"They didn't see anything? Nothing to confirm for us what we're up against?"

"They're young, Governor Winborne. Ten and eight. Based on that and what they lived through last night, I don't know that what they had to say would be of any value to us. It's nothing that we haven't heard before."

"That may be true, Captain Rensom, but I'd still like to hear it." Winborne's expectant and hopeful look convinced her to continue.

The Captain nodded. "The children didn't have much to offer. Their parents got them into the haystack during the attack. They were in the barn to start. Their father put them there when he went to help their mother, who had fallen. They heard virtually nothing except for a few screams. When the fog cleared, they found their parents."

"Just like all the other survivors. Those few that there have been."

"Correct. They dug into the haystack on their own initiative. The oldest child peeked out once she thought they were safe. She reported seeing several grey shapes in the fog. Very tall. Standing there for quite some time. As if they were waiting to see if there was anyone else to kill."

"They stayed hidden. Smart children."

"Indeed, Governor Winborne. They were able to tell us no more than that."

"The infamous Wraiths visited us again."

"It would seem so, Governor Winborne."

"From which direction did the fog come, Captain?"

"From the north. As always."

That last comment earned a raised eyebrow from the Governor. He had never quite understood why that was the case. He had heard stories of the Wyld and the fog that covered that forbidding land, but he had yet to find any people who had seen the Murk with their own eyes to confirm his suspicions.

"Don't you find it strange, Captain, this fog," began Winborne after chewing on what was percolating in his mind for a little while longer. "I grew up in the Southern Marches on the coast of the Silent Sea. Fog is commonplace there. A thick fog, like what we're seeing now, always comes off the ocean. Here, it should do the same. The Sea of Mist is just to our east. The name itself highlights that fog is a regular occurrence on those waters, and we know that it is based on experience. Yet here this fog comes from the north. Why is that? What is so different about this fog compared to the fog from the east?"

"I do find it strange," replied Rensom, "and I apologize, Governor Winborne. I don't have an answer for you. I was raised not far from the Bay of the Dead. I agree with you. The heaviest fog always came off the water."

Winborne grunted his agreement. Seemingly lost in thought, his eyes took on that faraway look that Captain Rensom noticed was becoming much more common these last few months. A slight movement behind Winborne caught her attention.

A door concealed within the wall opened, the Lady of the Northern Territory walking through. She held a finger to her lips and made a circular motion with her other hand, telling the Captain to just ignore her as she stopped next to her husband, resting a hand gently on his arm.

Nothing about what was happening in Winborne's Territory made sense. In his experience, fog like what they were encountering now usually stayed on the coast, maybe came in a few miles at most, but that was it. It was dependent on the water for its existence. Not so the dreaded mist that smothered them from the north. There was no natural reason for the fog to behave in this way.

In fact, based on all the reports that he had received, the fog coming from the north was thicker and denser than that smothering the Trench. Of course, he couldn't really say whether that was true or not. He had never been to the Trench.

No one he knew had been to that dreadful place, except perhaps for his niece if the latest letter that he had received from his brother was accurate. And knowing his brother it likely was. He wasn't one to exaggerate, providing the barest of information required to get his meaning across.

Why was it that everything of interest and import seemed to happen to Kevan and his family and not to him? He had come to the Territories for a reason. Yet instead of fighting great battles, instead of making a name for himself, he was ...

Winborne forced himself back to the present, his mind, always filled with grand ideas and even grander fancies, had an annoying habit these days of wandering off at the least auspicious times.

He needed to focus now on what Captain Rensom was saying. Perhaps this might be the opportunity that he had been waiting for. The opportunity to prove that he wasn't just the younger brother of a great lord.

That he was so much more than that. That he was a man of action. A man of bravery. A man who could make history just like his brother. A man who could ...

He shook his head, trying to clear the dozens of disparate thoughts clouding his mind. Why did this happen to him now? Why did he have so much trouble concentrating on any single thing at a time? He gripped his forearm with his right hand, digging his nails into his wrist.

The brief spike of pain pushed the haze into the background, allowing him to return to the present and concentrate on what his Captain had to say.

"From all reports," Captain Rensom was explaining, "the fog almost reached Shadow's Reach this time, stopping no more than a league away. It's as if we're being tested, the fog pushing farther to the west and the south each time rather than staying closer to the coast."

"Why would you say that?" asked Kendric, curious, because he had been wondering the same thing himself though he had not yet given voice to his theory.

"I believe that the creatures are trying to determine if we have the ability to respond to their attacks. To counter them."

Winborne couldn't disagree with his Captain's logic, having no choice but to acknowledge that they had yet to come up with an effective method for preventing the horrors of last night. "How many attacks in just the last month?"

"Seven."

"They're getting bolder indeed," said Winborne, putting together the frequency of the attacks with how close they were coming to the capital of the Northern Territory. "They'll come for Shadow's Reach within the next month. You can count on it."

"I believe that you're right, Governor Winborne," agreed Rensom. "If I might make a suggestion?"

"Of course," said Winborne. "Please. We need some way to deal with this."

"I understand that the fog is reaching even farther down the coast," she began, "so much so that the Highlands face the same problem that we do."

"Is that so?" Winborne asked, though he seemed to recall having heard that somewhere before. But from whom, he couldn't remember.

"It is, Governor Winborne," Rensom confirmed. "It seems that the people living in the northern Highlands have implemented a type of warning system."

"How so?"

"Pyres and bells to get everyone to safety before the fog covers the land. Towers made of stone that the Wraiths can't crack."

"The Highlanders can't fight what's in the fog either."

"They can't, Governor Winborne. They face the same challenge that we do. So they've taken other measures to defend themselves. From what I hear, it's working so long as no one is caught out in the fog. I suggest that we do the same."

"Yes, indeed, I must say that we should ..."

Winborne's eyes took on that faraway look once again.

Rensom waited, at first believing that her lord was simply lost in thought, then beginning to worry as the seconds passed with no response from him. Was there more to the Governor's strange behavior than just what she was noticing? An illness, perhaps? "Governor Winborne?"

"Yes, I agree with you," said Winborne with a start, suddenly coming back awake. "Please make that happen. My apologies. I was just thinking of all that would be required for us to mount an effective defense."

"As you command, Governor Winborne," said Captain Rensom. She glanced at the Governor's wife to see if she had noticed her husband's odd behavior.

Apparently not, the Lady of the Northern Territory simply giving the Governor a warm smile, her full attention focused on him as if nothing was amiss. Her hand continued to rub his arm gently, her touch obviously comforting to her husband. Not knowing what else to do, Rensom offered Winborne a nod of respect and then exited his office.

"Kendric."

It took almost a minute before the Governor of the Northern Territory turned his gaze toward his wife and away from whatever he had been staring at through the large windows running across the far wall, his expression more of confusion than clarity.

"Oh, Ursina," he said with a smile. "When did you get here?"

Ursina stood right next to him, but he didn't recall her

joining him in the study. She usually preferred to meet with him outside or in her own library.

Winborne's study was his one space in the entire keep that hadn't come under his wife's influence. Besides serving as his office, it was the only place to display the daggers that he liked to collect. The weapons, purchased from every corner of Caledonia, sat on tables or were mounted on the walls, Kendric's latest acquisitions scattered across his desk.

He thought that Ursina had been in the gardens on the west side of the plaza and wouldn't be joining him in the keep until lunchtime. Evidently, he had been so distracted by the pressing matter at hand that he hadn't heard her come in.

His feeling of confusion slowly shifted to annoyance, anger not too far beyond that, though he worked hard to prevent that from happening. Ursina didn't like it when he lost his temper, which she had told him was becoming much too common these days.

"At the end of your conversation with the Captain of the Guard."

"My conversation with the Captain?" His face brightened as it all came back to him. Or at least pieces of it. "Yes, my conversation with the Captain." He took a quick look around the large room. "Where is Captain Rensom? I feel as if there is more that we need to discuss. These creatures in the fog are becoming much too bold. We must deal with them now before they breach the walls of Shadow's Reach."

"Have no fear, my love. I believe that you gave Captain Rensom very specific guidance on how to handle the Wraiths. If I know the good Captain, she's already hard at work implementing those instructions."

Kendric looked down at his petite wife, who barely came up to his chest, somewhat baffled. He didn't recall doing anything of the sort.

Ursina continued. "I have no doubt that thanks to your

good thinking the Wraiths will be dealt with. The larger plan that we discussed that will guarantee the safety of the Northern Territory and those Territories to the south is already well underway. Your idea will work. It will just take time to implement."

"It will?" Kendric responded uncertainly, struggling to focus again, bits and pieces of what he wanted to discuss darting about in his mind.

"It will, my love," said Ursina, rubbing his arm more vigorously. "Of that I am certain. We will both gain what we want and what we need once everything is in place."

Kendric nodded agreeably, satisfied with his wife's answers. With a distant look in his eyes he stared at the blade mounted to the wall opposite his desk, the centerpiece of his collection. A wedding gift from Ursina.

It was a unique weapon, both in its design and use. It was actually three daggers forged into one, the grip in the center, each of the blades a foot and a half in length, each one spaced evenly from the next.

It was said that someone truly skilled in the dagger's use could throw the weapon and, because of its perfectly symmetrical design, catch it when the spinning daggers circled back to them. Even more impressive, the blades would never cut the person bonded to the weapon, thus the ability to reclaim it out of the air.

It was quite a claim. He didn't believe it, of course. Not after he tried it once, only succeeding in almost slicing off one of his fingers on one of the blades when he threw it and then having to stanch the gush of blood as he chased after the weapon so that he didn't lose it in the long grass of the Northern Steppes.

It was also said that the small notch in the center of the grip was a repository for the blood of the user, hence the weapon's name. The Blood Dagger. Crafted by the Giants of the Rime, the weapon was linked by blood through the Blood Ruby, a missing piece that fit into the grip, to the person charged with unlocking its power for use against the Ancient One.

Kendric had found the tale quite entertaining, although hardly believable. In large part since the Ancient One was a being who played the role of the villain in so many of the myths and fairy tales that parents used to get unruly children to go to bed at night.

The threat of a visit from the evil master of the Spirit World usually calmed boisterous children instantly, although nightmares also were a distinct possibility. He had discovered that when he was a child, his father more than happy to employ any tactic necessary to get him and Kevan into bed at a reasonable hour.

But also because when he had tried the Blood Dagger again after his errant throw, the grip still coated with his blood, much to his disappointment nothing had happened. He had attained no special powers as a result. From that point forward, he assumed that it was just a blade like any other though its design certainly was pleasing to the eye.

"When the darkness surrounds, the light will prevail."

Kendric's brow furrowed with worry. He could remember what was inscribed on a weapon that his wife had gifted to him, yet he could barely recall the conversation that he had engaged in just moments ago with his Captain of the Guard.

"You seem troubled, my love."

"Troubled?" asked Kendric, not understanding the question. "Me?"

"Yes. It's as if your mind is elsewhere."

"I am never troubled when you are near, Ursina. You know that."

"You are deflecting, my love," said Ursina, her dazzling smile broadening his own. Kendric's wife was a handsome woman with a strong nose and a hawklike countenance, due in large part to her sharp eyes, which seemed to see everything that was going on around her, even what she wasn't meant to see.

"I was just thinking."

He was certain that Ursina was correct. That they had discussed how to defend against the Wraiths, and that she had agreed that his idea for dealing with the monsters in the mist was a good one. Even so, he struggled to recall what that idea had been.

Why was he having such a difficult time remembering such a critical matter? Why did his mind feel the need to flit about like a fly trying to escape through a closed window, pounding against the glass hopelessly?

He would raise it with Ursina if he could. She was skilled in healing and he believed that she could help him. Yet every time he attempted to do so words failed him. He couldn't get them out.

"That can be a dangerous thing to do, my love."

She said it in jest, trying to replace his look of consternation with a smile. She realized her mistake too late.

A spark of hot anger flashed behind Kendric's eyes. Just as quickly as it appeared, it was gone. Barely there. Still, it was enough for her to feel just a touch of worry, an emotion that she hadn't experienced in quite some time. She had not expected such a reaction from her husband, not in his current state.

Kendric fought to control his temper. He enjoyed her humor most of the time. Not now. Not when it hit so close to the cause of his irritation. If only he could remember what that was. Why was he having such a hard time concentrating?

"It can, you're right," Kendric said with a smile, although that smile never touched his eyes.

"What is it that's bothering you, my love?"

Ursina stepped in front of Kendric, reaching for his hands with her own. The flash in her dark eyes and her uneven smile sent a surge of heat through him, just as it always did. His thoughts immediately began to wander down a path that was quite pleasant though thoroughly unproductive to the conversation he was attempting to have.

"I just never assumed that it would be like this here in the Territories."

"Like what?" wondered Ursina, even though she already knew the path the discussion would take. This wasn't the first time that they had engaged in this conversation.

"Like we're pushing a rock up a mountainside and that just when we're about to reach the crest we roll back down all the ground that we had covered already," replied Kendric. "It's as if everything is harder here than it needs to be. Nothing is ever easy."

"Nothing worthwhile ever is, my love," Ursina explained warmly. "We are building a New Caledonia, my love. We knew that it wouldn't be easy."

"Yes, but some of these challenges go beyond the pale. Addressing them takes so much time and attention. So much effort. It should not be this difficult. Every time we remove an obstacle another one appears. It shouldn't be that way."

Kendric had always wanted to come to the Caledonian Territories, what most had started calling New Caledonia, ever since the sailors who had made the long passage across the Burnt Ocean and returned to Battersea filled his mind with images and tales of adventure and excitement that he couldn't escape. That he didn't want to escape despite the many dangers they spoke of.

It was a difficult and treacherous voyage across the Burnt Ocean, a sea notorious for deadly storms and other threats. More than a few shipwrecks washed up on the Isle of Mist or the Fal Carrachian coast with not a crew member to be found, the signs of struggle and splashes of blood along the deck and in the holds and cabins suggesting that those who were lost were not always taken by the sea, unless what took them came out of the sea.

Those terrifying stories only ensnared Kendric in a tighter web of fancy, Kevan's younger brother always having preferred to live in his own world rather than the real one.

And then he finally had the chance to merge the two. Kendric remembered how excited he had been when King Corinthus Beleron began issuing grants to the Territories, seeking to rebuild his treasury through these new fees and the taxes the Crown collected on anything imported to or exported from New Caledonia.

The continent, rich in natural resources, began with the Northern Peaks where he ruled and stretched south to the Territory of Benewyn and the Endless Ocean, and from there all the way to the west and the far-off lands of Ferranagh to the south, Kashel north of that, and then just above what some were calling Inishmore even though the Crown had not yet approved of the name because so few adventurers had settled there.

Beyond those Territories was the Western Isle and far to the north the Distant Islands in the bitter Winter Sea. In between were more Territories with border towns sprouting up like weeds along the shores of the Heartland Lake and the Inland Sea.

New Caledonia sang to Kendric of opportunity and freedom, so he had jumped at the chance when Kevan offered him the Governorship of the Northern Territory, the province extending from the northern boundary of the Northern Peaks south across the Northern Steppes to the edge of the Clanwar Desert and the Highlands.

Kendric viewed his appointment as his chance to demonstrate what he could do. To step out from beneath his older brother's prodigious shadow and prove that the Winborne blood ran through his veins.

Besides, the Southern Marches held nothing of substance for him anymore, not after the birth of Kevan's daughter. Nothing but memories, in fact, and not all of them good.

He didn't care if his brother was giving him the Northern Territory because he cared about him and knew how much this meant to him or it was simply the best way for Kevan to get him out from under his feet. Kendric had been waiting for a chance like this all his life, and he had seized it with both hands, refusing to let go.

Yet, when he had gotten to his new home and the bustling and growing town of Shadow's Reach nestled within the imposing Northern Peaks, he had been shocked by what he had found.

He had wanted a fresh start, and he had gotten it. More of a fresh start than he had bargained for actually.

The first Caledonian settlers had been in the Territory for only five years before he had arrived. Leaderless for the most part, although that didn't seem to faze the farmers, miners, and traders who despite the lack of official order had made good progress in building a vibrant center of business. Still, there was so much more to do.

Expand Shadow's Reach so that the village, now a town and on its way to becoming a city, could meet the needs of the growing populace. Establish the tools of governance. Ensure that roads were built to allow for the easy flow of goods to the other Territories and to the port cities so that they could do business in Caledonia. Develop trade agreements with the other Territories so that commerce could be conducted seamlessly. Impose taxes, an unpopular though necessary task if public works projects, such as building a wall around Shadow's Reach, were ever to be undertaken.

So it went. A constant list of requirements that for every item completed two more were added.

And now the most challenging task of all. Protect against a

threat that they couldn't see and couldn't hear. A threat that they had yet to prove that they could kill.

It had been so hard and not at all what he thought it would be. The demands on his time and his dwindling treasury never ended.

He had believed that as soon as he assumed his position as Governor, he'd need to do little more than make a decision now and then. To settle disputes. Attend the openings of new buildings and marketplaces. To be the face of the Northern Territory and not actually have to ensure that the bureaucracy put in place to manage the affairs of the province functioned effectively and met the basic expectations of its residents.

The Northern Territory wasn't like the Southern Marches as he thought it would be. It was rougher, not as sophisticated, with little of the structure needed to ensure that everything worked as it should. The Northern Territory required that he dip his feet into issues and business with which he had no experience. With issues and business that he had little desire to have any experience.

But he had no choice. Not if he wanted to achieve his own goals. Not if he wanted to build his own reputation, one that could rival that of his brother.

He would have drowned beneath the weight of all the demands made upon him if not for Ursina, who had arrived in Shadow's Reach just months after he did. Just in time, too, because he had learned almost immediately that he did not have a knack for governing. That he needed competent people around him if he was to succeed. And she was more than competent.

When Ursina had appeared to pay her respects to the Governor at the Shadow Keep, then no more than a single story structure, now a towering fortress built with the black stone of the Northern Peaks, it had been love at first sight for both of them.

The two had been inseparable ever since, Ursina demonstrating a unique talent for ruling that Kendric didn't have, her organizational skills and her ability to build relationships with the local merchants and townspeople, something that he had struggled to do, helping him to finally get the Territory moving in the direction that he wanted. That he needed if he was to have any chance of proving that he was nothing more than the younger brother of the accomplished, much better known Duke of the Southern Marches.

"Difficult, yes," agreed Ursina, "although not impossible, Kendric. Think of all that we have accomplished. All that you have accomplished in such a short period of time."

"We have been quite successful, haven't we," mused Kendric, his focus, poor though it was, returning to the present for the time being.

"Your brother not only would be impressed by all that you have done, but he would be envious as well."

"Envious?" asked Kendric, his smile broadening. The thought of turning his brother green, his brother who could do no wrong in the eyes of their parents when they were growing up, was quite appealing.

"Indeed," she replied. "Few could have done what you have in so short a period of time."

"You're right," said Kendric. "You're always right, Ursina. But we still have so much more to do. Separate from all the challenges that we face with the Territory, we can't even get things done closer to home without running into problems."

"You're still upset that the fortress isn't complete."

"I am," admitted Kendric. "The masons are having difficulties getting all the stone needed so that they can complete the dome for our audience chamber. The stained glass for the hole in the center has yet to arrive from Roo's Nest. It should have been here months ago, yet we have received no word on when that key resource will make its way across the Burnt Ocean.

The stone cutters haven't even started on the figurines destined for the parapets. The main ..."

"Kendric," said Ursina in a strong voice, one that immediately stopped her husband's list of complaints.

"Yes, my love." The agitation that had been building up within him began to disappear when his wife's eyes caught his own.

"That will all be worked out, Kendric. Don't waste your time on it. I will deal with it myself. You have larger matters to attend to."

Kendric smiled and nodded, feeling a sense of calm wrap itself around him, his thoughts beginning to drift again as his anxiety dissipated.

"Thank you, Ursina." Yet before all his fears slipped away, a new concern popped into his head. "And what are we to do with the miners and farmers in the western peaks who are balking at paying the taxes they owe? Can you believe it? They say that they are gaining nothing from us that would justify the taxes they are required to pay. They say as well that they are not receiving the protection they need from the creatures terrorizing the mountains. They seem to think that it's our responsibility to give that to them. I find that completely ridiculous. How they could ..."

"Have no worries, my love," said Ursina, her hands rubbing his. Gently. The warmth of her touch seeping into other parts of his body. "I will look into that as well. Those farmers and miners will be made to understand why they need to pay their taxes on time. You need not burden yourself with such mundane matters."

"Thank you, Ursina," he replied, his smile broadening as another wave of cool calm drifted into him, that and the light, sensual touch of her hands making it difficult for him to concentrate, his thoughts and worries simply fading away into a nothingness of bliss. "I also wanted to talk to you about ..."

There was another matter. What was it? It was driving him crazy not being able to remember. Why did he want to remember whatever it was anyway? His wife's eyes had snagged him now, promising him things that were better left unsaid.

Yes, that was it!

"These Wraiths encroaching on our Territory. If what Captain Rensom says is true, how are we to deal with them? We can't fight these beasts if we can't see them."

"A valid concern, my love."

"I know it's a valid concern," grumbled Kendric. "But you're missing my point. How can we solve this problem? The Wraiths thrive in the fog. We are helpless within it. We must find a way to challenge them within their own domain."

"Don't you remember, my love? We already discussed the solution to the Wraiths. Several times, in fact."

"We did?" Kendric couldn't recall a word of that conversation.

"Yes, not so long ago. We have nothing to fear."

"We don't?"

"No, my love. I have no doubt that the plan we developed, that you developed, will work."

"It will?"

"It will, my love."

"You're certain, Ursina? The Wraiths present a grave threat. We must manage it deftly and show those creatures they have no place in the Territories."

"Spoken like a man who one day would be king," said Ursina with a throaty laugh, her words sticking within Kendric's mind like a seed planted into the ground. "And I am certain, my love. I'm sure the Captain will do all that we've required of her. I have no doubt that the Wraiths won't be a bother for much longer."

"That's good to hear," said Kendric, nodding his head in approval. "I'm glad that we worked that out."

"It is, isn't it," Ursina agreed amiably, her hands still rubbing her husband's, Kendric's face beginning to flush from the rising heat within him.

Confident that she now could do so, Ursina finally shifted her gaze from her husband's eyes and glanced down between them. Just as quickly, she recaptured Kendric's eyes, her smile suggestive now. A smile against which her husband had no defense.

"Why don't we go to our rooms, my love? It seems now that we've discussed the business that we needed to regarding the issues facing our Territory, your mind has drifted toward issues of a more personal nature." Ursina leaned into Kendric, brushing her lips against his, the power of her fleeting touch taking his breath away. "Perhaps we should continue our conversation where we won't be disturbed."

4

LANDING AT BALLINASLOE

"So what do you think?"

"About?" The reply held a hint of annoyance, as if he didn't want to be bothered with a conversation right then.

"You don't have to be difficult all the time, you know. Just some of the time would be fine with me."

His son still mourned. He understood that. Dougal only hoped that Jakob hadn't been scarred too deeply by all that had happened when they left their home.

"As you've reminded me many a time, it's something I'm good at, and you always tell me to focus on what I'm good at. Make the most of my strengths."

Dougal forced himself to bite back a reply that might lead to another argument. He could only shake his head, not knowing if he should be amused or irritated. His son was nothing if not consistent, and he certainly took a great deal of pleasure in throwing his own words right back at him.

He decided that it was best just to let it go and leave his son be for a few minutes. It had been a long journey across the Burnt Ocean, and thankfully, for the most part, an uneventful one. They had suffered through only a handful of storms, none of the tempests the ship killers for which the seemingly endless sea, which turned the color of smoldering orange when the sun touched the horizon, was known for.

Even better, the terrors that the sailors had filled their heads with when they first started out on the months-long voyage had kept their distance. Either that or the captain had done a magnificent job of navigating around them.

Dougal had heard many of the stories before they even left Roo's Nest. It seemed like there was no shortage of sailors in the taverns lining the docks willing to share tales of passage across the Burnt Ocean that were filled with blood, terror, and death.

The only evidence of those many ships that failed to reach the Fal Carrachian coast usually washed up on the Strand or the Isle of the Mist. Of course, that was whether there was even any wreckage at all.

Dougal had no desire to be among those unfortunates. Every few weeks they had glimpsed far off in the distance a few large shapes bursting out of the water. At first, Dougal thought that they were harmless creatures of the sea such as the whales he saw on occasion, many of the animals launching themselves out of the water and demonstrating a rambunctiousness that he appreciated.

The worried cries from the lookouts in the crow's nest told him otherwise, the men in the rigging shouting instructions to the captain at the helm so that they could turn the ship away from the only partially seen monsters. None of which, for whatever reason, took an interest in them.

The sailors also seemed to take great pains to stay out of the fog that became more frequent as they approached the New Caledonian coast, the Sea of Mist that bled into the Burnt Ocean well named. They often shared stories over a cup of ale on the stern deck, a place that Dougal frequented in the evening, of the strange and frightening occurrences that had been reported during the last few years, such as ghost ships appearing out of the fog, crewed by creatures with only a passing resemblance to men.

Because of all that, Dougal was glad to have arrived in Ballinasloe with nothing more than a few scares, not regretting in the least taking Jakob across the sea on what often proved to be a treacherous journey. Besides, the risk was necessary.

There had been too much working against them back home. Dougal needed to get them out of Caledonia. Swiftly. Despite the risk. Despite the danger.

Now he could only hope that they'd have the chance to build a new life and that the reasons for their leaving didn't feel the need to follow them to the Territories.

Pulling his thoughts away from the concerns that had chased him across the water, Dougal turned his gaze to the very busy port that they had just entered, their ship gliding slowly toward its berth once it had curled around the breakwater. Dozens of vessels were tied off to the piers that jutted out into the water, soaring cranes lifting massive crates of cargo from the holds, some ships even larger than their own.

Beyond the docks, seemingly endless markets were nestled along the water, traders aided by stevedores moving goods from the ships and onto wagons as fast as they could. Several large crowds formed around those merchants seeking to sell the products they had just received. Clearly, there was no lack of interest.

Gazing past the bustle of the waterfront, Dougal studied how the town spread out into the surrounding hills. The stone wall that rose thirty feet in the air and had been built closer to the port already was obsolete.

More of Ballinasloe was outside the defensive barrier than within it. And far above the very top of the surrounding hills, the snow-capped mountains of the Highlands off to the north touched the horizon.

His and Jakob's destination. The sight made him breathe

easy for the first time since they fled their cottage nestled in the crook of the Shattered Peaks.

Looking away from the town for just a few seconds, Dougal's gaze was drawn to the impressive and as yet incomplete fortress that belonged to the ruler of Fal Carrach. The keep barely fit on the small island that sat in the center of the harbor. Once finished, the huge citadel, its walls already well over one hundred feet tall and still rising, would dominate the town and the coast.

Several barges were tied up to a makeshift pier that extended from the rocky shore, the dockworkers struggling to offload large blocks of stone, mortar, wood, and other required materials. In Dougal's opinion, it seemed the continuing effort to increase the height of the walls was more an acknowledgment of the Governor's pride than of necessity.

The sailors told him that the people of Ballinasloe were calling it the Rock, as the builders were trying to make the towering fortress appear as if the thousands of carved blocks being used to construct the outer walls were actually a single stone. Ambitious. Yet to Dougal's practical military mind, aesthetics were of little importance.

As their ship navigated around the northern side of the isle so that they didn't ground themselves on the sandbar that ran through the channel between the island and the mainland, Dougal thought that instead of worrying about the keep's appearance, perhaps whoever ruled Fal Carrach might instead want to think about building a bridge to connect the island to the shore.

A span such as that would make it a lot simpler to get to and from what was to be the governing center of the Territory. Besides, it would be quite easy to defend such a causeway.

Dougal silently laughed at himself. Now wasn't the time to allow his thoughts to focus on useless practicalities. He should be worrying about more immediate concerns.

Like his son, who was leaning against the railing and taking in everything that slipped by them as the ship neared its berth. Jakob hadn't said anything, although Dougal could tell that his son was intrigued by what he saw.

After what had occurred back home, Jakob had not opposed coming to the Territories as he had before that terrible incident. He had lost too much to want to stay trapped within those nightmares.

Still, Jakob had a lot of questions about what had driven them here and with such urgency. Dougal answered some of his questions, hoping that his doing so would allow him to avoid several others.

Dougal knew that Jakob hadn't missed his many deflections, still his son hadn't pushed for all the answers at once, which Dougal had appreciated. There were some things that Dougal didn't want to explain, and there were others that he couldn't explain.

Even though Jakob appeared to be off in his own world as the harbor slid by, Dougal knew that his son's mind was working hard. It was always working. His biggest tell was the dagger that Jakob was flipping in his hand.

Sometimes Jakob caught it by the tip of the blade. Sometimes by the handle. Sometimes he balanced the steel so perfectly that he spun it on a fingertip. When Jakob had a dagger in hand, if he wasn't throwing it, he was thinking about something.

It was a unique skill that Jakob had demonstrated with the dozen daggers he carried on him, a few on his thighs, a few on his wrists and his belt, several hidden, the largest strapped across his chest.

Jakob was already quite accomplished with the sword and the bow, so Dougal had decided to give his son something new to master during their long voyage. It helped to pass the time and, more importantly, helped to assuage Dougal's concerns regarding his son's readiness if his fears about what might come after them proved justified.

During the last few months Jakob had perfected his skill with a dagger, often juggling three or four blades at a time. And not long after he had begun to practice, he became so accomplished that he never missed with a throw.

He could hit the center of the target from thirty yards. Every time. Even when the ship was rising and falling through rough water, Dougal believing that such challenging circumstances were particularly useful when learning a new weapon.

He had gotten so good, in fact, that many of the sailors and other passengers watched him during his training sessions, betting on his throws. They had discovered quickly that it didn't pay to bet against him, something that Dougal was more than happy to benefit from, at least in the beginning, before the sailors wised up, as he added golds and silvers to the little money that remained after they had booked their passage to the Territories.

Yet none of his success and celebrity on the journey had gone to Jakob's head. He remained quiet and unassuming, even offering a helping hand to the sailors when there was a need, giving lessons on how to throw a knife to the children who were enthralled by his newly acquired skill.

"I'm sure the Highlands will offer more opportunities than what Caledonia gave us," said Dougal, reading his son and realizing that he was quite fascinated by what he saw happening in Ballinasloe. Although Dougal could sense Jakob's excitement, he knew that his son wouldn't show it, and he got the response that he expected.

Jakob just grunted in reply, though his sharp green eyes continued to absorb every aspect of the waterfront as the sailors began to tie off the ship.

"Our twenty acres in the Highlands are to the northeast,

near the coast, so we've got a ways to go. The sooner we get out of the harbor, the better."

Jakob offered his father another grunt, waiting as the sailors began to maneuver the ramp that would allow them to disembark. He was listening to what his father was saying, just not responding. He had heard it all before during the last few days, his father never really satisfied unless he could explain the same thing over and over.

Studying his son closely, Dougal wondered for the thousandth time if this was the right decision, coming across the sea.

Then he tamped down on his concerns. There was really no point in wondering if they were doing the right thing. They had no choice. They couldn't stay in Hardholm. They were here now and there was no going back.

He didn't need to think about from where they had come. He needed to think about what to do next.

Even though his father was trying to turn his thoughts to the future, Jakob was still thinking about the past. He had been thinking of joining the Guards of Roo's Nest, wanting an option if Senna couldn't be persuaded to leave her family's farm. His father had desired something more for him, not wanting him to take the same path that he did, so Dougal had decided that a new direction that led out of Caledonia was necessary.

His father's desire to keep quiet certain things about him, which had been getting harder to do in Roo's Nest, even with the instruction that he had been receiving, had accelerated the timing of the decision. That and a few other unanticipated and unwanted events that still darkened his dreams and made a good night's sleep difficult if not impossible.

Better to start fresh. To escape some of the rumors that seemed to be trailing them like a wolf pursuing its prey. To get away from the problems that were not easily addressed and could prove fatal.

Jakob couldn't fault his father's reasoning. It just took him time to adjust to a new environment. Even so, he realized that wasn't good cause to make his father's life more difficult than it already was. With that in mind, Jakob turned toward Dougal and gave him a smile.

"I'm sure we can make this work," Jakob said finally.

Yes, his father had wanted to come here because he believed that it would help to protect him and give them a better life, but he knew that there was more to it than just that. He could see the pain behind his father's eyes. It was always there, and he doubted that it would ever disappear.

Perhaps the Highlands would offer them both what they were seeking. A path away from the losses that haunted them.

Jakob's smile brought a smile to his father's usually serious countenance, as well as a look of relief, which was what Jakob wanted. His father had done a great deal for him. He had made a lot of sacrifices after his mother had died. They both deserved the opportunity to begin anew.

As soon as the sailors fixed the gangway in place, Dougal and Jakob stepped onto dry land for the first time in three months with nothing more than their weapons, rucksacks holding only a few personal items, blankets, and the clothes on their backs. It was slow-going as they worked their way through the throng toward the gentle hills of Ballinasloe.

"Why don't you wait here," suggested Dougal as he walked into a general store after they had reached the northern border of the town. "I'm just going to get enough supplies for a few days."

Jakob nodded, then sat on a barrel that was set off to the side of the entrance to the general store. As was his habit, he pulled one of the daggers from his belt and began flipping it between his fingers as he had when their ship had entered the harbor.

He spent the next few minutes watching all the people go

by. Merchants, soldiers, sailors, miners, tradespeople. No two were alike, and all of them were busy. All of them were on the move. All of them had places to be.

Except for the two men who had the look of soldiers about them standing farther down the street near the entrance to an alley.

Something about the two grabbed Jakob's attention. He caught one of the men, the larger of the two who had a long beard and deep-set eyes, glancing his way from time to time, though never long enough for Jakob to confirm that he was the target of their interest.

"You ready to go?" Dougal asked, coming back out of the store and distributing the supplies he had purchased -- hard tack, biscuits, a small frying pan, some vegetables -- between their two packs.

"Yes, let's get going," said Jakob, the two men in the alleyway making him nervous. "What are our chances of getting some horses?"

"Poor," Dougal replied. "They're more than we can afford even with what you won on the ship."

"What if we came upon them through other means?"

"Jakob ..."

"It is a busy town, after all. I'm sure things go missing all the time."

"Maybe so, but not horses."

"It would certainly help us get to where we're going that much faster."

"Jakob ..."

"And it likely wouldn't take more than a few minutes."

"Jakob," Dougal said with an exasperated sigh, interrupting his son, "I thought that we discussed this. You need ..."

Jakob sheathed his knife, then offered his father another smile. "I'm just making a joke. No more than that."

"I really hope ..." Dougal began again.

"I was just making a joke," Jakob confirmed. "Really. I left all of that in Caledonia."

Dougal nodded. He wasn't sure if he believed his son.

That didn't matter now, however. They had a long way to go and could put in a few hours of travel before they'd need to stop for the night.

The sooner they reached the Highlands, the better. And the fewer temptations there would be for his son to employ some of his less reputable skills.

THE SMALL FIRE crackled and snapped, Dougal adding a few more branches to the greedy flames to keep them going for a few hours longer. Once he and Jakob had reached the outskirts of Ballinasloe, they had used the last few hours of light to hike into the foothills of the Highlands. They would look for one of the many trails that would lead them deeper among the peaks in the morning.

Jakob tried to enjoy the dark and the quiet, laying down on the grass, his rucksack his pillow, as he stared up at the stars, the chill night air refreshing. Yet no matter what he tried, the peace that he was seeking eluded him.

He was uncomfortable, an itchiness buzzing in the back of his head that warned him that something wasn't quite right. Even more frustrating, he had no idea what it could be.

It reminded him in a vague way of the threat that had begun the chain of events that had brought him and his father to the Territories faster than they had planned. Rather than lie there and allow his uneasiness to fester, he decided that he needed to wander for a bit.

He wanted to find out what it was that was bothering him. He hoped that he was mistaken, that he was simply on edge, but there was only one way to find out.

"I'm going for a walk," Jakob said, pushing himself up. Then he called over his shoulder to his father who sat against a large rock staring at the fire. "I won't be too long."

Dougal nodded, used to his son's habits. "Don't go too far. And keep your eyes open. That shopkeeper said that it wasn't safe beyond the city walls."

"Did he say why?"

"He didn't offer much in the way of specifics. Just that people are going missing."

Jakob grunted as he headed down the slope. Not very helpful.

He took his time, the steep decline and the darkness complicating his efforts, sliding more than walking down the grass. When he reached the base of the knoll, he stood in place for several minutes, doing as his father had taught him.

When you were in unfamiliar territory, if you could, it was always a good idea to take some time to get a feel for what was going on around you. He closed his eyes, extending his senses around him, focusing on the movement and the sounds, the breeze gusting off the mountains, the crickets singing in the scrub, the mice scurrying around the stalks of grass likely worried about the soundless owls hunting them.

Jakob opened his eyes, then slowly turned his head, studying everything that extended out from the knoll. He knew what was bothering him, why the alarm was going off in the back of his head.

He was being hunted.

Why that would be the case, he didn't know. It didn't seem that there was anything out here in the wilderness with them. And they had seen nothing along the way that gave them cause to worry.

The Highlands was known not only for the massive kestrels that he had observed gliding on the warm air currents where the mountains met Fal Carrach, but also for bears and wolves.

Yet none of these predators worried him. They had no interest in humans.

Whatever was bothering him, it was something else entirely.

He could sense it, just at the edge of his consciousness. A touch of corruption. There, then not. Dodging about with an incredible speed.

It was a familiar feeling, but at the same time unfamiliar.

Keeping his eyes peeled, he walked slowly around the knoll, moving from the south to the west, then to the north, the feeling of being stalked intensifying with every step he took. Yet nothing had changed other than his position. He could see nothing or hear nothing that would suggest that there was anything out there hiding in the darkness.

He should have been better prepared.

He felt naked. It was foolish of him not to bring anything more than his daggers with him.

Rather than giving in to his rising irritation, he tried to lock onto that faint corruption. He couldn't do it. Whatever it was, it was moving too fast.

Jakob cursed under his breath. He wished he had more time to train with Aloysius. He had learned a great deal in the short amount of time that he had spent with the old Magus, and clearly not all that he needed to know.

As he came to the northeastern side of the knoll, he stopped, startled, thinking that he had seen something move in the long grass just a dozen feet to his front. At least he thought it was movement.

Even with the bright moonlight, he couldn't tell for sure. It had just been a brief flash that cut through the dim illumination.

Feeling a slight disturbance in the air to his left side, Jakob ducked just as something darker than the night slashed through the space where he had been standing. His eyes widened in alarm when he realized that it was a monstrous claw that could have taken his head from his shoulders with a single swipe if the strike had connected.

Jakob immediately scrambled backward, wanting to put some space between him and his attacker. He only succeeded in tripping over the trunk of a fallen tree in his haste, although his clumsiness actually worked in his favor as another claw slashed into the wood just a second after he had rolled over the tree, the powerful blow ripping out huge splinters that exploded into the air.

Jakob wasn't very tall, though he had a wiry strength, and he was quick with both his mind and his movements. All of which were useful attributes for dealing with his current circumstances.

Of course, none of that would matter if he couldn't get his feet back under him as the massive shadow leapt over the log, following after him as he scuttled away through the grass.

He could barely see the beast. Whatever was attacking him was no more than a vague shape in the darkness as it stalked toward him.

A cold fear rippled through him when his back slammed against a boulder, halting his attempted escape and knocking the breath from his lungs. The creature growled softly, a flash of white fangs revealed in the moonlight. Based on where he saw the gleam, if he was right, whatever was coming for him must stand well over eight feet tall.

He needed a solution to this dilemma. Now.

He didn't have his sword with him, and even if he did he doubted it would be of much use against this monster. Refusing to give up without a fight, Jakob pulled one of the many daggers he carried with him. Taking the steel tip between the thumb and the forefinger of his left hand, he threw it with all the force that he could muster.

As the steel spun toward the shadow, flashing in the moonlight, Jakob's hope rose, the monster not seeing what was streaking right toward it. Jakob's sense of hope immediately disappeared, replaced by one of despondence when the sharp point of his dagger hit the creature right in the chest, sticking shallowly in its flesh for just a second before dropping to the grass.

It was then that the creature finally stopped. The monster loomed over Jakob, the bright moonlight revealing what was trying to kill him. Its body was the color of black granite and was covered at the shoulders, chest, and thighs by raven-black scales, which allowed it to merge seamlessly with the night. The only feature that was easily discernible were its blood-red eyes.

As another large claw flashed down toward him, Jakob rolled away right before the beast shattered the large boulder, slivers of stone shooting in all directions. When Jakob regained his feet, he hustled backwards a few more steps, finally putting some space between him and his attacker and now holding a long dagger in each hand.

The sight of the steel he grasped tightly didn't seem to have much of an effect on the creature, the monster standing there for a few breaths, staring at him, hesitating. It wasn't because of concern. Jakob was certain of that. It seemed to be more out of curiosity.

Although the monster's eyes were the unnatural color of blood, for just a moment there appeared to be a slight touch of humanity behind them.

Then just as fast as it was there, that recognition vanished.

The monster stalked toward him.

Jakob swallowed nervously. Remembering how his first dagger had failed to penetrate the creature's natural armor, he didn't think that the daggers he held now would be of much use. The only real benefit they offered was that he could tell himself that he went down fighting when the monster's claws tore into his flesh.

Unable to focus as his death approached, disconnected thoughts shooting through his mind, something that Aloysius had taught him just before he left Caledonia came to him. It just might work, he thought. Besides, he had nothing to lose by trying it since he had no other ideas and his time was running out.

Infusing both daggers with the Talent, he threw the one in his left hand, immediately shifting the steel in his right hand to his left so that he could throw again if necessary.

The flash of light shot through the space in between Jakob and the monster, the creature hissing in pain when the dagger struck, the hilt of the blazing steel slipping right through the armored scales and sticking out from the very center of the monster's chest. The creature halted uncertainly then, just a few feet away from Jakob, its frightening eyes looking down at the weapon protruding from its torso.

Before the monster could reach for the hilt with one of its claws, the power of the Talent blasted out from the blade and into the monster's core, burning through the beast's insides. The monster dropped to its knees in agony, trying to pull free the dagger, the pain too much for the beast as its claws scrabbled weakly for the steel, the blood-red eyes already dimming.

The white-hot energy Jakob had placed within the blade burned through the beast until in just a matter of seconds the monster had collapsed onto its side, its eyes closed, faint wisps of heat drifting up from what now appeared to be a slightly overcooked carcass.

Jakob stared at the corpse for several minutes, the sense of danger and corruption that had been teasing him fading away just as the monster breathed its last.

He assumed that this beast might be what the shopkeeper

had referenced. He had no idea what it was. He did know that he didn't want to run across another of these monsters.

Knowing that he wouldn't find any answers by standing there in confusion, the sickly sweet smell of charred meat making him feel slightly ill, he reached down, pulled free his dagger, wiped the black blood off the blade in the grass, and then sheathed both weapons.

He needed to warn his father. This was something that neither of them had anticipated. If one of these monsters had found them, there was nothing to say that there weren't more out there waiting for them.

As he climbed back up the hill, his thoughts were elsewhere. He had never heard of anything like what he had just fought and killed, and his father had been quite methodical during his training to ensure that he knew how to fight anything, man or beast, that he might ever come across. Yet this monster was something that even his father, after years of service in various Caledonian Guards, had never mentioned.

When he finally reached the top of the tor, almost falling backwards a few times when he missed a step as he scrambled up the slope, his worried thoughts distracting him from what he was doing, he saw that the fire had burned down to a very low flame.

His father appeared to be sleeping. But rather than being rolled up in his cloak and blankets, he was draped uncomfortably over his pack, as if he had fallen there, his arms behind his back.

His mind trying to catch up to the dissonance of what he was seeing, Jakob turned when he heard what sounded like a twig breaking behind him.

With a quick swing, the figure who appeared out of the gloom before him slammed the hilt of his dagger into the side of his head.

As Jakob drifted off into unconsciousness, he realized that

he had seen his attacker before. The familiar face belonged to the large, bearded man who had been lounging by the alley while Jakob had been waiting for his father in Ballinasloe.

"Back on your feet, lad."

Dougal reached down and lifted up his son before one of the guards walking beside them had a chance to hurry them on.

Jakob had been struggling all day. His balance was still not right because of the sharp hit to the head that he had suffered the night before.

"I'm fine," Jakob mumbled. "I just need a few minutes to rest."

"We'll rest tonight," said Dougal, half of the words his son had said barely comprehensible thanks to his concussion. "Just focus on your feet. Keep your feet moving, and I'll keep an eye on you."

Dougal and Jakob had been added to a chain gang of two dozen men and women who slowly made their way deeper into the Highlands on what appeared to be a trail that was well used. The dozen men guarding them had said no more than a few words to them since they had begun their journey early that morning.

The only time that the slavers really ever came alive was when one of the prisoners fell. That usually led several of the hard-looking men to unleash a string of curses, the more aggressive and sadistic in the lot letting loose with a few cracks of their whips across the fallen person's back if the prisoner didn't get up fast enough. Or, as Dougal had discovered, if they felt the need to amuse themselves on what had so far been an uneventful journey.

It had happened to Jakob the fourth time that he had fallen, angering several of the slavers because he was slowing the entire group down and he was having a particularly hard time getting back up. His son suffered through three strikes that ripped through his shirt and marked his back with three bloody stripes that extended from his shoulders down to the base of his spine. Dougal suffered twice as many for having the temerity to try to protect his son by throwing his own body over Jakob's.

"I can try to break us free ..." Jakob said, though the rest of what he wanted to say was lost, the thought drifting away from him, the words that he had gotten out sounding garbled as he said them.

"No, not now. You can't do that now." Dougal started walking with the group again, holding Jakob up by the arm, his son needing help with his first few steps before Dougal could give him the chance to walk on his own again.

Even then, Dougal stayed right next to Jakob. They both wore steel manacles around their wrists that connected them to a long chain. Their legs were free, which allowed them to keep pace with the slavers, but there was little point in trying to run.

Dougal had no doubt as to how things would play out if two dozen people, all connected to a single length of welded steel, tried to make their escape all at the same time. They'd be falling over one another, all making a break for it in a dozen different directions.

The slavers probably wanted them to try. It would break up the monotony of the day. Give them a little fun.

"I can," mumbled Jakob, who placed a boot wrong and almost fell again, Dougal catching him by the arm in the nick of time. "I can. I promise you."

Dougal shook his head no and kept his son moving, holding tightly to Jakob's arm now, whispering into his ear because one of the overanxious slavers had sensed an opportunity when Jakob almost fell again, the man's hand caressing the whip curled around his belt.

"Not now, Jakob. Focus on where you're walking." Dougal stared at the slaver, his eyes hard, full of nasty promises if the man got too close or ambitious. The slaver actually moved away from them then, apparently uncomfortable under the harsh gaze of a man who was shackled. "Later. You can try later when your head is clear. You've got a concussion. If you try what you want to do now, you might kill yourself."

Jakob mumbled something in response to what his father had said that even he couldn't understand, so he shifted his attention to placing one foot in front of the other as his father had suggested.

Satisfied that his son had his feet back under him, Dougal took a quick look around. They had hiked probably three leagues since he and Jakob had been added to the chain, the path leading up, only up, and now winding its way between the snow-capped peaks of the Highlands like a very long snake.

Dougal had no idea who these men were or why he and his son had been taken. All of the men guarding them had the appearance of strongarms, though that was a bit deceptive.

Looking more closely, Dougal believed that in a former life many of them had been soldiers, one even having a scabbard across his back that marked him as once serving in the Royal Guard. Therefore, he assumed that they knew how to handle their weapons.

Of course they all seemed to prefer the whip at the moment, its familiar crack ringing out farther up the chain. Dougal could only hope that whoever had fallen got back to their feet before they were badly hurt.

The only hint as to where they were going had been provided by the man stumbling along behind them. From what Dougal could tell he was a trader. He had been waylaid by a few of the slavers before he could reach Ballinasloe, losing his horses, wagon, everything he owned in just a matter of minutes. What he had told Dougal had sent a sliver of ice straight into his heart.

"I heard rumors, but I didn't believe them. Bands of slavers and criminals in the mountains. Stealing people. No one coming to help. You'll need to help yourself. It's a long trip into the Highlands. Get you and your boy free. If they take us where I think they're taking us, we're all dead. It's just a matter of time. No one lasts long in the mines."

5

A FINE LINE

"Has your opinion of this vessel changed, Captain Kenworthy?"

"Not in the least Lady Carlomin." The Captain of the *Swift* turned slowly, a broad smile on his sunburned face as he looked from the bow back across the sleek lines of his triple-masted clipper. "This ship and the others," motioning to the two identical vessels that tracked them on each side, one called the *Lightning*, the other the *Rapid*, "are well named. Based on our progress to date, I think I can safely say that we'll have cut a month from the standard travel time across the Burnt Ocean when we reach Ballinasloe."

"That's excellent news," replied Talia, "since my family has invested so much in this effort and this particular journey is so important to our future endeavors."

Talia's mother had convinced her father that when it came to shipping goods between Caledonia and the Territories, there was a market for speed. Rather than acquire some of the massively large merchant vessels that carried a huge cargo and made a ponderously slow voyage between Fal Carrach and the eastern ports of Caledonia, the Carlomins had spent their money on building smaller, sleeker vessels that conveyed less on each run but shaved critical time off the crossing. The success of their current test certainly was proving the validity of their belief in such an approach and boded well for the future.

"An excellent investment, indeed, Lady Carlomin. The three ladies even handled themselves well in the few gales that we sailed through."

Talia nodded her agreement. They had fought their way through two storms, each one a swiftly approaching sheet of black flung across the horizon. Despite the howling winds, the driving rain, and the waves that sometimes reached as high as the masts, the three ships had handled the rough seas with an almost unheard of dexterity, coming through each tempest unscathed, only those few men and women with stomachs not hardened to the vagaries of the sea the worse for wear.

Another victory, in her opinion, since storms were so common on the Burnt Ocean and one of the most dangerous hazards to their business.

"What do you make of that, Captain?"

Talia pointed to the north, her eyes fixed on what appeared to be several large humps floating on top of the water. She was curious, wondering if they might be a pod of whales. The Captain, however, appeared to be concerned.

"Ollie, off the starboard bow!" the Captain called to the sailor in the crow's nest built atop the center mast.

Ollie didn't need to ask what to look for. If it wasn't icebergs when they were this far south, there was only one other reason to worry about what might be in the water with them.

Sensing the tension in Captain Kenworthy's voice, Talia felt a spark of exhilaration shoot through her. Finally, perhaps something exciting was about to happen. So far, except for the storms, the journey had been relatively uneventful.

Her mother had thought that a good thing for the maiden voyages of these three new ships they had just added to their small but growing merchant fleet. Talia had a different perspective, growing tired of the monotony of each passing day.

"Most likely blue whales!" Ollie yelled down to the Captain.

That was something that Talia would like to see. Blue whales could grow to twice the size of her ship, which was one hundred and fifty feet in length.

It wasn't to be, however, Captain Kenworthy proving his cautious nature once again.

"You're not sure?"

"As sure as I can be from this distance!" Ollie shouted.

Captain Kenworthy thought about that for several seconds. Having made his decision, he shouted back across the deck to Emelina, the helmswoman. "Signal the other ships! Hard to port for two leagues, then back on course."

The sailor standing next to the helmswoman responded immediately, raising several differently colored flags and whipping them about his head, sending orders to the ships behind them. Then, after waiting for one minute, Emelina turned the wheel, the *Swift* heading to a new course, the ships behind them gracefully mimicking her movement.

"You're afraid of blue whales, Captain Kenworthy?"

"No, I'm afraid of what feeds on blue whales."

"A Bakunawa will attack something so large?"

"Without a second thought, Lady Carlomin," he replied. "They'll attack anything if they're hungry or they believe we're encroaching on their territory."

"Bakunawa are territorial?" She had never heard that and found it curious.

"Indeed, Lady Carlomin. They view the entire ocean as theirs. They have no challengers."

Talia remembered the description that Captain Kenworthy had given her the first time that they had discussed the apex predator who ruled the Burnt Ocean. The gigantic sea dragons, a blue scaly back and white underside allowing them to blend in with the colors of the ocean, were exceedingly aggressive to begin with, even more so now because it was their mating season.

"Have you ever come in contact with a Bakunawa, Captain?"

"Thankfully, no, Lady Carlomin, not directly, and I don't want to." Captain Kenworthy kept his eyes to their stern now, looking for any sign that might reveal that the sea creatures Ollie had identified were something other than blue whales and much more dangerous. "Anything to worry about, Ollie?"

The sailor in the crow's nest took his time before responding. Talia knew what he was searching for.

The Bakunawa were stealthy hunters. Often the only sign that they approached was the serpentine wake of their passage through the water.

A very small part of her was hoping that the lookout was about to yell down a warning that one of the famed beasts had turned in their direction. The saner part of her called her a fool for wanting to take such a risk.

"No, Captain!" Ollie finally replied. "All clear! For now!"

Captain Kenworthy nodded with satisfaction, then turned back toward Talia. "As I said, I have never experienced an attack by a Bakunawa, and I'd like to keep it that way. I have seen it happen, though. A ship that was no more than a few hundred yards away from mine. We had just come out of a storm, and we needed to repair some ripped sails and tangled rigging, so we were enjoying the calm of the ocean that often follows a tempest. My crew did the job faster than the other, which proved to be a good thing for us and an unfortunate occurrence for the sailors on the other vessel. We got underway just in time."

"What happened?"

Captain Kenworthy took a moment before continuing, grimacing as the horrific memories played through his mind.

"As I said, the water was relatively calm since we were on the back end of the storm, almost glassy. We were just about to catch the wind, our mainsail filling with a steady breeze, when there was a thunderous roar off our port side. A Bakunawa shot up out of the water and slammed down onto the deck of the other ship. Its coiled, serpentine body was as wide as the ship, its sharp teeth ripping apart the rails, the masts, the sailors unable to get out of the way on the slick deck. The monster must have been circling beneath us for quite some time, and we had no clue that it was there until it decided to show itself. It could have picked our ship. For some reason it didn't."

"The other ship didn't escape?"

"No, they had no chance. That monster must have taken a half dozen sailors into its gullet before they knew what was happening, slithering across the deck, shattering the helm with its body, then dropping back down into the ocean. It happened so quickly, just a few seconds at most to do what it did, that many of us simply stood there stunned, having a hard time believing in what we had just witnessed."

"Did you try to help them?"

"We didn't have time," Captain Kenworthy replied sadly. "Just as quickly as the Bakunawa appeared the first time, it did so a second time. Everything was calm again, the water still, the wreckage of the ship floating on the gentle waves. And then the Bakunawa burst out of the water at the stern, its weight pushing the vessel down, the seawater rushing over the rails and flooding the holds. As soon as that happened, the ship and its crew were done for. The ship itself slowly began to sink, and we had no chance to save any of the sailors who jumped off the broken vessel and were trying to swim to ours."

"The Bakunawa continued to hunt?"

"Yes, it was almost like a game to the beast, slowly sweeping across the water with an easy motion, swallowing them whole. We had no choice but to make our escape while the beast was feeding." Captain Kenworthy closed his eyes for a moment and shook his head in sadness. "The screams of the sailors begging for help stay with me to this day."

"You still regret doing that?"

"I do. Even so, if I had it to do again, I'd do the same thing. Otherwise, the Bakunawa would have slaughtered two crews that day."

"And with the *Swift*, Captain? What would happen if a Bakunawa attacked?"

"We'd likely already be at the bottom of the sea. This is a fast ship, Lady Carlomin, but not as fast as a Bakunawa, and it doesn't have the size or the weight that might cause a Bakunawa to rethink its decision to attack. One of the larger monsters could probably wrap itself around this vessel several times, breaking us in two with a couple of squeezes."

"A less than pleasant thought."

"Indeed, Lady Carlomin. Still, better that we know what we're facing, don't you think? Better to know our enemies than not."

"I couldn't agree with you more, Captain."

TALIA REMAINED at the bow when Captain Kenworthy left to make his rounds on the deck. He hoped that Emelina might allow him a few minutes at the wheel, as he loved both the speed and the maneuverability of the newly constructed and uniquely designed vessel.

The double hull gave the lady a stability that was only surpassed by its agility, the *Swift* cutting to the side at the barest touch of the wheel in a way that he had never experienced before. But as he took in his wife's broad grin as she held the helm steady, he doubted that she would be so kind. She had fallen in love with the ship just as he did.

What Captain Kenworthy said before he walked away stuck with Talia, and it brought to mind the night before she left Roo's Nest, a night that she wanted to forget. Yet she couldn't. Just as Captain Kenworthy couldn't forget the screams of the friends that he had lost.

"You belong to me now!" he had shouted at her. Just as always occurred, a shiver ran down her spine as the nightmare played through her mind. The nightmare that had plagued her every night since they left Roo's Nest before dawn. "You will always belong to me!"

She had tried to get away from him, scrambling for the door. He wouldn't allow it, quicker than his size suggested, forcing her to the ground, one very large hand gripping her throat, holding her in place while also closing off her airway.

She had no other choice.

It wasn't the first time that he had gotten aggressive. But he had never acted like this, blinded by rage, a killing look in his eyes. A man who had little to lose and little fear of the consequences of what might happen next.

She had done the only thing that she could to save herself, black spots beginning to form in front of her eyes as she struggled to breathe. She had kneed him in the groin, gaining her freedom, although only briefly.

She had tried to crawl away, kicking with her free foot, digging her hands into the thick carpet as she tried to pull herself to the open doorway.

It was no use.

Ronild was too strong for her. Despite her best efforts, he flipped her over and straddled her, careful to protect his groin this time. He tried to take his pleasure with her, enjoying the fight she was putting up.

He had been a fool.

She had gotten the better of him, almost biting off his

tongue. She had gained her freedom again, and this time she made the most of the opportunity.

He had given her a jeweled dagger as an engagement present. She had pulled it from the sheath hidden at the back of her belt, then with the last of her fading strength slashed it across his face right after he had swung at her with one of his favored throwing axes.

He swung again with his axe. This time, when Talia ducked, she punched up with her dagger, stabbing the blade into his side right between his two lower ribs. Right where Tennyson, who at that very moment was climbing the rigging above her, had taught her to strike if she wanted to make sure an attacker was put down with a single blow.

After her betrothed crumpled to the floor, a look of betrayal in his eyes, she had fled from the manor and gone straight to the docks. She hadn't been planning to go with her mother to the Territories, but after that night she had no choice. She couldn't stay in Caledonia.

She'd be charged with murder. He was a lord. The City Watch in Roo's Nest wouldn't listen to her side of the story. They wouldn't care. She didn't have the power and connections her fiancée and his family did.

As her dead betrothed had so liked to remind her, he had been only a dozen places away from obtaining the Duchy's seat of power. She lived in the harbor.

In hindsight, although that had been a terrible night for her, it had also been an enlightening one. It had given her a clarity with respect to what she had been doing with her life and what she should have been doing.

Her father was already in Ballinasloe, setting up the base of operations that they would need to run their shipping company. Her mother was bringing over the first three new ships as well as the first batch of spices and other commodities that made up the cargo and were in short supply and in high demand in the Territories.

They'd be able to sell their stock at a premium. In fact, most of it had already been purchased by other traders who stood to make a killing.

Time away from the man she was supposed to marry, the man she had killed, had given her the perspective that she had been missing when she had been with him. She had always been a strong person, doing things on her own, making her own decisions, her parents raising her that way.

Yet when she had met her fiancé, she had changed. She had become what he wanted. She had lost herself, so taken with the handsome young lord who treated her so well that she forgot who she was and who she wanted to be.

She didn't know why, and she had hated herself for it. She became a meeker version of herself, seeing herself through his eyes rather than her own.

It wasn't until she had been aboard the *Swift* for a few days and had time to think about it that she had realized that although her fiancé may have pushed her in that direction, she had allowed it to happen. She was responsible for the person she had become for him, not him.

He had guided her, yes, but she had followed willingly. That would not happen again.

Ronild Magnison.

Very handsome. Very accomplished. Very high opinion of himself.

Making a name for himself in Roo's Nest as he sought to broaden his family's business interests. Peculiarly curious about her and her family's plans for the Burnt Ocean and New Caledonia.

She had been such a fool, acting like a lovestruck teenager rather than the competent young woman that she was. She should have realized what Ronild was after.

It wasn't love as she had allowed herself to believe. It was her family's company and the wealth that it could bring him and his own family.

She had fallen for Ronild the first time she had set eyes on him. He had been kind. Considerate. Interested in her. Her opinions. What she had to say. What she wanted to do with her life. Asking questions. Making her laugh. Making her feel special. At least at the start.

Ronild had lavished her with kind words and gifts, rides in the countryside, picnics on the beach. He had proposed marriage after a whirlwind courtship of just two months. Entranced as she was, she had accepted before speaking with her mother, whose opinion of Ronild differed from hers.

Talia saw what she wanted to see. Her mother saw who he really was before she did. Although not before she too was taken in for a time by the chance such a pairing presented to the Carlomins.

Isana had thought that Ronild would be a good match for her. A young man who would broaden her horizons, give her access to a part of Caledonian society to which the Carlomins hoped to ascend. And his connections would be good for the family business.

Despite all that, looking back, Talia realized that her mother had her doubts from the very beginning, hinting at them whenever she could. Isana, knowing that trying to change Talia's mind only made her want all the more whatever it was that she shouldn't have, had asked her to wait before scheduling the wedding. Wait until after she and her father returned from the Territories.

Isana had suggested as well that Talia convince Ronild to join them in the Territories. He had refused, nicely of course, noting that he couldn't leave his many interests in Roo's Nest.

She should have known then that Ronild's desire for her wasn't based on her, but on what she could give him.

And then on the night before her mother was to set sail for Ballinasloe, she finally saw Ronild for who he really was.

She had almost made the worst mistake of her life.

She almost didn't recognize in time that he was more interested in her name than in her.

She realized that when he was choking her into unconsciousness. When he was making clear that she was no more than a possession to him. Something to be acquired. Something to be used. Something that belonged to him. Something to be discarded when she was no longer of use.

She realized then that he wanted her business. He didn't want her.

She had escaped, although just barely. He hadn't escaped her. And she kept the dagger that he had given her close at hand, always in the sheath at the small of her back.

The jeweled weapon had proven handy once. She had no doubt that it would prove useful again.

"You need to get out of your head. If you spend too much time in there you'll get lost and never find your way out."

"I don't know how to take that, mother."

"Take it for what it's worth."

"So not all that much."

Isana patted her daughter's hand warmly. "It's that sharp mind and even sharper tongue that will get you into trouble, Talia."

"It already has, mother. Many times. And it likely will again, just as you say."

"And yet you still have done nothing about it."

"I've smoothed out the edges just a bit."

"That doesn't seem to have stuck for very long."

Talia shrugged. "I can't change who I am."

"Nor should you," Isana agreed. She was an older version of her daughter, with a strong presence, pixielike face, and blond hair that sometimes flashed pink when it caught the light a certain way. "Although there's nothing wrong with picking your moments. Some would call that maturity."

"You know I can't remember the last time that we talked and you weren't trying to impart advice or share a lesson."

"All of life is a lesson, Talia. You should know that by now."

Talia held her tongue, though she couldn't keep a smile from her face. Her mother was a force of nature. Always so sure of herself. Never wavering. Always seeing the forest for the trees, or the trees for the forest, depending on what the situation required.

She so much wanted to be like her mother.

And yet there were also times when she needed her space, needed her freedom, chafing under the expectations placed on her by Isana.

She had mulled that thought almost every night since she had boarded the *Swift*, wondering if her falling for Ronild so quickly and so heedlessly had resulted in part from her desire to forge her own path no matter where that path might lead her.

Talia shook her head to clear it. She didn't want to think about any of that anymore. That had happened in Caledonia. She would begin anew in the Territories. She would build the life that she wanted and learn from the mistakes that she had made.

As her mother liked to say, you weren't really living if you weren't making mistakes. Just don't make the same ones twice.

"I was just speaking with Captain Kenworthy. He is quite pleased with the *Swift* and the other ships. He believes in what we're doing now."

"That's good to hear, particularly since we have three more of these ships coming behind us from Roo's Nest and your father has three more under construction in Ballinasloe."

"You were willing to take a risk like this without a real test?" Talia was shocked. Her parents rarely moved forward with a venture until they'd tested and evaluated it, almost to the point of overkill, working out any of the potential hiccups before investing their hard-earned money.

"In this case, yes. We believed that we could make this work. We also believed that speed was of the essence, not only in terms of what we wanted from the ships, but also in how quickly we implemented the concept. If we can create the market for fast transport across the Burnt Ocean, we can keep our competitors in our wake for a longer period of time."

"That's very cutthroat of you, mother," said Talia teasingly.

Her mother didn't take the comment in that way. When she talked business, she was always serious.

"I am being realistic." She then pointed off their port bow. "And we may have come across another situation where our speed will be essential."

Talia looked to where her mother pointed. Three ships, just dark blots at the moment because of the distance between them, were coming up on them fast.

From the direction they were approaching, Talia knew that they could be only one thing.

Pirates.

"Can we outrun them, Captain Kenworthy?" asked Isana, she and Talia having joined him at the helm.

"We can," he replied with absolute confidence, leaving his wife at the tiller, his focus on the three ships that were seeking to cut them off from the south. "The problem is that we're not running neck and neck." His brow wrinkled as he ran through some calculations in his head. "The question is will we get past the point where those three ships are trying to intercept us before they do. If they miss us, they have no chance of catching up to us."

Talia looked to their port side. A strong wind from the southwest was aiding the three vessels angling toward them. If not for the sleek lines and innovative hull of their new ships, Talia was certain that the pirates would already be boarding them.

She picked out the features of the pursuing vessels as they increased in size. Three masts for each one. Black sails. And high prows upon which stood a handful of men, crossbows in hand.

She shook her head in irritation. They should have assumed that this would happen. Her father had written about what was going on off the eastern coast of the Territories. The increasing number of well-coordinated attacks by pirates who were aware of where the fattest targets would be and when.

It was all very suspicious, in her opinion, and much too convenient. And now it was all too real.

"If we do, it will be very close," said Talia, judging the rapidly decreasing distance between them and their pursuers and how the angles would collide.

"I'll signal the other ships," said Captain Kenworthy, the three pirate frigates now no more than a few hundred yards away, curling toward them on a steep arc, the pirates on the prows and along the starboard rails winching back their crossbows, preparing to attack. "Perhaps you could take the lead trying to keep them off us? Your mother has told me quite a bit about your skill with a bow."

"With pleasure," Talia replied, racing belowdecks to retrieve her bow and quiver of arrows. When she reappeared seconds later, she called to the several sailors charged with defending the ship to follow her as they ran onto the deck with their crossbows.

They reached the port side with only seconds to spare. The approaching cutters sliced through the waves, now no more than thirty yards to the south and closing on a curve that would bring them alongside.

Talia pulled an arrow from her quiver. The sailors worked as fast as they could to pull back their shorter bows by placing the head on the deck, holding it in place with their feet planted on the steel bars at the front of the weapon, and then pulling back the taut cord. Not an easy task for even the strongest of fighters.

Just in time too as the lead pirate ship rose and fell right in front of them, pounding through the waves, no more than twenty yards away now. The crossbowmen along the side already had begun firing across the water.

One of the sailors just a few feet away from Talia screamed in agony, dropping his crossbow when he himself fell to the deck, a bolt sticking out of his arm. She ignored that and the several other quarrels that slammed into the wood around her and sent sharp, thin splinters flying into the air.

She knew that she only had one shot, so she needed to make the most of it. Crossbows would keep the pirates' heads down, but they didn't have the accuracy at the current range to do what she needed to do. To do the only thing that might prevent the pirate vessel from smashing against their hull.

Pulling back on the string, arrow fixed in place, Talia took a deep breath. She wasn't interested in the pirates on the prow or along the rail. She had a different target in mind.

Blocking out everything around her, the noises died away. The men and women moving around her vanished. Everything disappeared but for the motion of the ship cutting through the waves.

Taking one more deep breath, having attained the calm that was so critical to her efforts, she released.

The effect was almost immediate.

She smiled in pleasure, knowing that she had made the shot, a shot that she didn't think she could.

The cutter, about to scrape against the side of the *Swift*, heeled sharply to port, Talia striking the helmsman in the chest, the man collapsing to the deck. The unattended wheel spinning wildly. The waves slamming into the faltering ship's port side, threatening to swamp the vessel. Even worse for the pirates, that brought the cutter square to the two ships just behind it.

As the *Swift* and then the *Lightning* and the *Rapid* shot across the imaginary line that ensured that the pirates couldn't snare them, Talia watched in morbid fascination as one of the other vessels curled farther to the west, avoiding the floundering cutter by just a few feet. The second ship wasn't so lucky, slamming into the port side near the stern with a sickening crunch of cracking and splintering timber.

In seconds, both ships were taking on water, the floundering vessel with a large hole near the stern, the other cutter with a large slice in its hull just below its prow, water rushing in.

As her mother had taught her, everything in life was a lesson.

For her, it was that her mother tended to be more right than wrong.

She chose to ignore the irritation that accompanied that finding, more pleased by what they had just confirmed.

Speed was the key on the Burnt Ocean.

6

THE HONOR WAS MINE

Banshee's squawk brought Bryen out of his reverie. He had been on the ship for only a week. Even so, it hadn't taken long before it had begun to feel confining. To remedy that, he now flew with Banshee daily, getting away from the *Freedom* to explore the world around them from above.

He relished the freedom of his hours' long flights. Even more, the opportunity to get some time to himself. The constant activity aboard the vessel drained his energy. Leaving all that with Banshee helped him to relax.

Banshee squawked again, finally catching Bryen's attention. They had decided to head to the east that morning and out over the Silent Sea. The ocean appeared endless, the waves never smaller than ten feet at the crest. Every so often dolphins skimming across the water and pods of migrating whales broke the grey and blue expanse. He even glimpsed the broad back of some creature that was clearly bigger than a whale diving beneath the water before he could get a good look at it.

"You sure you want to keep going in this direction, Banshee?"

The Griffon screeched once more in reply, seemingly unconcerned about what blocked their path.

"Have it your way," replied Bryen.

In response, Banshee banked more toward the east and the fog bank that blanketed the horizon. As they approached, the air became noticeably cooler. It wasn't long before the bright sunlight shifted to a sickly yellow, dimmed further by the thick wisps of grey as Banshee flew along the edge of the billowing mist.

"Do you mind if we go in for a few minutes?" asked Bryen, now curious about the billowing grey.

The fog was denser than what he was used to on the coast of the Southern Marches. Darker, even forbidding. It was as if some menace lurked within.

Apparently just as curious as Bryen was, Banshee turned sharply, diving right into the fog.

They both regretted the decision immediately.

The instant the sun disappeared, the swirling grey consuming them, Bryen and Banshee stiffened, on the alert. He had been right. It felt as if a threat hid within the mist. That they were being hunted.

Although he couldn't see a thing, Bryen was certain that they weren't alone in the fog.

A wrongness had joined them, a presence that radiated evil. What it could be, though, neither he nor Banshee could determine.

It was ephemeral. Barely there, just at the edge of Bryen's consciousness. It reminded him of what it was like trying to catch a shadow.

Even so, it was inescapable and all-encompassing, infusing the grey haze with an unmistakable malevolence.

Bryen could tell that it was affecting Banshee much as it was him, a darkness settling over them, a touch of fear beginning to play through them.

Everything about the fog felt wrong. Tainted.

Needing to know what it could be, Bryen reached for the Talent, crafting several balls of energy that played around his fingers before he threw them to their front with the goal of lighting their way. Neither Bryen nor Banshee anticipated what happened next, the Griffon halting her flight, her powerful wings beating just to hold them in place.

The spheres of energy didn't just brighten the fog as Bryen thought they would. Instead, the Talent burned through the mist, clearing a space around them. And then, even more remarkably, the fog began to retreat, pulling even farther away from them, giving them more room, allowing a hollowed-out space to form, the haze reluctant to draw closer to them once again.

What had just happened could mean only one thing. Bryen wasn't sure that he was pleased that he was right.

The fog wasn't natural. It was made of or at least laced with the Curse.

How that could be he didn't know. Why that would be ... that worried him even more. He would need to speak with Rafia about his findings, because his suspicions were leading him down a dark road and one that he didn't want to venture on by himself.

"Why don't we head back to the ship, Banshee," Bryen suggested.

The Griffon was more than happy to comply, curling around in a tight circle to fly through the fog, Bryen sending several more balls of energy to their front, the grey tendrils pulling back, not wanting to come in contact with the Talent. As soon as Bryen and Banshee shot out of the fog, relishing the warmth of the sun once again, their spirits lifted, the soul-crushing essence that plagued the thick mist leaving them.

Bryen took a deep breath, glad to be free of whatever lurked in the mist, even as his curiosity continued to tease him.

The experience immediately brought to mind his struggles with the Curse when fighting the Ghoule Overlord, in particular when the Dark Magic had been just seconds away from making him its own.

The Seventh Stone had cleansed him just before he turned. Just before he joined with the Curse.

But it had been close. Way too close, and certainly not something that he wanted to have to deal with again.

He had been grateful to come through that experience without being corrupted by the Curse. Even so, a small part of him, a very tiny part, had been disappointed as well.

He had felt the power contained within the Curse. The seductiveness of that tainted power. The pull. What the Dark Magic offered him. Promised him.

He had known in that instant what he would have lost if he had acquiesced to what was trying to take him, if he had given in to the Curse.

He had known as well what he would have become. What he would have gained.

He had learned an important lesson in that moment.

You didn't have to touch the Curse to be turned by the Curse. It was more subtle than that. It was all about power, yes, but it all really came down to intention.

His intention.

How he intended to use the Talent and the Seventh Stone.

His decisions in that regard could lead him down a path to his own destruction.

He didn't need to touch the Curse to become the Curse.

No. There was another way.

A way that was much more devious. One that was difficult to avoid if you failed to pay attention. If you failed to consider the consequences of your decisions. If you failed to see how a moment of indecision, of weakness, could take you down a path from which you could never return.

The Curse was so very enticing.

No more rules. No more restrictions. No more morality.

He could do what he wanted, when he wanted, however he wanted.

He shivered at the thought.

He didn't like what he had just experienced. He didn't like what he was thinking. He didn't like how easy it was for his thoughts to move down a trail upon which he didn't want to tread.

He didn't like how good the promise of the Curse made him feel.

~

THE *FREEDOM* HAD BEGUN its turn around the far southeast cape of Caledonia after heading south down the coast of the Southern Marches, making for the Endless Ocean to the west. From there, once past Caledonia, the massive vessel would sail into the Burnt Ocean and then on to Ballinasloe, the primary and only port of consequence in the Territory of Fal Carrach.

In all, a journey of more than three months, assuming they weren't caught up in any of the powerful storms for which the Burnt Ocean was famous.

Banshee circled the ship several times before alighting onto one of the special decks at the stern built just for her and the other Griffons. All of the other animals were enjoying a late afternoon nap under the large oilcloths that gave them shade from the sun. The strong ocean breeze ruffled their feathers and kept them cool in the heat of the day.

The Griffons had taken to the large ship with little difficulty, enjoying the space provided to them and the new environment. They spent their mornings fishing, often bringing back massive, fanged eels and even an occasional swordnose to feast upon.

"She's a magnificent animal."

Bryen turned, taking his fingers from beneath Banshee's feathers, the Griffon growling gently, unhappy that the attention that she was receiving was coming to an end sooner than she would have preferred.

"She is that," agreed Bryen.

"May I?" Captain Gregson asked.

"That's not a question I can answer."

Captain Gregson nodded, then looked at Banshee, taking in the animal. Banshee stared right back at him. The contest of wills continued for more than a minute, then Captain Gregson, courage still in place although beginning to wane because of the strength of Banshee's gaze, stretched out his hand, holding it just a foot in front of the Griffon's very sharp beak.

Banshee continued to stare at Captain Gregson, not blinking, her auburn eyes blazing brightly in the waning sunlight. Finally, tentatively, Banshee stretched out her neck, sniffing at Captain Gregson's fingers, then huffing.

"She likes you," Bryen said. "She likes to be scratched along the jaw. Slowly."

Captain Gregson waited a moment more before taking that risk, swallowing a few times, still uncertain. The Griffon was a magnificent animal. A deadly one as well.

Even so, his courage never flagging, he reached out and began to run his fingers where Bryen had suggested, Banshee purring in response. He did that for several minutes before finally stepping away, a broad smile cracking his often serious visage.

"Looks like you made a new friend," said Bryen.

"That's good to hear," said Captain Gregson, a note of satisfaction in his voice. "Because I'd hate to be anything else to a Griffon."

"Very wise," said Bryen. "They do tend to hold grudges, and

they tend to approach their enemies in a very singular manner."

Captain Gregson nodded as if he knew what Bryen was talking about, though he really didn't. He had approached the Griffon for a very specific purpose. Many of the sailors were still uncomfortable with the five animals traveling with them, knowing nothing more than the stories told about the beasts who lived in the mountains where men rarely trod, most of those stories unsettling if not outright terrifying.

Appreciating that his crew trusted his judgment, he had wanted to show them that they had little to worry about from their feathered and furry guests. He assumed that if he did this now, they might see that the Griffons weren't to be feared. Or at least the ones aboard the ship. So long as they treated the magnificent animals with the respect they deserved.

Bryen had assumed as much, watching as a small group of sailors stopped to watch as Captain Gregson introduced himself to Banshee. A good captain, and a smart one, Bryen had learned, knowing what his crew needed and then trying to give it to them.

"Might I ask you a question, Captain Gregson?"

"Of course, Captain Keldragan."

Bryen's next thought fled for just a second, then his eyes sparkled with an unexpected mirth. "Did Captain Klines put you up to that?"

"You mean calling you by your title as commander of the Blood Company?"

"Yes, that's exactly what I mean."

"Yes, he did."

"Who knew the Blademaster had a sense of humor," mused Bryen.

For some reason, Captain Klines took a particular pleasure in addressing Bryen by the rank given to him by Duchess Noorsin Stelekel when she named the gladiators of the Pit the free Blood Company in recognition of their role in the overthrow of the Beleron dynasty. Why the very serious Blademaster found it so amusing, Bryen had no idea.

Although he assumed that since the Blademaster was friends with Declan there was more to it than that. Likely a lesson for Bryen and an effort to help him get more comfortable with his responsibilities with respect to the gladiators who had sworn allegiance to him.

"I certainly didn't," replied Captain Gregson. "Though he certainly does know how to spin a good yarn."

"Something else I wasn't aware of," replied Bryen, "but good to know." Bryen stepped off the deck, Captain Gregson scratching Banshee's beak for a few seconds more before joining him. "I was hoping that you could tell me more about something I discovered while flying with Banshee."

"What might that be?"

"Just to our east, maybe no more than a handful of leagues distant, we came across a dense fog."

"That's not uncommon for where the Silent Sea meets the Endless Ocean."

"I expect not," nodded Bryen. "This fog was different, however, from the fog that I was accustomed to when I was in Battersea. This fog was ..."

"Alive," Captain Gregson finished very quietly. He looked around quickly, making sure that none of the crew were close enough to hear what he had just said. Sailors tended to be a superstitious lot after all.

Bryen nodded, catching the distant look that came to the Captain's eyes. "Exactly so. The fog was incredibly dense though that thick moisture you would expect coming off the ocean wasn't there. And within it ... the best I can explain it is that it felt like there was an evil lurking within that thick mist. Strange, I know, but there it is."

"That's an excellent way to describe it," said Captain Gregson. "I've only seen that fog a few times myself, and always at a distance thankfully, but just looking at it ... it's not right, as you say. I'd rather face off against a Bakunawa than enter that fog."

"In the Silent Sea? That fog is common here?"

"No, actually, I'm surprised you ran into it where you did. I've only come across it in the Burnt Ocean when needing to take a more southerly course to New Caledonia."

"Do you expect then that we'll come upon it during our journey to the Territories?"

"There's no way to know, although I certainly hope not. There are dangers aplenty already. I don't want to add another to the list. And certainly not one against which we have no defense."

"Why do you say that?"

"It's as you said, Captain Keldragan. There's an evil lurking within it. An evil I'd prefer not to meet."

"What do you know of this fog? And what do you know of this evil?"

"Just stories, Captain Keldragan. You know how sailors like to talk, especially after they're a few sheets to the wind."

"Indulge me," said Bryen, feeling the need to know more. Feeling as if whatever lived within the fog wasn't a threat that they would be able to escape during their journey to the west. And not knowing why he did so.

"No one really knows what might be in the fog, if anything at all. All I know is that no one in their right minds will enter that murk. It's not natural. There are too many stories of ships vanishing in that grey haze and never being seen again to not give them at least some credence."

"You must have at least a guess as to what might be in the fog," prodded Bryen.

"A guess, yes," replied Captain Gregson. "Some of the other captains I've talked to say that there are monsters in the mist."

"What kind of monsters?"

"Kraken."

"Isn't a Kraken a mythical sea creature that's even bigger than a Bakunawa?"

"It is," agreed Captain Gregson. "It's also what people around the shores of the Burnt Ocean have been calling whatever it is that inhabits the fog. Kraken. Haven't seen anything myself, don't really want to, so I can't give you a definitive answer. Supposedly they look somewhat like men, though definitely not human. I don't know any more than that. I'm just telling you what I've heard."

Bryen nodded, thinking about what Captain Gregson had just told him. There was no reason to think that the Curse was restricted solely to the Lost Land. In fact, it would be foolish to believe that it was. And likely dangerous. Fatally so, in fact.

"What happens if we enter the fog?" asked Bryen.

"You want to enter the fog?"

"I already did with Banshee."

"You did?" Captain Gregson's eyes widened in disbelief. He then spoke in a hushed whisper. "How did you make it back out?"

"The Talent," Bryen replied simply.

"Right, yes, sorry," stammered Captain Gregson. Bryen had knocked him a bit off balance, not used to being around people skilled in the use of natural magic and never having heard of anyone ever entering the fog willingly, much less surviving what lived within that grey swathe when they did. Then again, the young man standing before him was the Volkun, and no one likely had flown into the fog on the back of a Griffon, so it certainly stood to reason that he'd be able to escape whatever it was that made the fog its home.

"So what happens if the fog catches up to us?" Bryen rephrased his question, understanding that Captain Gregson would never willingly enter the fog.

Captain Gregson gave him a sour look, then sighed. There

was no reason not to tell the lad the full truth. He wasn't the typical merchant or traveler who'd piss his pants if he or she received some frightening news.

The lad had fought in the Pit. Captain Gregson had even watched one of his combats, leaving the Colosseum with a sense of awe and relief. Awe because he had never seen anyone move so quickly on the white sand, relief that he wasn't the one tasked with fighting the Volkun.

"Most likely we don't come back out," replied Captain Gregson quietly. "The ship might. Often a ship taken by the fog will be found floating somewhere in the ocean or grounded on a shore. But the crew and any passengers will be gone, the signs of a slaughter visible throughout whatever is left of the vessel."

"And still no one knows what might be lurking within the mist?"

"No, I don't think anyone wants to know."

"Then we should stay out of the fog," suggested Bryen.

"That we should," agreed Captain Gregson, who gave him a smile. "Although whatever might be lurking in the fog hasn't run across someone like you. That might be a fight worth seeing. You might make these Kraken, or whatever they are, think twice about challenging you."

"Maybe so, Captain."

"Anything else I can help you with then?"

"No, thank you, Captain Gregson."

"Glad to help. One other small matter, Captain Keldragan, if you don't mind."

"Of course," replied Bryen, realizing that Captain Gregson hadn't approached him just because of the discomfort his crew was feeling regarding the Griffons.

"The sailors who make up this crew have experienced more than most. A few Griffons won't be a problem after a few more days have passed, especially now that they've seen how your Griffon responded to me. But you're a different matter."

"Me?" asked Bryen, not understanding. "How so?"

"They're a bit nervous around you."

"Around me?" asked Bryen. Why would they be uncomfortable around him? He was no different than they were. Bryen shook his head in resignation. He realized that just because he told himself that didn't make it true. "Did you have something in mind to ease their concerns?"

"I did," said a strong and quiet voice from right behind him.

Bryen turned, the Blademaster standing there, his green eyes flashing with anticipation and the faint hint of amusement that always seemed to be there.

"I can understand how people are uncomfortable around the Griffons," continued Captain Klines. "They are unique and beautiful animals. Even so, they are nothing compared to the stories they've heard about you, about what you have done, Captain Keldragan. They know of the gladiator, the Volkun. They know of the Protector. They know of the man who freed the men and women of the Pit and then saved Caledonia. They see you and they see a story come to life."

"You think they need to see me as more human."

"I do," admitted Captain Klines.

"And I take it, Blademaster, that you have in mind a way to do that?"

"I do."

Word of the practice combat spread like wildfire through the *Freedom*, the excitement among the crew almost palpable. It was a welcome break from what could often be days of nothing more exciting than the broad expanse of the ocean stretching out before them in all directions.

With the help of several sailors, it hadn't taken long for Declan to create a training ring on the center deck just beneath the helm. Now every member of the crew who wasn't on duty or assigned to the watch surrounded the space, the crowd ten rows deep, the rigging packed with those who couldn't get a good view from the deck.

All of them waited with a hushed anticipation. The only noise came from a smaller group opposite the helm who were talking animatedly as they placed their wagers, Emelina serving as the bookmaker.

"Did you make a bet?" Captain Gregson asked of Lycia.

The two stood at the helm, Captain Gregson at the wheel, pleased that his wife finally relinquished control of the ship to him, the combat between the Volkun and the Blademaster the only reason that Emelina would allow her husband to take a turn.

"Of course," replied Lycia. Her gaze never wavered from the two men about to face off against one another. Both seemed inordinately calm and composed. She wasn't surprised in the least.

"The Volkun?" asked Captain Gregson.

Lycia nodded. "I always bet on the Volkun."

"I saw him fight once in the Colosseum. Do you believe that he stands a chance against the Blademaster? I would think that a combat on the white sand differs from one against the best swordsman in Caledonia."

Lycia turned toward the Captain, intrigued by the question. She could understand his logic, even though she didn't agree with it.

"A fair point, Captain Gregson. But you forget two key points."

"What would those be?"

"First, the Volkun has never lost. That's why he's still alive."

"There's a first time for everything, and neither has the Blademaster."

"There is that," admitted Lycia.

"And the second point?"

"We're no longer in Caledonia."

Captain Gregson chuckled at that. "Point taken. Still, I wonder if you might like to make a side wager."

"What did you have in mind?" asked Lycia.

While Lycia and Captain Gregson worked out their own gamble, Declan stepped into the center of the training ring, his stentorian voice ringing out across the deck.

"This bout will not be to three touches. We will treat this as a combat. First touch wins."

That statement brought an appreciative murmur from the crowd. Few combatants would ever allow such an approach, as they always preferred to have a chance to recover if they made a mistake.

Not so the Blademaster, who held onto the hilt of his sword loosely, blade pointing to the deck, nor the Volkun, who leaned against the Spear of the Magii, the haft gripped comfortably in his hands. That condition seemed to be of little concern to either of them. Nothing more than a small detail.

"Are you sure this is a good idea?" asked Declan in a quieter voice so that the sailors around them couldn't hear, directing the question toward his friend.

"Why wouldn't it be?" replied Jurgen Klines, his eyes flashing with anticipation. No one but Declan had offered him much of a challenge for decades. He guessed that was about to change with the Protector.

"You're not as young as you used to be."

"I appreciate your concern," said Klines, "but with all respect I must point out that neither are you."

"That's beside the point," Declan grumbled, not appreciating his friend's comment because of the truth it contained. "I'm not the one matching steel with Bryen."

"I'll be fine, Declan," sighed Klines. "I'm sure I can hold my own against the Volkun."

Declan looked across the small space at Bryen, the young man's eyes hard, emotionless, fixed on the Blademaster. Although his posture suggested that Bryen was adopting a casual approach to this combat, Declan knew the young man too well to be taken in by the façade he presented.

Bryen approached a combat in only one way. Having competed against both men, Declan had no doubt as to how this bout was going to end.

It seemed that Klines hadn't reached the same conclusion. Declan knew that the Blademaster would and likely sooner than he would prefer.

"Let's hope so," Declan murmured under his breath. Then he stepped back so that both Klines and Bryen could hear him. "There's only one rule."

"Don't kill each other," Davin yelled out from far above them, having taken his preferred place in the crow's nest.

"Right." Then Declan stepped out of the training circle. "Begin!"

The Blademaster almost lost at the very start of the combat, Bryen launching an immediate, blazingly fast attack, the Spear of the Magii a swirl of grey steel as he swung low, then high, then low again, steadily advancing, his weapon a blur in front of him.

Each time, Klines got his blade up in time, though just barely, sparks flying when the sword and spear met. The Blademaster had no choice but to retreat around the circle, pivoting and turning, ducking, dodging, even rolling to the side, exhibiting an agility at which few would have guessed in large part because he had not had to demonstrate it for quite a long time.

Bryen barely made note of the Blademaster's impressive display, staying with him, his steel singing through the air. He had no intention of allowing the Blademaster to do anything else but dance to the tune that he selected.

As a result, the Blademaster continued to backpedal, always getting his blade where it needed to be and his body away from where it shouldn't be just in time. Yet Klines realized almost right from the start that perhaps he should have listened to what his friend had been trying to tell him.

Because Declan may have been right. Challenging the Volkun may not have been Klines' best decision.

Even so, there was nothing for it now. Klines had wanted to test himself against the Protector for quite some time, having listened intently to what the Lady Winborne had told him of the young man and what he could do with a length of steel, hoping that information might help him when he finally got his chance.

Klines certainly wasn't disappointed as the Protector guided him around the training circle. The Volkun was revealing a skill that he had rarely seen. It didn't seem like the Protector was even sweating while his own shirt was already sticking to his back.

Probably not the best decision on his part. True. But even though he had yet to do anything other than defend himself, he was thoroughly enjoying the combat. If he was going to lose a duel, something that hadn't happened in years, he couldn't think of a better way to do it.

In a combat with the Volkun.

"Bryen's not even letting Captain Klines take a breath," said Aislinn.

"Would you?" asked Lycia, her eyes never leaving the combat, tracking every movement, every decision made by the two combatants, thinking about what she would do if she were in the practice circle with either Bryen or the Blademaster.

"No, I wouldn't," admitted Aislinn. "Not after spending so much time working with Captain Klines."

"It's how I trained Bryen," explained Declan. "I'm sure he's heard quite a bit about the Blademaster's reputation."

"Likely from the Lady Winborne," offered Davin, the gladiator having just joined them after placing a bet on the fight with Emelina, certain that his friend was going to win, climbing down from the crow's nest because he couldn't see from far above as well as he would have liked.

"I might have sung his praises a few times. He is quite skilled with a blade."

"That he is," agreed Davin.

"I wouldn't have survived Tintagel without Captain Klines," said Aislinn. "He's a good friend. Even more, he's an excellent instructor."

"He is that," grunted Declan.

"And he taught me quite a bit while in the Corinthian Palace."

"Of that I have no doubt," murmured Declan, his eyes tracking the combat playing out before him.

Bryen took control of the fight right from the beginning and had yet to relinquish it -- collected, calm, focused -- just as Declan expected that he would. Jurgen Klines was coolheaded as was his habit, even as Bryen continued to apply more pressure to him.

Both were masters of their respective weapons. The only real difference between them was the speed.

Klines was holding his own. For now. Declan could tell that it wouldn't last. Bryen was too fast for him.

"And I may have told Bryen a bit about my training sessions with Captain Klines," admitted Aislinn.

"Well, it looks like he took some of what you said to heart," nodded Declan. "He's approaching the Blademaster the right way. Most can't match Jurgen cut for cut. Bryen can. So it's the right move to keep Jurgen on the defensive. If you give the Blademaster too much time to think about how to defeat you, you're done."

"How do you know that?" asked Davin.

"From hard experience," Declan said. "Didn't you watch any of the training combats between me and the Blademaster in the Pit? Every Monday afternoon, the Blademaster and I were on the white sand."

"A few, yes," Davin admitted. "Sometimes other things got in the way."

"Like what?" demanded Declan. "That was the perfect opportunity for you to learn how to improve as a fighter. Bryen was always there. Lycia. Many others as well."

"A nap," Davin replied much too calmly for Declan, who had to work to control his simmering exasperation. "The only time that we had to ourselves during the week was when you were on the white sand."

"What did you take away from those sessions that you did watch?" asked Declan, his voice grating, clear to everyone but Davin that he was irritated.

"To not get into a fight with either of you."

Declan thought about Davin's response for a moment, then nodded, taking a deep breath to release his building tension. A small smile even broke through his look of disapproval. "You're smarter than you look."

Davin briefly shifted his gaze toward Declan as if he were insulted, then gave his instructor and mentor a self-satisfied grin before he turned back toward the combat. He didn't want to miss the conclusion, which he sensed was coming soon.

"Should I take that as a compliment?"

"Take it any way you want, lad," Declan said with a smile, not feeling the need to offer any further explanation.

Before Davin could say anything else, Lycia's words cut him off.

"Bryen's about to finish it."

"How can you tell?" asked Davin.

She didn't even bother to look at her brother. She and Davin had spent most of their time training with Bryen in the Pit. If she could see it, he should be able to as well.

THE CHEERS of the crowd rolled across the deck seemingly in time with the motion of the ship as it cut through the waves, the vessel's huge size blunting the impact of the deep troughs it slid through and the towering crests it surged over. Several of the sailors had watched the gladiatorial games in the Colosseum. None had ever observed a combat such as this, every one of the sailors enthralled by the speed and skill demonstrated by the Blademaster and the Volkun.

Bryen didn't hear any of it. He was focused solely on his opponent, pressing forward, refusing to give the Blademaster the opportunity to shift the momentum against him.

The Blademaster had tried, several times, exhibiting an ability honed by decades of experience, showcasing the skills that had earned him his title and the acclamation that went with it. Yet, in each instance, Bryen halted the Blademaster's attempt to go on the offensive before he could gain any traction.

Klines had sensed the work of Declan each time the Protector fought off his bid to take control of the combat, recognizing that it was taking very little effort on the part of the young man to do so. The Master of the Gladiators had trained the Volkun so thoroughly that Bryen barely needed to think about what he was doing. His actions and decisions were so ingrained within him, so much a part of who he was as a fighter, that all of it contributed to his fluidity, both in thought and movement.

He sensed as well how this combat was going to end. He

was just trying to delay the inevitable for as long as possible because he was having so much fun.

As he kept the pressure on the Blademaster, Bryen finally saw his chance. It was a tiny opportunity at best. Still, it was the first crack in his adversary's defenses, and he didn't want to miss it, because he had no doubt that few others would become available to him.

Swinging with the Spear of the Magii for the Blademaster's shoulder, at the same time he pushed on the indentation in the center of the haft of the Giant-crafted weapon.

The Blademaster parried the strike Bryen made with the blade in his left hand. A remarkable feat in and of itself, the Protector's steel no more than a blur as it sliced toward him.

Unfortunately, it proved to be only a partial victory. Klines was so focused on that one move that he saw too late the other blade that cut toward his neck from the other side.

He didn't fully realize what had happened, the Volkun's speed astounding him, until he felt the cold steel pressed against his throat.

"You're a very dangerous young man," said the Blademaster.

"I'll take that as a compliment."

Bryen stepped back, the crowd roaring its approval and its pleasure, the sailors in the rigging shouting at the top of their lungs, even those who had bet against the Volkun thrilled by the combat. He then pulled back the steel from the Blademaster's throat, brought his blades back together, and remade the Spear of the Magii. That done, Bryen brought the steel to his forehead and gave the Blademaster a nod of respect.

"As you should," Klines replied, bringing his blade to his forehead and then offering his opponent a nod of respect in return. "As it was meant."

"An honor to spar with you, Blademaster."

"And you, Captain. Or Gladiator. Or Volkun. Or Protector. You have acquired many names. Is there one that you prefer?"

"Bryen," he replied simply.

The Blademaster smiled at the response, liking the young man's unassuming personality and the humility he demonstrated even after all that he'd accomplished.

"The honor was mine, Bryen."

HIDDEN ON THE DOCK

"Why did we have to meet here so early?" demanded the woman. "This is ridiculous."

She usually started her day closer to noon, not when the sun had yet to rise. That habit and the cold wind that made her eyes water and her body shiver even with her thick cloak, hood bunched around her shoulders because she didn't want the heavy covering ruining her intricately styled hair, had put her in a foul mood.

The hulking man standing next to her shrugged. He didn't enjoy the cold either, pulling his cloak tighter around him as he was hit by another burst of bitter air. The wind had a habit of shooting through the gap that led into the cove and then whipping around the encircling cliffs before meeting in the very center of the tiny lough, exactly where he and his companion, who had not stopped complaining since they had arrived, stood.

He had little patience for complaints, unless, of course, he was the one making them. His first admittedly unhelpful thought as her tirade continued for more than fifteen minutes had been to push her into the water so that she'd finally shut her trap. He held back, however, realizing that though that might be fun, and perhaps even keep her quiet until he hauled her out of the water and back onto the dock, it would not help him in the future.

A future in which he thought there might be a place for her. The woman had caught his eye the first time he had met her upon his arrival in the Territories. Since then, whenever they were together, just as they were doing now, his thoughts immediately traveled down a path that helped to warm him despite the frigid chill.

"It's a small price to pay, is it not?" he finally asked, tiring of the woman's constant stream of invective, although he certainly enjoyed the spark in her eyes and the flush on her cheeks. "For what we hope to achieve. We must all make sacrifices on occasion, just as we're doing now."

"That's not the point," huffed the woman, her dark eyes finding his as she stomped her feet on the pier in an attempt to get her blood circulating again.

She was angry, he could tell. But he couldn't tell if this was a common aspect of her personality being revealed or just a bit of pique because of her current circumstances. Probably the former, he decided.

This wasn't the first time he had seen her like this, and that was fine with him. He liked a woman with a bit of fire in her. That gave him the chance to tame her, and in his experience that was often much more fun than the actual consummation of the conquest.

"Then what is the point?" he asked. "You've been saying quite a lot since we got here. Then again you haven't been saying much at all."

That comment halted the string of curses that she was about to utter. Her eyes narrowed, her expression, already shrewish to begin with, becoming even more so as she peered at her companion in a new light.

"You would dare to say such a thing to me? A person of my birth? Of my position?"

"I didn't dare," he replied calmly, giving the woman an insolent grin. "I just did." He then leaned down toward her, as if he was going to share a secret with her. "And keep in mind, we're both of the same standing in Caledonia. So harping on all that makes you come across as spoiled and a bit out of touch with the common people, which is fine, because we both are, but also as foolish, which isn't a good thing. You might want to keep that in mind."

They had both arrived at the large dock anchored in the center of the secret cove less than an hour before. There was no way to get there but by water because of the sheer cliff face that angled around the cove in such a way so that some tricky maneuvering was required to enter the lough from the Sea of Mist and thus could only be attempted in a ship of a certain size. Any vessel too large for the slot in the scarp would run aground on the sandbars just beyond the entrance or fall prey to the rocks haphazardly shooting up from the ocean floor, most just beneath the surface and usually not discovered until a ship was taking on water because of a rip in the hull.

The location was a preferred meeting place for smugglers, although no honest smuggler would be caught dead with the two people waiting there now, their schooners tied off on two sides of the floating pier, their crews huddling together belowdecks in search of some warmth.

"You're quite confident, aren't you?" asked the woman, her gaze now calculating, almost as if she had misjudged her partner and was now seeing him for who he truly was.

"Why wouldn't I be?" the man replied impudently, his grin broadening, enjoying the give and take between them.

The woman stared at the man for several seconds more, not saying a word. He felt as if he were being appraised just as someone would when looking to purchase livestock in the market. He didn't like it, feeling distinctly uncomfortable. He was used to placing a price on others, believing that he was above being priced himself.

"I know what you want."

"Do you?" he asked, intrigued. He wanted many things, in fact. He was curious as to which items on his very long list she might be referring to.

The woman stepped closer to the man, facing him, looking up because of his great height, no more than a hand separating them. She smiled brightly, although that smile still didn't warm her eyes.

"I do."

"Then tell me, my Lady, what is it that I want?" The cold of the cove had vanished, his body warming nicely, both because of the conversation and his proximity to this beautiful young woman.

"You're not satisfied with your Territory. You want more."

"I'm never satisfied," confirmed Torstan Sharperson, Governor of the Highlands.

"I know," the woman replied, "because I'm never satisfied either. I always want more." It was her turn to lean in now, her breath warming his cheek as he leaned down instinctively to catch her words. "Have you ever considered that you might not be able to take everything that you want?"

Torstan Sharperson smiled at that, then licked his lips. Why this woman was captivating him so, he didn't know. But he so wanted to find out. He leaned in close to the woman this time, so that he could whisper in her ear. "I have not yet been in a situation where I have not taken everything that I've wanted, Hakea. You should keep that in mind. That's not going to change. If I want something, I will take it."

He said it with the confidence of a man who placed himself above others, as if the normal rules of the world didn't apply to him. Another woman might have been troubled by the statement or the aggressiveness of his tone, but not her.

She had been dealing with men like him all her life. Men who viewed others as tools, as possessions, to be thrown away when they were no longer of use. Dangerous men, unless you knew what to expect. Unless you knew how to deal with them. And she believed that she did.

"I will," replied Hakea Roosarian, Governor of Fal Carrach. "You can count on it."

Torstan nodded, his grin becoming a leer. "May I ask you a question, Hakea?"

She took a moment before responding. "You may, although I offer no guarantees that I will answer."

"Fair enough," he replied, leaning in again to close the space between them. He so wanted to reach out to her, but he restrained himself, knowing that now wasn't the time to take such liberties. "Would you enjoy being taken?"

A long silence stretched between them, Hakea staring challengingly into Torstan's eyes. Then she chuckled, Torstan stepping back, a look of confusion on his face, because that wasn't the response he had expected.

"Behave, Torstan. We have larger matters to attend to this morning."

"For now," he agreed, several inappropriate comments coming to mind after Hakea's latest statement, impressed that he was able to keep them to himself.

"He's doing this on purpose," said Hakea, shifting the topic, tired of Torstan's insinuations and wanting to move on to the business at hand.

Torstan looked at Hakea with his characteristic smirk, knowing what she was doing and deciding to allow it. For the moment. The game he played would take time to reach its natural conclusion, and that was fine with him. He enjoyed the hunt much more than he enjoyed the kill.

"He'll get here when he gets here," Torstan said nonchalantly, apparently unconcerned by the delay, even though it bothered him as well. He was not accustomed to waiting on anyone.

He had to remind himself that he wasn't in a rush. He rarely was, in fact. He was a Governor of a Territory after all, a Duke in everything but name. So he wouldn't allow little annoyances like this to mar his perspective.

Besides, he was thoroughly enjoying his conversation with Hakea, what was left unsaid just as exciting as what was said. Their current interaction only strengthened his resolve to take what he wanted from her when the time was right.

Even though Hakea tended to be irritated most of the time, that only made her more attractive in his eyes. That and her mass of almost uncontrollable curls, her hair a brown so dark that it appeared black and her hooked nose reminding him of the kestrels that flourished within his Territory. Torstan definitely had a weakness for strong and beautiful women, in large part because he so enjoyed breaking them.

"So this doesn't bother you?" she asked, surprised. "I thought that you would have lost your temper by now."

She knew Torstan better than he thought she did. She could see through the image he presented quite easily. And it was just an image, in her opinion. There was little substance to the man. That, in itself, didn't bother her. No, actually it pleased her. Because she believed that she could use Torstan to her advantage when the time was right, though not in the way that Torstan so obviously wanted to use her.

"No, it doesn't bother me," Torstan answered almost flippantly. "Particularly since I have you to amuse me."

Hakea kept her immediate, sharp retort to herself. Instead, she decided to find out if she could prick him in another way, to test him and perhaps confirm her suspicions.

"Why the hair cut?" asked Hakea, nodding toward Torstan's

scalp, which had been closely shaved. The last time they had met together his red hair had flowed below his shoulders. It had been a source of pride for him.

"I was getting tired of it," he replied, waiting a moment before replying because he was taken off guard by the strange and unanticipated shift in the conversation. "I wanted a change."

It was Hakea's turn to smirk. She knew the truth. She had seen the evidence the last time when she looked at the back of his head. Torstan, though a young man, was balding prematurely. And his vanity, which knew no bounds, had pushed him toward an extreme measure. Useful information, and certainly something that she could use against him when the time was right.

"I'm getting tired of waiting," Hakea offered, filing away the information that she had just obtained for future use.

"That's quite obvious."

"Are you trying to antagonize me, Torstan? That's not something that I would recommend."

"No, there's no need for me to do that, now is there? You're doing a fine job of it all by yourself."

"You know, you really can be infuriating at times," said Hakea, her eyes flashing, hinting at her volcanic temper.

Although not with the invective that Torstan had expected. Rather, Hakea said it warmly, as if she viewed it as a positive trait. And maybe she did. That thought sent a faint surge of heat through his body from the tips of his toes to the top of his bald head, his mind once again turning down a quite enjoyable road.

"And charming at others," Torstan offered with a slight bow and a lift of his eyebrows to punctuate his words.

"You give yourself too much credit, Governor Sharperson."

"And you don't give me enough, Governor Roosarian." He stepped closer to her once again, his height and bulk putting her in shadow. He thought that this tactic was a way to get what he wanted, something that he did quite frequently when he felt the need to intimidate, not realizing that she was well aware of what he was trying to do. "Have you considered my offer?"

"It was barely an offer worth considering," Hakea replied in a soft voice, the sultriness laced within it sending a shiver of delight through him.

"It was an excellent proposal and one that shouldn't be dismissed so easily," Torstan said. "Think of what we could do."

She reached up, rubbing his forearm gently. She could feel the heat coming off him, pleased that she could affect him in this way so easily. She was willing to admit to herself that she was enjoying the game that they were playing now just as much as he was, in large part because she believed that she could get the better of him when the time was right.

"I'm thinking of what I could do without you."

It was Torstan's turn to chuckle, though it came out more as a cackle.

"That's very harsh though quite an alluring picture," he replied, his eyes narrowing. Although not in anger. No, Hakea's recalcitrance and how she was teasing him only increased his interest in her. He was never one to be satisfied once he had gained what he wanted. Rather, he preferred the chase, and this was a hunt that he was thoroughly enjoying. One that he believed would continue for quite some time, the prize at the end well worth the wait.

"Perhaps," Hakea admitted, releasing his arm, clasping her hands demurely across her belly. "Then again, we must do what is necessary when we are on our own."

"And that's exactly my point," said Torstan. "We don't need to be alone."

"Yet we are," said Hakea, her voice sharp once again. "He should have been here before us. He was the one who called this meeting."

Torstan smirked again, nodding. It was his turn to appraise the woman standing across from him. She was clever. Very clever. Perhaps too clever, which she would likely learn to her sorrow, and he hoped that he was there when she realized it. Hoped that he was the cause of it.

"He's just delayed," he finally said. He knew that she was trying to turn the conversation away from the direction that he had taken it. He decided once again to permit it. There was no need to rush the issue. Where was the fun in that? "That's all. There was a squall forming to the north when I left the Highlands. He probably got caught in it."

"Maybe, but I still don't like it. Arriving last is a clear way to make it seem as if he holds a position of primacy in our partnership. He's up to something. You know it as well as I do."

"He's not up to anything more than what he's agreed to," scoffed Torstan. "He doesn't have it in him to try to play us. With him, what you see is what you get."

"How could you think that?"

"I don't think it. I know it. He's not a devious person. Yes, he wants power, respect, privilege, but no more than we do. Actually, he's crippled by the fact that he cares about what people think of him. So there are certain things, such as subterfuge, that are well beyond him. It's not in his nature. You can see it as well as I can. You just don't want to."

"And you're certain of that?"

"Yes, completely certain. As I said, you just don't want to see it. You want to think the worst of him, but he's not like us."

"If you believe that, then you're a naïve fool."

Torstan stepped closer to Hakea before she had taken another breath, his surprisingly fast movement catching her off guard. She didn't even have the few seconds she required to place her hand on the hilt of the dagger hanging from her belt, which she felt the need to do now because of the rapid and threatening change in her companion.

Torstan's temper had taken hold in an instant, his carefree indifference replaced by a coldness in his eyes and his voice that reminded her of some of the more nefarious elements she used to work with in Roo's Nest when circumstances required it. Men and women who were just as likely to slit your throat as they were to shake your hand depending on their mood, and often you didn't know what mood they were in until you felt their steel slide across your flesh.

"Be careful, Hakea. You have a habit of underestimating other people. Eventually, that failing will come back to bite you in that lovely ass of yours."

"I do not," she hissed. "How dare you!" She desperately tried to project the confidence that was so much a part of her, but she failed, her voice much softer than she wanted, almost meek.

Torstan was so close now that she could feel his breath on her face. She didn't like that. Not in the least. But she couldn't show weakness. Not now. Because it seemed that she may have indeed underestimated what Torstan Sharperson was capable of, what he would do to gain what he wanted. That conclusion dominating her thoughts, she made herself stand in place, her body rigid, refusing to give him the pleasure of seeing her fear.

"You think you're smarter than everyone else, but you're not," Torstan said casually, though the coldness of his eyes suggested something else. Something darker, more dangerous. "Eventually that's going to cost you, Governor Roosarian. It will cost you dearly."

Hakea had no response, or at least not one that she believed that she could offer. Her holding back only increased her anger, making her feel as if she had lost control of the situation. And that was something that she could not permit.

He had taken her by surprise, put her at a disadvantage. She felt the need to balance the scales between them, although she didn't know how to do that at present because she was still feeling quite flustered.

Because of that, she was thankful that Torstan stepped back then, giving her some space so that she could breathe again, just as a cutter glided between the rocks and into the cove. Hakea realized that the opportunity to reclaim what she had lost had passed. That Torstan Sharperson had won that round between them. That fact both enraged and intrigued her.

"Besides," Torstan continued, "Kendric doesn't need to be devious to be successful. He can leave that to his wife."

Torstan gave Hakea a wink then turned toward the oncoming vessel, offering a perfunctory wave as the ship drifted to a stop against the dock at one of the two remaining open berths, sailors scrambling along the side to tie the vessel off to the posts that lined the edge.

Kendric Winborne, Governor of the Northern Territory, stood at the prow of the clipper in all his finery, a well-made cloak around his broad shoulders, a sword with a jeweled hilt hanging from his belt. He offered his two partners standing on the dock a wave.

Hakea and Torstan ignored it. Hakea Roosarian clearly impatient and wanting to get down to business. Torstan Sharperson more amused, though his expression soured just a bit when he saw the Lady Winborne step up next to her husband.

"You see, my love," said Ursina, grasping her husband's arm warmly and then smiling down upon the two who had been waiting for them. The forced smiles of Hakea and Torstan, who had to stretch their necks to look up at them, made her smile grow. As she was trying to teach her husband, perception was just as if not more important than reality. "The delay was well worth it."

"Yes, they do seem to be a bit put out," Kendric agreed as he continued to smile. His eyes were clear this morning. He felt good. More like himself, better than he had in days, an almost uncontrollable energy coursing through him.

The fog that had plagued his mind for so long vanished as soon as he had stepped aboard the ship and headed out into the Sea of Mist. Maybe the cause was the sea air and the time away from Shadow's Reach, the opportunity to dig out from beneath his burdens of leadership if only for a short time.

"As I said, my love, it's little things like this that can have a big effect," Ursina explained, rubbing her hand along her husband's forearm, the bright light in his eyes fading for just a moment at her touch. "Set the tone for the deliberations to come. You have other matters to deal with, larger matters, so you can leave these little things to me."

"Of course, my love," Kendric replied, a bit more subdued now, feeling a little less in control of himself and not really knowing why. He tried to shake off the feeling, but found it difficult. Then his wife caught his eyes, her bright smile filling him with a surge of warmth on what was proving to be a very cold morning, his clarity back in a flash. Ursina was right. They had business to attend to. "Shall we?"

Ursina nodded and then allowed her husband to guide her to the side of the ship. The entire time her gaze never left that of Hakea Roosarian and Torstan Sharperson. If little things like a slightly late arrival could so easily throw off their partners, then the few concerns that remained about the arrangement that she and Kendric had negotiated with the two Governors were not really concerns at all.

It wouldn't take her very long to turn what was supposed to be a balanced arrangement between them to one that favored her and her husband. And the two upstarts wouldn't even realize it was happening until they could do nothing about it.

When the cutter was made secure to the dock, Kendric jumped over the side, landing deftly for such a large man. He then reached up for his wife, not wanting to wait for the ladder to be put in place.

Ursina permitted him to hold her about the waist and lift her down to the floating pier, smiling, even giggling softly, as he swung her through the air. She knew the effect that their light-heartedness would have on Hakea and Torstan, both of whom appeared to be on edge.

"So good of you to meet us as we requested," said Kendric, assuming the role of good-natured host, just as his wife had suggested. "I trust your journeys were uneventful?"

"Why all the drama?" demanded Hakea. Torstan had unnerved her. She didn't like being taken by surprise in that way. Combined with a temper that was rarely far from the surface, she was finding it difficult to control her irritation now when she had what she viewed as a less imposing target. "Why can't we meet as we usually do?"

"That might give them cause to suspect, my dear," replied Ursina, Kendric looking to her for a reply. He tended to avoid conflict if he could. His wife, on the other hand, thrived on confrontation.

"Give who cause to suspect?" continued Hakea. "And suspect what?"

"Suspect us, my dear."

Ursina's voice was calm, soothing, almost motherly. Her eyes weren't. It was clear that she didn't like to be challenged, a trait that Hakea missed as she stood there fuming.

Torstan did not. Ursina reminded him of his brother Talus, who was much the same way. Seemingly under control, until he wasn't. And you didn't want to be around him when he lost control. You never knew what might happen, but it was never good.

"Suspect what we're doing," chimed in Torstan, feeling the need to defuse what had instantly become a tense situation.

It didn't work, Hakea continuing along her chosen path.

"The three Governors of the Territories on the eastern coast of New Caledonia meeting to discuss issues of trade and security? How could that be suspect? We wouldn't be suspected of doing anything other than what we're expected to be doing."

"Yes, my dear. You're right." Ursina's gentle smile didn't match the sharpness of her eyes. "But we are not scheduled to meet again for three more months. To do so prior to that might lead to questions that we don't want to answer. It might make people worry, even make them think that we are weak, that we don't know what we're doing."

"You might come across as weak, but not me," argued Hakea, "and we don't have to answer any questions we don't want to. We're the Governors, after all. We can do what we want when we want."

"I understand your perspective, Hakea," said Ursina, her voice no longer soothing. It was hard now, almost brittle, finally matching her expression. "And you're right, we don't have to explain ourselves. But why make things more difficult for us than they need to be?"

"You mean Governor Winborne," said Hakea, clearly not seeing or not caring that Ursina had lost patience with her.

"What?" Ursina didn't understand Hakea's comment, or at the very least she pretended not to.

"Governor Winborne, not you," said Hakea, her natural irascibility coloring her thinking and her actions. "You're not the Governor. You're not a partner in our little cabal."

The smile that Ursina gave Hakea in response to her declaration could have stripped paint from the wall. Before the tension escalated any further, Torstan inserted himself into the deteriorating conversation, fearing where it might lead if the two women continued to bite at one another.

"Why the concern now? No one can challenge us here in the Territories. And from what I understand, Old Caledonia has its own problems."

"Yes, my brother sent word," said Kendric, finally speaking up. "Ghoules."

"That's surprising," admitted Torstan. He had heard rumors of Ghoules coming down from the Shattered Peaks before he took a ship across the Burnt Ocean, but he had believed that they were no more than rumors. And if they weren't it still didn't matter to him. His life, his future, was here. He didn't care about anything else but that. "Although it's not our concern."

"Agreed," grumbled Hakea, her anger still plain.

"All has been going well," continued Torstan before Hakea could ramp up her temper once again. "No one can touch us. We are too powerful."

"But perhaps not for much longer," Kendric said sadly, believing that he needed to lead the dialogue, if for no other reason than to defuse the animosity between Hakea and Ursina.

"What do you mean?" asked Hakea, not liking the possibility that their plans that were moving forward quite smoothly could be derailed.

"We have two problems. One in the Highlands, the other from the north."

"There is no problem in the Highlands," challenged Torstan, insulted that Kendric would suggest as much. "All is going as it should."

"Word of people being taken as soon as they arrive in the Highlands is a problem," countered Kendric.

"How could that be a problem? It's only rumors."

"Rumors that spread all the way across the Northern Steppes to Shadow's Reach aren't really rumors," argued Kendric.

"My husband is correct. Rumors are always based in truth, are they not?" suggested Ursina. "Worse, these rumors are spreading well beyond Shadow's Reach."

"They're right, Torstan," said Hakea, her anger at Ursina apparently just at a simmer now. She hated the fact that she had just agreed with the irritating woman who was meddling in what was proving to be a profitable and useful arrangement. "I've been hearing much the same in Ballinasloe, and much too often."

Torstan thought to continue to protest, then realized that it was a waste of time. Shaking his head in resignation, he tried to offer an explanation that would assuage their concerns.

"I need the workers as few of those coming across the Burnt Ocean want to dig for a living, particularly when they don't get to keep anything that they dig up. It's the only way I can obtain what we need from the mines. If I don't do this, then we won't have the iron ore that we need or the other riches hidden in the Highlands. We'll be dependent on Caledonia for weapons. And we won't have the precious metals that are so much a part of our building our power. Without all that, we will only succeed in building a house of cards to be blown down at the whim of someone who can challenge us."

"That simply won't do," agreed Kendric. "The precious metals and other riches are a must. You make a compelling argument."

"So a necessity," said Hakea.

"Yes, a necessity. Besides, we select our workers carefully. None of these people are missed."

"Maybe, but I wouldn't be surprised if some of them have family here," said Hakea.

"I won't deny it," Torstan admitted. "But quite a few have no connections in New Caledonia. No one knows them. And for those who do, there is nothing connecting me, connecting us, to what's going on. It's a wilderness beyond the towns. Accidents happen all the time. Bandits. Perhaps even something worse. And even though we do our best to keep the people in our Territories safe, we can't be everywhere at once, now can we?"

"Fair enough," replied Kendric, nodding his acceptance of Torstan's argument. "Just keep in mind that if word gets out somehow, we'll face a problem that I'd really prefer to not have to handle. We would have much to answer for. You would have much to answer for."

"It won't become a problem," said Torstan, trying to infuse his voice with as much confidence as he could, and not missing how Kendric had just cut himself out of the possible repercussions for what they were doing. "You have nothing to fear."

"What's the problem to the north?" asked Hakea, her thoughts already moving away from the Highland mines that were Torstan's responsibility.

"A strange fog coming down from well beyond the Northern Peaks and often reaching into the northern Highlands."

"Why so much concern over a fog?" scoffed Hakea. "There's fog on the coast every day. That's why it's called the Sea of Mist."

"It's not the fog itself," clarified Kendric. "It's what's in the fog."

"Don't tell me you believe those stories?" Hakea failed to keep the incredulity from her voice. "Monsters in the mist leaving behind the remains of the people they slaughter. Never seen. Never heard. All powerful."

"Unfortunately, it's all too true," confirmed Kendric.

"Kendric is correct. It's happening in the northeastern section of the Highlands," added Torstan. "I've received several petitions for assistance against what the Highlanders are calling Wraiths."

"What are you going to do about it?" asked Ursina.

"Nothing," Torstan shrugged. "I need to focus on the mines. From what I've heard, the people living in that part of the High-lands have developed several strategies for protecting themselves. What they're doing seems to be working. And since I can do nothing to stop a fog from covering the land, there is nothing more for me to do."

"Are you certain you want to allow that?" asked Hakea. "Once your people realize that they don't need you anymore, that they have to and can defend themselves, they start thinking about why they need you at all."

"They will always need me," hissed Torstan.

"And you know this how?" Hakea challenged, pleased that she had regained some measure of control and was now making the Governor of the Highlands uncomfortable, much as he had done to her before Kendric and Ursina arrived.

Before Torstan could offer a cutting retort, Kendric interrupted. "Torstan must focus on ensuring that the Highlands produces what is essential to our success. So we need to focus on these Wraiths. Eliminate these monsters and we eliminate one of our primary threats."

"You are right, my love," said Ursina, her hand on his arm again, rubbing gently, filling him with a confidence that he rarely felt. "Just as you always are. These monsters put everything at risk."

"Leave that to us," said Kendric. "My wife and I have discussed this issue at length. We will make the creatures in the fog regret coming into our Territory."

"Good," said Hakea. She didn't trust Ursina when it came to the partnership they had all agreed to. But she did trust her to do everything that she could to ensure that her husband gained the power that she believed he so deserved. And with these Wraiths threatening that power, she was certain that Ursina would keep her word and do whatever was necessary to disperse these creatures and the fog they came in. "The longer this takes, the more our business will be affected, and we don't want that. We want our business to function without any hitches getting in the way."

"Good business means more money," offered Torstan. "More money means ...""More power," finished Hakea.

"And with the Beleron dynasty at an end, apparently taken down by a gladiator known as the Volkun, Caledonia will have eyes only for Caledonia," said Kendric.

"Which means we have free rein to do whatever we need to do," explained Ursina. "Whatever we want to do."

"We should move faster then," suggested Torstan. "Speed is essential now to consolidate our gains."

"True," acknowledged Hakea. "Though we still need to be careful. If we move too swiftly, we could make a mistake or miss something important."

"Stop worrying so much," chided Torstan, not understanding Hakea's hesitation. "There are times when speed is the key to success, and right now is one of those times."

"As much as I hate having to admit it, Hakea is correct," said Ursina, already tiring of the argument between Torstan and Hakea that had the potential to escalate into another problem that needed to be dealt with, and they already had enough problems as it was. "Caledonia is distracted, and likely will remain so. The journey across the Burnt Ocean is a long one and the distance between the continents creates a natural separation. Speed is important, yes, but it must be applied with patience as well. If we can find the right balance between the two, New Caledonia can become greater than the old world, so long as we do things the right way."

"Do things our way," murmured Kendric.

8

NEW JOURNEY BEGINS

"Stay focused on where you're walking, son." Dougal reached out with a strong hand, gripping Jakob's elbow right before he tumbled to the rocky ground, his hand staying there until Jakob had his feet back under him. "It's going to be rough going for just a while longer. You can't afford to take another spill."

Jakob nodded groggily, not wanting to speak. He was nauseous still. He had been ever since he had been hit in the head, and he feared that if he tried to utter even just a couple of words, the few bites of gruel that he had eaten that morning would come right back up.

To distract himself from the sourness that always lurked in the back of his throat, Jakob allowed his gaze to slowly take in the landscape around him. He knew exactly what would happen if he moved his head too quickly.

He was completely taken with these mountains, feeling as if he belonged here as soon as he set foot in the Highlands. He even preferred the clouds here compared to Caledonia. The bright sunlight that peeked through the grey overcast every so often made his already splitting headache even worse.

They had left the foothills earlier that morning, taking a narrow trail that led them deeper among the peaks. It had taken several hours to get where they were now, climbing a path that switch backed up a steep slope, the valley they were seeking that would offer them an easier route for a time just a few hundred yards above them.

Although Jakob couldn't see above the crest, he could see the massive heart trees standing guard between the two mountains that he now skirted. He had already walked through several groves during the last few days, awed by the trunks that were a hundred feet or more in diameter and rose hundreds of feet into the sky.

Impressive as the heart trees were, Jakob was more enthralled by the massive kestrels flying among the peaks. He had never seen the like in Caledonia. Every time he heard the ear-piercing screech from one of those majestic raptors echoing off the mountains, he experienced a jolt of excitement that settled within his heart.

He always tried to find the kestrel when the animal announced itself. Yet even with a wingspan stretching seven feet or more, he often struggled to pick out the white feathers speckled with grey on the bird's underside that blended perfectly with the sky. It was easier when a kestrel banked during the few moments during the day that the sun peeked out from the clouds, the orange-brown feathers on its back flashing with an unexpected but unmistakable brilliance.

Unfortunately, Jakob and his father hadn't arrived in the Highlands as they had hoped they would. They were supposed to be traveling to what would be their new home, not chained to two dozen other unfortunate souls being taken farther into the Highlands to some unknown destination. No one knew for certain where they were going, but they had worked out by listening to the guards' conversations that they were to be put to work in one of the many mines that was now operating within the Territory.

Even though the Highlands was rich in valuable iron ore and other precious metals, as well as jewels of various types, he and his father had never been interested in prospecting or mining. They were hoping to farm and hunt. To create a homestead of which they could both be proud.

Now, thanks to their bad luck, they would be tasked with digging out for someone else the riches hidden by the rough, dangerous terrain. Likely dying for their effort if the stories circulating among the prisoners were correct, miners never surviving for very long.

Expediency was the driving factor in the mines, not safety. An early death because of a cave in, noxious gas, or some other kind of accident was bad enough. Although it might be preferable to the fate waiting for some. Listening to some of the slavers last night when they talked about what they hoped to do to the women once they reached wherever it was they were going had sickened him.

As he followed unavoidably the prisoner who was several feet in front of him, he imagined the chain linking all the prisoners together to be a snake several hundred feet in length slithering along the trail.

Hearing another loud screech that reverberated off the surrounding peaks, he turned his head slowly to the sky, locating the kestrel drifting in the air just off to his right.

He realized that his mind was doing much the same thing as the kestrel. Drifting.

The slaver had knocked him out several nights before, yet he was still feeling the effects of the concussion. In addition to the nausea and his aversion to bright light, he was having a difficult time concentrating.

He had considered trying to use the Talent almost every second of every day since he had been captured. He had learned enough from Aloysius to melt the shackles and the chain to which they were attached. With that thought in mind, he had reached for the natural power of the world whenever they stopped for a short break.

The energy was there, he could feel it running through him, giving him some additional strength every time he touched it, helping him to heal faster than he might without it. But he acknowledged reluctantly that his father was right. Trying to do anything of consequence with the natural magic in his current condition was dangerous.

His head was still too foggy. He didn't want to risk using the Talent, at least not yet, fearing that if he did he'd be more of a threat to the people around him than a help. He would need to wait a little while longer, until he could actually hold on to one idea for more than just a few seconds.

Aloysius would be impressed by his restraint. Thinking of the Magus brought a smile to his face. At first, Jakob had believed that the old man was no more than a healer in the hills just beyond their small cottage.

His father knew better, Dougal telling him that he had come across Magii several times in the past, even working with a few when required. Dougal had explained that in Caledonia the Magii tended to maintain a low profile, often using their knowledge of herbs and natural remedies, along with the Talent though in a circumspect way, to assist those in need of care.

For some strange reason as he continued to follow the man in front of him along the rough path that wound between the mountains, Jakob's initial meeting with Aloysius played through his mind. The old man had balked at first, refusing to train Jakob in how to manage the power that was available to him.

Time after time, Aloysius protested that he was only a

healer. Dougal hadn't bought it, continuing to push for the result that he wanted for his son.

"He needs help," Dougal had explained. "You and I both know that you just can't shut off the Talent. It's a part of him. It will always be a part of him. He needs to learn how to control it, use it, so that he's not a threat to himself or anyone else. Unless, of course, there's a need for him to be a threat."

"So you want him to become a Magus. You understand what that means? What his learning about the Talent could lead to?"

"I didn't say that I wanted him to become a Magus," his father had explained. "I don't like the Magii. I don't trust them."

"I'm a Magus," the old healer had finally confirmed after several minutes of incessant wrangling with Dougal. Jakob simply had watched the entire exchange with a slightly amused expression as his father wore down the old man.

"Yes, but you're different," his father had said. "You're out here on your own. You're not a part of the Order from what I can tell, and if you still are, you're so far removed that I have little fear with regard to my son."

"Why do you fear the Order?"

"Why wouldn't I? The Order does what needs to be done for the Order. Not for the people who are a part of it. Not for Caledonia."

"Why would you say something like that?" the old healer had asked.

"Because I saw some of the worst that the Order of the Magii has to offer firsthand. I lived some of it."

"But you're not a ..."

"No, I'm not. The woman I loved was. I saw what was required of her. What she had to do. What led to her death."

That last had caught Jakob's attention, though he didn't have long to think about it.

"You seem to know a great deal."

"I wasn't always a soldier," his father had replied cryptically.

"Well, if that's the case, why don't you teach your son how to use the Talent?"

His father had chuckled at that. "My son's ability in the Talent doesn't come from me. Besides, you have nothing else to do here, Aloysius, other than heal those in need. And I'm sure that's not a daily exercise."

"Maybe I like it that way," the old man had countered. "Maybe I want to be left alone. Maybe I'd prefer to live in the past."

"You're bored, Aloysius. I can tell."

"That may be," the old man had admitted, "but why would you assume that I'd want to train your son?"

"You need something else in your life, and I'm giving it to you."

"Thank you so much," Aloysius had replied, his sarcasm plain. Then he had pointed toward Jakob, their eyes locking. For just a second, it appeared as if the old man had seen something in him that he hadn't expected. "He could be thick for all I know. If that's the case, trying to train him would be a massive waste of my time."

His father had smiled at that comment, demonstrating a patience with which Jakob was quite familiar, simply allowing the old man to work his way through the arguments he apparently felt the need to make.

"Why don't you do whatever it is you do to judge how much Talent a person can manage at one time," his father finally had suggested. "I'll wait."

"How do you even know that we can ..." Aloysius had left off what else he had been about to say, simply shaking his head. Although from what Jakob could decipher, the old man had appeared to be more pleased than irritated, possibly even enjoying the interaction with his father. For just an instant, Jakob had thought he was watching them act out a scene that they had practiced.

Aloysius had turned toward Jakob next, and he had seen a shocking sharpness to his gaze that he hadn't seen before. Reaching for the Talent, the old man had sent a small thread of energy toward him.

Jakob had stood there quietly the entire time, staring right back at the old man. Calm. Collected. And just a touch curious.

Aloysius had seen the intelligence behind the young man's eyes just moments before. And then Aloysius' own eyes had widened. The power that this young man could manipulate with the Talent was immense, greater than he had ever thought possible. Greater even than Sirius Keldragan, the current Master of the Magii, and to his knowledge the most powerful Magus still alive.

"You see what I mean?" his father had asked.

"I do," Aloysius had replied, nodding his head as he considered all the possibilities of what he had just discovered.

Jakob had been able to tell that the old man had considered hesitating a little while longer, though really only to extend the dialogue because he appeared to be relishing the give and take with his father so much. Even so, the old man had decided against wasting any more time.

As he had told Jakob after they had been working together for a while, Aloysius had decided to train him not when he had judged his strength in the Talent, but rather when he had judged what lay behind his quiet gaze.

"I'll want the lad ..."

"Jakob," Jakob had said sternly.

Aloysius had stared at him then for almost an entire minute. The old man's often dull eyes had sharpened, seemingly pleased that Jakob had stepped in to clarify rather than his father. Then he had nodded, Jakob guessing that Aloysius liked the fact that he was willing to speak for himself.

"I'll want Jakob here by first light every day. To pay for the training he'll do chores around the farmstead and any other work that I might require of him. When that's done, we'll work on his use of the Talent. He doesn't leave in the evening until I say he can go."

"Fair enough," Jakob had answered, his father nodding in agreement.

Aloysius had reached out a hand toward the soldier to seal the deal. Dougal had ignored him, Jakob stepping forward instead. It had been his agreement to make, not his father's, so he would be the one to seal it.

Thinking back now, Jakob found the entire exchange amusing, his father and Aloysius putting on a show with the hope that the truth wouldn't come out. But it had, and in a way that Jakob had never anticipated. Just thinking of that other terrifying experience made him shiver with unease, so he tried not to.

Jakob had learned quickly from Aloysius that healing was so much more than what the old man could do with the Talent. Every day the Magus instructed him for hours on end after he completed the work required of him. He often didn't make it home until well after dark.

Aloysius had been quite clear from the very beginning. In his opinion, you could never master the Talent. You could borrow it. You could use it. But you could never make it your own. Any attempt to do so would take you down a dark path that was to be avoided at all costs.

Jakob had taken that lesson to heart.

Thinking about Aloysius now made him miss the old Magus. He had wanted to train with Aloysius longer. He had wanted to learn more. Although he had worked with Aloysius for more than a year, he knew that he barely knew anything at all.

Aloysius had confirmed it for him daily, liking to remind him every time he left for the night that he was barely scratching the surface of what one day he might be able to do with the Talent. The old Magus often told him, "You know just enough to get yourself into trouble."

Jakob scratched at his chest through his dirty shirt so that any slaver who might be watching didn't suspect his real motive for the action. The necklace with the gift – though at times Jakob viewed it as anything but – given to him by Aloysius right before he and his father had left for Roo's Nest was still there, the shape exceedingly familiar.

He was thankful that the slavers who had captured him hadn't searched him beyond taking his weapons. They were too intent on getting into the Highlands before anyone saw what they were doing to perform anything more than a cursory check to ensure that all their steel and money had been taken from them.

Lost in his thoughts, Jakob missed a step. Feeling himself fall, the ground rising up to meet him, he extended his hands, hoping to break his fall. But before he felt the sharp scrabble beneath his feet cut into his palms and his knees, he was suspended in the air for just a moment, then pulled back up gently, his father's strong hand once again holding onto his forearm, his other hand gripping his shoulder. The only discomfort he felt came from the steel shackles digging into his wrists.

"Try to focus on where you're walking, son," said Dougal. "It's rough going for a while and you can't afford any more knocks to the head."

Jakob nodded, fighting the nausea and dizziness once again. He kept his eyes to the trail as it snaked around a ledge that had been washed out. What was left of what was obviously a much larger waterfall, likely caused by the warm temperatures of spring melting the snow and ice that had accumulated farther up the mountain, still trickling down the mountainside.

He continued to concentrate on where he placed each boot,

not wanting to test his father's strength on this section of the trail, when he heard a scream just a few places to his front. One of the other prisoners had slipped on the loose stone, sliding off the path and down through the mud and shattered shale, only coming to a stop when he slammed into a very large boulder with a shout of pain.

Dougal, Jakob, and the prisoners just in front of the unlucky fellow had no choice but to follow thanks to the chain connecting them all, although because of its length they were able to slow their descent and avoid any injuries themselves.

Dougal leaned into the man, taking one look and closing his eyes for a brief moment in sympathy. The older prisoner clearly was in agony, one leg twisted and facing the wrong direction, the other showing white bone sticking through the skin of his thigh.

"Easy, fella," he said. "We'll do what we can."

Jakob looked down at the man's injuries, the nausea that he had been experiencing for several days worsening at the sight. He fought the urge to bend over and wretch, not understanding why the man wasn't screaming at the top of his lungs from his horrendous injuries. Then he realized that the prisoner was in shock, what had happened to him still not yet having fully registered.

The slaver in charge of this chain gang, who had captured Jakob and his father, appeared. He took his time as he stomped and slid down the slope, cursing up a storm with every step that he took.

"How bad is it?" hissed the large, bearded slaver, his ever-present whip in his hand.

"I've seen worse," Dougal said. And he had. He had seen more than he cared to in the battles that he had fought.

"What's the matter with him?" demanded the slaver.

Dougal held back the sharp retort that came to mind. All you needed to do was take one look at the man to know what was wrong, his injuries hideously obvious. Instead, Dougal answered calmly, not wanting to increase the slaver's already simmering agitation.

"Both his legs are broken. I can splint the legs, and we can build a stretcher to take him with us. It shouldn't take more than a half hour at most and then we'll be back on our way."

The hulking slaver with the beard extending all the way to his belt stared down at the injured man as if he was no more than an inconvenience, nodding his head as he did so, apparently weighing his options. Then he reached for a key that hung from his belt and knelt down, unlocking the injured man from the chain. By the time he was done, a couple more slavers had scrambled down the rough slope to join them.

"I'll take care of him," the large slaver said to his compatriots.

The other men nodded and then began to herd Jakob and the other prisoners connected to the chain back up the incline.

"You don't have to do this," Dougal said, calling back over his shoulder. "I can help him."

Dougal had realized what was going to happen the instant the slaver had reached for the key. He also knew that there was little that he could do to stop him. Still, he had to try.

"You can get him to where we're going," said the slaver as Dougal reached the crest of the trail with the other prisoners. "Of that I have no doubt. But he won't be able to work when we get to where we're going, and that's all that matters. If he can't work, he's of no use to us. He's just a mouth to be fed."

The big slaver then attached his whip to a hook on his belt and pulled the sword from the scabbard he wore strapped to his back. The injured man, his eyes still glazed over by shock, didn't make a sound when the slaver drove the point of his weapon through the fellow's throat.

"He's no good to us now," explained the slaver. "It's only worth our effort to take you sorry lot to the mines if you can work. If you can't work, you're just dead weight. So this should serve as a warning for all of you."

In a matter of minutes the slavers had the column of prisoners moving again along the trail that led them steadily toward the north.

Dougal walked closer to Jakob now, worried about him, ready to help if it appeared as if his son was going to tumble to the rough ground again. He didn't want what had happened to the unfortunate man who had slipped off the trail to also befall his son.

Jakob barely noticed his father walking beside him. He was in a daze and not because of the concussion. He couldn't believe what had just occurred. The callousness demonstrated. And he couldn't believe how angry he was. How badly he wanted revenge on the slaver. To make him pay for the murder he had just committed.

"Be ready," his father whispered to him. "If any chance comes our way to get free, we need to take it."

9

TEMPTATION VS. INTENTION

"Were you tempted?" asked Aislinn.

Her eyes gleamed brightly, suggesting that she had already guessed at his answer. Bryen had just explained to her and Rafia what he had detected when he had flown with Banshee into the strange fog off to the east.

The evil contained within the dense murk triggered memories of Bryen's struggle with the Curse since he had become the Seventh Stone. Struggles that she knew still tortured him, even though he was free of the Curse ... for now.

"Of course not," he replied with a smile that failed to reach his eyes. "Not in the least."

"You're lying," laughed Aislinn.

"I am," Bryen admitted with a bark of a laugh. "Of course I was tempted. I will always be tempted. That's what the Curse is."

"What do you mean by that?" asked Rafia, the Magus staring at him, intensely curious as to why he said what he said.

"The Curse is power," Bryen replied, "just like the Talent. But it's more than that."

"How so?" asked Aislinn, recognizing that Bryen was

working to bring his thoughts together.

"At its very core, the Curse is temptation," he explained. "The Curse is testing you whenever you use power. If you give into the temptation of the Curse just once, you will lose your ability to make your own decisions. The Curse will make them for you."

She and Bryen had just finished their training session with Rafia, the Magus instructing them daily in the Talent since they left Battersea. She had suggested that they approach it as informal apprenticeships.

Neither had minded, both wanting to enhance their skill in the natural magic of the world. Both also wanting to keep Rafia occupied so that her thoughts didn't drift to past events that continued to bother her in her dreams.

Their lesson that morning had consisted of using the Talent to work in a variety of different ways with the ocean surging and frothing around them. By the end of the session, neither had any difficulty using the Talent to shoot geysers of water in all directions that rose several hundred yards into the air or form massive balls of water that they lifted a hundred feet or more into the sky and then dropped wherever Rafia instructed.

Bryen understood that it was just another way for him to practice the precision that Rafia pecked at him about with unerring regularity. He didn't mind her pushing him. He had enjoyed the last few hours, just as he did most mornings, always thinking about how he could employ in a fight each new skill that he was learning.

That was to be expected considering his background. He had been raised and trained in a certain way. His perspective on life and the world wasn't likely to change, even with the struggles of Caledonia behind them.

"Do I have to kill you now?" asked Rafia, a hint of humor in her voice. A weighty question when the Magus had first begun to ask him, not long after he had revealed that he was the

Seventh Stone. The question had become more of a running joke between them now that Bryen had destroyed the Ghoule Overlord and locked away the Curse in the black diamond, though the seriousness of the inquiry was not lost on either of them.

"Not yet."

"Good, because I've grown quite fond of you. I'd hate for things to end between us in such a bad way."

Rafia left unsaid the fact that she probably didn't have the strength to do the deed as well as her fears with respect to Declan if, indeed, there was ever a time when she needed to worry that Bryen had been touched by the Curse. How would the man who viewed Bryen as his son react? The man whose loyalties were never in doubt and who continued to aggravate her and enthrall her both at the same time?

"Me as well," replied Bryen.

"I thought we had gotten past all that," said Aislinn. "Bryen is free of the Curse. The Seventh Stone cleansed him of the Dark Magic."

"We'll never get past the Curse," Rafia replied with a frank honesty. "Bryen is the Seventh Stone. As he just said, the temptation is there. It will always be there. Because that's what the Curse is. He's absolutely right. You don't need to touch the Curse to be infected by the Curse. It often comes down solely to intention. It's a matter of free will, and as we've seen in the past, there are many who are more than happy to exercise their free will with little in the way of a moral compass to guide them."

"That's a very uplifting thought," Aislinn murmured sarcastically.

"It's the truth," shrugged Rafia. She pushed herself off the railing, wiping her hands together as if she had just finished scrubbing the deck. "Now if you'll excuse me, I'll leave you both be. I sense you've had enough of me and my positive nature for a time."

With that the Keeper of Haven gave them both a nod and a smile before walking farther down the deck toward the helm, where they saw that Declan was preparing the circle for the daily training session. The Magus rarely missed these combats, although she never participated herself.

Bryen had wanted to ask her why that was the case, knowing how good she was with the daggers that she favored, then thought better of it. He realized that her interest wasn't driven by any desire to improve her martial ability. Rather, it was something else entirely. A compunction in which he had no desire to pry.

"Do you think that it will ever happen for them?" asked Aislinn.

"Who knows," Bryen replied. "Regardless, it's out of our hands."

"True," agreed Aislinn, though she was nodding in a way that suggested to Bryen that maybe she really didn't agree with him. "You know, there are ways that we could ..."

"We could," he cut in. "But we shouldn't."

Aislinn stared after Rafia until she was lost among the gladiators who were circling the ring. "I guess you're right."

"I am right."

Aislinn turned her sharp gaze on her Protector. "You say that with a great deal of certainty. How can you be so sure? I didn't know you were so knowledgeable in matters of the heart."

"I never said that I was."

"My question still stands. How can you be so sure?"

"It's just another one of those lessons that I learned from Declan when training on the white sand."

Aislinn scoffed at that. "How could Declan have taught you anything about matters of the heart while you were in the Pit?"

"He didn't."

"Then how can you be so sure?" Aislinn asked a third time,

her voice rising in conjunction with her irritation. It seemed like Bryen was purposely trying to bait her into losing her temper. It was one of his unique skills, in fact, among so many others.

"I'm just likening the situation between Declan and Rafia to something that I learned in the Pit, that's all."

"What would that be?" Aislinn demanded. "I can't wait to hear."

"Both are strong people with strong personalities, right?"

"They are," Aislinn agreed, though her patience was wearing thin.

"On the white sand often when two strong opponents charged at one another, they usually just succeeded in pushing the other away."

Aislinn stared at Bryen, her confused expression telling him that she had no clue what he was talking about or how it related to their topic of discussion, so he sought to clarify before their conversation became an argument.

"What I'm trying to say is that when you force two people with strong personalities together, then more likely than not they'll bounce off one another. But, if they come at each other in their own time, in their own way, on their own terms, there's a better chance that won't happen."

Aislinn continued to stare at Bryen, her confusion gradually shifting to an expression that might be described as compre-hension, although Bryen couldn't tell for certain.

"That kind of makes sense in an illogical sort of way," she said finally. "Why didn't you say that in the first place?"

Just then a large splash shifted their gaze beyond the railing of the *Freedom*. A pod of orcas had just appeared only a hundred yards off their starboard side, large black fins slicing inconsistently through the waves as they dipped beneath the surface after taking a breath, every so often one of the younger whales leaping out of the water entirely to crash down into the ocean and create a magnificent splash.

For several minutes, Bryen and Aislinn simply watched as the whales stayed with them, enjoying how the large mammals moved so deftly through the water, the larger bulls always swimming on the flanks to protect against any threats.

"What's on your mind?" asked Bryen, noticing that Aislinn was distracted despite several of the whales doing their best to keep them entertained.

"I was just thinking."

"As you've told me before, quite often in fact, that can be a very dangerous thing to do."

"Very funny."

"I do my best," Bryen replied with a grin and a lift of his eyebrows.

"I was thinking about intention," Aislinn explained, smiling even though she tried not to. "About what that could mean."

"You mean with respect to the Curse."

"Yes."

"How so?"

Aislinn turned away from the killer whales that continued to track the *Freedom* and faced Bryen, leaning against the railing as she did so. "If the Curse is also about intention, then how you plan to use it is key, correct?"

"Yes, that's my take on it. In its purest form, power is neither good nor bad. It's all in how you use it. If you use power to corrupt, then you corrupt yourself in the process."

Aislinn nodded her agreement. "Then let's take that thought to the next logical step."

"All right."

"You are the Seventh Stone. Although you don't have the Curse within you now, there is the possibility that at some point in the future you may have to take the Curse within you once again."

"Certainly a possibility," Bryen admitted, "though not one that I care to think about at the moment."

"Fair enough," Aislinn replied, not eager for him to do so either, knowing how hard it had been for him to maintain control over the Dark Magic when it resided within him. "So if intention is a key part of the application of power, what happens if when you take in the Curse, you try to shift the intention of that power?"

"I don't follow."

"You just said that power is power. If intention plays a role in its use, can you convert the Curse into something you can use without fear of corrupting yourself?"

"You mean removing the taint from the Curse so that it's no different from the Talent?"

"That's exactly what I mean," confirmed Aislinn, her eyes sparkling as she considered the possibility. Assuming, of course, that she was correct. "The Seventh Stone used the Talent to cleanse you of the Curse. Could you not cleanse the Curse itself?"

"That's an interesting thought," mulled Bryen, letting his mind meander down several intriguing paths Aislinn's proposal led him. "Based on what you're suggesting, Dark Magic is simply a power to be used, and so long as I use it in a way that isn't self-serving, that doesn't adhere to the demands of the Curse, then I have nothing to worry about if I remove the taint. I should be able to make use of that power without fear of corrupting myself."

"Yes, you said before that the Seventh Stone is a receptacle for power." Aislinn shrugged her shoulders. "What type of power really not being relevant. What if you could use the Seventh Stone to cleanse the Curse if you must take it within you? Then you can simply add it to the Talent that you already control."

"I'm going to need more time to consider what that might

mean," said Bryen, his mind already working through the full ramifications of what Aislinn was suggesting. "On the surface, you're right. I should be able to do exactly as you suggest. That's really quite an interesting idea you've proposed."

"I do have my moments."

"Attractive and an incisive intellect. I am truly a lucky man."

"That you are," Aislinn agreed, leaning in to brush his lips with hers. "Don't ever forget it."

THE GLADIATORS of the Blood Company who circled the ring didn't say a word. They simply watched, taking everything in, obviously captivated by the two combatants who stalked around one another for a time.

It didn't last for long. One or the other or both lunged forward, a flurry of blows following, the clang of steel meeting steel reverberating across the deck, the slashes and cuts so fast that they were difficult to track with the naked eye.

Then the two stepped back, beginning the dance once again.

Neither rushed. Neither felt the need. They knew each other too well. Besides, the combat was less for them and more for the men and women watching them so intently.

"Did you see that?" asked Declan as he glided away from his opponent with a grace that seemed quite incongruent for a barrel-chested, tree-trunk-armed soldier. Having knocked away the Blademaster's sword during the last series of attacks, he circled back around, staying on his toes, perfectly balanced, ready for whatever Jurgen Klines might try next. "How did I know that the Blademaster was just testing me? That he wasn't fully committed?"

"His feet!" shouted Jenus, his baritone voice resembling the sound of a rockslide.

"Exactly," Declan said. "How so?"

"The Blademaster would have taken a longer stride if he meant to continue with his attack," offered Kollea.

"Correct," confirmed the Blademaster. "The longer the step you take the less time you have to adapt. A shorter step will allow you to keep your options open until you find what you're looking for."

Before he had even finished his explanation, the Blademaster attacked again, this time committing himself to the assault with a long stride as he closed with Declan, trying to get in tight with the Sergeant of the Blood Company.

Rather than drifting away, Declan also advanced, happy to engage in this manner. For the next few seconds their blades were no more than steel streaks, the two men refusing to budge an inch as they sought to score a touch on the other.

Then, as if through some silent agreement, they disengaged from one another, large grins on their faces. Neither had expected to break through the other's defenses, and neither had. But they had enjoyed immensely their attempts to do so.

"I think it's time for some others to have a go in the ring," suggested the Blademaster.

"I couldn't agree more."

Declan stepped back then, the Blademaster taking over the session and motioning for Asaia and Dorlan to enter the training circle.

Finding a place at the edge of the ring, Declan crossed his arms, observing the gladiators challenging one another under the strict instruction of his friend who commented every so often on how they could improve their performance.

"You might as well ask."

"What do you mean?"

Declan's comment caught Rafia by surprise. She didn't think that the Sergeant of the Blood Company noticed when she slipped up beside him. He hadn't taken his eyes off the training circle.

"I can tell you want to ask me something." Declan's gaze never left the two gladiators facing off against one another. He nodded slightly, approving of Dorlan's tactics as he blocked Asaia's barbed whip with his shield, then immediately rushed forward, knocking her to the ground, poised to offer the final blow, which clearly upset her. She wasn't used to losing during a combat. "Asaia, remember, if you overextend with that whip of yours, you'll leave yourself vulnerable to the counterattack. Short and sharp strikes, just like with any other weapon."

"I know that, Declan," Asaia grumbled as she pushed herself off the deck, preparing for another go at Dorlan.

"Then perhaps you should apply what you know."

Several of the gladiators standing around the training circle chortled at that, which earned them a hard glare from Asaia. It also seemed to help her focus, which had been Declan's intention.

Asaia attacked again, yet this time just flicking the tip of her whip at Dorlan, forcing him to back away around the circle, not giving him the chance to attack this time.

"I don't know that this is the best time," said Rafia now that the interaction with the gladiators in the ring had ended. "You seem too busy."

"You can ask. I can do more than one thing at a time." Declan finally turned away from the training circle, satisfied that Asaia was employing his advice effectively. He then smiled as if he knew something that no one else did. "Besides, you can't help yourself."

"What do you mean by that?" protested Rafia, not sure if she should be offended by his comment.

"I mean that when you want to find something out, you find it out. You don't stop until you get the answer that you want."

"And you view that as a good thing?" she asked.

"I do," he replied without a second thought.

Rafia studied Declan for a moment. "Why can't I intimidate you?"

"That's the question you wanted to ask?" replied Declan, somewhat surprised.

"It is."

"Why would you want to intimidate me?" countered Declan.

"I don't. It's just that when most people learn that I'm a Magus they get uncomfortable. Nervous. Even flighty."

"I'm not uncomfortable because you're a Magus. Besides, I've had more experience with Magii than you might expect."

"That's good to know." Rafia thought about what Declan had just said a moment more, not sure what to make of his veiled response. Curious about why he answered as he did. Then her mind latched onto a very specific part of his response. "Wait a second. You're uncomfortable with me? If so, you don't show it."

"I fought in the Royal Guard for a decade and then in the Pit for another decade. Because of that, very little intimidates me. Does that answer your question?"

"If you're not intimidated, then why are you uncomfortable?"

Declan placed his full attention on Rafia then, his hard eyes catching hers. She felt the urge to reach for the strands of curly hair that always escaped the scarf she wore, pushing them back behind her ears, the habit helping to calm the butterflies that had begun flitting about in her stomach.

Declan watched her do it in silence, allowing the seconds to drag on. When she worried that he wasn't going to say anything, he finally did.

"Because you're a beautiful woman, and I have little experience with beautiful women. So I feel the need to step carefully."

For almost a minute, Rafia didn't know what to say, shocked by Declan's honesty, although she should have expected it. He certainly wasn't one to mince words.

"You speak your mind, don't you," she finally said, feeling an unexpected rush of heat coloring her face. Now she was the one who felt uncomfortable.

"Unavoidably and often irretrievably," Declan confirmed.

"I like that about you."

"Glad to hear it."

Declan was about to say more when a laugh far above him cut through the noise of the combat, Chesin and Kollea now testing their skills against one another. Examining the crow's nest on the mast he stood beneath, Declan cursed under his breath. If it wasn't one thing, it was always another.

"Perhaps we could continue this conversation later?" Declan asked as he turned back toward the Magus.

"By all means," said Rafia, wanting some time to think about why she felt so flustered with this man. "And I will hold you to it."

"I wouldn't have it any other way."

"He's at it again?"

Declan came to stand right next to Lycia, her head turned toward the crow's nest, a hand in front of her brow, squinting because of the brightness of the sun. He shook his head, his irritation plain.

Davin had perched himself on the crow's nest, toes curled around the edge of the railing, one hand holding onto the mast, a look of wild abandon on his face. Just as he had done yesterday. And the day before. And the day before that. It was becoming an obsession with him.

"He is," replied Lycia, several choice curses running

through her mind, struggling to keep them to herself. She loved her brother, even though he had a unique ability to drive her crazy. "He can't seem to help himself."

Declan and Lycia had discussed Davin and his current issues several times already. Yet despite all the discussion, neither had found a good solution.

Not surprisingly, after fighting as a gladiator for almost five years, Davin was having trouble adjusting to life outside the Pit. Addicted to the adrenaline that was so essential to his survival while fighting on the white sand, now, with the Pit no longer available to him, he was trying to find ways to fill that hole. That meant taking risks that he might not take normally.

Declan understood what Davin was going through, having worked his way through a similar experience when he was taken from the Pit to serve as Master of the Gladiators. In the months that followed, he had felt out of sorts. Jittery. As if a part of himself was missing. As if that critical part was still on the white sand.

True, he no longer had to fight for his life. Yet that seemed a small gain compared to what he had lost.

He had felt so alive when fighting on the white sand. So in control of himself. His decisions. His actions. He had been less concerned about staying alive and more concerned with trying to achieve the high that he attained when he defeated his opponent.

It was addictive, maybe even more so than the poppy root that the now deceased Marden Beleron had preferred. Although he could not tell for certain, never having indulged.

All his decisions he made in the Colosseum were driven by the adrenaline rushing through his veins. And he hated the feeling that a slice of himself had been cut away.

He hadn't found his balance again for quite some time, not until he had directed all that energy, all that drive, into helping the gladiators he was responsible for stay alive. And now Davin was in the same position that he had been. The Crimson Giant needed to find his equilibrium again, and clearly he didn't know how.

"He's a fool," Lycia grumbled, clearly unhappy with what her brother was about to do.

"He can be that," Declan agreed. "Just keep in mind that as we discussed, his acting out comes from a larger issue. What he's doing is just a symptom of what he's really struggling with."

"That doesn't make it any easier."

"It doesn't," Declan agreed. "That's why patience is so important."

"Yes, well you know how patient I can be," said Lycia, her tone suggesting that she was anything but patient at the best of times.

Just then a screaming Davin sped by, the rangy gladiator diving off the crow's nest, a rope tied around his waist and trailing behind him.

Declan struggled to keep a smile from breaking his stern countenance as he locked eyes with Davin for just a split second before he disappeared into the water. The look of utter joy on the young man's face had tugged at him in a way that nothing else had in quite some time.

Hearing the splash, Declan looked over the side of the ship, confirming that Davin had survived the plunge when he saw his bright red hair pop up above the waves. His head vanished almost immediately, only to appear once again about a hundred yards behind the stern. The *Freedom* would drag Davin through the water until he pulled himself back up the rope and on board. It could be a few minutes, it could be an hour, depending on Davin's mood.

"He's playing with fire," said Lycia. "One mistake and he's dead."

"It was the same way in the Pit."

"Yes, but at least then we didn't do it to ourselves."

"You're right. Still, there's little that we can do about it. If we tell him to stop, he'll just want to do it more. Or he'll find something else to try that might be even more dangerous. You know how he is, how his mind works when it's actually functioning."

"Can't you just keep him in the training circle all day? If he's doing that he can't do something so stupid as he's doing now."

"We already tried that," said Declan. "It didn't end well."

Davin had taken down seven gladiators in less than an hour, injuring three in the process. It wasn't so much a viciousness on the part of the Crimson Giant. Rather, Davin found it difficult controlling the energy flowing through him, an energy that he desperately wanted to feel and didn't want to let go.

Declan had needed Bryen to join the training and actually challenge Davin in the circle, as he was the only one who could defeat him.

Bryen did, ending Davin's reign of terror and having to break one of his wrists to do it. Even then, Davin refused to concede despite having no chance at victory. He was lucky that Aislinn was willing to heal him, just as she had healed the gladiators who Davin had injured.

Afterward, Davin had sulked for several days, refusing to enter the training circle again. Finally settling on his latest escapade as a way to break himself out of his doldrums.

"So what do we do?"

"Keep him busy. So busy he doesn't have time for stunts like this."

"You have some thoughts on that?"

"Of course I do." Declan's smile wasn't very welcoming, almost coming across as cold-blooded.

"And when we run out of things that will keep him busy?"

Declan shrugged, not having an answer. "Then we hope that he comes across someone who can tame him before he kills himself with his foolishness."

10

ALWAYS A PRICE

"We are free from Caledonia, Talia. Free. There is nothing for us to do but create the new path that we desire."

Talia gave her mother a sideways glance. It was a nice thing to say, and she knew that her mother said it more for herself than for her. Because the words held little meaning for Talia, the statement no more than a hope at best. And she knew from experience that hope had little meaning in the real world. In her world.

"We'll never be free, mother, you know that." Their business spanned the Burnt Ocean and was dependent on both Caledonia and the Territories. "No matter how much we might want to, we will never escape Caledonia. We are tied too closely to that Kingdom, even if we have moved our center of business to Ballinasloe."

"You misunderstand me, Talia."

"On purpose, yes," Talia agreed. "I do."

Isana smiled at her daughter's comment. She understood Talia's perspective. It pained her every time that she thought about it, which was every second of the day when she wasn't distracted by something else.

She had not forgotten what her daughter had been through. She never would. Of what she was truly trying to escape by coming to the Territories.

"We will do well here," said Isana, reaching for Talia's forearm, gripping it warmly. "I can feel it. We will make the life we want here. We will make a life that we can all be proud of."

Talia held tightly to her mother's hands. She hoped that her mother was right. She wanted to believe her. More than anything, she needed to believe her. But her recent experiences made it difficult for her to do that. Impossible, in fact.

"We will do well here," continued Isana, not noticing the dark shift in her daughter's mood as Talia took in the bustling town of Ballinasloe that gained greater clarity with each passing second. "We will be free from the constraints of Caledonia. Free of those who would seek to hold us back. Free of those who are jealous and want to take what we are trying to build because they have no capacity or desire to make such an effort on their own."

Talia was barely listening to her mother now. She had heard the same monologue several times while they crossed the Burnt Ocean. Instead, she focused her attention on the primary port on the eastern coast of the Territories and the capital of Fal Carrach. As their ship passed through the breakwater and finally entered the Ballinasloe harbor, she smelled the sharp, salty sea air mixed with the undeniable and unavoidable smells of so many thousands of people forced to live together in a very tight space.

For some, after weeks at sea, it could be a nauseating stench that required a quick exit to the countryside. For Talia, it smelled of something else entirely. For her, the stench was one of opportunity.

Despite her dark thoughts, Talia couldn't stop herself from

smiling. She didn't want to, either. She wanted to enjoy this moment for as long as she could, her calculating eyes surveying every aspect of the harbor.

It was hard to miss the unfinished fortress in the center of the port. All the bustling activity along the crowded piers. The dozens of busy taverns, inns, and various businesses necessary for a town to grow that began at water's edge and stretched up into the hills where hundreds of homes were being built at the same time to add to what was an already densely packed landscape.

The port was thriving. The piers were crowded. A dozen or more vessels of all sizes waited to find a slot so that they could unload their cargo and passengers. Large cranes dotted the docks. Wagons and porters filled the streets taking goods to the ships or away from the harbor to who knew where in the Territories. Makeshift markets littered the avenues and even the alleys, having taken shape where there was any available free space.

Talia smiled even more brightly as she took in everything she saw. With their clippers and their new approach to shipping, once the routes between the Territories and Caledonia, and from the Territories to the many other kingdoms and empires to be found on the other side of the seas, had been tested and perfected, this would be the place for them.

Her father had been right. Definitely a risk worth taking.

Talia and her family could not escape Caledonia, nor would they try. To do so would be foolish.

She could never escape what happened to her there. Her mother was wrong about that.

But Talia did believe that they had a good opportunity here. One that she planned to make the most of.

"WHAT DO YOU THINK?" asked Abram Carlomin, his eyes glowing with anticipation and just a touch of worry.

He hadn't expected his family to cut so many weeks off the voyage, so he wasn't ready for them. It was a welcome surprise, however. Not only because his wife and daughter had joined him, but also because their new ships had crossed the Burnt Ocean faster than he had ever imagined possible, which only boded well for their business.

Talia had always enjoyed the very marked differences between her parents. Both Abram and Isana had a knack for business and building the relationships so essential to ensuring the success of any new venture. From there the similarities ended.

Isana had long blonde hair and was a head taller than her husband. Abram was short, very broad, and had a darker complexion, his hair tightly curled and thinning. Abram was calm and even tempered, slow to anger. Isana at times struggled to control her sharp temper that if left unguarded could go off like a teapot on the stove. Yet their union, combining their love for one another and their business acumen, each bringing something different to their relationship, clearly worked.

Abram offered a running commentary as he walked his wife and daughter down their pier, which revealed a flurry of activity as sailors and dockworkers scrambled to and fro, obviously knowing what they were about. Although it all appeared to be quite chaotic on the dock that extended for almost a quarter mile out over the water, Talia could sense the structure within the activity going on around her, knowing that her father's calm, ordered mind had much to do with it.

"The *Resolute*, here to your left, just returned from the Distant Islands, which are off the far northwest coast of this continent in the Winter Sea," explained Abram. The ship was an exact replica of the one Talia and Isana had used to cross the Burnt Ocean. "It will be refitted and restocked by the end of today, and then it will sail for the Western Isle with a special shipment. It then returns with spices and some other goods that are in high demand here on the eastern coast. And the *Constellation*," motioning to the ship they were passing on their right, "just returned from making a run into the Inland Sea, stopping in Tinnakilly, Newry, and Rosecrea along the way. It took her no more than a week to make a journey that would usually take three." The pride in Abram's voice was clear. "That ship will leave on the tide tonight and begin its run to Caledonia."

Talia was impressed. Her father and mother had jumped into the shipping business less than a decade before, out of necessity more than any real desire to begin a new enterprise. They had needed to find some other way to make a living because the Duke of Sharston had decided that he wanted to take for himself the wineries that had sprung up all along the western coast of his Duchy.

To do that, Talus Sharperson had started imposing heavy taxes that had driven most of the original owners from the industry, even those whose families had founded their vine-yards centuries before. There was little point in fighting against what appeared to be an inevitable change. Or as Talia's parents had called it, theft.

The few independent wineries that remained had no choice but to form a partnership with the Duke, Sharperson buying the property after paying barely anything for the valuable land, the original owner allowed to continue to run the business while earning a salary that didn't come close to what they had made on their own. That arrangement had not appealed to the Carlomins.

They had no intention of sharing their business with a callow fool who had no clue as to what it took to run a winery. So they had taken the pittance that the Duke had offered for Carlomin Winery and invested it in a small shipping company that had distributed their wine across Caledonia. They quickly built up the business, making the most of their knowledge and experience, all with an eye toward creating an enterprise that would not be held hostage by the desires of the often greedy rulers of Caledonia.

A tall task, they knew. Yet one that they believed was worth trying. And one that they went at with a will.

Talia's parents had started with short runs along the western coast of Caledonia, focusing on smaller cargos and delivering those shipments faster than any other shipping company from Roo's Nest to the Bay of the Dead. Both Abram and Isana believed that they would succeed if they concentrated on creating a niche market, and they did. They discovered almost immediately that many merchants and traders would pay a premium to get certain products, especially those that were high end or perishable, where they needed to go if they could get them there faster and safer.

From there, they had taken their model, which had proven so successful after less than a year of practice, and applied it to the larger challenge of trading across the Burnt Ocean.

"Very impressive," replied Isana, who walked down the pier at the very southern end of the Ballinasloe harbor with her arm tucked within her husband's, marveling at all that he had accomplished in just a few short months. Her pride could barely be contained.

Just as she and Abram had wanted, there was nothing beyond their pier to the south but the rocks of the breakwater and a sandy beach running for miles farther down the shore. It gave them a measure of privacy that no other location in the harbor enjoyed. Moreover, because of the deeper water to the south of the island, Abram had already added a shipbuilding facility, demonstrating the industriousness that had served them so well when they ran their winery in the hills just outside Sharston.

"The location is perfect, Abram."

Talia could only agree. Her father had done exactly as he said that he would. Along the pier, in addition to the three clippers that had taken Isana and Talia across the Burnt Ocean, five more were tied up to the dock distinct from the *Resolute* and the *Constellation*, all in various stages of being loaded or unloaded, sometimes both at the same time.

She knew how her father prided himself on his ability to use a variety of methods to cut the time to transport goods anywhere they needed to go. The new clippers were certainly a key aspect of that strategy, the primary tool in fact, but the new systems that he had implemented with the introduction of the ships that had removed many of the logistical challenges that often delayed vessels during their crossings were proving to be just as important.

Even more impressive, perhaps, was how Abram had transformed the very end of the pier into a drydock. Three more vessels were under construction, dozens of shipbuilders scrambling across the wooden frames, the three masts for each ship already in place.

Talia's father liked to apply his attempts to achieve greater efficiency to every aspect of their business. He did so here as their new ships were constructed, knowing that he could save costs by having skilled workers apply their talents to more than one project at a time, many carpenters and other tradespeople often willing to give him a discount for the guaranteed work that would take a month or more to complete.

"And we will continue to expand during the next few weeks. I have contracts in place for us to purchase the two piers closest to us so that we will have space for all the ships joining our fleet, as well as all the buildings lining that section of the harbor. It won't be long before we will have the largest presence in the Ballinasloe harbor compared to any other shipping or trading company."

Isana looked at her husband with a mixture of pleasure and shock. She was more than familiar with his unique skills. She just hadn't considered how effectively he could apply them. Then a hint of concern seeped into her voice.

"Where did you get the funding for that? We weren't supposed to consider such a possibility for another year at the earliest." Abram was about to reply, but Isana didn't allow him to do so, her worry gaining strength. "You didn't leverage any part of the business, did you?"

She and Abram had talked about that before they had formed the Carlomin Trading Company. They had put in place a long-term plan for expanding their business, and they both had agreed that they would not accept outside funding in order for them to do that.

They didn't want to be beholden to anyone but themselves, not after what had happened in Caledonia. If that meant that they progressed at a slower pace than they desired, then so be it. It was the price they were willing to pay to maintain complete control over their business.

"No, Isana, of course not. You need to give me more credit than that."

"Then how did you do it?"

"There has been more demand for our services than either of us anticipated," he replied. "That's why I've already gotten started on more ships here in the Territories in addition to the ones that are being completed in Roo's Nest. We can't handle all the orders that we are receiving now as it is. As soon as we proved to the merchants that we could get their products where they needed to go faster than the traditional, larger vessels, they've been knocking at our door nonstop ever since. I already have ten different offers from larger trading houses that want to form exclusive partnerships with us."

"You haven't accepted any of those, have you?"

"Of course not," he replied, easing Isana's concerns. "However, I did put in place with several of our better, very consistent customers who never fail to pay on time preferred shipping agreements."

"Meaning?"

"Meaning they pay a premium to get space on one of our ships whenever they want, the cost of which goes up or down based on the demand for a particular run, which we determine based on an agreed-upon sliding scale."

"So that's how you did it," laughed Isana, beginning to understand and clearly excited by her husband's creativity as she rubbed his arm warmly.

"Yes, the premium fees are what's allowing us to move forward faster than we expected. Those fees have doubled our profit and make up more than half of our net."

Isana stopped walking, then reached up with her hands, gently grasping Abram's cheeks and pulling him in for a very long kiss. Talia felt the need to turn away until they were done, uncomfortable with public displays of affection to begin with and not needing to see that aspect of her parents' relationship.

"I'm very proud of what you've accomplished," said Isana once she finally released her husband's lips from her own.

"What of the pirates along the coast?" asked Talia, feeling the need to return the conversation to safer waters, figuratively speaking of course. "We had a close call on our way here." She spent the next few minutes telling her father of the pirate attack just a few days outside Ballinasloe and how they escaped. Abram's eyes filled with pride upon hearing how Talia's skill with a bow had aided their escape.

"Yes, it's becoming more and more of a problem," Abram admitted. "So far we have not been affected, if only because the pirates can't catch our captains. The same can't be said for many of our competitors."

"Their ships," said Isana, nodding her head sagely.

"Indeed. All the other merchants have larger, slower vessels that can't outrun the pirates. They've taken precautions, such as adding armed men to each vessel to fight them off and trying to keep each of their runs a secret, though that last is a faint hope at best. There are few ways to keep a secret in a port like this one."

"How many ships have been lost?" asked Isana.

"In the last month," said Abram, nodding his head slightly as he calculated the number, "fifteen."

"All by pirates?"

"For the most part, yes. But we've received reports from all of our captains of a strange fog drifting down the coast through the Sea of Mist."

"What would a fog have to do with this?" asked Isana.

"You would think not much," admitted Abram. "A fog is not uncommon. What is uncommon is that if a ship is ever caught in the fog, we never see it again, at least not as it was before it entered the fog."

"What do you mean by that?" asked Talia, curious as to how her father framed his response, but she didn't get an answer as her mother spoke over her.

"You don't think that those losses are the pirates as well? Or just a captain misjudging her or his position in the fog and running into the rocks along the coast?"

"If it was the latter, we would find some evidence of that. We haven't."

Talia could tell that her father wasn't telling them everything. "What have you found?"

"Vessels floating in the sea, their sails destroyed. Weirdly, the cargos are intact. Nothing has been removed, other than the crews."

"What happened to the sailors?"

"We don't know," groused Abram, the mystery clearly upsetting him. He had a very analytical mind, and he liked to put everything in its proper place. He couldn't do that with this mystery, and it clearly bothered him. "What's even more worrisome is that we always find signs of a struggle. Blood on the decks. Strange scratch marks along the railings and the walls. Perhaps even a few body parts lying about, although never an entire body. Very strange. Very ominous."

"So definitely not pirates," said Isana, apparently not affected by her husband's gruesome recounting, her thoughts instead focused on what might be the cause of what was happening in the Sea of Mist.

"No, not pirates."

"But no idea what it could be?" asked Talia.

"Not yet," her father confirmed. "And until we do know, that unknown threat and the pirates along the coast mean we need to be careful. Very careful."

"Have you discussed this with some of the other merchants and shipping companies."

"I have, almost every day, especially since they're dealing with the brunt of the hazards," Abram confirmed. "We've been talking about how we might be able to combine our efforts to defend our ships, such as hiring small companies of soldiers, placing lookouts along the coast, a host of other possible options. Still, nothing that we have agreed upon, nothing that doesn't come with enormous cost. We have another problem as well."

"What would that be?" asked Isana.

"The lords and ladies of Caledonia have little interest in what's going on here and these new threats that we face, nor do the Governors of the Territories."

"The Governors don't care? How could they not? Our taxes fill their coffers."

"That may be, but some of us believe that there is more going on with the pirates than is obvious. That perhaps there is more to the pirates than meets the eye."

"What do you mean by that?" demanded Isana, wanting to know more of what was on her husband's mind.

"We'll talk about it later," Abram said. "Not now."

Isana and Talia followed his eyes down toward the entrance to their pier. A petite woman dressed in fighting leathers, a short sword on each hip, strode down the dock right toward them. A dozen soldiers, all very large men who had the look of veterans, trailed her. The workers on the dock skipped out of the way as she and her escort demonstrated no intention of allowing anyone to slow them down.

Talia noticed the woman's mass of almost uncontrollable curls. Yet what was most unmistakable about her was the hooked nose and the sharp eyes split by it.

The woman had the look of a raptor, and Talia got the feeling that she and her parents were the prey.

"Governor Roosarian," said Abram, offering a brief nod of respect in greeting. "You honor us by visiting Carlomin Trading Company today."

"No need for such formalities, Abram," replied the woman, the strength of her voice and commanding posture displaying her confidence. "Are we not friends by now?"

"Of course, Hakea," corrected Abram. "Force of habit. What can I do for you?"

"I'm just making my daily rounds, Abram. You know how I like to keep my finger on the pulse of my city. The best way to do that is to ensure that the commerce that makes Ballinasloe what it is functions unhindered."

"Indeed, a worthy and necessary objective."

"And may I ask who these two lovely women are?"

"My apologies, Hakea. My wife Isana and my daughter Talia."

"A pleasure," Hakea Roosarian said, reaching out and grasping their hands firmly, although both Talia and Isana noted that the warmth of her greeting never appeared within her eyes, the dark orbs remaining cold, unyielding, predatory.

"The pleasure is ours," responded Isana. "We have only just arrived, but it is obvious that you have done great things here in the Territory."

"I have," Hakea agreed. "And I have so much more to do. Once the Rock is completed we will turn our attention to the wall surrounding the city."

"The Rock?" asked Talia.

"The fortress in the center of the harbor," explained Abram.

"Yes, the Rock will be my center of power. From there, Fal Carrach will become a force to be reckoned with, both here in the Territories and beyond."

"You seem quite certain of that," said Talia, her tone slightly challenging, both her parents giving her warning looks as soon as she uttered the words, though Hakea Roosarian didn't seem to notice. Instead, it appeared that the Governor of Fal Carrach liked the direction the conversation had taken. It allowed her to focus on herself and her plans for her Territory.

"I am," she replied. "And you're right to question, but you will see once you've been here in Ballinasloe for a while that I do what I say. Always."

"You've certainly made good progress so far," offered Abram. "I and all the other merchants have been quite impressed by your efforts on our behalf."

"As you should," agreed Hakea with the bark of a laugh, though it seemed forced. "Speaking of doing what I say, Abram, have you considered my proposal?"

Abram smiled graciously. Even so, Talia could tell by glint in his eye that her father was not happy. In fact, he appeared to be angry, although he was hiding it well.

"I have, and I thank you for the offer. I apologize. I am not in a position to give you a reply presently, what with all that's going on here on the dock. I need to study it some more. And I need to discuss it with my wife now that she's finally here. We are business partners after all."

"Of course," acknowledged Hakea, her eyes narrowing. "I understand. Just don't wait too long to get back to me. As I've said many times, your success is my success. Working together ..."

"Of course, Hakea. I will get back to you shortly. Once my wife and daughter are settled."

"Good," replied Hakea. "Then I'll leave you and your family to it." She headed for the far end of the dock, taking a few steps before turning back toward him. "Just remember, Abram. I do what I say. Always."

The Governor of Fal Carrach didn't give him a chance to respond as she whipped back around, her soldiers following her as she moved through the bustle of the dock and then out into the larger port.

"What was that about?" demanded Isana once she was certain Hakea Roosarian was too far away to hear their conversation.

"She's seen how well we've been doing here."

"She wants in?" whispered Isana, a look of cold fear flashing across her beautiful face.

"She does. And the sooner the better in her opinion."

"That could be a problem," grumbled Isana.

"It already is," confirmed Abram.

11

A SACRIFICE

The small fire offered the only light on the craggy ledge, and a dim one at best. The low flames only lit a radius of ten feet, no more, leaving the rest of the stone outcropping that jutted out from the bluff in shadow.

Jakob didn't mind the darkness. It gave him a good view of the Highlands as night slowly draped itself across the range of mountain peaks that played out before him. They were not very far from the coast. Just as the last few flashes of a fading orange light kissed the western horizon, he glimpsed a glimmer of the Silent Sea no more than a league to the east.

Closing his eyes, Jakob took a deep breath, enjoying how he disappeared into the gloom. He felt better than he had in days. He was thinking more clearly. Even so, he was tired. It had been a long hike, starting before the sun had risen until just a few minutes ago, the terrain getting steeper as they moved deeper within the peaks.

The slavers had finally allowed them to stop when they reached this ledge. The trail they were taking curled higher up the mountain into what appeared to be a narrow pass, although it was difficult to see from where they were located.

A hike of several hours at the very least, Jakob assumed. So he was happy for the break, even though the ridge stuck out from the side of the peak for several hundred yards, a drop of more than a thousand feet waiting for anyone foolish enough to get too close to the crumbling edge.

The slavers had herded Jakob and the other prisoners toward the far end, away from the fire, which blocked the narrow defile that led to the ridge. There was nothing but shadows and dim shapes where the exhausted men and women sat or lay, trying to find a comfortable position on the rocky ground for the few hours of sleep the slavers would permit them.

Only one of the slavers was currently turned in their direction, sitting on a large stone with his back to the fire, hunched over in a way that made his bulk obvious. His hands twisted his leather whip into a circle, then let it go. Again and again he would coil it into a circle and release the leather strap.

And so it went. The repetitiveness of his actions, which were beginning to become sluggish, suggested that the man was distracted. Perhaps even falling asleep. If he was, it likely didn't matter.

The slavers didn't seem all that concerned about the potential for escape. Justifiably so. Chained together, a steep drop on three sides, only one way off the ledge, where were Jakob and all the other prisoners to go?

"We need to escape, lad," whispered Dougal, who sat right next to his son, his eyes staring daggers at the slavers arrayed around the fire. "I don't know how much longer until we reach wherever we're going, but our time is running out. I know it."

Jakob nodded, pleased that the slight motion didn't cause him as much distress as it had during the last few days. The intensity of his constant headache, what had felt like a hammer pounding against his skull, was lessening, his nausea diminishing. He was even able to keep down some of the watery gruel the slavers provided.

Even better, his mind was no longer as clouded as it once had been. He could actually concentrate for several minutes at a time now.

Pleased that the effects of the concussion that he had suffered were beginning to recede, Jakob began to consider how he might use the Talent to gain their freedom from the chain and then from the slavers.

"It won't be easy," Jakob finally offered.

"Nothing worthwhile in life is ever easy, Jakob. Remember that."

Jakob smiled. His father was always offering platitudes, always willing to give him another one whenever the mood struck him or the situation called for it. From what his father said the few times he spoke about him, his uncle had been much the same way, a witty and memorable saying always on the tip of his tongue.

He often wondered how many of the sayings that his father so liked to tell him actually came from his uncle, who was a few years older than his father. Of course, Jakob couldn't ask. His father refused to speak of his brother, the shame of what his uncle had done tainting the family name.

"You should write some of these sayings down," said Jakob. "You've got enough to fill a book. I'm sure there are others desperate for the knowledge you're willing to share so freely."

Dougal shifted his gaze away from the fire and the slavers, his eyes settling on his son. "Your dry wit returns. You must be feeling better after all."

"I am," Jakob confirmed. He was actually hungry again, although not for what the slavers passed off to them as food.

"That's good to hear," said Dougal. "I was worried for a time." He leaned in even closer, his voice at Jakob's ear even though no one was sitting within ten feet of them. "Remember what we discussed. Don't do anything that would reveal what you can do. At least not yet. Not until I tell you. Not until we can make the best use of it. We're only going to get one chance."

"I understand your concern, father, but I'm certain ..."

"No argument, Jakob," said Dougal, his dark eyes unwavering in the dim light.

Jakob stared at his father for several seconds, not agreeing with him, but not having the energy to disagree. Finally, he grumbled his assent.

He was angry that his father didn't trust in what he could do. Didn't trust him. It hurt more than he was willing to let on.

Dougal nodded. "The trick will be getting the key, and only the big bastard who took us has it. It's going to be a challenge to get it away from him."

Jakob spent the next few minutes listening to what his father had in mind, having heard much the same for the last few nights. Admittedly the first few times his father had told him he couldn't remember much of it at all thanks to his concussion. Every so often Jakob tried to add a few ideas of his own, though he knew that it was wasted effort.

His father had a strategy worked out, and he would stick with it. It was just like every other time that Dougal made a decision. Jakob's suggestions rarely diverted his father from the plan he had devised for their escape before they reached the mines.

His father was overthinking what they would need to do, unwilling to acknowledge that Jakob's skill in the Talent could simplify the strategy that he had concocted and improve their chances of success. Jakob was fairly certain that once the effects of his concussion disappeared entirely, and he could reach for the natural magic all around him without feeling as if the world wouldn't stop spinning and he was about to pass out, he could use the energy that he could call upon to snap the steel attaching the shackles to the chain.

Snap all the shackles and chaos likely would ensue. Jakob could then do a few other things that he had learned from Aloysius that would help to even the odds against the slavers.

There were only a dozen guards, after all. If he moved forward with what he had in mind at a time like this, when the slavers were tired and unfocused, the darkness would aid him. That and the fact that many of the other prisoners still appeared to be fairly fit, and he believed that they wouldn't hesitate to take their anger and fear out on their captors.

Despite how his father might argue, with the numbers in their favor and the use of the Talent, Jakob thought that he could get everyone away, not just themselves as was his father's plan. And that was Jakob's goal.

He had no connection to the people chained to him other than the fact that they had all been placed in a terrible situation. Nevertheless, he wanted everyone to gain their freedom, and he would do what he could to make that happen. No one deserved to suffer the destiny waiting for them in the mines.

His father thought that they needed to obtain the key in the next few days, realizing that each step they took brought them closer to a place from which they would likely never be able to escape. Jakob believed that he just needed an opportunity.

One chance.

If he did what he knew that he could do, they would be free. All of them.

His father was right about the importance of one variable, however.

Time.

Would he reach a point physically where he could make use of the Talent before they arrived at the mines? And before his father decided to put his own plan into motion? Two key questions for which he had no answers.

Jakob sat there quietly, allowing his father's words to wash over him. There was no point in trying to interrupt Dougal.

Once he made his mind up, there was nothing more to discuss. Words didn't matter then.

Jakob would have to show his father what he could do when the time was right. That would be the only way to convince him to change his approach.

As his father continued to talk quietly from just a few inches away, running through several possible adjustments that might need to be made to his plan by whispering out loud, although really only to and for himself, and not loud enough for the slavers or any of the prisoners with them to hear what he was saying, Jakob turned his focus in a different direction.

Although he still struggled to concentrate for long periods of time, he was finding it easier to latch onto a few coherent thoughts. One of which kept playing through his mind, and it filled him with an unexpected sense of dread.

What it brought to mind took him back to Aloysius' cottage several leagues outside of Hardholm to a night much like this one. A night that had set him and his father on the course that had taken them across the Burnt Ocean.

Unconsciously, his right hand reached toward his hip. But the dagger wasn't there. The gift from Senna. The only piece of her that he had left.

It was strange how that memory seemed to have become real in just seconds. And because of it, this night felt different from the others he had spent in the Highlands. This night felt just as it had when he had lost the woman he loved.

When they were working their way up toward the ledge, darkness just beginning to settle within the snowcapped-peaks, a blood-curdling howl had sounded no more than a few miles away to their north. That had stopped everyone for a moment, even the slavers. And then another chilling howl echoed through the mountains that sent a shiver down Jakob's spine, this call from the south.

That gave the slavers an urgency that Jakob hadn't seen

before. They rushed the prisoners forward, their whips, which had barely been used that day, cracking in the dying light. When they finally made it to the ledge, the slavers got the fire going quickly, clearly unsettled by the baying.

The howls coming from opposite points of the compass began to occur closer together. Every time there was a howl, another followed only a few seconds later.

The consistency of the baying suggested that whatever animals were causing the eerie noise were in fact tracking the party as it made its way along the rugged trail.

And then, after more than an hour, there was silence.

Even the slavers began to breathe easier until the two ear-splitting howls echoed off the peaks, this time at the exact same moment, shattering the temporary calm.

Jakob listened intently, the sense of dread that had filled him months before building within him. He couldn't use the Talent effectively at the moment, but he could do just enough to sense the evil that had settled around them. An evil that was similar to what he had come across on that fateful night just a few months ago.

How he knew that, Jakob couldn't say. But he knew it for a fact.

He also knew with absolute certainty that the two creatures with their last cries shared the location of the slavers' camp with whatever else might be lurking in the dark. Because he also was sure that there were more than two of the creatures out in the night, even though only two had revealed themselves.

Strange as it may sound, Jakob believed that the beasts were talking to one another. He just wished that he knew what they were.

Dougal had taught him how to track, and he had seen quite a few signs of wolf packs, bears, badgers, even mountain goats. Other wildlife you would expect living within peaks such as these. Most of the tracks were barely visible, usually just a few prints in the mud to suggest that the animals had been there.

The wolves were still there, in fact. But the wolves didn't worry him. There was plenty of game in the Highlands, and wolves tended to shy away from people.

Whatever these creatures were, he was certain that they were nothing that he had ever come across when he had gone hunting with his father.

The howls were nothing like those of the wolves that haunted these mountains. And if his fears were correct then these creatures were not animals. They were something worse. Something unnatural.

Jakob turned his gaze back toward the fire. The slavers were talking animatedly around the flames, their backs turned. Several had pushed themselves up from where they had been sitting or lying down on the ground, now walking about, clearly agitated, their hands never far from the hilts of their swords or the whips that they liked to use so much to keep their prisoners in line.

His eyes naturally shifted to the tallest of the slavers, the man so broad that he would have to turn sideways when he walked through most doorways. Every so often the other slavers called him Sergeant. Because of that, Jakob assumed that he was the one in charge, his and the other prisoners' experiences of the last few days confirming it.

When he had mentioned to his father that there was more to these slavers than met the eye, Dougal had agreed with him.

Perhaps these slavers weren't just slavers. Maybe they were soldiers, either doing this on the side or in a way that they wouldn't be seen as being affiliated with any particular lord. That possibility had taken Jakob's thoughts in several worrisome directions.

Jakob tilted his head toward the fire, the slavers' increasingly loud voices beginning to travel on the wind, which had picked up when the sun had dropped beneath the rocky crags. The slavers' concerns regarding the howls that now echoed intermittently among the peaks were intensifying, their postures suggesting a level of fear that Jakob hadn't expected to see.

What would cause a dozen experienced fighters to become afraid so readily?

Despite his father's constant, quiet dialogue, Jakob was able to pick out a few pieces of the disjointed conversation being conducted by the fire.

"I thought we would be safe from those beasts."

"We were supposed to be safe. That's what he said. He said that we had nothing to worry about."

"I thought so too."

"They won't come close. We're too many. We should be fine."

"Against two of them?"

"Yes, we should be fine against two of them."

"What if there are more than two? What if we're only hearing two?"

"Yes, what if there are more? There probably are."

For just a few heartbeats, Jakob wondered if he might be able to take advantage of the slavers' concern and growing distraction. Then he became curious.

The one they called the Sergeant had stood up on the far side of the flames, placing himself in front of the narrow defile that led away from the ledge, turning his broad back toward the prisoners as he stared off into the darkness from which any threat would have to come.

The other slavers arranged themselves around him. Jakob could see what the Sergeant was trying to do. His men were nervous, probably even afraid. He was hoping that a show of strength would calm them. But as best as Jakob could tell, the Sergeant's efforts weren't working.

The conversation among the slavers became more subdued, even as their anxiety appeared to increase, none of the men wanting to anger the Sergeant, who appeared to be looking for something farther down the trail. He had little chance of finding it in the pitch black, the moon blocked by a heavy overcast.

Still, he remained where he was for several minutes. Searching for what, the men huddling behind him didn't seem to know.

Jakob thought that he heard the term Stalkers a few times, although he couldn't be sure. Then his still slightly addled mind returned to the night that the slavers had taken him and his father. To the combat that he had fought against the creature that had almost killed him at the bottom of the knoll.

The creature that had made his blood run cold. The monster had blended almost perfectly into the darkness, its claws longer than the daggers that Jakob then had on his belt.

Could that have been a Stalker?

When he had mentioned what had come for him that night to some of the other prisoners, none of them knew what it could have been either, except for one woman. Most of the prisoners had only just arrived in Ballinasloe, heading out into the hills the same day they set foot in Fal Carrach just as Jakob and Dougal had done. Not so with the woman. She had stayed at an inn for several days, frequenting the tavern, waiting for some friends who never arrived.

She had heard tiny bits of conversation from the other patrons, admitting that she had spent most of her time there deep down a bottle or two or three of wine. She had paid little heed to what was said around her then, yet she hadn't forgotten some of what she had learned.

Most of the gossip came from the small clusters of farmers living outside the town who had stopped in for a drink. They had brought their crops to the town market, selling what they could, before heading back to their farmsteads. Every one of the farmers had enjoyed their wine or ale quite a bit and then had left well before dark, wanting to get home before night fell.

The woman had been curious about that, so she had paid more attention to what they had to say.

The farmers had spoken of creatures terrorizing the countryside, supposedly coming down from the mountains or out of the forests to hunt anyone unwary or foolish enough to be out on their own. The farmers had called the beasts Stalkers. The woman had thought it nothing more than an interesting rumor until Jakob had shared his story with her.

He hadn't paid much attention to it until now, not having cause to do so. And though he didn't know for sure what was hunting them, that part of him that he tended to listen to when danger threatened told him that it was most likely Stalkers. The obvious agitation on the part of the slavers and the murmurs from the men that linked the cries echoing off the peaks to the descriptions of what he had seen himself confirmed it for him.

Another howl shattered the silence of the night, this one closer, quickly followed by two more with slightly different timbres. The two Jakob had heard many times before. The first sounded different.

It was a deeper call. More dominating. More menacing.

If he could have used the Talent without having to empty his stomach at the same time he would have searched around them to confirm his suspicions, but he couldn't. Not yet.

Even so, he didn't really need to get a sense of what was happening. He simply needed to close his eyes and visualize it.

The two beasts located to their north and south, Stalkers he assumed, had snuck closer, probably no more than a hundred feet to either side of the narrow ledge. One higher up on the trail, one where he and the other prisoners had already climbed.

That louder, more strident howl told Jakob that a third creature had arrived. That beast was likely lurking right on the trail just beyond the small gap between the rocks that led to the ridge.

With his eyes still closed, Jakob listened as best as he could to what the slavers were saying now, his father's private dialogue sometimes making it difficult.

"I told you!" hissed the slaver standing closest to the Sergeant. "Two, maybe we stand a chance. Three ..."

The Sergeant grimaced. "I know, you're right. You're right."

"Those beasts aren't supposed to be here. We were promised that."

"And yet they are here," hissed the Sergeant.

"What do we do?"

"This is it, Jakob. Be ready." His father patted him on the shoulder, then pushed himself up so that he was perched on one knee. With the howls distracting the slavers, he sensed an opportunity.

"Wait," whispered Jakob, realizing that his father thought that he could take advantage of the distraction caused by the creatures hidden within the darkness.

Dougal was about to make his move toward the Sergeant, his goal the key on his belt and then his sword. He would throw the key to Jakob once he freed himself from the chain then hold off the slavers while Jakob released as many of the other prisoners as he could to create confusion.

In the chaos that followed, Dougal and Jakob would make a break past the fire and then through the cleft in the rocks. The slavers would never be able to catch them.

For just a second, Jakob wondered if maybe his father had been hit on the head as well when the Sergeant had taken him. It would be a doomed effort right from the start.

The slavers might be distracted, but they were primed for action. And if the howls that were now so close that they echoed off the surrounding rocks came, indeed, from Stalkers, he and his father would stand little chance against so many of the beasts if Jakob couldn't make use of the Talent effectively.

Even worse, in Jakob's opinion, Dougal's effort now helped no one but themselves. The strategy of using the other prisoners for their own benefit, not helping them, sickened him.

Before his father could get to his feet, Jakob grabbed his forearm, pulling him back down to the ground.

Dougal hadn't expected such a response from his son. He was about to pull free from Jakob's grip and push himself off the ground once more, but Jakob held strong to his forearm. Then Dougal understood why.

The Sergeant had turned away from the fire and was staring at the shadowy figures positioned farther along the ledge. After a quick nod to himself, apparently having made a decision, the Sergeant walked down the overhang, his beady eyes settling on the woman who had shared what she had learned about the Stalkers with Jakob.

"If we put something out that might be of interest to them, maybe they'll leave us alone," the Sergeant said to no one in particular.

Several of the slavers who had followed the Sergeant nodded, a few of them grinning maliciously, all of them staring at the woman. Clearly, they liked the plan that their leader had proposed.

Without another word, three slavers strode purposefully toward the woman, two of the men grabbing her, the third unlocking her from the chain, then all three dragging her toward the defile that led back to the trail.

Through it all, the woman screamed at the top of her lungs, fighting against the slavers, hitting, kicking, scratching, all of her efforts to no avail. The men were too big and too strong for her, handling her with an easy, casual violence.

Tiring of the woman's hysterics, one of the slavers punched

her hard in the side of the head. The blow stunned her, her attempts to fight what was happening to her slackening.

Wracking sobs soon replaced her screams, which only annoyed the slavers even more. The one who had hit her once before did so again, and then again, until finally she fell into a dazed silence. Even so, the slaver's ire was still up. He pulled back his fist for one more punch.

Much to the slaver's surprise, a strong hand grabbed the man's fist before he could connect, holding his arm in place.

"Leave her be," Dougal demanded, his voice not threatening, just insistent. Commanding.

Jakob had rarely seen this side of his father before. He had glimpsed it only recently when he had begun to talk about his desire to join the Roo's Nest Guard, his father disliking the idea.

Jakob was impressed.

He was also concerned, because he knew what was coming next. The Sergeant now stood right behind Dougal, his father unaware of his presence as he locked eyes with the slaver.

In an instant his father was on the rocky ground, one hard punch to his jaw from the Sergeant knocking him off his feet. The slavers holding the woman dropped the barely coherent prisoner, now focusing their attention on Dougal, kicking him in the legs, the back, the gut, his chest, his ribs. Anywhere they could, their fear caused by whatever waited for them in the darkness and their anger at being challenged driving them into a frenzied rage.

Jakob pushed himself up off the ground, stumbling more than rushing to aid his father. Before he could reach him, three more slavers came out of the darkness, holding him back. One of the men punched him in the ribs, and then all of them did, taking turns, releasing their fury, until finally he collapsed, barely able to breathe, the pain almost too much for him.

The slavers left him there, no longer concerned, instead moving to assist their friends as they finished working over

Jakob's father. Despite the agony, despite the fact that he could barely get any air into his lungs, Jakob rolled himself over onto his other side.

His father was nothing more than a crumpled mass in the darkness. The only thing that Jakob could see with any certainty was the steel blade shining brightly thanks to the flames of the fire.

"We can't afford to lose more slaves if we can avoid it," said the Sergeant softly to the slaver who pressed the tip of his sword to Dougal's throat. "So leave him be. He'll do just as well as the woman. Give him to the Stalkers and when we get to the mine we can enjoy the woman."

For several seconds the slaver didn't move, his bloodlust and panic mixing into a dangerous combination. Then the slaver nodded. He sheathed his sword and with the help of a few of the other men, grabbed Jakob's father beneath the arms and by the legs, carrying him out beyond the fire and into the darkness.

"What are you doing?" demanded Jakob, struggling to his feet, wobbly, only making it to his knees before he felt the need to wretch.

Jakob needed to go to his father, to help him, but he couldn't. He could barely stand. Then he tumbled back onto the ground, the Sergeant standing over him. His boot pressing down onto Jakob's aching chest.

"There's nothing you can do about this, boy, so let it go," said the Sergeant in a strangely sympathetic voice. "We're using him as an offering. If your father is there in the morning, then we keep making for the mines. And if he isn't, we keep making for the mines. So it's best to worry about yourself now. You're not in a position to do anything for anyone else but yourself. Hear me?"

The Sergeant pushed down a bit harder with his boot just to make a point, the pain becoming excruciating for Jakob, before he walked away. Jakob lay there for a long time, struggling to breathe.

Not so much from what the slavers had done to him. No, that was only a part of it. He could barely breathe because of the shame that coursed through him.

Jakob turned his head toward the flames, trying to pierce the darkness that lay just beyond.

Another chilling howl pierced the night. The Stalkers were close now. Very close.

Jakob hoped that his father made it through the night. But he knew from hard experience that hope offered little more than a false promise.

As he turned his head away, his eyes taking in the stars that were finally revealed now that the clouds had thinned, Jakob promised himself that he would gain his revenge.

He would start with the slavers who had harmed his father. And then the Sergeant.

He wouldn't stop there, however.

He would find the people responsible for all this, for taking his father and him to the mines. He would make them pay as well.

All of them.

That's what he focused on as he stared up at the stars, his mind drifting once again.

He knew that what he was thinking was no more than a hope, a wish, and not real. Just a false promise.

But he didn't care. He only cared about his father.

12

WORRISOME SIGHTING

"Must you always do that?" protested Aislinn, her voice a mix of irritation and veiled amusement, although the former was gradually gaining dominance over the latter.

For the third time in just the last few minutes, Bryen cut straight down in front of her and Astuta, Banshee squawking in triumph as she shot by, wings tight to her body, before tipping a wing to curl right back around and next to the Griffon who had befriended Aislinn.

"It's not me," Bryen replied with a much too pleased grin. "It's Banshee. She just wants to have a little fun."

Whether that was the truth or simply an excuse, Aislinn didn't know. Banshee did have a penchant for diving down toward the water as if the Griffon was going to crash into the sea and emerge with a tarpon between her claws, always pulling away at the very last second, allowing the crest of the ten-foot waves that rolled across the Burnt Ocean to kiss her paws. So she assumed it was a little bit of both.

Banshee screeched again as if she was agreeing with what Aislinn was thinking. Of course, it also sounded as if she really didn't care.

Aislinn shook her head in resignation. She had learned that was a common attribute in Griffons. A touch of arrogance, which suited their personalities well. As she spent more time with the Griffons Aislinn had discovered as well that they were brave, determined, trustworthy, and incredibly loyal to those they deemed honorable.

Banshee had demonstrated that time and time again with respect to Bryen, the Griffon always there when he needed her. Astuta appeared to be much the same, having attached herself to Aislinn, seemingly treating her like a friend and as someone she needed to watch over.

In many respects the two Griffons were much alike, the only obvious difference between the two their appearance. Banshee's coat and feathers were a tawny gold. Astuta's coat was broken by two rows of white feathers that ran down both sides of her neck from just below her beak to her chest.

"I find that hard to believe," said Aislinn.

"It's true," Bryen said with a roguish smile. "Banshee is Banshee. She does what she wants."

"An easy excuse to offer," noted Aislinn. "And I don't accept it. You two are in league with one another. I can't believe that you'd stoop to corrupting a Griffon simply so that you can irritate me."

Bryen didn't bother to reply, simply adding a wink to his now even broader smile.

Aislinn wanted to be angry with him. But she couldn't be, her own smile breaking out. Bryen was usually so reserved, keeping his emotions and thoughts in check. The look that he wore now suggested that he was relaxed and enjoying himself, which was a nice switch.

Of course, it made sense. While they were in Caledonia, everything that he had done had been geared toward a specific goal, whether it involved surviving in the Pit, protecting her, rebuilding the Weir, or destroying the Ghoule Overlord.

Now, out here on the Burnt Ocean, the Territories still a month or more off, there was little for him to worry about. There was little that required his attention.

And therein lay the rub. Bryen wasn't the type of person who could relax. Who could let things go. Who could allow others to do what he could just as easily do himself.

He needed to stay busy. He needed to have a goal to achieve, even just a small one. He needed to have a purpose. It was too much a part of who he was. Too much a part of his core.

Though his circumstances may have changed, who he was hadn't.

That's why she was thankful that Banshee enjoyed her daily flights with Bryen so much, because not only did they break up the monotony of their voyage, but they also gave Bryen something to do. Scouting around the vessel as they made their way to the west filled a need within Bryen.

Yes, she, Bryen, and Rafia used the Talent to extend their senses regularly, checking to make sure that all was well in their very small part of the very large Burnt Ocean. Even so, she couldn't disagree with his argument that there was much to be gained when you saw what was around you with your own eyes rather than relying on the Talent.

Being out over the water gave her a different perspective, a better feel for her surroundings, something that no soldier would ever dispute, as knowing the ground you were going to have to fight on was often the key to survival.

There was nothing to suggest that the Blood Company had anything to worry about as their ship sliced through the waves toward Fal Carrach. Then again, there was nothing to say that they didn't have cause to worry. So better to be prepared than to be surprised. Just another of Declan's many sayings that had become ingrained within Bryen.

A screech by Banshee that was answered by Astuta pulled Aislinn free of her musings.

Storm clouds billowed to the north, although Aislinn determined after a cursory glance that there was little reason for concern. Threatening skies were commonplace on the Burnt Ocean, and their ship was well beyond the strengthening tempest, the sheets of rain and blasts of lightning that illuminated the black mass for just a blink of the eye moving off to the east at a speed that indicated the squall had the potential to become a cyclone within the next few hours.

What caught the eye of the Griffons were the several pods of dolphins skimming across the surface of the water, diving in and out of the waves in silver and blue streaks. The mammals raced steadily to the south, ignoring several massive schools of fish that were swimming near the surface.

"I've never seen so many dolphins at one time," said Aislinn. "There are hundreds."

"Nor have I," replied Bryen, studying the marine mammals a bit more closely. "Do you notice anything else about them?"

"Other than the fact that there are so many together at one time and that none of them have attempted to feed?"

"Yes, besides that."

It didn't take her long to figure it out. "I don't think they're playing." Every other time they had come upon a pod of dolphins in the Burnt Ocean, some of the younger ones always had been enjoying themselves, leaping out of the water, crashing back with impressive splashes.

"Exactly. All of that gives me a bad feeling."

Aislinn stared at the dolphins as they surged through the water, all of them clearly aligned in intention. Strange.

Dolphins rarely turned down the opportunity to hunt, and the younger ones always had an unruly streak. So what could have pushed the animals into such a focused behavior?

At first glance, it seemed almost as if the dolphins were migrating. Then she realized what else had seemed out of place to her as they had flown to the north.

"We didn't see any whales when we came out in this direction," Aislinn said, her voice carrying her surprise. "We always see whales, even if just a small pod."

Bryen nodded in agreement, his concern growing. As soon as they had entered the Burnt Ocean they had observed several pods of whales every day. Always. Without fail.

Captain Gregson explained that was common for this time of year, the whales migrating south down the Caledonian coast and then west across the Burnt Ocean. Thousands of them. Some pods would even track the ship for a few hours, just as curious about the humans as the humans were about them.

Aislinn was right. They hadn't seen a whale at all this morning. It was as if they had disappeared. And maybe they had done just that if the whales were doing much the same as the dolphins.

"So no whales and the dolphins are acting differently than they have been," said Bryen. "You know what that means."

"Something is wrong. They're fleeing."

"Yes, they're frightened," agreed Bryen, voicing the same conclusion that Aislinn had reached.

Her mind searching for an answer to her question, Aislinn caught a glimpse of a dark blot floating on the water just a mile to the east. With a gentle nudge, Aislinn turned Astuta toward the blemish in the sea, Bryen following on Banshee. When they reached the large shape, Banshee and Astuta pumped their wings powerfully to stay in place only a few dozen feet above the waves.

They couldn't be certain exactly as to what they were looking at, but the massive size limited their choices. The shape appeared to be a mutilated blue whale, the biggest species in the ocean.

This one had to have been more than a hundred and fifty feet from the tip of its rostrum to the end of its fluke, though it was difficult to tell because only half of the animal was still floating in the water, and what was left of it was disappearing quickly down the gullets of some very large great white sharks. The animals bit into the carcass, ripping into the fat and the flesh with their bone-crushing jaws, then rolled their white-bellied bodies as they tore free the meat, taking several hundred pounds in a single gulp.

"What could have done something like this?" asked Aislinn, slightly sickened by the feeding frenzy taking place below them.

"I wouldn't know," said Bryen, "though I could guess. There's really only one possibility."

"You think it could be what Captain Gregson was talking about?"

"A Bakunawa? That would be my first thought. My only thought really, what with the whale cut in half in what looks to be just a few bites."

Captain Gregson had been more than willing to detail all the dangers they could expect to face during their passage across the Burnt Ocean. In fact, he seemed to enjoy telling them all the ways that they could possibly die.

The Bakunawa had been the most frightening. He had described the creature as a sinuous sea serpent that preferred the deepest water of the ocean as its hunting ground. The monster was so large that it could destroy most ships in seconds.

Although, because of the size of the *Freedom*, it might take a minute, maybe more, for the top predator in the Burnt Ocean to bring their vessel to the bottom, so at least they had that. A strange kind of logic, they both thought.

He had taken particular pleasure in noting that the monsters were rarely seen, then explaining that wasn't necessarily a good thing, because usually you only saw a Bakunawa right before it attacked. If you were lucky. Or unlucky, depending on your perspective.

If what Captain Gregson said was accurate, and they had no cause to doubt him, then a Bakunawa would likely have little trouble with a blue whale, even one as big as this one. As Bryen continued to inspect the carcass, he confirmed what he had suspected. The jagged cuts in the flesh and blubber where the front half of the whale had disappeared had not been made by sharks. Those bites were too clean and too large even for the great whites feeding below them.

"We should head back," said Aislinn, Astuta already dipping toward the west. "Captain Gregson needs to know what we found."

"How are you, girl? Doing well today?"

Captain Gregson stood on one of the five specially constructed decks at the stern of the *Freedom*, scratching the feathers that ran along Fuerza's jaw. Of all the Griffons, he liked her the best. She was the calmest of them all, which suited his own temperament, and he loved the streak of auburn feathers that ran down her neck on both sides.

In his opinion, the markings hinted that the beautiful animal had a touch of attitude, which he certainly appreciated. You couldn't be a successful captain without a calm demeanor and more than just a little mettle.

When Duke Winborne had told him how they were going to refurbish the ship he would be sailing across the Burnt Ocean, building the additional platforms that allowed the Griffons to come and go as they pleased and gave them a comfortable place to rest and sleep, he had been worried.

He didn't like change to begin with. And he certainly didn't like being told that the ship that he had sailed at least ten times to and from the Territories was being remodeled. The decks being added were bad enough, but when he learned what the

Duke had in mind with respect to integrating two smaller skiffs as a part of his vessel he had barely been able to restrain his temper.

From the standpoint of seaworthiness, he feared that the new construction would negatively affect the stability of the ship, making what was already a beautifully balanced vessel ungainly and prone to capsizing in bad weather, an unavoidable reality when crossing the Burnt Ocean. He wanted to make his opinion known to Duke Winborne, but he held back, deciding to wait.

As he thought about it some more and watched the construction progress, he began to understand how the changes actually improved the massive vessel's equilibrium, the decks and the two smaller ships broadening the *Freedom's* beam and allowing it to cut more smoothly through the rough water of the Burnt Ocean thanks to the narrowing keels and additional rudders.

Somewhat mollified now about his initial concerns, as was his nature, he began looking for the next worry. He had found it immediately.

The Griffons themselves.

They were rare animals. He and his sailors had never seen one before. So to have five appear out of the sun, gliding down to their manmade nests when the *Freedom* was only a few hours outside of Battersea, had been a bit of a shock.

He had heard stories about the Griffons. How the animals kept to themselves in the wilder and higher places of the Kingdom. How they swooped down to steal sheep, perhaps even a shepherd if the person was in the wrong place at the wrong time. How they attacked miners or explorers who came too close to their nests. How they killed cattle with a single swipe of their massive paws. How the animals preferred to eat human hearts and could peck it out of your chest with a single strike of their razor-sharp beaks. How a plucked feather ensured good fortune for the rest of your days.

Whether those stories were true, Captain Gregson didn't know. He didn't think so. Not after getting to know the five Griffons who had joined them on their journey.

He was a familiar face to them now. They accepted him, even trilling quietly whenever he visited, which was often several times a day.

He had learned the value of these magnificent animals. They provided him with information that he couldn't get any other way. Information that, in fact, he believed he was just about to receive as he watched Banshee and Astuta circle the ship a few times before deftly and gently landing on their platforms, the Lord Keldragan and the Lady Winborne on their backs.

Those two spent as much time in the air as they could, yet they had returned hours earlier than usual. That could mean only one thing.

Trouble.

"How worried do I need to be?" asked Captain Gregson, his fingers still stroking along Fuerza's beak, the Griffon purring contentedly.

"You'll have to tell us," replied Aislinn, who spent the next few minutes explaining what she and Bryen had discovered during their daily sojourn.

She could tell almost immediately that they had been right to return when they did. Captain Gregson's habitual look of concern had already deepened to something that more closely resembled a thundercloud.

"Could it be a Bakunawa?" Aislinn asked after she completed her recounting.

Captain Gregson didn't reply right away, instead staring off in the direction from which Aislinn and Bryen had come. The waves were fairly calm for the Burnt Ocean at the moment, the swells no more than five or six feet.

A bit uncommon for this time of year, Gregson thought. Usually it was a lot rougher. But perhaps the uncommon was actually the common today, a thought that filled him with a chilling foreboding.

"Based on what you described, Lady Winborne, I can't see how it's anything except for one of those monsters. How far away again was what was left of the body?"

"A league. No more than that."

Captain Gregson nodded to himself. "Farther south than the monster normally would be this time of year." He then shook his head like he did when one of his sailors wasn't quick enough to respond to one of his commands, more displeasure in that single glance than could be shared in the flurry of curses that would soon follow. "Then again, I shouldn't be surprised. The monster might just be following the whales. If it's had its fill, it will leave us alone. Probably."

"And if it hasn't?" asked Bryen, his mind always taking the more pessimistic road.

"Then we've got a major problem if the sea dragon is still hungry or gets curious."

"Not a comforting thought," said Aislinn.

"It wasn't meant to be, Lady Winborne. Bakunawas are nasty creatures."

"And is it possible that there could be more than one Bakunawa in the vicinity?"

"Have you ever heard the expression, lad, don't ask a question you don't want to know the answer to?"

"I have, actually," Bryen replied with a smile. "Declan taught it to me."

"That doesn't surprise me," grumbled Captain Gregson. "I knew as soon as the Sergeant walked aboard that he was a man after my own heart."

"So I take it by your response that there is a distinct possibility that there could be more than one Bakunawa in the immediate area," Bryen replied.

"There very well could be. Bakunawa are not solitary creatures by nature. If there is one, there is always another. It's just a matter of whether or not we see them."

"Anything we can do to keep them from us?" asked Aislinn.

"No, Lady Winborne," said Captain Gregson with a defeated shrug, "there's little for you to do against beasts like that. There's little that any of us can do. I would simply ask that you continue to keep an eye on what's around us with that Talent of yours."

"Easily done, Captain," Aislinn replied, already beginning to extend her senses below the surface of the water so that she could see what might be lurking beneath them.

"Thank you, Lady Winborne. In the meantime, I'll increase the number of lookouts and make sure that we're ready in case that monster comes closer, which means that I need to find Declan so that we can talk."

Captain Gregson offered Fuerza a final few scratches before giving Aislinn and Bryen a nod, jumping down from the deck, and stalking off toward the bow where Declan had set up the day's training ring.

"Let's talk to Rafia," suggested Bryen. "We can share the responsibility of searching around the ship. I'd hate to be surprised by a monster like the one Captain Gregson has described."

"Sounds good. But before that, could we talk about something else?" She hadn't found anything out of the ordinary beneath the waves, though she would keep looking.

Bryen nodded, not sure what could be on her mind beyond the prospect of being attacked by a sea dragon that could be twice as long as their ship.

"You remember when I was telling you about the conversation I had with my father before we left?"

"The multiple conversations, you mean?" asked Bryen. For a moment, he thought that Aislinn was going to bring up Duke Winborne's concerns about her going with him, which had been many. Much to his astonishment, he discovered the issue didn't involve from where they were leaving, but rather where they were going and what they might be sailing toward.

"There was actually one discussion right before we left that I wanted to talk with you about. It has to do with my uncle."

"Your uncle?" asked Bryen. He knew that Duke Winborne's brother was the Governor of the Northern Territory, the capital of which was Shadow's Reach. Beyond that, he knew very little about him.

"Yes, Kendric Winborne, my father's younger brother."

"We're supposed to visit him, aren't we?"

"We are," replied Aislinn. "Although it's to be more than just a visit."

"Meaning?" Bryen was getting a bad feeling as to where this conversation was headed.

"Meaning that my father had some concerns about what was happening in the Northern Territory. When Uncle Kendric first arrived in New Caledonia, he sent regular dispatches about what was going on there. Updates on the progress that he was making, in particular how Shadow's Reach was transitioning from a small town to a much larger city."

"Then what's the cause for concern?"

"Those communications stopped more than a year ago, and that's been worrying my father. He hasn't heard a word from his brother in all that time."

"Maybe your uncle is just spreading his wings," suggested Bryen. "He's the Governor, right? He's responsible for the Territory. Maybe he doesn't feel the need to report back to your father, or he doesn't want to. Maybe he's enjoying the freedom that being several thousand miles away from Caledonia gives him."

"Maybe," agreed Aislinn, although her response was only halfhearted. "My father purchased the title to the Northern Territory from Corinthus Beleron specifically for Uncle Kendric, so he assumed and hoped that he would demonstrate some independence. Not feel as if being a Winborne was a burden."

"Your father wanted him out from beneath his shadow."

"Blunt as always," murmured Aislinn, "but yes."

"Then why is your father worried if your uncle is exhibiting that desired independence?"

"The last few communications before they stopped referenced a white mist or fog coming down along the coast that contained within it strange and deadly creatures."

"A fog like the one that Banshee and I explored a few days ago?" Bryen's gaze sharpened. He had sensed the evil lurking within that grey haze, although he still had no idea as to the cause.

"Keeping in mind that we're still a thousand leagues or more from New Caledonia, I can't say for sure," said Aislinn. "Of course, it's certainly possible."

"You've got that look in your eyes."

"What look?" asked Aislinn innocently.

"The look that tells me that you're not telling me everything."

"I have no such look," protested Aislinn.

"You keep telling yourself that," replied Bryen with a wink.

"You think you know me so well," said Aislinn, a sly smile breaking out.

"In this regard, I think I do," Bryen said with confidence.

"Just don't let it go to your head," replied Aislinn.

"Never."

In that moment, and with the certainty that was obvious in Bryen's reply, Aislinn knew that he was speaking matter of factly. One of his attributes that she liked the most was that overconfidence was anathema to him.

"You're right," Aislinn said finally. "I do have more to share with you. And I wasn't holding it back. I just hadn't gotten to it yet."

"Of course," replied Bryen. "You just needed to wait until right before a massive sea dragon attacks us to fill me in on whatever all this is."

The upward tilt of his eyebrows suggested to Aislinn that he was teasing her, and she didn't mind in the least. Although it was one of his attributes that she didn't always appreciate.

"My father asked Noorsin to see if she could get any other pieces of information that would be useful to us before we arrived."

"Her eyes and ears extend to the Territories," Bryen nodded. "I'm not surprised."

"Neither am I."

"What did she learn?"

"She was able to gain a few useful morsels. Apparently, the fog coming down the coast and then spreading deeper into the Northern Mountains and then into the Highlands is becoming much more common. At first, it happened once every few months. Now, it's smothering the land several times each month. And there is no disagreement whatsoever that there's some kind of creature prowling within it."

"Any idea as to what it could be?"

"No, no one is certain. The only thing that is certain is that if you're caught out in the fog, you don't survive."

"Whatever is hunting in the fog is hunting people?"

"By all reports, yes, that's what her eyes and ears are telling her. Noorsin reported that people in the areas affected by the fog lock themselves into strongholds whenever the dense mist begins to drift down from the north."

"Is there any evidence of what happens when you're caught out in the fog?" asked Bryen.

"When it first began, just spatters of blood and maybe a few signs of a struggle, although the former was a lot more common than the latter. Since then, still a good number of people missing and a few bodies, often with their throats cut. A few dismembered, just bits and pieces left."

"And no one has any idea as to the cause?"

"Unfortunately not."

"It sounds like a ghost story," said Bryen, though he said it in a way that suggested that his mind was working through everything that he had just learned, his curiosity piqued. "Have you talked to Captain Gregson about this? He seems to know everything that's going on in Caledonia and the Territories. If anyone could provide more information on the fog, it would be him."

"Not yet, but I will. That's a good thought."

"I have them from time to time."

"Yes, although they seem to be few and far between." It was Aislinn's turn to give Bryen an upturned eyebrow and a knowing grin.

"Funny," replied Bryen drily.

"I thought so."

"Try not to hurt yourself patting yourself on the back."

"Do I note a touch of petulance?" asked Aislinn, pleased that she may have gotten a rise out of Bryen, who usually kept his emotions rigidly under control.

"No, just a bit of advice." Bryen quickly shifted back to the primary topic of their discussion, not wanting to get too far off on a tangent. "So your father wants to find out what's really going on with respect to your uncle and the Northern Territories, and if we can dig out anything to do with this fog he'd like that as well."

"He would," Aislinn confirmed.

"That works for me with respect to the grey mist," said Bryen. Having entered the fog while over the Burnt Ocean, he didn't know if it was the same as that affecting the Territories since they were still so far away from that distant shore. Nevertheless, he was intrigued by the possibility that there could be creatures lurking within, quite deadly creatures in fact. "But he doesn't want us to do a little snooping just because it's a good story. I'm assuming that there's more to it than that."

"You're right. He's worried about my uncle and what it could mean if the other stories he's heard are true."

"What other stories are these?"

"Rumors of monsters in the Northern Peaks, the Highlands, even at the border of Fal Carrach."

"You mean distinct from whatever might be hunting within the fog?"

"Yes. It was a tidbit that Noorsin unearthed. Strange creatures roaming the wilds." Aislinn shrugged her shoulders as if to say that she didn't know what to believe. "I guess it's not surprising when you consider that the Territories, until just a decade ago, were essentially an uncharted wilderness except for the traders and other merchants who came here on occasion looking to make their fortune. It wasn't until Marden's father started doling out grants that gave title to those coming across the Burnt Ocean that we started to see a larger migration as people looked to make a new start in a new land. So who knows what could be roaming the wilderness."

"Declan explained that to me in the Pit," said Bryen. "An opportunity that most people never imagined that they would have. For less than a gold they could purchase twenty acres of their own land. A once in a lifetime chance. So why not risk whatever danger might be involved? It certainly captured our attention when we were in the Colosseum, even though then it was only a dream. We never thought that we'd ever be on the way to the Territories."

"Yet here you are," said Aislinn, giving him a radiant smile, proud of how far Bryen had come in such a short time.

"Here I am."

"I really want this to work out for us," said Aislinn. "I want you to get what you want in life."

"I already have what I want," Bryen replied, his eyes finding hers, his meaning unmistakable.

"So do I," said Aislinn, a slight blush warming her cheeks. She turned the conversation back to its original direction, knowing what could happen if she didn't. Although that would be quite pleasant, it would have to wait until things quieted down. "And my father wants it to work out well for my uncle. He wants him to succeed as Governor."

"But ..."

"But with these stories, which may be more than stories, there is talk of unrest within his Territory and a few others."

"Because of these stories about monsters?" Bryen didn't see the connection.

"Not entirely," replied Aislinn. "It seems that some of the Governors are flexing their muscles. Or at least they're trying to. With Marden dead, and the historic lack of oversight from the Caledonian throne exacerbated by the distraction caused by the Ghoule invasion, the Governors may be trying to expand their authority in a way that's riling up or upsetting some of the people who have settled within their Territories. Taking away some of their freedoms. Not providing the services that are required as part of their charters."

"Like what?" asked Bryen.

He could understand why the Governors would do such a thing. He believed that it was the natural human instinct for people who were habituated to a life of privilege and power. The temptation for more of both was rarely resisted when that was all you knew and it could be gained without any real resistance.

"It's a mish mash of information, from what my father said. People upset because the Governors in the affected Territories aren't providing a real defense against whatever is hunting within the fog. Stories of other strange and dangerous beasts roaming the land, but again, just stories, as no one has seen what these other creatures might be, and those who have are dead. Forced labor. People taken from the streets and sent to the mines as punishment for crimes they didn't commit."

"Your father wants us to discover the truth about these stories," said Bryen, nodding, finally getting the entire picture. "We're working for him. Again."

Aislinn didn't respond immediately, seeing the dark look that Bryen was giving her.

"He asked that we explore it," she admitted finally, reluctant to do so but not wanting to hold anything back from him.

"Aislinn, you know that I didn't come to the Territories to ..."

Before Bryen could finish what he going to say, Aislinn cut in. "There have also been stories about people disappearing not long after they arrive from Caledonia. Why they are taken and where they are taken, or whether they simply disappear, no one knows. And then there are stories about farmsteads being ravaged and burned. Businesses destroyed. People who don't adhere to a Governor's or their underlings' demands being targeted."

Bryen's initial irritation began to shift to an inquisitiveness that was tinged by anger as he took in these new pieces of information. He was beginning to see how they all might fit together.

Monsters, real or imagined. Unrest. Governors seeking to expand their power beyond that guaranteed by their charter, overreaching when there was no one to get in the way of them doing so. Employing force at the expense of those who couldn't fight back if it proved necessary to gain what they wanted.

Strongarming had, of course, long been a favorite tactic of many a lord. Why not here in the Territories?

Even so, with this many disparate threads, no matter what he might want to believe, he didn't know if or how they could all be tied together, or whether they even should be.

He had told himself that he was done with this. That he was coming to the Territories to start fresh. To make a new life for himself with Aislinn. To break away from the strictures of Caledonia and not solve everyone else's problems. He had his own life to live, and he wanted to do just that.

Then why was his anger brewing? Why was he beginning to feel some responsibility for finding out what might be happening? Was that innate sense of right and wrong that Declan had infused within him once again rearing its head?

"Aislinn, you know that I didn't come here to help your uncle or your father," cut in Bryen as she took a breath, knowing that she was going to continue to make an argument as to why she wanted to do as her father asked.

"I know," said Aislinn quietly. "I should have told you all this sooner. It's just that with everything else that was going on, it didn't rise to the top of the list of issues that we needed to discuss, at least not until now."

"Thank you for that," said Bryen, appreciating her honesty. "We were going to Shadow's Reach anyway. That hasn't changed. So we'll be meeting with your uncle. And since we're landing in Ballinasloe, I'm sure we can dig around a bit to see if we can pick up any more details on what might be going on in the Territories. But beyond that, I'm not making any promises. I have no reason to involve myself or the Blood Company in someone else's fight unless there's good cause to do so. Fair enough?"

"Fair enough." Aislinn visibly breathed a sigh of relief. "Thank you."

Bryen nodded. "If nothing else, everything you've said --

assuming there's some truth to it -- just confirms that when we get to the Territories we don't know really what we're walking into and that we'll need to be careful."

"I couldn't agree with you more," said Aislinn.

"I just wish that we had more information. I don't like heading toward a potentially dangerous situation blind."

"Neither do I."

"With that in mind, do you know your uncle very well?" asked Bryen.

"As a young girl, yes. He was very fun loving. Always had a smile, a joke, and a treat for me when he visited. Although I haven't seen him since I was a child."

"I have seen your uncle in just the last few years actually." Jurgen Klines stepped up to join them at the rail. "My apologies. I couldn't help but overhear some of your conversation. And I certainly didn't mean to intrude."

"No intrusion at all, Captain Klines," said Bryen.

"You're too kind, Captain Keldragan."

"Are we going to do this every time we meet, Blademaster?" Bryen's tone insinuated that he was getting tired of the game.

"A bit too much, I take it?"

"Just so," Bryen replied.

"Then I'll put that humor to the side so that we can talk of Kendric Winborne. Your uncle was just as you said, Lady Winborne. But when I last spoke with him, I noticed something else about him that I hadn't seen before."

"What was that, Blademaster?" asked Aislinn.

"Drive. Ambition. For the first time, he seemed unsatisfied with his position in life. That he wanted more than what he had been given."

"People can change," suggested Bryen. "They usually do."

"Of that I'm well aware," agreed Aislinn.

"Do you trust your uncle?" asked Bryen.

If he was going to start digging into what sounded like a

jumble of different threats, some most likely real, others probably imagined, they would want to start with Kendric Winborne, because based on the charter granted by the Caledonian Crown, he exercised more authority than any of the other Governors, actually having oversight of them, and therefore was perfectly positioned to affect his and Aislinn's efforts, either for good or bad, to uncover the truth of what might be happening in the Territories.

"There's no reason not to," Aislinn said, although she had hesitated before replying, and her words and tone did not inspire much confidence.

Bryen nodded, understanding her meaning. He had a feeling that when they arrived in Fal Carrach, he and the Blood Company would be walking out onto the white sand once again. Worse, they wouldn't know what kind of adversary they'd have to fight. That didn't appeal to him in the least.

"But there's no reason to trust him," concluded Bryen. He shook his head in irritation.

"Duchess Stelekel and her eyes and ears certainly have proven useful, although only to a point," said Aislinn, her tone of frustration mirroring Bryen's. "I feel like I'm stumbling about in the dark, and I don't like it."

"Perhaps I could help with that," interjected Klines. "Before I rose to Captain of the Royal Guard and then Blademaster, I made my way in the world with some skills that I haven't had to use in quite some time that might prove useful now."

13

BAD OMEN

Standing at the bow of the *Resolution*, the newest three-masted clipper added to his family's growing fleet, Abram kept his eyes closed, attempting to block out the noises around him. The shouts and conversations of the sailors as they went up and down the rigging, scrubbed the deck, and did the myriad other jobs required to maintain the sleek vessel. The snapping of the ropes and the sails at the insistence of the wind. The seagulls cawing loudly as they circled the crow's nest.

Although it proved difficult, he succeeded, cutting out all the distractions around him and concentrating only on the ocean. Enjoying the touch of the warm sun on his face, he relished even more the rhythm of the vessel cutting through the rough waves, the crests not as high as they would be for a ship not of his new design, the troughs not as deep.

The unique design of the hull did more than allow the ship to glide through the sea with an unmatched grace. It also added several knots to their speed, what was becoming the primary distinction of Carlomin Trading Company compared to their competitors.

He heard only the pounding of the waves and the *Resolution's* sleek hull sliding through the water. To his ears, it was the sweetest of sounds.

Eyes still closed, he smiled broadly. Every time the bow dipped into a trough a salty spray shot up over the prow. He enjoyed the refreshing mist as it dampened his hair and his clothes.

This was where he preferred to be. On deck. Not in his office, reading documents, reviewing charts and numbers, and dealing with the almost inexhaustible issues that he needed to address on a daily basis in order to keep his business afloat ... literally.

No, he much preferred being on one of his ships. Out on the water. Seeing everything with his own eyes. Judging for himself how things were going. He couldn't do that from his dock in Ballinasloe.

Joining his captains and crews on their routes was the only way to get a feel for what was working with his business and what wasn't. What practices needed to be established, what practices needed to be refined, and what practices needed to be eliminated.

That meant that he had to listen to what his sailors had to say. He had to keep his eyes open. So for the first time since he had settled himself at the bow, he did, shielding his gaze from the glare of the bright sun. For as far as he could see, there was nothing in all directions but a rough blue sea.

Abram had been a soldier before he had become a vintner, trading in his sword when he met Isana. He had learned quickly during his time as a scout in the Royal Guard that the only way to make good decisions, especially before a fight, was to get the lay of the land. He had applied that practice to his business, and he was doing that right now.

After speaking with many of his peers about the several dozen merchant vessels that had been taken by pirates in just the last few months, he wanted to see for himself what might be occurring along the eastern coast of the Territories. The soldier in him was thinking of ways to use the speed of his new ship, this being her maiden voyage, against any vessel that might seek to attack them, almost hoping to come up against the marauders haunting the Sea of Mist, the businessperson in him arguing that that was a very bad idea. His men and women were sailors, not soldiers.

"See what you want to see, but do no more than that." That's what his wife had told him. "Why risk a fight if the pirates can't catch you?"

He had to admit that once again Isana was right.

He had every confidence that all of his vessels, including the *Resolution*, could outpace any other ship on the water, which was likely why none of the Carlomin clippers had been seized yet. The pirates preferred the larger, slower vessels that lumbered from port to port.

A few of his captains did report being chased by ships that at first didn't fly a flag denoting their merchant house. The expected black sails and flags only became visible when the pirates drew closer, although never close enough to attack.

Abram let his gaze track the fuzzy shore that was passing by swiftly on his starboard side. They were close to the coast, not feeling the need to curl farther out into the ocean because of their belief in their ability to evade any ship that might display hostile intentions.

But not too close.

It could be a dangerous journey if you didn't know the particulars of the Sea of Mist. In addition to the all too common fog that could come up on you quite unexpectedly, there were a host of other dangers.

The rocky coastline, towering sea stacks often rising out of the water a quarter mile or more from the shore, the channels between the rocky pillars and coast often becoming a muddy beach when the tide was out. Shifting sandbars that could extend for miles in any direction. Shoals that could tear out a ship's hull hidden beneath the waves. Large rocks barely visible in the shallow water reaching for the unwary.

Only a skilled and experienced navigator was aware of all the threats and how to avoid them.

Confident in the abilities of his captain, Abram spun around slowly, scanning the horizon. He didn't see anything that would give him cause to worry, at least not in that moment. Although he knew from experience that could change in an instant. So he would enjoy the peace of their voyage, away from the cares that clambered for his time when he was on land, for as long as he could, the movement of the ship beneath him almost lulling him into a rarely attained calm.

Unfortunately, his constant worries swiftly worked their way to the surface like monsters rising from the deep. Inevitably, his mind, as it had been doing as soon as they had left port, had shifted its focus to the offer from Hakea Roosarian.

Of course, it really wasn't an offer. It was an ultimatum cloaked as a proposal.

The Governor of Fal Carrach wanted Abram to sell her at a cut-rate price half of Carlomin Trading Company so that she could become a partner in the business that he and his wife had built up during the last few years. In fact, the Governor had the audacity to suggest that she didn't even need to pay any golds for her shares, arguing that the real value of the partnership that she proposed came from her position as ruler of the Territory. Her political standing provided benefits that the other merchants doing business in the Territories couldn't match and, as she stated with absolute confidence, that was more valuable than any money she could offer him.

She could be right, Abram admitted. Perhaps Carlomin

Trading Company would come out ahead from such a partnership. Although he doubted it.

Hakea Roosarian did nothing that didn't benefit her to the greatest degree possible. Her record of engagement with the other merchants certainly proved that.

Those who partnered with her, whether willingly or not, rarely saw the same success that she did. In fact, usually those partners sold what they still owned of their companies to the Governor not too long after going into business with her, rarely getting back the golds they had invested in the first place.

Abram could not truly measure the value of a partnership with Hakea Roosarian. However, he could conclude that if he accepted her proposal, it wouldn't be long before he lost the other half of his business. His supposed partner would take it all, and he would not be able to do anything about it.

Her being the Governor.

It would simply be a repeat of what happened to his family in Roo's Nest.

When he had told his wife about how Roosarian had approached him, Isana had agreed with his initial take, their conversation replaying in his head.

"You can't trust her."

"I don't trust her."

"Why does she want our business? She's not busy enough as it is making everyone's life difficult in Fal Carrach?"

"She wants to make money. And we are making good money. She knows that. Everyone knows that based on what we're doing with our dock and the new ships we're bringing into service."

"Yes, but so are all the other merchants doing business across the Burnt Ocean and along the coast. There are so few of us and the demand is so great that we control the market for a time. You'd have to be a fool to not make money in this trade."

"All too true," Abram had said, taking some time to think.

His wife had been right. Roosarian could make the same proposal to any of the other merchants doing business out of Ballinasloe because all of them were making a good profit. So it wasn't just the business that she wanted. "She wants something else. Something that only we can give her."

"Our ships?"

"Yes, that would be my guess. Our ships are the fastest on the water."

"Which is why our business is so good and no one can compete with us in terms of what we offer."

"Yes, but there's more to it. She might see a purpose for our ships beyond how we're using them now."

"What do you mean?"

"She wants our ships not just because of what they add to our business. She has another reason. I'm sure of it."

"How so?"

"The pirates."

Isana had nodded sagely, taking in what Abram had said, mulling his comment. Abram had waited for her to catch up to his thinking. It hadn't taken long. Isana had a sharp mind, a better mind for business than he did, which was one of the reasons that he had married her, in addition to the fact that he had lost his heart to her as soon as he had laid eyes on her.

He could tell by the expression on Isana's face that it was all beginning to come together for her.

"You believe ..."

"I think," he had corrected. "I don't have any proof."

"Have you talked with any of the other merchants about your hypothesis?"

"Not yet. I wanted to obtain some proof before I did. Our peers prefer facts, not supposition."

It was that conversation looping through his head along with Governor Roosarian's proposal that kept him from achieving the peace that he was seeking, making him think that he couldn't wait any longer, proof or no proof. He had few options for keeping the Governor's grasping hands from his business other than trying to work with his competitors to block her efforts.

The argument was quite simple for joining together into a loose coalition. If she could take his business, she could take theirs. When it came to the demands of Hakea Roosarian, they were all in the same boat.

Abram was pulled from his thoughts when he heard the tell-tale thunk of Captain Jennison's wooden leg hitting the deck in a steady rhythm.

"Thinking thoughts deeper than the sea, Mr. Carlomin?"

"Why would you say that?" he asked, turning to greet his friend. Captain Jennison had worked for the Carlomin family from the very beginning, commanding their first ship.

Abram trusted Jennison with his life. He had been there when the Captain had lost his leg. They were lucky that was all that was lost during that unforgettable night.

What they had discovered then had made them both question whether they wanted to stay on the water. Inevitably, and not unexpectedly, they both did. The pull of the sea was too much a part of them to let go of their often demanding mistress despite the terrors that she offered.

That experience had bonded them, and it had made them look at the world differently. It had made them believe in things that they never would have believed in if they hadn't seen them with their own eyes.

"When you're out here on the water it's hard not to."

Abram smiled and nodded. He couldn't disagree. "Nothing that you need to worry about."

It was Jennison's turn to nod. "Not yet, you mean."

"Not yet," confirmed Abram, not ready to share more.

Jennison trusted Abram with his life. He would be dead if not for him, and he knew from experience that his employer and friend would talk with him about what was bothering him when the time was right. That could wait for now, however, a more immediate concern requiring their attention.

"There was something else I wanted to talk with you about," said Jennison, motioning to the grey mass that was rapidly blotting out the eastern horizon and speeding toward the coast.

"A storm?" Abram was used to squalls taking shape fast on the Sea of Mist, but he didn't glimpse the lightning that he had seen so many times before when these gales came in from the east.

"Worse," grumbled Jennison. "A fog thicker than you've likely ever seen before. It'll be on us in just a few hours."

"Can we outrun it?"

"In this beautiful clipper," said Captain Jennison, from the tone of his voice clearly already enamored with his new ship, "we just might be able to ... if the front wasn't so broad. The fog bank must stretch for a hundred leagues."

"So no chance to get beyond it?"

"No, it's coming in too fast, even for the *Resolution*. Better to wait it out."

Abram nodded. "Do what you need to do. It's your ship."

Jennison nodded and smiled, pleased by Abram's comment. Without another word, he walked off, wooden leg knocking on the deck, issuing a series of commands once he reached the helm.

The helmswoman spun the wheel, turning the ship hard to starboard, making for a small cove that was a favorite of the merchants and traders traveling up and down the coast on this section of the Sea of Mist that was just south of the Strand.

Anchoring in Mermaid's Cove would slow their journey, keeping them there until the fog dissipated. Even so, better that than risk their lives sailing blind along such a treacherous shore.

When they reached the hidden cove, Jennison would make

certain that they stayed well out in the deeper water, near the entrance to the small, protected bay, keeping a good distance away from the shore.

He had heard the stories, the tales growing larger and less believable as his fellow captains drank more ale in the tavern. Stories of what walked in the fog like the one that would smother them in just a few hours. Stories regarding the dangers of not keeping a wary eye on what could come out of the mist if they were too close to the shore.

He would set a strong guard for the night as well. Just in case. And he was sure that his sailors would take their responsibilities seriously. They had all heard the tales as well. Besides, Jennison's missing leg proved to many of them that monsters were real.

He and Abram certainly believed that. They knew that out here in the Sea of Mist, pirates weren't the only danger they needed to worry about.

ABRAM COULDN'T SLEEP. His mind refused to turn off. He had tried to calm himself for the last few hours, to think of other things. He only succeeded in wrapping himself in his blanket as he rolled around on his small bed with all his worries, some real, some imagined, weighing down upon him.

The lack of air didn't help. He was hot, sweaty. The cabin was humid, the air just hanging there. In large part because there was no breeze, which was strange along the eastern coast of the Territories. The many portholes that were open along the length of the aft wall, one of the few comforts he incorporated into his private quarters, gave him no relief.

In every Carlomin ship Abram had included space for a private office that also served as his cabin that was located in the stern just below the main deck. Some of Abram's peers and competitors had called the small stateroom a frivolity, nothing more than wasted money.

They believed that the additional chamber reduced the square footage of the hold, thereby limiting the amount of cargo that could be taken on board. And as they were all so willing to tell him, multiple times in fact as if he didn't understand what he was doing despite running his company for almost a decade, the more cargo you could carry, the more money you could make.

Abram had conceded that was true on a standard cargo vessel, where the size of the hold usually determined the profit to be made. Not so with the new approach to ship design that Abram and his wife had implemented.

In their opinion speed was more important than size. The traders who reserved cargo space on his vessels paid a premium for the privilege since his clippers could cut the standard shipping time across the Burnt Ocean in half.

He didn't need a full cargo hold to make a good profit. He just needed the right customers and the right freight.

To date, finding both had proven easier than he thought it would be, creating a formula for success that none of his competitors could match. So much so that several of the other traders were seeking to become his partners, something that he would talk to Isana about when he returned to Ballinasloe.

A few strategic alliances might not hurt. In fact, they likely would give them a chance to increase their profitability while also helping to ward off Governor Roosarian's interest.

Abram pushed himself up from his bed, running a hand through his damp hair. He knew why he couldn't sleep, the same conversations continually running through his head. One in particular that had left him more worried than the time his Captain in the Royal Guard had ordered him to make a full circuit of a bandits' cantonment even though there was little cover other than the long grass that encircled the small grove where the thieves had made their camp.

Seeking to shift his mind to other matters, if only for a time, he pushed himself up off his bunk, although he didn't extend to his full height, wary of the large beams that ran across the ceiling. Pulling on his shirt and pants, and then his boots, he walked over to the portholes, staring out into the darkness.

There was no illumination other than a faint glow from just above him, a lantern set in the hook on the railing. Even that light was muted, however, thanks to the heavy fog that had draped itself across Mermaid's Cove.

His inability to sleep because of his constant worrying wasn't in itself all that surprising. He was always worried about something, which his daughter loved to tease him about. Relentlessly, in fact.

Yet, at the moment, he believed that his worrying was more than justified. How was he to deal with Lady Roosarian and her ridiculous offer?

He had to keep the Governor's grasping claws from their business at all costs. Allowing her to get even a fingerhold would mean the end of Carlomin Trading Company. All their work and effort to make their company a player in the trade crossing the Burnt Ocean would have been for naught.

And with Roosarian so intent on taking their business, how was he to protect his wife and daughter now that they were in Ballinasloe with him? If it was just him, he had few concerns, as he was more than capable of defending himself.

His wife and daughter changed the equation, however. Their being in the Territories gave the Governor leverage that she couldn't obtain otherwise.

Once he told the Governor that he wouldn't be accepting the deal she had proposed, he had no doubt that Hakea Roosarian, in exhibiting her displeasure, wouldn't hesitate to make the issue personal. She would seek to use his family to apply more pressure on him with the hope of his acquiescing to her demand.

Better that Isana and Talia had stayed in Roo's Nest, free of the Governor.

Abram pushed that thought from his mind.

He knew that hadn't been an option. Something had happened there to Talia, though his daughter had yet to speak to him about it. He hoped that she would when she was ready.

Abram was thinking that the best way to deal with his concern regarding Hakea Roosarian was to speed up the work on the concept that his wife had put forward with respect to creating an enclave at the port. Perhaps they could even begin building before he had to respond to the proposal.

At Isana's suggestion, they had purchased the dock and the warehouses next to it as soon as Abram had arrived in the city. They had expanded the pier swiftly, adding the shipbuilding facilities at the very end.

But that was only the first step in their plan. Now they were working to extend their foothold along the Ballinasloe waterfront.

When he returned to the port he would accelerate the process to do that. Their goal was to create a sanctuary of sorts, a section of the docks owned by his family that was like a village within the larger town, though with walls of their own. Roosarian's threats would mean very little if she couldn't reach her targets easily.

One problem addressed, at least for now.

Turning away from the porthole that he had been staring through and seeing nothing the entire time, Abram opened the door to his cabin. His brief spark of pleasure because of what he believed would be at least a partial solution to the issue that was plaguing him didn't last long.

His thoughts naturally moved on to some of the other challenges he faced, his mind continuing to work at a furious pace.

Needing some fresh air, he walked down the passageway, stopping at the very end of the hallway.

It was quiet. Too quiet. He couldn't even hear the gentle waves of the cove lapping against the ship's hull. The silence sent a shiver down his spine.

The incredibly thick fog hiding the *Resolution* deadened any noise. The swirling mist, heavy to begin with when he went to his cabin just a few hours ago, was much denser now. So substantial, in fact, that just for a second he thought that he could reach out and rip free a piece of the grey blanket.

The worries that had kept him awake disappeared in an instant. The fog felt wrong. Unnatural. As if it didn't belong here.

He didn't know why he thought that. Still, he believed it.

The billowing murk reminded him of the night that was more nightmare than memory. The night that neither he nor Captain Jennison had any right to believe that they would survive. Yet they did, thanks to a strong dose of courage and a large helping of luck.

After several seconds of surveying what lay before him, Abram, unable to see much at all in the impenetrable gloom, walked out from the hatch. Glancing behind him, he glimpsed Captain Jennison standing at the wheel, his form drifting in and out of the mist. Several sailors stood there with him, all of them staring out into the fog in various directions.

It was as if they actually expected to see something. No, that wasn't quite right. They all had weapons on their belts. Swords. Daggers. A few held maces and axes.

They were anticipating an attack. But why?

Despite an overwhelming sense of misgiving, Abram began to walk down the deck toward the bow. Whenever he came across a sailor standing watch, he spent a few minutes speaking with him or her. He was impressed. They all seemed to appreciate his taking an interest in them.

Even more telling, and a credit to their training, when they talked with him none of the sailors ever looked at him directly. They always kept their eyes staring out beyond the railings.

That discipline came from Captain Jennison, he knew, and probably just as much from the sailors' own fears. They knew better than anyone what might come out of the fog, which might explain the sense of foreboding that pervaded the ship.

When he reached the bow, Abram peered out into the gloom, searching for the faint line of the shore that was more than a quarter mile off. He couldn't see a thing. He could barely see a few feet in front of him, if that.

He felt like he was in a cocoon, and he hated it. He hated the feeling of being cut off from the world. Even more so, the sense of being isolated from the sailors on the deck, who were no more than faint shapes in the mist even with the handful of lamps set along the rails.

Abram had been a soldier for almost a decade before leaving the service upon meeting Isana. A scout. Always sent well ahead of the main body of troops, sometimes with a partner, often on his own because of his skill at moving stealthily and his ability to identify anomalies and opportunities that most other people missed.

After that experience, he didn't mind being alone. It didn't bother him like it did other soldiers. Even when he was behind enemy lines he had few concerns when he was by himself.

But then he could see clearly. He could get the lay of the land.

Now, he was in his own world, a strange, hidden world, and it made him distinctly uncomfortable. Right at that moment, the voice in the back of his head that had warned him of danger so many times in the past chose to speak up, the soft murmur of warning becoming a scream.

He could see nothing that alerted him to why that would be the case. Nevertheless, he respected the voice. He always did.

The unexplainable tremor of danger had saved him many times.

Wanting to focus on the only sense that might help him while he was enveloped by the fog, he closed his eyes. All he did for the next few minutes was listen.

Just as he couldn't see anything, he didn't hear a sound.

Nothing. Nothing at all. Until ...

When he finally identified the all-too-familiar sound, his eyes widened and his breath quickened. He hadn't heard a noise like that in quite a long time. It reminded him of a knife sliding into a melon, and that realization sent a jolt of terror through his entire body.

Abram opened his eyes then, turning around slowly. The deck spread out before him, the helm at the far end of the clipper all but invisible in the fog. He could barely make out the first mast of three, and that only a large vertical shadow in the thick fog.

Then his gaze went to the railing to his left, pausing for a few seconds, before shifting to his right.

Squinting, Abram took a few steps toward the helm, trying to get a better look. There appeared to be several large, form-less lumps on the deck.

The voice of warning in the back of his head was screaming at him so loudly now that it threatened to drown out his own thoughts.

There was only one explanation for what he was seeing. He could only assume that the lumps on the deck were the sailors assigned to the watch.

Then several flashes of movement closer to the mast caught his eye. What he discerned in the blanketing mist, vague though it was, terrified him.

One huge shape that appeared to be taller and larger than a man stalked away in the fog toward the helm, dripping water as it went. The other figure stood over one of the fallen sailors for a few seconds, then knelt down.

At that very instant, the fog thinned just enough for Abram to gain a peek of the greyish black skin of a clawed hand lunging out from the hulking shadow and disappearing in the lump. He heard again the sound that had caught his attention and made him turn when he stood at the bow, the sound that reminded him of a piece of steel sliding through flesh.

Unable to take his eyes away, he watched, horrified, as the shadow dug into the sailor's gut. The monster ripped free pieces of intestine and other organs that disappeared down the creature's throat in only a few bites.

Abram's first thought was that they were being victimized again by the creatures in the mist that he and Jennison had come upon when they were sailing not too far from the Jagged Islands. A similar fog had draped itself over their vessel on that fateful day, forcing them to seek refuge in a large bay that sailors had the misfortune to name Solace Sound.

Jennison had lost his leg that night when the monsters came out of the water. They both had been lucky to escape with their lives.

The creatures that boarded their ship then had looked like men for the most part. From what Abram could pick out of the mist, they had been about the same size as them, thinner, however. And their skin, a mixture of pale grey, white, and blue, allowed them to hide in the thick fog. Most telling, those monsters had carried cutlasses and knives in their clawed hands.

He realized that they faced a different terror now, not a length of steel to be seen. A horror that he had never expected to meet here.

He had heard of these beasts. Stories about them were endemic from Shadow's Reach down to Benewyn and every-place in between. These monsters were the reason they had anchored far out from the shore, believing they would steer clear of these terrors by doing so.

He had not heard that they could swim. Yet here they were on his ship, dripping water and feasting on his sailors.

What he stared at now, and what was now staring back at him, seemed human, but clearly wasn't. It was almost as if the creature had once been a man and had been stretched somehow, elongated, expanded, so that the monster stood at least a head or two taller than the tallest man and was wider than a doorway.

Because of the fog Abram couldn't see much beyond the overall shape of the monster, except for one defining characteristic that had frozen him in place. The one characteristic that confirmed for Abram what was attacking his crew.

The eyes. The blood-red eyes that held no mercy within them.

Abram pulled the sword from the sheath that he had been carrying in his hand, throwing the scabbard off to the side so that it wouldn't get in his way. He took a deep breath, preparing to shout a warning.

He couldn't get the air out in time, a thump to his side followed by a splatter of drops startling him. Without needing to turn, he knew what stood behind him.

There was a third monster on board, this one having jumped down from the rigging.

Without even thinking, Abram pivoted, slashing with his sword, aiming for the creature's neck. At the same time he glimpsed the burnished flesh, a mix of black and grey that looked almost like wax, as if it had been placed over a flame to be melted down and then allowed to harden into what resembled a rough, rudimentary armor.

Still, it was those eyes, those blood-red eyes, that pulled Abram's gaze, the former soldier struggling to break free from the hateful gaze so that he could focus on staying alive.

Abram's slash, though swift, never connected. The monster was too fast for him.

The beast blocked his blow, the strength of the creature's parry so powerful that it knocked the sword from Abram's hand.

Screaming in pain, his wrist broken, Abram fell back on his training as a soldier, keeping his wits about him.

Abram felt the air blow past him as the beast's clawed hand cut right above his head when he ducked the swing that he had seen coming. Ignoring the pain of his injured wrist, which he held against his chest, Abram whipped out the dagger at his hip.

He attacked blindly, the beast blending into the fog much too easily, an already difficult target to hit becoming even more so.

With what he knew was a great deal of luck, Abram slammed his dagger into the beast's groin. The stab gave Abram some small pleasure, particularly when the creature hissed in agonizing pain.

His first thought was that he had taken the monster out of the fight. His second was that he should have never made such an assumption, the monster ignoring the wound and responding with a speed for which Abram wasn't prepared.

The monster swung a backhanded blow with the claw that had just missed taking off Abram's head.

Abram tried and failed to dodge out of the way, the monster's talon-like fingers ripping into his chest and sending him flying through the air.

Moaning in agony, Abram collapsed to the deck. He felt himself going into shock, not realizing how severe his wound was, several of his upper ribs and his sternum exposed.

Barely able to see and think through the pain, Abram forced himself to look up.

He knew what he was going to see.

The monster stood over him, peering down, its fanglike teeth revealed in what Abram could only assume was a smile. The monster reached for him, the beast's bloody claw moving toward his throat.

His vision beginning to blur, black spots sparking in front of his eyes, Abram refused to give up despite the inevitability of his coming death. He still had the presence of mind and wherewithal to stab with the dagger that he clutched in his hand.

He jabbed blindly. Even so, he hit the target he had been hoping for, his scream of rage using up what little air he was able to pull into his damaged lungs.

The monster reared back, pushing himself away from Abram, clutching at the dagger that had sliced across his nose and then been driven into his eye when the creature turned his head at the first touch of searing pain. The beast's terrible shriek shattered the quiet of the night before dying away.

Now feeling a heavy weight on his chest, Abram knew that the end was near. Yet when he opened his eyes again, he saw nothing but the fog.

The monster was gone.

Abram heard the shouts then, Captain Jennison screaming orders, the sound of steel whipping through the air, the blood-curdling cries of the monsters still on board, and the responding shouts from the sailors as they tried, and often failed, to send the creatures to a watery grave, before a welcoming darkness finally took him.

HE FELT the bright sun on his face, warming him, keeping him from opening his eyes even though he was desperate to do so. He couldn't remember the last time he'd felt warm. He'd been cold for so long.

Stuck in a freezing place. A dark place. A silent place. He never thought that he'd find his way out.

Abram guessed by the sound of the waves lapping against the pillars and the rough surface of the wooden planks against his back that he was lying on a dock. But which dock? Was he back in Ballinasloe?

It was the chorus of voices he heard that answered the question for him. The voices that brought him back from that cold, lonely place.

The hand that was gripping his own pulled him closer to the surface. He could never forget that touch. The warmth and feel of the skin. That spark the first time that he had held Isana's hand.

It had happened innocuously enough, Isana stumbling on a rough patch of road, Abram reaching out to steady her. He had known then that he was going to marry her, even if she didn't.

Abram wanted to turn his head. He could sense Isana kneeling down next to him, her hand still in his. But he couldn't. No matter how hard he tried, he couldn't.

It took too much effort. Too much strength that he no longer had. His body didn't want to listen to him.

Why?

Then he remembered what happened on the deck of the *Resolution*. The creature that he had fought. The monster that he had never expected to see there. That shouldn't have been there.

Abram groaned softly, a bolt of pain shooting through him, then fading into the background once again.

The pain was still there. Even with the cold, it had been there. Although just barely except for that brief spike.

As soon as the pain faded, the numbness returned, and with it the sensation that he was encased in ice.

Even with the warmth of the sun on his face, the rest of his body was cold. So cold.

He was about to drift away, to allow the cold to take him, tired of trying to keep it at bay. But then another voice grabbed his waning attention.

He could hear Captain Jennison now. His friend had survived. That pleased him.

If Jennison escaped the beasts, then maybe some of the crew did as well. They must have. Jennison could never have sailed the *Resolution* back home on his own.

"WE LOST HOW MANY?" asked Isana.

"Twelve," replied Captain Jennison. "Half the crew before we even knew the monsters had boarded us."

"What were they?" asked Talia, staring down at her father, her eyes wide with fear and shock. She desperately wanted to shift the topic, knowing what was going to happen next and not ready to deal with it, fighting to maintain control over her emotions, which threatened to burst forth.

Her father had been unresponsive ever since the sailors had carried him off the ship and laid him down gently on the dock. She had seen the claw marks along the railing of the *Resolution*. The large chunks of wood that had been torn out.

Taking that damage into account, she could only imagine what her father's chest looked like, dark red blood staining the bandages wrapped around his torso. And it was all fresh, the physick having already come to see him just minutes before, doing all that she could to help him, although that proved to be very little based on the seriousness of his wounds.

"We couldn't say for sure," Captain Jennison grumbled.

He was irritated that he couldn't provide more useful information while also feeling a heavy burden for all the sailors who had died, even more so for what had happened to his friend.

Abram had sounded the warning, killing one of the creatures. The remainder of the crew had dispatched another of the beasts, the third leaping into the water after being wounded several times.

They had thrown the bodies overboard and then set sail as quickly as they could, leaving the cove behind, more fearful of coming face to face with more of those monsters than of running into a shoal in the cursed mist.

"With the fog, we couldn't get a good look at them," explained Jennison. "Big. As tall as a draft horse. Vaguely human in shape. Long claws as sharp as a cutlass. We didn't see much more than that."

"So it wasn't pirates?" asked Isana, seeking to confirm her suspicions. She gripped her husband's hand tightly, using that action to hold back the grief that was welling up within her, knowing that she could succeed for only so long.

"Not the human kind," the Captain replied. "We didn't get a good look at them. The fog was too thick and they were too fast. All I can say with any certainty was that they came out of the fog like the monsters of lore. You didn't know they were there until they were right next to you, so how Abram was able to fight one off on his own ..." Captain Jennison left the rest unsaid, still marveling at his friend's small victory, though not believing that the cost of achieving it was worth it. "The only characteristic of these monsters that we could see with any clarity were their eyes."

"Blood red?" asked Isana.

Jennison nodded. "Just so. Those eyes burned through the fog hotter than a fire. Even when we were throwing the dead ones into the water."

Isana dipped her head, nodding sadly. "Stalkers."

"I believe so," sighed Jennison, his voice revealing his exhaustion. "I never heard that these monsters could swim. None of the stories speak of it. Clearly, they can. They reached us at the entrance to Mermaid's Cove. We stayed well away from the coast. We made sure of it."

Talia took in everything that Captain Jennison had said, just listening, not commenting. Trying to make sense of why this horrible tragedy had occurred.

She knew that the Captain had done everything he could to keep her father and the crew safe. There was no doubting that.

And she couldn't fault his actions, knowing that her father would have agreed with every decision that Jennison had made. Yet despite their best efforts to stay clear of any threats, the deadly peril had still found them.

Something else was going on here. She was sure of it.

Stories of these Stalkers were running rampant throughout the eastern Territories. True. But none of the tales ever suggested that more than one Stalker attacked at a time. It was always a single Stalker.

Three boarding a ship well off the shore at the same time? And Mermaid's Cove no less? A remote place that was shielded by sheer cliffs on all sides and offered no easy way to get to the small beach other than the Sea of Mist?

It didn't make sense to Talia. She was missing something, yet she didn't know what it could be.

It was almost as if the attack had been premeditated. But how that could be, Talia didn't know.

How could the monsters know that her father and his ship would be there exactly then?

It's not like the Stalkers could control the fog. She had no satisfactory answer for how those monsters had any idea that the fog would come in then and force the *Resolution* into that specific cove.

None of this made sense.

Maybe it was just luck. Good for the monsters, bad for her father and the sailors who had lost their lives.

Maybe it was something else entirely. Something more sinister.

She looked at her father's drawn and pale face. She needed to know why this had happened. She needed to know if someone was responsible. If it was more than just an amalgamation of separate events leading to a terrible, heartbreaking result.

She struggled to make sense of it all, how what had occurred could even be possible. How it could be planned.

At present, it seemed like a waste of her time and her focus. She had no good answers to the myriad questions that shot through her mind.

Yet the more Talia thought about it, the more she believed that it had to be more than just happenstance.

Didn't it? It couldn't just be bad luck. Could it?

She looked at her mother and realized by the expression on her face that many of the same questions that Talia was struggling with were running through her mother's mind as well. Although it looked as if her mother had reached a conclusion already.

Isana's gaze had hardened, having analyzed everything that Captain Jennison had explained and linking it to the conversation she had with Abram right before he had left on the *Resolution*. She understood now. Or at least she believed that she did. She didn't need all the pieces to fit together perfectly to believe that she was right.

That her husband had been right all along.

She didn't believe that it was a random attack. There was no reason for the Stalkers to be at Mermaid's Cove other than to be there for her husband.

She couldn't explain how the monsters knew to be there then. She couldn't explain how the fog could have formed at such a perfect time to force Captain Jennison to seek refuge there that night. She couldn't explain many things.

Yet in her heart, she knew. She knew she was right. Sometimes instinct trumped reason, and in her opinion this was one of those times.

The Stalkers had been waiting for Abram.

That was the only explanation that made any sense to her. Somehow, the monsters knew that he would be there. They were waiting for him. They were there to kill him. To kill all of the crew if her husband hadn't killed one of the Stalkers himself and raised the alarm.

If she spoke what she believed aloud, she assumed that Captain Jennison and the sailors with him would think that she was losing her mind, driven there by the grief that was pushing its way to the surface.

She looked down at Abram, her eyes softening. She had never thought that this would happen. That the end would come this way. Not after he had left the Royal Guard for her.

But it had.

Abram had left a world of death and violence only for that death and violence to find him.

Her husband's eyes remained closed, his breathing becoming more labored with each passing second. His color was poor. In fact, in just the last few minutes Abram had paled considerably, his chest rising more slowly, his breaths shallower.

Isana had examined his wounds with the physick when the woman had removed the bandages. She had known with just a quick glance that there was little that the physick could do. Not only because the damage was so extensive, revealing much of her husband's rib cage, but also because of the thin streaks of black that spread out along the edges of the wound.

That's why she had assumed that it was Stalkers. That's why she had believed Captain Jennison's description of the attackers so readily.

Few survived a fight with a Stalker. Whenever there was an

attack by one of those monsters, at least around Ballinasloe, very little of the victim was ever found. Just pieces.

The monsters were frighteningly efficient killers. Hungry as well.

Isana recalled the story of a family attacked in their farmhouse. The father had fought the Slayer, trying to give his wife and children time to escape. The children had gotten out in time, the mother as well, though not without a slight scratch across the back of her shoulder from an errant strike by the Stalker while it was killing the father.

The children had lived. The mother had died the next day.

The monster's claws carried a poison for which there was no known cure. Not even the physick, who Isana knew to be a Magus, could do anything to save the woman. Once the poison got into her blood, she was doomed.

Based on the putrid smell that drifted up from her husband's chest, she understood that nothing could be done for him. She hated having to acknowledge that conclusion, but it was the truth, and no matter how hard she tried she could not escape the truth. Abram's fate was sealed the moment the Stalker cut into his sternum.

Isana forced down the anguish that threatened to engulf her, crushing the emotion, locking it away, if only for a little while longer. Now was not the time to grieve.

Isana looked up at Talia, her daughter staring down at her with a grim expression. She wasn't surprised by what she saw. Her daughter was much like her, which was both a good thing and a bad.

She could tell that just like her, Talia was attempting to suppress her emotions, allowing nothing more than her eyes to water, a single tear streaking down one cheek. With a nod from her daughter, Isana understood that Talia had reached the same conclusion that she had, and that she too would deal with what had happened at the right time.

Not now, however. Now they needed to deal with other issues.

Yet recognizing the emotions that her daughter fought to hold back, Isana almost lost control over hers. Needing a distraction, she gripped Abram's hand even more tightly, seeking to will some of her strength into him though knowing it was a false hope right from the start.

She turned to Captain Jennison, who along with all the surviving crew had circled around them. They, too, understood that Abram's time was coming to an end and that all of them owed their lives to him.

"Tell me what my husband did." Isana needed to know. It was the last piece that she had to hear before she could let him go.

Captain Jennison, his face pale, tears running freely down his cheeks, provided a brief explanation. His sentences were short and clipped. His voice thick with emotion.

"Abram saved us," Jennison concluded. "If he hadn't warned us, we'd all be dead." The sailors standing around them nodded their agreement. "Your husband is a true soldier. That might not sound like much, but I fought in the Royal Guard for more than a decade. That's the highest compliment I can give him."

"I know your history with my husband, Captain Jennison," said Isana. "That compliment means something coming from you. My thanks. I will treasure it."

Jennison nodded, unable to say anything more, not wanting to shed even more tears in front of his crew.

Just then, Abram gasped, drawing everyone's attention. For the first time since he had fallen in the fight against the Stalker, his eyes opened. With a surge of fading energy, he gripped Isana's hand with the last of his strength, bringing tears to her eyes. Not because of the power of his grip, but because she knew that this would be the last time that she would feel his touch.

"I love you," whispered Abram with his last breath. "You and Talia. Stay safe. She did this. She's coming for us."

With that warning, Abram settled back onto the rough dock, his hand slipping from Isana's, his eyes closing. With a final shudder, Abram was gone.

Isana tried to maintain her composure, she was desperate to do so, but she couldn't. They had been together for twenty years. Twenty years. And now she had lost him.

Bending over her husband and laying her forehead against his, her tears streamed down. Many of the hardened sailors joined her in her grief.

Talia watched her mother, unable to move. Unable to speak. She felt numb inside. She couldn't believe that her father was gone. Heartbroken and angry, Talia's mind worked furiously.

The same day that they had arrived, Hakea Roosarian had appeared on their pier. Her father had deflected the woman's attempt to take half their business. Abram hadn't said as much, but they had all known that was going to be the result. Even the Governor. Yet her father wasn't one to cave in to veiled threats.

Then, within days, her father had been attacked. Stalkers. And though she couldn't connect Hakea Roosarian to the Stalkers, in her mind she didn't view the seemingly unconnected events as a coincidence.

Somehow, Hakea Roosarian and the Stalkers were linked.

Her father was rarely wrong. She didn't think that he was incorrect now.

Talia promised herself that she would find the truth. No matter what it took.

Once she did, she would make those responsible pay.

If Hakea Roosarian was indeed the cause of her father's death, then she was living on borrowed time. And before she finished with her, Talia would make the Governor of Fal Carrach suffer just as her father had done.

"We need to make this happen," said Isana. "We don't have time for delays."

"We can only go so fast, mother," replied Talia. "I spoke with the owners this morning. The earliest we can get these deals done is by the end of the week. They are both willing to work with us, they liked father, so we should have no more obstacles other than getting the paperwork in place."

Isana grunted. It wasn't as quick as she wanted. She wanted those agreements completed now, this minute, her patience for any delay frightfully lacking after Abram passed just a week before.

But it would have to do. To her credit, Talia had succeeded in shaving months off a usually drawn-out process, condensing the two major acquisitions to no more than a few days.

"And the other matter we discussed last night?" asked Isana.

"Captain Jennison and Captain Kenworthy have already gotten started. They both said not to worry. They have everything under control."

"Good, I'm not surprised."

"We'll be ready, mother, have no fear of that."

"I have no doubt that we will be," Isana replied as she turned back toward the large table that she had pushed up against the open windows so that she could focus on her work and also look out onto their pier, which extended for quite a good stretch into the Ballinasloe harbor.

Her eyes scanned the blueprints for the hundredth time just that morning. She could hear the construction taking place below her, the gates well on their way to completion and the walls extending out from the entrance to be started tomorrow. Even though her impatience continued to plague her, she had to admit that they were making excellent progress.

The somberness that had settled over their pier upon Abram's death remained, all of their employees saddened by her husband's death. Nevertheless, that hadn't stopped them from doing their work. In fact, it had energized them.

Captain Jennison and the sailors who survived the attack had spread the word about what had happened. What attacked them. What Abram had done for his sailors. Everyone working for the Carlomins wanted to make his memory proud. They didn't want his death to be in vain.

Talia was about to move on to another topic that was at the top of her mind, one that had kept her up at night since her father's murder, when, sensing a presence in the doorway, she held her tongue.

Isana didn't bother to turn around as the person strode into her office. She could tell who it was based on the sweet perfume that had drifted in with the visitor.

"Governor Roosarian."

"Mrs. Carlomin," she replied. Hakea then turned toward Talia. "I'm sorry, young lady, I know that we were formally introduced when we first met. I don't recall your name."

"Talia," she replied softly, her voice filled with a sharp venom that the Governor couldn't fail to miss.

Roosarian smirked briefly, more amused than insulted. She shifted her attention back to Talia's mother, Isana having turned away from the window, now leaning back against the table with her arms crossed after rolling up the blueprints, not wanting Roosarian to have any idea as to what they had planned.

Talia took that moment to study the woman who ruled Fal Carrach. The arrogance in both her expression and her posture was unmistakable. The Governor held herself with an easy confidence, as if she expected others to recognize her superiority right from the start.

None of that was surprising. What was surprising to Talia was how young Hakea Roosarian was, probably no more than a year or two older than she was.

"I want to offer my condolences," said Roosarian. "Abram was a good man, and I was certain that he would be a good business partner. He didn't deserve to die in the way that he did."

Isana stared at the Governor, parsing her words, her tone, her bearing, everything that went into what she had just said and how she said it.

"No, he didn't," she replied finally.

Roosarian stood there, waiting, expecting the widow to say more. Instead, Carlomin's wife simply stared at her. She saw a cunning there, and a toughness, which when combined Roosarian realized could make it quite difficult for her to achieve the goal she had set for herself in coming to the Carlomin pier.

Nevertheless, that wouldn't stop her. If nothing else, it was an opportunity to measure a woman who could be her primary opponent, at least for a time.

"If there's anything you need," offered Roosarian, "you need only let me know. I understand this is a difficult time for you. I stand ready to help in any way that I can."

Isana nodded shrewdly, which made Roosarian uncomfortable. It was as if the woman saw right through her.

"We have no need of assistance," replied Isana, not bothering to offer any thanks, which set Roosarian's quicksilver temper to a simmer.

Silence fell in the office for a time then, Isana feeling no need to say anything more, unwilling to aid the Governor in reaching the real reason for her visit. Because offering assistance clearly wasn't it.

"Yes, well," began Roosarian, at something of a loss as to how to handle this woman, deciding to simply plow forward, "I know that you have more important matters on your mind, so I hoped to ease your burden."

"Really?" asked Isana, clearly amused. "How would you do that?"

"Rather than buying half your company, I am willing to purchase all of it," replied Roosarian in a voice that hinted that to not accept her offer would be a foolish error. "You have invested a great deal in your business, as can be seen by the work that you're doing on your dock, so I know that your debt is rising. I am willing to overlook that. I will take on your company and your debt and provide you with a generous stipend so that you and your daughter can live out the rest of your days free of any concerns. Think of it as a way to honor your dearly departed husband's memory. A fitting tribute, in my opinion."

Isana struggled not to laugh at an offer that was no better than an attempted theft and also to restrain the anger that was rising within her. This woman, Governor or no, had no right to speak of her husband. Not when she was likely the cause of his death if Abram was correct. Before she could say anything, however, her daughter stepped in.

"I think not," Talia replied through gritted teeth. "The Carlomin Trading Company will always be owned by a Carlomin."

Roosarian bristled at Talia's obvious impertinence, several choice responses popping into her head. Even so, she held her tongue, ignoring the daughter, keeping her eyes locked on the grieving widow.

Isana stared back at her, unafraid. She could respond sharply. She wanted to. She wanted to put this upstart lord in her place. She understood, however, that now was not the time.

"I appreciate the offer, but I cannot accept. My husband

would not want us to sell the company so soon after his death. We must honor his wishes."

Roosarian's face twisted into a scowl. She should have assumed as much. And hiding behind the memory of a dead man? That was rich.

"You're making a mistake," Roosarian said finally, after quelling her initial instinct to take a harder tone with these two recalcitrant women, one that would be less than pleasant for them. She was the Governor of Fal Carrach, after all, and she was not to be trifled with. Still, she understood that this moment required a more delicate touch. She could take a more heavy-handed approach later if that still proved necessary. So she offered a veiled comment instead of what she really wanted to say. "As we've seen with the death of your husband, the dangers in this Territory can be great. Why risk further pain and suffering if it can be avoided?"

Isana stiffened at Roosarian's question. Talia watched her mother closely, then she smiled. Roosarian had no idea what her mother was capable of, especially now. Isana was not one to let a threat lie.

"A risk perhaps, yes," Isana replied pleasantly, "though maybe not." Then she shrugged, as if the conversation they were having was of no real consequence. "In this case, I believe that I am making the right decision, regardless of the danger. Regardless of the threat. Because I know the truth."

"Think hard on this, Mrs. Carlomin," said Roosarian, not missing what the woman was telling her, her eyes blazing in anger. "I will only make this offer once. If you refuse, I can't guarantee your protection ... or the protection of your daughter."

"We will see to our own protection," replied Talia instantly. "Thank you for your offer, but we must refuse."

"Prideful girl," said Roosarian, not bothering to look at

Talia, her eyes still locked with those of the widow. "I hope you both don't pay the price for your lack of vision."

With that, Hakea spun around, exiting the office with as much dignity as she could muster, her dozen guards, who had been waiting in the anteroom, forming up around her as they headed for the stairs.

Mother and daughter looked at one another. Neither needed to say a word. They understood the real purpose of the conversation and the meaning hidden within it.

Both knew what was coming next.

And that was all right with them.

They would be ready. They would welcome the chance to gain some revenge.

14

RISK VS. REWARD

"Quite a combat the other day, Captain Klines," said Bryen, nodding to the Blademaster. "It's just how I remember your practice combats with Declan on the white sand."

"I'm sure my display lacked the luster of yours, Bryen," replied Klines. "Declan told me a great deal about the lengths that he went to train you. He said that by the age of fifteen he began to realize that you could do more than match him in the Pit."

"That's kind of him to say, Blademaster, but I believe the credit for that belongs to Declan. If not for him, I would likely not be here today."

"Probably true," Klines agreed.

"Before you two continue to sing one another's praises, and mine for that matter, I assume, Lady Winborne, that you wanted to speak with all of us for a reason. And I'm assuming as well that there's a reason we're in one of the holds rather than up on deck."

"I did, Declan," replied Aislinn, thanking him with a nod

for putting their conversation on the right track. "Thank you all for joining us."

Wanting to ensure their privacy, Aislinn had selected one of the holds near the stern. The storage area ran for a hundred yards beneath the main deck, almost all of it but for the first twenty feet near the hatch they had used to enter the space filled with cargo that had been boxed up in crates of various sizes that then had been fitted onto a skid and wrapped in a net with a rung at the top for a hook for easy offloading. Every single bundle of goods had been chained down to ensure that nothing could break free in a storm and potentially put the entire ship at risk.

"I take it that we're here because of our previous conversation, Lady Winborne?"

"Indeed we are, Blademaster," said Aislinn.

"What conversation?" asked Declan.

"The one in which we both agreed that we were distinctly uncomfortable arriving in the Territories without having some sense of what really is going on there," explained Klines.

"The information we've received certainly is sketchy at best," admitted Declan.

"It's also the information that the Governors of the Territories were willing to share with Aislinn's father and the Duchess of Murcia," added Bryen.

"You think they might be hiding something?" asked Declan.

"I wouldn't be surprised," said Aislinn. "Having been raised by my father, I learned quite early in my training as the heir to the Southern Marches that the information provided in missives usually is incomplete, at worst incorrect, and in all circumstances likely just one piece of a much larger puzzle. The only way to know what's really going on somewhere is to walk the ground yourself."

"I don't dispute your logic in the least, Aislinn," said Declan. "Moreover, I fully agree with you and Jurgen. I have no desire to stumble into an environment in which we can be taken unawares. That being said, do you have a solution?"

"We do, possibly," replied Klines. "Have you figured out how to make this all happen, Protector?"

"I did with some help," Bryen replied. "It should work."

"Should work?" asked Klines, not thrilled by the lack of clarity in Bryen's response.

"Well, when you're trying something new with the Talent, there are never any guarantees. So that's the best I can tell you."

The Blademaster stared at Bryen, looking for any sign of levity and seeing none. The Protector simply was speaking as he normally did. Honestly and to the point. Telling you what he knew and what he didn't know. Another habit he had acquired from Declan. Klines really couldn't ask for more than that.

"But it is doable?"

"From what my friends are telling me, yes, it is doable. It's just more difficult than what I anticipated originally. Even with the Seventh Stone, because of the distance involved, I will be limited in terms of how large a gateway I can craft and how long it will stay in place."

"What are you talking about?" asked Declan, the concern in his voice almost palpable.

"I would use the Seventh Stone to craft a portal that would allow the Blademaster to step into the Territories. He could then prepare the way for us, digging up information that we wouldn't be able to obtain otherwise."

"I like the idea," said Declan, nodding his head as he considered the possibilities. "Nevertheless I thought there were some restrictions with respect to using portals that you couldn't get around. For example, you never having been to the Territories, so there's no guarantee that you'd be able to create a gateway that led to the right place, and the fact that the distance between the Territories and Caledonia is so great. That if you actually succeeded in crafting the portal and placing it in the correct location, you weren't sure you'd be able to keep it open long enough for someone to walk through, the natural magic failing without warning and slicing right through the unlucky person."

"We did discuss that," Bryen confirmed.

"We had talked about that when we were discussing whether we could use a portal to bring the Blood Company to the Territories," Declan continued. "Even with the Seventh Stone, even if you could somehow create a portal somewhere in the Territories, you said that was an impossibility."

"All true," admitted Bryen, now trying to assuage Declan's obvious concerns. "But I spoke with a few other people knowledgeable in the creation of portals, and I believe that I've found a solution that would at least allow me to get the Blademaster to the Territories."

"What other people? Rafia was with us when we were having that conversation."

"Well, not really people," Bryen tried to clarify. "More like guides."

"What are you talking about?" demanded Declan, his patience, never good to begin with, already wearing thin.

"Viktor Keldragan and Mikayla Benewyn."

Declan stared at Bryen for several long seconds. He really shouldn't have been surprised. The Ten Magii had helped Bryen to recreate the Weir. Why not assist him with this task as well?

"Explain."

"The rules for portals still apply," said Bryen. "Because of the distance, even with the use of the Seventh Stone, I would only be able to craft a gateway large enough for a single person and only for a few seconds."

"So if you create the portal, Jurgen steps through, and if he's in the wrong place, he's out of luck. He probably doesn't have the time to get back through. He's stuck."

"That's the risk, yes."

"One of the risks, I would argue," said Declan. "And how could Viktor and Mikayla help you with the portal?"

"They've both been to the Territories. Working with them, I at least should be able to get the Blademaster to the right location."

"Where would that be?"

"The Crag," said a soft voice right behind Declan that almost made the Sergeant of the Blood Company jump up from the deck. It took all of his self-control not to, Bryen obviously drawing on the Seventh Stone to release the spirits now standing behind him.

Not wanting to give Bryen the satisfaction of letting him know that he had taken him by surprise, Declan gave Bryen a look that told him they'd be having a conversation about this later. He then turned his attention to the two Magii.

"Viktor Keldragan and Mikayla Benewyn, I presume?"

"You presume correctly, Master of the Gladiators," replied the hazy figure standing to his left who bore a striking resemblance to Bryen.

"We can assist the Protector," confirmed Mikayla. "Be certain of that."

"How so?" asked Klines, curious as to what the next step might be.

"When the Protector uses the Seventh Stone," began Mikayla, "we can provide him with the location of the Crag in the Territories. That will enhance his chances of success. We can guide him there since we have both been there before."

"And the possibility that after a thousand years the Crag isn't there isn't a concern?"

"It is still there," Mikayla replied confidently.

"You're certain?" asked Aislinn. This had been her idea, well, hers and the Blademaster's. So if anything went wrong, she would be the one responsible. "You can ensure that the portal opens at the Crag?"

"As certain as we can be," answered Viktor.

"You really are full of surprises, Protector," said the Blademaster, turning his cool gaze toward Bryen.

"You have no idea," muttered Declan.

"Can you do this?" Klines asked, ignoring Declan's less than useful comment.

Bryen didn't rush his response, instead taking his time, working through in his mind one final time the conversation that he had engaged in with Mikayla and Viktor and then with Aislinn and Rafia, wanting to make sure that he hadn't missed anything. He was all for trying new applications of the Talent, although not at the expense of a good man's life if his experiment went horribly wrong.

"I can," he replied finally, certain that he could accomplish what would be required of him.

The Blademaster took a moment to think as well after hearing the Protector's quiet, confident response. The young man clearly was competent, and when he said he could do something, he always did it. So there was no reason not to believe in him now.

Besides, the necessity of the assignment pulled at Klines. He believed that it was too important not to at least try.

After all, he had promised himself that he would aid Aislinn Winborne to the best of his abilities, and he refused to allow her to walk into a situation in the Northern Territory for which they weren't prepared. Kendric Winborne was her uncle, yes, but she hadn't seen him in years. Since she was a child.

The opportunity to exercise power could change a man, something that Klines knew all too well, having watched it happen many times before. Rather than welcoming his niece Governor Winborne might view her as a threat instead. That was a concern that he wanted to gain clarity on before she set foot in Shadow's Reach.

"Then how do we get started?" Klines asked.

"You're certain of this, Jurgen?" asked Declan, fearful for his friend, although curious as well as to whether what the two Magii proposed would work.

"As certain as I can be," the Blademaster replied. He then reached down and slipped one strap of his pack over his shoulder, his scabbarded sword held in his other hand.

"It seems that you made your decision before this conversation, Blademaster," said Aislinn with a gentle smile.

"For the most part, yes, Lady Winborne. The Protector's honesty just now simply confirmed my thoughts on the matter."

"Thank you for your confidence," nodded Bryen. Then, not wanting to think too much about what he was about to do, he turned his focus to the two spirits who had joined the conversation. "Shall we?"

Both Viktor and Mikayla nodded. "Open yourself to the Seventh Stone and begin to craft the portal. We will join you, giving you the location," said Bryen's uncle.

"Be ready, Blademaster," urged Mikayla. "The Protector will only be able to hold the gateway open for a few seconds. When I say go, go."

"As you command, Magus."

Bryen wasn't really listening to the conversation anymore, instead focusing on the latest challenge that he had set for himself. Reaching for the Talent, he then opened himself to the Seventh Stone, relishing the rush of power that surged through him. Remembering his conversations with Viktor and Mikayla, he pulled in as much energy as he could possibly hold, the quantity daunting, even terrifying, yet also thrilling.

Not knowing how long he could safely manage so much of the Talent, he began crafting the portal, a misty white energy taking shape right in front of the Blademaster, the haze spinning faster and faster as Bryen added more power to his creation.

At the same time, Mikayla and Viktor added their expertise and knowledge to the partnership they had formed with Bryen, instilling the location of the Crag within the Protector through their memories.

Bryen nodded, letting the Magii know that he had what he needed. He then sent a final burst of energy into the gateway, and with a small grin, he realized that he had succeeded.

The hazy mist sharpened. Through the portal he glimpsed a plateau with a single mountain rising into the sky that was surrounded by a green forest that extended to the horizon. Just to the side rose a glimmering tower.

It was a mirror of both Viktor and Mikayla's memories. Yet though Bryen was pleased by his success, already he was feeling his creation wavering. The strength demanded of him to keep the portal open over thousands of leagues was already affecting him.

"Now, Blademaster," Mikayla ordered. "Now or never."

With a nod and an uncharacteristic grin for Declan and Aislinn, the Blademaster stepped through swiftly. As soon as he did, the gateway closed behind him, the Protector holding on to the portal for as long as he could before the strain became too much for him. Still, it had been enough.

The Blademaster was exactly where Bryen and the Two Magii said he would be.

The Crag.

Mikayla Benewyn had explained to him that it was much like the Aeyrie in northeastern Caledonia, though a much smaller version. It was first built by the Magii as an outpost in the Territories before they were even known as the Territories so that some in her Order could study what at the time was a wild continent uninhabited by man.

It likely still was in most areas even with the settlers coming across the Burnt Ocean seeking to conquer this wilderness, mused Klines, as he stared at the tower crafted of almost translucent stone that rose about fifty feet into the sky, a massive mountain of what appeared to be black granite towering right behind it.

He would camp here for the night, the sun already dipping below the peaks in the west. Then he would begin his journey in the morning through the Highlands and then across the Northern Steppes.

15

THE DEADLY FOG

"Take it easy, father," cautioned Jakob. "No need to rush. I'm here with you."

Dougal didn't bother to reply. Instead he kept his head down, careful as he could be as to where he placed his feet. He had fallen several times already. He knew that if not for Jakob's assistance, he wouldn't be getting back up.

And just as had happened to those unfortunate prisoners who had collapsed on the trail during their journey deeper into the mountains, the slavers would cut their losses and move on. Especially now that they were intent on reaching their destination as quickly as possible, willing to lose the little profit to be made on the weak and injured if it meant that they could push a little harder and faster.

"And so it begins," Dougal murmured, "the son assuming the role of the father."

"What was that?" asked Jakob, unable to hear most of his father's mumbled words as he helped Dougal shuffle along a steep trail that wound its way down into a wide gulley.

After several days of brutal exertion, having to work their way over or around more patches of trail that had been washed out by the torrential rain that was never far off or covered by rockslides than Jakob cared to remember, they were finally coming down out of the larger peaks in the Highlands toward the coast.

Smelling on the breeze the salt of the Sea of Mist, Jakob couldn't stop himself from smiling, though he only allowed the extravagance for a brief moment. The difficulty of their trek should be less here, which was both good and bad. Good because it should be easier going now that they were emerging from the more daunting peaks. Bad because that meant they were getting closer to their final destination, a place from which there was likely no escape.

It had been a long day, just like all the others. The slavers had forced Jakob and the other surviving prisoners onto the trail before the sun rose. And only now, with the sun about to fall below the western horizon, the shadows in the gulley making it seem like it was already night, was there any talk by their captors of stopping for the night.

The slavers pushed because they wanted to get to the mine as fast as possible, primarily because they were concerned about keeping clear of the beasts that had been shadowing them for the last few nights. The beasts, what Jakob assumed were Stalkers, hadn't attacked. But they hadn't left them alone either, which had surprised the slavers and put them on edge.

Just then, a howl echoed through the small canyon, sending a shiver of fear down the spines of prisoners and slavers both. Right on time, thought Jakob. The monsters had been tracking them ever since that night on the ledge, never getting too close, never very far away, always making their presence known as soon as darkness fell.

The beasts would continue to howl now and then through the cold hours of the night, just to let Jakob and those with him know that they were still there. Watching. Waiting. For what, Jakob wasn't sure.

He was curious as to why the Stalkers had not assailed them yet. If three of the beasts were out in the darkness, he doubted that they would have any trouble slaughtering all of them. Considering how hungry the Stalkers sounded, he had assumed that they would have come for them by now.

Even more perplexing, although Jakob certainly was grateful for it, the beasts hadn't gone after Dougal when the Sergeant had staked his father to the ground outside of the campsite a few nights past. Though the Stalkers clearly were interested in the party traveling through the Highlands, they were holding back for some unknown reason.

What that reason could be, Jakob didn't know. But he really wanted to find out.

"Faster!" ordered the slaver known as the Sergeant. "We'll stop around the next bend, just a mile farther down the trail. If you can't make it, we'll leave you for the beasts, so pick up the pace." The Sergeant flicked his whip out, striking several of the prisoners to urge them along. "I'm not dying here just because you're tired and can't lift up your feet. So get moving, blast it!"

"Come on, father, we're almost there," urged Jakob, supporting Dougal under one arm, taking as much of his weight as he could since his father couldn't stand straight, his injuries keeping him in a painful, crouched shuffle. "Then you can rest for the night."

Jakob had to give his father credit. No matter how badly he was suffering, Dougal stayed with him and the dwindling group of prisoners. Never stopping. Never complaining. Never allowing his injuries to slow them down. Refusing to join the growing list of casualties left behind on the trail.

Two healthy prisoners had died in just the last two days. One slipping on some loose shale when trying to clamber over a mound of large rocks and hitting his head before falling off the side of the cliff, the other prisoners having to pull his body back up so that he could be removed from the chain.

The other made the mistake of sitting down during a break on a large rock that jutted out over the packed dirt of the path, not realizing that right beneath the stone was a rock viper, the snakes native to the Highlands. It had only taken one bite from the incredibly poisonous snake for the woman to die a slow, agonizing death.

Jakob had stayed close to his father every day, trying to keep him safe and help him along. Dougal had been struggling since the beating the Sergeant and several of the slavers had given him on the ledge.

Besides the obvious bruises and crushed nose, which led to a sharp wheezing noise whenever Dougal sniffed in air, he had a broken wrist, stomped on by one of the slavers – Jakob had cut a strip off his shirt that he had wrapped around the injury in an attempt to stabilize it, and one knee was twisted badly in the wrong direction, swollen and still twice as large as the other one.

Those were only the visible injuries. Jakob feared that Dougal was bleeding internally, the blood that he spit up on an all too regular basis revealing that one or several of his cracked ribs were poking into organs that they shouldn't.

Yet despite their current circumstances, Jakob considered them lucky. When the Sergeant had forced his father out beyond the fire on the ledge, staking him to the ground and leaving him for the Stalkers, Jakob never thought that he would see him again. But he had.

The next morning, his father was barely alive and slightly delirious from the battering that he had taken. Still, he was alive. For whatever reason, the Stalkers had left him alone.

Jakob gently shook his head in irritation as he helped his father over a large landslide of loose rock that covered the trail for more than fifty yards, the obstruction forcing the entire group to slow down. He was feeling better. He was thinking clearly again. He believed that the more serious effects of his concussion were gone.

Just that morning, he had succeeded in reaching out and connecting to the Talent, if only briefly, barely touching the natural magic of the world although just that slight taste filled him with a welcome confidence. Most important, he had only suffered a minor headache for his efforts.

He desperately wanted to make use of his hidden skill, yet now he couldn't. Not with his father so badly hurt. Even if he used the Talent to break their chains, theirs and all the other prisoners, there was no way that he could escape all the slavers, not with his father barely able to put one foot in front of the other without collapsing.

He had no choice. He would have to bide his time and hope that his father's health improved enough so that they could try to make a break for it before they reached the mine.

Jakob's hopes of that happening had been diminishing day by day. After a much too brief resurgence, his father's health had not improved. In fact, Dougal's injuries and the constant strain of their hiking had only served to worsen his condition.

Just that morning Jakob had spent almost ten minutes trying to get his father moving from where he had fallen into a fitful slumber, simply getting him to his feet a challenge. It was almost as if Dougal had decided to give up in order to give his son a better chance at getting out of their likely lethal predicament.

With no other option but to continue on their trek, Jakob had spent just as much time studying the slavers as he did assisting his father. Their guards had been jumpy and out of sorts ever since that night on the ledge when the Stalkers first made their presence known.

They weren't as boisterous around the fire as they had been the first few nights. They had become more somber, several even sullen, every howl burrowing deeper into their bones.

The Sergeant now set a stronger guard when the darkness fell. Clearly, based on past practices, these guards were more concerned by what was stalking about in the darkness just beyond their fire, paying little mind to their prisoners.

The slavers were afraid. They weren't used to what was happening. They didn't like it. It made them uncomfortable, tense.

Maybe Jakob could use that. He'd just need to figure out how.

"Just a little farther, father," said Jakob, urging Dougal on, his father more stumbling than walking now, the last of his energy having left him. "We can rest in just a few more minutes."

JAKOB ONLY HAD BEEN DOZING for a few hours when he came awake with a start, the moon not having traveled very far across the sky. He assumed initially that he had awoken because he was hungry, having had scarcely anything to eat in the last few days. His stomach protesting the lack of sustenance was common ever since he had entered the Highlands, made worse because the slavers were saving the last of their rations for themselves, none of the guards willing to hunt with the Stalkers never more than a quarter mile away.

But that wasn't it. No, it was too quiet.

The howls that had been a staple of his sleep for the last few nights had stopped. He listened for a few minutes, expecting a blood-curdling shriek to shatter the silence. Nothing.

He didn't hear anything except for the crackle of the slavers' fire, and that just barely since most of the logs were now no more than embers.

The quiet bothered him. It didn't feel right. He could sense that something was off.

He didn't hear any of the nighttime sounds that were so familiar to the Highlands -- the crickets in the grass, the owls in the trees, the bats flitting through the air, the occasional wolf or mountain cat prowling through the undergrowth.

There was only an eerie silence. A hush that had draped itself across the land. It was as if the world was waiting for something to happen.

He began to understand when just a few seconds later he felt the first faint, cool touch of the fog that rolled in incredibly fast, smothering the land in just minutes. Jakob could barely see his hand in front of his face, his father just a vague shape next to him. The slavers' fire now was no more than a muted, dying glow.

"This fog didn't come off the Sea of Mist as it should have," Dougal whispered, not wanting to be the one to disturb the stillness. For some irrational reason he feared drawing attention to himself and his son. Then again, maybe he wasn't being irrational. The sense that something exceedingly dangerous approached pounded in his head just like it had while serving as a soldier in Caledonia. And it had come with the fog. The trick would be getting away from whatever was the cause of his rising fear, if they could. "It came from the north, which is strange, and it's not as wet as it should be." Dougal groaned softly as he rolled from his back onto his side. "Be ready, Jakob. Whatever this is, it isn't right. There's an evil lurking in the mist."

Jakob nodded, not bothering to reply, scanning around them. With the thickening fog, colors had dulled and shapes had lost their definition. But that wasn't the most worrisome aspect of his new environment.

His father was right. He could sense the evil in the murk. It reminded him of what he had discovered at Senna's farmhouse and then Aloysius' cottage, although it had a corrupt taste all its own.

Something was terribly wrong with this fog. At the same time, Jakob worried even more for his father. He could barely hear what his father said because of the weakness of his voice, and he was listening just as much to Dougal's words as he was to how his father was saying them, confirming through the raspy wheeze that was his voice that his father was finding it harder and harder to draw breath.

As the silence around them deepened even more, Jakob noticed that several of the slavers and prisoners had noticed the fog as well. Their nervous energy was beginning to dominate the small encampment, a few snatches of anxious conversation drifting through the stifling haze, although even those sounds were muted by the grey mist.

"Father," whispered Jakob into Dougal's ear, "did you catch that?"

Despite the challenge of seeing anything with any clarity in the enveloping grey, Jakob had caught a flash of movement not too far away from them in the gloom. Really just a brief disturbance of the swirling grey tendrils, nothing more. Even so, something about that motion worried him.

"I saw it," Dougal replied softly, pushing himself up to an elbow with some difficulty. "Eyes open, mouth shut. No rapid movements if we can avoid it. Be ready."

Father and son remained where they were, waiting, not making a sound, not moving, the sense of foreboding building within the both of them. They wanted to get away, as fast as they could, the fog filling them with an irrational fear.

Every sinew in their bodies was telling them to flee. Now. Don't wait.

To wait meant certain death.

Yet despite that burgeoning insistence, they forced themselves to stay still when they heard the first sharp, piercing scream that tore through the fog, coming from no more than thirty feet to their left.

Then just as quickly, silence once more.

Almost a minute passed, neither father nor son willing to move any part of their body, not even their heads, for fear that they would be discovered by what lurked within the fog. They only moved their eyes, seeking to catch any other disturbances in the mist, anything that might reveal what was hunting them, fearful of what might be coming at them from their backs, although unwilling to take the risk of looking behind them.

Another scream rang out, this one short, cut off before the person could give full throat to their pain and their terror.

Then a groan by the slavers' fire, followed by several quick exchanges of steel meeting steel.

The clash lasted just seconds.

Silence reigned again.

For the next several minutes, as he and his father stayed low to the ground, Jakob noticed a terrifying rhythm to the night.

A scream of terror, often accompanied by a whimper or a groan.

The clash of steel, although only for a few seconds, whatever combats were occurring ending just as rapidly as they began.

And then another scream ripping through the night immediately after the meeting of metal ended.

Then silence once again.

Over and over the cycle ran. A disjointed, terrifying song of slaughter.

Through it all, Jakob could see nothing more than a few faint hints of movement in the fog. He had no other way to try to get a sense of what was going on around them than through what he heard, and that was proving to be incredibly difficult and potentially fatal.

"We can't stay here," whispered Jakob, tired of waiting for

the inevitable. If he was going to die, he wanted to make whatever was hunting them work for the kill. "They'll find us eventually. Come on."

Dougal didn't bother responding, acknowledging that his son was right by dragging himself across the ground. Better to be away before the hunters completed their grim work and combed the campsite for any prey they may have missed.

Slowly, very slowly, Jakob crawled away from the slavers' fire, holding his chains carefully so that they wouldn't make any noise and reveal his position. He had only gone a few feet when he felt a light kick to his leg.

His father was slightly behind him. With a quick flick of his head, Dougal motioned in the other direction, wanting to head for the fire. Jakob tried to protest his father's decision. He didn't get the chance.

Dougal already was moving in his desired direction. Jakob had no choice but to follow, even though he didn't agree with his father's decision.

While Dougal had been lying on the ground, he had been facing toward the slavers' fire, focusing his attention on the Sergeant before the fog covered the Highlands. He knew what his injuries meant. He had known as soon as he had received them, using the knowledge and experience that he had gained as a soldier to determine whether he had any chance of escaping from the fate that awaited him in the mines, assuming, of course, that he survived the journey to get there.

The simple, harsh truth was no. There was no way that he was going to get out of his current predicament alive. Although disappointed, he didn't allow that to keep him down. His thoughts shifted immediately to how he could help his son escape. That was all that mattered to him.

Both of them didn't need to die at the hands of these slavers or in the mines.

Not wanting Jakob to harm himself by using the Talent

while he still suffered the aftereffects of his concussion, as soon as Dougal had heard the first scream in the mist a plan had come to mind, and he meant to see it through because this would likely be Jakob's only chance of gaining his freedom.

As he crawled toward the fire, Dougal took his time, not rushing, knowing that with the threat lurking in the fog that slow was fast, pleased that Jakob had reached the same conclusion and was mimicking his actions. They only worked their way forward a few feet at a time, then they settled back down toward the ground, allowing the fog to drift over them, to hide them, waiting for another scream or the sound of a clash to break the silence so that they could crawl a few more feet forward.

Although it took Dougal longer than he would have liked, he and Jakob finally made it to the slavers' fire, what was now just a few glowing embers, the flames having been kicked out by either their attackers or the slavers themselves.

Just a few feet from the smoldering fire, Dougal found the Sergeant. He had fallen into the long grass by the side of the trail. He was lying on his back, two large blossoms of blood staining his shirt and leather armor, another long slash opening a streak of red across his belly.

"Please, help me," the slaver begged.

His voice was too loud for Jakob's taste. He placed a hand over his mouth to shut him up before he drew any unwanted attention toward them. The hulking Sergeant was so weak, he could do nothing to prevent it.

Dougal ignored the slaver as he quietly rummaged through the man's pockets. He cursed under his breath. The keys weren't where he assumed that he would find them, either already taken or missing in the grass.

"No luck?" asked Jakob quietly.

Dougal shook his head in irritation.

"Leave it to me," whispered Jakob.

Dougal tried to stop him, attempting to get his son's attention.

Jakob ignored him, intent on his task. Time was short. They needed to get moving. Any delay could cost them their lives.

Jakob reached for the Talent, doing so as gently as he could, knowing that he couldn't handle the huge rush of energy that normally surged through him every time he touched the natural power of the world.

Even with the dire circumstances he currently faced, he couldn't help but smile.

He had taken control of the Talent with a precision that evaded him at times and not like an elephant stomping across the earth as Aloysius had liked to say, a skill that the old Magus had feared he would never achieve, calling his technique heavy-handed much too frequently.

Jakob would congratulate himself later. Now he had work to do.

Concentrating on the irons linking his manacles together, he focused a thin stream of the white-hot Talent on the steel. In seconds, he was done, the metal melting and freeing Jakob from the chain.

He left the manacles in place around his wrists. He could deal with those later. He then performed the same procedure on his father, who perked up noticeably once he was free.

How long his father's small surge of energy would last, Jakob didn't know. But they would use it for as long as they could.

With the job done, Jakob released his hold on the Talent, only having to deal with a deep pounding in the center of his forehead as a result of his efforts rather than being overcome with a paralyzing pain as had proven to be the case ever since he received his concussion.

Although the Sergeant couldn't lift his head, he was able to twist his neck just enough to watch what Jakob was doing, his eyes widening in disbelief.

"You're a Magus," he whispered, half in fear, half in awe.

"No, he's not," clarified Dougal, his voice barely heard above the soft breeze playing through the fog. "He just happens to have some skills that other people don't have."

Dougal nodded to Jakob, then began rolling away from the slaver, slowly, intent on moving away from the campsite. Right now, in his mind, he equated distance with survival.

The slaver reached for Dougal's legs, not having the strength to grasp hold, just able to give Dougal a light touch that stopped him.

"Don't leave me. Please. They'll butcher me."

"What are they?"

"I don't know," whispered the slaver.

"They're not Stalkers?"

"No. I've never seen the like before, though I have heard a few tales."

Dougal didn't have time for a story, so he changed the subject, wanting a specific piece of information.

"Tell me who you are," Dougal demanded, his voice quiet but insistent.

"I'm a slaver. Isn't it obvious?"

"No, you're not," whispered Dougal. "They don't call you Sergeant as an affectation."

The wounded man hesitated before responding, a look of consternation crossing his face. Then, not too far away, Jakob and Dougal caught another flash of movement. Seconds later a scream ripped through the fog, followed by a silence that was almost more frightening than the wail of torment that had preceded it.

"You won't leave me?" asked the slaver, fear loosening his tongue.

"I won't leave you," said Dougal. "Have no fear of that."

"I'm a Sergeant in Governor Sharperson's Guard."

Jakob glanced over at his father, their eyes meeting. They understood now.

It all made a terrible sense.

The mines were critical to Sharperson's goal of building his Territory into something that resembled a Duchy, yet even with the huge influx of settlers coming across the Burnt Ocean, there was not enough labor to do the necessary work. Few of the settlers were interested in risking the danger of the mines, instead intent on building a homestead of their own.

The Governor had come up with another way to solve his problem. Ingenious and insidious, both at the same time.

Jakob hoped that he might survive long enough to have a chance to speak with Sharperson about his approach, up close and personal ... and alone.

Dougal started to crawl away, getting no more than a foot before the Sergeant called him back.

"You promised that you wouldn't leave me," he pleaded.

"I won't," replied Dougal, who lifted the dagger that he had found not too far away in the grass, then twisted back around and drove the steel tip through the Sergeant's throat.

Jakob watched his father kill the Sergeant, understanding what Dougal was going to do as soon as his hand grasped the hilt of the weapon. He felt as if he should have some remorse for what needed to be done, but he didn't.

The Sergeant was responsible for their enslavement. The man had beaten his father to a whisker of his life and had done the same to several other prisoners who had slipped to the other side. And the man was more than willing to take them to a place where they likely would be worked to death. No, Jakob felt no sympathy at all for the man.

What had happened to the Sergeant was deserved. A rough form of justice.

In reality, his father had put the Sergeant out of his misery.

Yes, Dougal was likely driven in part by a desire for vengeance. Nevertheless, his father was also being practical and kind in an exceedingly ruthless way.

The Sergeant was badly wounded, he couldn't move, and it would only be a matter of time before the creatures in the fog returned for him. His father had done the Sergeant a favor, speeding up his death, which was only inevitable, and causing him less pain and suffering than the creatures hunting in the fog likely would.

"Come on," whispered Jakob, who began crawling slowly through the fog and away from the Sergeant's corpse, pulling himself deeper into the long grass, hoping that the additional natural cover might give them some protection before they exposed themselves again on the open ground closer to the trail.

Employing the same approach that he and his father had used so effectively to make their way unnoticed to the Sergeant, they worked their way slowly, painfully so, through the reedy grass, stopping after advancing no more than a few feet at a time to listen, to make sure that none of the creatures in the fog approached, their attention still drawn toward easier prey.

When they reached the border of the long grass, they waited there for several minutes. They searched the fog, looking for any movement, any disruption in the mist that would suggest a creature with a deadly temper waited for them.

Nothing.

Just the grey mist barely drifting, the wind having died away.

Not wanting to wait any longer than necessary, Jakob and his father moved back out onto the rough ground that gradually fell away from the trail toward the coast. They maintained their rhythm, although it was a bit slower now, Dougal beginning to flag. His strength was fading.

Jakob's worry for his father increased, staying at his side as they worked their way across the ground, wondering whether their slow pace actually aided them. They crawled no more than a few feet before they stopped and stayed still, listening, not starting up again until they were certain that there was nothing around them. The required tactic gave the monsters in the mist very little to pick out in the gloom.

Through it all, the terrifying tempo of the night continued to play out.

Silence.

A scream of terror.

Sometimes, but not always, the sound of steel striking steel.

Another scream or groan.

Then silence once again.

Every few minutes.

Jakob began to worry that they might need to go faster. Based on the number of screams, there couldn't be very many of their fellow prisoners still alive. Once he and his father were all that was left, whatever was hunting in the fog could focus their full attention on them.

Even so, he couldn't bring himself to urge his father to go faster. Dougal was having a hard enough time as it was. So Jakob simply hoped for the best as he and his father wound their way slowly, quietly, through the mist.

All the while, they kept their eyes open for any other prisoners who might have survived. As they moved farther away from the trail and toward the east, they found a few bodies along the way.

All had been killed efficiently, a punch of a broad-bladed dagger into the heart or a slash across the throat. More often than not the slash. None of the victims had any real chance of escape, their manacles and chains eliminating their options.

Several times Jakob and Dougal were forced to stop abruptly, quick bursts of movement in the fog just at the edge of their vision demanding that they lie still. They dropped their heads as low to the ground as they could, wishing they could dig their way into the dirt, having very little to hide themselves with except for a scattering of large rocks, a few fallen trees, and some sparse brush.

As the sounds of struggle receded behind them, Jakob, who was once more in the lead, thought that they might be free of whatever had attacked them. He revised his opinion when his sixth sense, warning of danger, told him to stop sooner than he would have otherwise.

No more than ten feet away, he picked out a tall, hazy shape that resembled an almost impossibly thin man standing in the fog. Jakob, afraid to lift his head, kept his eyes to the ground, thankful that his father had stopped just as quickly and just as silently as he did.

For several minutes, they stayed there. Not moving. Understanding that even the slightest sound would draw the attention of whatever creature waited for them just ahead.

Jakob began to dread that the creature knew that they were close, just unsure of exactly where they were hiding. It seemed the hunter was going to wait them out. A good strategy, and, cursing silently, one that Jakob thought just might work.

If this creature didn't move, his greatest fear would become reality. Once the rest of their group had been killed, the other creatures who had participated in the slaughter could join this one and close the net around them with relative ease.

Wanting to avoid that, as their chances of surviving such an outcome were poor at best, he considered pushing himself up and attacking the creature even though he only had the dagger that his father had found near the Sergeant and given to him.

Thankfully, he didn't have to. A sharp rustle and a yelp about twenty yards to his left drew the creature's attention, the figure standing in their way launching itself at an incredible speed through the fog toward the noise.

Breathing a welcome sigh of relief, Jakob kept his head

down for a few seconds more, wanting to make sure that the creature didn't return. When it didn't, and as certain as he could be that there was nothing around him in the fog, Jakob began moving again, his father right behind him.

Three more times Jakob stopped. The screams and sounds of blade meeting blade didn't bother him anymore. He was used to it. Now several dozen yards off the trail, his focus was on getting as far away from the hunters as he could.

Instead of the cries of pain and fear that had become commonplace in the gloom, he was listening for the faint scrape, much like a snake moving almost noiselessly through the long grass, that sounded out of place to him now. What was the only hint of warning that one of the creatures in the mist was close.

The first two times Jakob thought he heard the rasp, he didn't see anything. No shape in the fog. No blur of movement.

Nevertheless, he and his father remained in place, not rushing, staying as calm as they could knowing that there were hunters all around them, letting the minutes drag by. It was only when the crackle of danger in the back of his brain dissipated that he moved forward again.

The third time he did see a figure flickering in the fog. The shape appeared silently out of the mist just ten feet to his left. His father, so intent on keeping his weakening body moving, stopped in the nick of time when he crawled into the heel of Jakob's boot.

Thankfully, Dougal didn't make a sound, both of them understanding that if the creature discovered them, they were done for.

Having no other options, Jakob and his father remained in place for almost half an hour, waiting impatiently for the figure to continue on its way through the fog. There were a few false starts, the creature moving a few feet in one direction, then a few feet in another, almost as if the hunter was trying to sniff them out.

Once, the creature even moved directly toward Jakob, a bolt of fear shooting through him, worried that the hunter had found them. But just as quickly as the creature shifted toward him, it glided back to where it had been standing originally.

Finally, the monster loped off into the mist, drawn by a soft, shuffling noise that sounded as if someone was struggling to pull themselves across the ground. Jakob could barely hear it, yet the creature homed in on the whisper of a body moving through the long grass as if a bell had been rung.

That was the closest encounter yet, and it was much too near for Jakob's taste.

Pressing his forehead onto the ground, sweat dripping off his brow as he took a deep breath, trying and failing to calm his nerves, Jakob decided that a new approach was needed. Although crawling was quite effective and it allowed them to stay as hidden as possible within the mist, it would only work for so long.

Eventually, the creatures would discover them. Making their escape even more challenging, Jakob could tell that his father's struggles were getting worse. He didn't know how much longer he could be expected to keep this up.

"Follow my lead," Jakob said, leaning into his father's ear, "and as quiet as you can. They hunt by sound and movement."

"What are you doing?" Dougal whispered urgently as he watched his son push himself up off the ground.

Jakob leaned back down, speaking softly. "One of those creatures knows that we're here. It's the same one that has made us stop three times now. At the rate we're going, before we escape the fog that monster is going to catch us. So we need to move faster now if we can and get some distance on whatever it is that's trying to zero in on us."

Jakob rose from his crouch, placing a hand beneath his

father's arm at the same time to help him to his feet. All Dougal could do was shake his head in amusement.

He had never expected that Jakob would take charge. He had heard about how the roles between father and son reversed as both got older. He just never guessed that the transition would begin at that very moment when both their lives were at risk.

Putting into play the same approach as they did while crawling, Jakob and Dougal began moving through the fog at a very slow but steady pace, taking just a few steps before they stopped again, both of them keeping their eyes peeled for any hint of movement within the mist. They weren't moving as fast as Jakob wanted to go, the sense that something was stalking them becoming more powerful as they shuffled through the fog.

Still, they were moving faster than they had been when they were crawling. So at least they had that.

With no sign of a threat in the fog swirling around them, Jakob extended the distance between their pauses to every twenty or thirty feet. Dougal now was paying less attention to what was around them and more to Jakob's back so that he knew when to stop as well, wanting to avoid a stumble at all costs, knowing that even the slightest noise could give them away.

When they stopped, Jakob listened for several minutes. Only when he was satisfied that it was safe to continue did they begin walking again as quietly as they could through the fog.

So it went for the next half hour. Walking for a brief distance, then stopping. Listening. Hearing nothing of concern and moving forward again.

Stopping. Listening. Moving.

Stopping. Listening. Moving.

Stopping. Listening. Moving.

This time, though, Jakob stopped after only advancing a

few feet. Dougal was about to ask what he was doing when a very slow shake of Jakob's head told Dougal to stay quiet.

They weren't alone. Jakob was sure of it.

He had caught the sound of an almost silent shuffle about thirty feet behind them and to his right. Even though he didn't hear anything now, and he couldn't see anything in the fog, he knew that he was right. As his father had taught him, he needed to trust his instincts.

Jakob waited for almost a minute, hoping that whatever was behind them would give itself away.

No such luck. Nothing moved. Nothing made a noise.

Still worried, still certain that one of the monsters was tracking them, but not wanting to wait too long, with a slight nod of his head, Jakob and his father started walking again through the fog. They had only gone about ten feet when Jakob stopped again.

He had heard that very faint rustle behind them once more. He was right. One of the creatures knew, at least generally, where they were.

And the monster was trying to find them.

Jakob waited a few minutes this time, wanting to see if the hunter at their back would reveal itself. When nothing happened, the fog billowing slowly around them, Jakob nodded. He and his father walked about twenty feet before they stopped this time.

He hadn't heard the noise that he had been listening for, although Jakob was certain that whatever was hunting them had moved with them. He had felt it, the fog shifting ever so slightly around him to suggest a disturbance not too far behind them.

The creature in the fog was mimicking them now. Moving when they moved. Stopping when they stopped. Keeping pace with them. Maybe even gaining a few feet on them. Likely waiting for them to make a mistake so that the creature could confirm their exact location and attack. Probably enjoying every second of the hunt.

Jakob wracked his brain, seeking some way to extricate himself and his father from the deadly and strangely slow chase that they had reluctantly become a part of. He cursed himself silently. Nothing came to mind that could possibly help them.

He had decided on their current path. They had no choice but to follow it to the end, wherever that end took them.

They started to move away from the trail again, though this time on an angle, Jakob changing the direction they walked with the hope that it might throw their pursuer off the scent.

For the next several minutes, Jakob and his father continued to play their game of cat and mouse. Walking no more than twenty feet at a time as quietly as they could. Then stopping, waiting, listening, before starting up again. Never moving in the same direction twice.

Each time they did, Jakob heard ever so faintly or simply sensed that the creature behind them continued to move with them. Even when Jakob turned to the left or the right, whatever was tracking them wasn't deceived.

The hunter had a general sense of where they were, and the monster was taking its time closing the gap. Obviously not feeling the need to rush the hunt.

If he was honest with himself, Jakob didn't really have any hope of escaping their pursuer, not with his father in such a bad way. They were only going as fast as Dougal could, and during the last few minutes, his father had begun to struggle even more.

Clearly, Dougal needed to rest. Yet they had no opportunity to do that, having no choice but to press forward with the creature so close.

Then something happened that Jakob hadn't expected. The last few times that they had advanced, he hadn't sensed the creature moving with them. Maybe his walking to the side or on an angle actually had drawn the creature in the wrong direction.

He was just about to urge his father to move a little faster if he could when he changed his mind and instead reached for Dougal's arm, gripping it strongly, a touch of warning.

Jakob had been right to exercise greater caution. The creature in the fog hadn't stopped tracking them. Rather, it moved faster than Jakob had assumed that it would and had looped around them.

The creature had determined where they were, so it had hurried on a curve to get ahead of them, believing that its prey would walk right into it. Jakob and his father almost did.

Jakob cursed himself for a fool, what was becoming a regular occurrence during their attempted escape. He recognized the shape in the mist now standing just twenty feet in front of them.

What was he supposed to do?

His father wasn't in a position to do much more than lie down and rest. He could barely stand on his feet, and Jakob had just watched him wipe a few drops of blood off his lips with his sleeve.

Dougal was almost done, his injuries only draining what little energy he had left. It was only a matter of time before they were caught.

His current strategy had proven fruitful, but its utility had come to an end.

So what to do now?

Try to go in another direction?

That was one option, although he doubted that such an approach would do anything more than delay the inevitable. They weren't moving as quietly as they had when they first had escaped in the fog. His father was dragging his injured leg now, that slight noise just enough to catch the attention of their pursuer.

Dougal had always been willing to offer him words of advice when he was growing up, usually when Jakob wasn't interested in hearing what he had to say. Of course, that never stopped his father, and every so often something that he said stuck with Jakob.

One of those pieces of advice came to mind as he thought about how to get out of what had become an almost impossible situation. "If you need to fight," his father had told him many times, "better that you start it."

"Be ready," Jakob whispered to his father.

"What ..."

Dougal didn't have the chance to get out the rest of his question, breaking out into a fit of coughing that sounded like a rockslide in the silence.

"Run!" urged Jakob.

Dougal took off in the direction that Jakob shoved him, moving at a slow shuffle just as the large shadow that had been standing near them sprinted through the fog directly for him.

With his father stumbling away from him, Jakob raced toward the hunter on an angle so that the creature had no choice but to face him rather than chasing after his father.

Only having in hand the dagger that his father had taken from the Sergeant, Jakob wanted to avoid getting into an extended fight. With that desire guiding him, as the creature silently raced toward him, barely disturbing the fog, Jakob's eyes drawn to the double-bladed dagger in his hand, he slid across the grass, slamming into the creature's knees with his feet.

Taken by surprise, the creature flipped head over heels, hitting the ground on his back, a hiss of air escaping him. Despite the hard fall, the creature still kept a grip on his weapon. The creature pushed himself up in an instant, resuming his charge toward Jakob.

Jakob only had a second to get a good look at the creature, and even then the fog hindered his view.

The hunter stood a foot or more taller than he was. Its face was drawn, the pale, white flesh that resembled the belly of a fish and likely had never felt the touch of the sun pulled back tightly, giving the hunter a skull-like appearance, his long white hair getting lost in the fog. The creature wore what looked to be a greyish-white leather armor that made it incredibly difficult to pick him out of the swirling mist.

That's what almost cost Jakob his life. He had become fixated on the armor, jolting himself awake just in time to duck beneath the creature's swing. He was back on his feet in an instant, parrying with his dagger the slice the creature aimed for his neck.

Jakob danced backward and continued to do so as the hunter maintained his attack. He realized quickly that his dagger was of little use against the creature's weapon, which was almost the length of a short sword. Besides, he was in no position to get into a prolonged fight.

He needed to catch up to his father. The sounds of their clash would draw whatever other creatures were hunting in the fog, and his father wasn't capable of defending himself.

With those concerns dominating his thoughts, and understanding that speed was essential to the creature's success as a hunter, Jakob decided that now was the time to try to remove or at the very least impede that critical advantage.

Anticipating the slash to come, Jakob ducked beneath it. In the same motion he dropped to one knee and then with all his might drove his dagger through the creature's clawed foot. He then ripped the blade free and rolled away, pushing himself off the ground and sprinting after his father.

The unexpectedly high-pitched shriek that burst from the

creature, which fell to the ground in agony, clutching at his wound, chased Jakob through the fog, sending a shiver down his spine.

It didn't take Jakob long to catch up to his father, startling Dougal when he wrapped an arm around his waist and tried to help him limp along at a faster pace. They couldn't manage a sprint, although Jakob was able to get Dougal up to a hobble that was a bit faster than a walk.

That would have to do.

Jakob caught glimpses of the creature trailing behind them. It had gotten back to his feet, unwilling to give up the chase. Just as Jakob had expected that the hunter would, glimpsing the determination in his dark, soulless eyes before he drove the steel blade through his clawed foot.

But with the wound that Jakob had given the hunter, the creature now could go no faster than they were, so they were able to maintain their slim lead on their pursuer. The key question was for how long they could do that, Jakob knowing that he could only expect so much from his father.

Jakob was pleased that he was able to slow down the creature. But he understood as well that it was only a partial solution. They needed to get out of the fog as quickly as they could, assuming they could even exit the mist, because based on the several shrieks that he heard echoing in the murk behind them, the sharp clamor setting his teeth on edge, the other monsters in the mist had joined the chase.

As they continued to shamble through the fog, his father almost falling every other step now, the creature behind them slowly catching up, Jakob finally saw a ray of hope. Literally.

A thin stream of sunshine blasted through the mist just a dozen feet in front of him.

It was growing brighter. The fog was thinning.

Then with a shout of surprise, Jakob and Dougal tripped on the crest of a gentle slope and rolled down to the bottom of it, the edge of a steep cliff reaching out just in front of them.

On his feet in an instant, Jakob grabbed his father's arm, not caring at the moment about any other injuries Dougal may have suffered, pulling him to his feet despite his groans and carrying more than walking his father to a large tree that jutted out over the ledge.

It was agonizing work to get his father to climb the branches until he was well above the ground, more often than not pushing him up from one limb to the next, finally after thirty feet of ascending the trunk finding several thick branches that resembled a latticework of wood that his father could lay back on.

The arduous work was well worth the effort. Now he could leave his father in place and face the creature who had been chasing them without having to focus on anything else other than killing their hunter.

Yet when Jakob spun around on his perch, he realized that they were alone. Only a few, wispy strands of the mist touched him here, and those were moving away from him. Even better, night was giving way to dusk. He could glimpse the last of the stars above him, that single ray of light increasing in intensity.

A growl from the top of the slope captured his attention. At the very edge of the fog stood the creature who had been chasing them, a handful more of the hunters lined up next to him. They were no more than dim shadows in the mist.

Jakob's natural curiosity wanted at least one of the creatures to step out of the fog so that he could get a better look at their hunters. He realized that was a foolish desire as soon as he thought it. He had encountered enough of a challenge against one of those creatures as it was. Six were well beyond his ability.

As he tamped down his dangerous desire, a strong gust of wind burst up and over the top of the cliff, blasting into the fog, pushing it a few feet farther away from the tree that Jakob had selected to make his last stand.

When that happened, the figures glided back as well, none of the creatures willing to step out of the fog.

Certain now that the creatures in the mist wouldn't be coming for him so long as the fog didn't drift his way, he turned toward his father. He began to minister to his wounds as best as he could, knowing that there was little that he could do for most of Dougal's worsening injuries, the effort expended during the last few days almost too much for him.

THE TALL, emaciated figure, his dimensions and appearance vague thanks to the grey mist that swirled around him and kept him hidden from view, had been hunting these two humans for the last several hours.

The slaughter of the other humans had bored him.

Too easy. Too fast.

He was a hunter. He had been his entire life.

He preferred a challenge. Killing his prey as if they were no more than cattle unable to defend themselves held no appeal for him.

He was not a butcher.

There was no fun in that.

No thrill.

Because it was the thrill of the hunt that drove him. That's what energized him.

These two had gifted him that. They had given him a sense of excitement that he had not experienced since he had started hunting in these lands far to the south of his own.

They had made him work for the kill, and rather than being irritated by that fact, he was pleased by it. He appreciated their efforts.

They were worthy adversaries. Or at least worthier than the rest of the chattel he and his scouts pursued.

He had been enjoying every second of this hunt, impressed by the younger human's abilities, his intelligence and cunning. He had known that he would take a particular pleasure in killing the human when he caught him because of that fact.

Until the boy had driven a dagger into his foot.

The creature took a deep breath, expelling the air slowly, trying to release the tension and anger that he could feel building within him.

These two humans indeed were worthy game. They had surprised him by escaping the initial attack.

None of the other humans did. All the others fell victim to his hunters. Even the humans who were free to move and had weapons at the ready. They had fallen just as quickly as the humans who had been chained together.

Except for these two.

They had escaped the chain and then evaded his hunters.

Impressive.

But they couldn't escape him.

He had watched them instead of killing them right at the start. Curious. Wanting to see what they would do. What they could do when faced with so many disadvantages.

The two humans had done better than he had anticipated.

The creature shook his head in annoyance, angry with himself for his arrogance.

He had treated the hunt as a game. That had been a mistake. The pain in his wounded foot, at first sharp, now a dull throb, testified to his foolishness.

Thinking about his injury, the throbbing worsened. It wasn't until he cleared his mind, pushing the heat of the stab away from him, that the pain subsided to a manageable level.

The wound was both an embarrassment and a hindrance.

His injured foot would slow him down. Worse, it would weaken his position with his hunters.

He couldn't allow that to happen.

Now, after hobbling after his prey, his irritation with himself increasing with each painful step, he only had thoughts of revenge. Of gaining retribution upon the boy who had wounded him. Who had lowered his standing in the eyes of his brethren.

That's what galled him the most. He had allowed the weak human to get the better of him. That should never have happened. Yet he had permitted it because of his overconfidence.

None of his targets had ever escaped him before. He did not want to carry the burden of that shame with him back to the north.

He needed to excise that weakness before it took hold.

The boy was, indeed, quite clever. He could not deny it. He would not underestimate that one again. It was because of the boy that the two humans were still alive. That they had not yet felt the caress of his steel.

Yet what was he to do now?

The humans had broken free of the Murk. They had escaped him.

They were safe.

That thought galled him. It pained him almost as much as his foot.

Giving in to the dangerous urge that had grown in intensity as he stared out of the mist, having eyes only for the boy who had gotten the better of him, the creature stepped to the very edge of the fog.

The wispy touch of the mist comforted the creature. Nourished him. Sustained him and the others of his kind who had now joined him at the very edge of the whitish grey brume.

His hunters had killed all of the other humans. And this

was just the beginning. A taste of what was to come as the Murk encroached farther and farther into this southern land that was rich in resources. Rich in prey.

The two humans were no more than a few dozen feet away. He could easily take them out of the tree. One was injured, hurt worse than he was. The older man would not be a threat.

The boy would be a challenge, though nothing that he couldn't handle. Nothing that he hadn't come across before.

He would not allow his overconfidence to get in the way this time.

The creature took another step, the thick threads of grey dissipating at the very boundary of the fog. Then another step. And one more.

He was where the mist thinned to almost nothing now, just a few traces of grey caressing him.

Even with his injury, he could do this. He was fast. Faster than any of his hunters. In just a few seconds he could kill the two humans, thereby wiping the shame from his name. Then he could return to the safety and the succor of the Murk.

Just a few seconds. No more.

With that desperate thought driving his decisions, the creature tried to step out of the Murk entirely.

Immediately, the creature felt an uncomfortable resistance, a pressure pushing back at him. Fighting against it, he sought to extend his foot beyond the Murk.

He couldn't do it, the fog holding him in place.

He pushed harder, attempting to force his entire body through the grey mist that now seemed to be twisting itself around him, restraining him. Unwilling to let him go, even if only for a few brief moments.

The Murk itself was holding him back.

Refusing to be denied, the creature set himself in the dirt and grass, leaning down the slope, straining, pushing as hard as he could even as the bonds of grey strengthened around him.

For several seconds, nothing happened, the creature frozen in place.

Then a jolt of pleasure surged through him.

He had succeeded!

He had forced his way through, at least partially, placing one boot beyond the comforting touch of the Murk.

The creature recoiled in a flash, burning pains shooting up his exposed leg. He fell back into the fog, several of his hunters going to his aid.

He shoved them away, pushing himself back to his feet even as the pain became more acute for a time, his limb feeling as if it was withering away, shriveling, the flesh burning, until it finally subsided to a dull ache.

The creature growled in anger.

He rarely failed. Yet today he had failed twice.

He had failed to kill his prey.

He had failed to leave the Murk.

He had also proven himself a fool.

He should never have treated this hunt as a game. Never!

Because of his conceit, the two humans had escaped.

And he should never have tried to step out of the fog.

He had seen what had happened to his kind when they were caught out from the Murk. Yet even so he had allowed his ego to reign.

He should never have permitted it. That was not the way of his kind.

The needs of the individual didn't matter in the Murk. Only the hunt mattered. Only the needs of all were of any consequence.

Even if he had escaped the Murk for just a few seconds, he would have died a terrible death, his entire body withering into a dry husk, the energy of the Murk that sustained him, that gave him his strength, his power, his vitality, drained from his body in an instant.

He knew that, yet still he had tried.

He had acted the fool.

He and his kind couldn't live without the Murk.

That meant that he and his kind couldn't leave the Murk.

As the dense fog began to drift away, back toward the north, the creature had no other option but to move with it. He had no choice other than to leave his prey where they were, treed like the cowards that they were.

The shame of his failure threatened to crush him.

Instead of allowing that to happen, he experienced a rush of renewed resolve, consoling himself that he would gain his revenge on these two humans who had shamed him.

He would find these two humans again. He would finish what he started.

And when these two humans were dead by his hand, his shame would be lifted.

He was the Wraith Hunter after all.

He had never failed to kill his prey.

JAKOB SAT on the thick tree branch, one leg hanging off the bark, dagger in hand, ready to jump down if the creature that hunted them in the fog stepped out and came toward them.

He was worried about the hunter who stared daggers at him, even more so by what came next.

His father dozed behind him. Dougal's breathing didn't sound right. Not just his struggling for a breath, but now also a bubbling every time his father exhaled, a loose string of bloody spittle hanging from his lip that only got longer.

It had to be his father's lungs. Bruised. Punctured. Both. He didn't know.

Worse, there was nothing that Jakob could do to help him other than try to make him more comfortable.

With his father's troubled breathing as a frightening backdrop, Jakob glared across the space separating him from the wispy grey. He locked eyes with the figure hidden within. It was the only feature of the creature that he could clearly see besides the curved double-bladed dagger grasped tightly in his skeletal hand.

The eyes were a pure black, filling the entire sclera. No white at all. That was the only distinct color to the monster. And those black eyes blazed with an all-consuming hate.

The creature barely moved except every so often when the hunter lifted his wounded foot off the ground.

Jakob's eyes crinkled with delight each time the monster did that, a broad grin breaking out for the first time in days as he watched the creature struggle to deal with the pain of the wound that Jakob had given him.

He heard the angry growl from the figure in the fog next.

That broadened his smile even more, which only earned him an even louder growl, much louder, in fact, thanks to the several other creatures who now stood with the hunter.

And so it went for the next several minutes. Jakob and the creature in the fog staring at one another, neither willing to look away first. Both locked in place.

Jakob refusing to leave his father's side. The creature unable to exit the fog.

The showdown continued until the sun broke completely over the horizon and set the Sea of Mist afire, the fog finally receding, the monsters in the mist reluctantly going with it.

Jakob sensed the spite radiating from the creature as it slowly hobbled away, staying at the very edge of the fog until the grey mist drifted off the slope. Only then did he break eye contact. He was glad to be free of the creature, releasing some of the tension building up within him for the first time since he had entered the Highlands, though he doubted that it would last long.

Jakob had a feeling that he would be meeting this creature again in the future. The anger so clear in the creature's eyes suggested that what had happened during the last few hours would not be forgotten. Nor would it be forgiven.

If that proved to be the case, so be it. He could deal with it then. Not now.

Now, he had other more critical matters to address.

Turning away from the fog, Jakob finally could breathe freely again. Yet even as he did, relief flooding through him, his entire body felt cold.

Maintaining eye contact with that creature had chilled him to the bone, the promise of pain and anguish in the hunter's black orbs. Because of that, he didn't think he was ever going to get warm again.

Whatever had attacked them in the fog, whatever that creature was, it wasn't human. Of that he was certain. Beyond that, he had only a limited sense of what the hunters really looked like because of the few brief glimpses that weren't distorted by the fog.

Nevertheless, he did learn some important facts about the monsters that had stalked them.

They were fast. They moved silently. They didn't appear to see any better in the fog than he did.

Instead, the creatures were attuned to movement and sound. Even the tiniest of motions caught their eye, the barest of whispers drawing their ear.

So you could hide in the fog, but you needed to remain silent and still. To do otherwise meant a dagger slicing across your throat.

Most important, and really the only positive that he could draw from the experience, the creatures couldn't leave the fog. He had watched as the hunter who had tried to kill him and his father had attempted to do just that, Jakob's anxiety rising as the creature tried to force his way out of the fog.

But the hunter couldn't do it. He heard the hiss of pain when the monster tried to break free, and then the growl of frustration and resignation when he was forced to pull his boot back within the grey.

The creatures couldn't leave the fog even if they wanted to. That was information that he could use.

Stay out of the fog, and you were safe. And if you were in the fog, stay silent and hidden, preferably in an easily defensible space with thick walls and a sturdy roof, though that last was probably more dream than reality in the Highlands.

"You all right to move a little farther down the slope?" asked Jakob. "Somewhere a little safer?"

He studied his father. He saw the pain creasing his brow, but beyond that Dougal didn't betray much of anything else. His father wouldn't complain no matter how much his injuries bothered him.

"Yes," Dougal replied weakly. "Shouldn't be a problem."

He tried to push himself up from the trunk of the tree, struggling to do even that, holding his broken wrist against his ribs because of the intensifying pain. Unable to gain any leverage when using just one arm, Dougal slipped and almost fell to the ground thirty feet below them.

Jakob caught his father's arm just in time. Once Dougal found his balance again, Jakob guided his father slowly down the branches, staying beneath him, supporting a good amount of his weight to ensure that Dougal made it down safely from his roost.

When they reached the ground after several minutes of energy draining effort, Dougal rested his forehead against the bark. Or rather tried to, a hacking cough sending shivers up and down his body, droplets of blood spurting up from his lungs. He wiped them away with his sleeve, thinking that his son hadn't seen, not wanting to reveal the severity of his wounds and cause Jakob to worry any more than he already was.

But Jakob hadn't missed it, cringing the entire time his father was bent over, the coughing fit not subsiding until his father had spit out a huge glob of bloody mucous into the grass.

"We'll wait a little while longer," said Jakob.

He knew that his father's injuries were bad. He just hadn't known how grievous they truly were until now.

The difficulty breathing. The sucking and rasping noises when he exhaled. The bloody discharge.

Jakob had spent enough time listening and learning while his father fought in the various Guards up and down the western coast of Caledonia to know what it meant. He just wasn't ready to acknowledge the truth.

"I'm all right, we can get moving," his father started to protest, another series of hacking coughs bending him at the waist.

Jakob held him up by the arm so that he didn't collapse to the ground, fearing that if his father did, he'd never get him back on his feet.

"It doesn't matter at the moment," replied Jakob. "We can wait. We can't go anywhere until that fog to the west and north lifts entirely. If it comes back this way and we get caught in it, we're dead."

Dougal nodded, not in the mood to argue with his son. He leaned back against the tree trunk, sucking in air, his pain worsening in just the last few minutes. The effort to get down from the tree seemed to have extracted what little vitality he had left to the point where he could barely function. "What were those monsters?"

"I don't know," Jakob replied, his eyes scanning back and forth between his father and the fog that continued to move to the north. With the sun rising in the sky, the grey mist was drifting away at a faster pace. A good sign. "I never got a good look."

"I just caught a glimpse of them," Dougal said, shaking his head in disbelief. "In all my time I've never run into anything like what we just faced. I'm not afraid to admit that whatever was hunting us made my blood run cold."

"Mine as well," agreed Jakob. "Come on."

Jakob was thinking that they should wait awhile longer. Then he decided against it. His father, pale to begin with, had lost almost all of his color. And without the tree to hold him up, he had no doubt that Dougal would have been lying on the ground.

His father needed to rest, regain whatever strength he could muster. That was the only chance they had to find somewhere safe in the Highlands.

Rather than try to gain some distance on the fog in which those fearsome creatures lurked, Jakob decided that they needed to locate a more defensible position where they could stay at least for a few days. If his father's health improved during that time, or at least didn't take a turn for the worse, they could think about moving away from the slaughter that had taken place here.

Because Jakob was certain that even if the fog and these creatures didn't return -- although he believed those hunters in the mist would be back, particularly the one he had wounded -- more slavers would be coming this way eventually. He may be young, but Jakob wasn't naïve.

He had little doubt that the Sergeant led only one of the slaver bands and that there were several more working the Highlands and the other Territories, taking their prisoners to the mines along this same route. He didn't want to be here when more of those bastards appeared.

Jakob had worn chains once, the manacles still encircling

his wrists, and though it was not for very long, only little more than a week, he refused to do so again.

With all that flowing through his mind, Jakob hooked his arm around his father's waist and slowly led him behind the tree and down a barely visible path that wound around the edge of the cliff. Thankfully, he didn't have far to go before Jakob found what he was looking for. With every step they took his father grew weaker, until Jakob was carrying and dragging his father through the loose rock of the trail rather than helping him walk the path himself.

"We need to hole up for a few days," said Jakob as he lay his father against a large rock in the back of the cave hidden below the ledge, the trail leading right to it. The large firepit in the center of the hidden space, though obviously not used for quite some time, gave Jakob hope that he and his father might actually have a chance of surviving the next few nights.

The nook in the cliff face was large and dry, the entry curling around a slice in the stone. From the entrance they could look out over the last few peaks of the eastern Highlands, the Sea of Mist just beyond.

Best of all, Jakob could build a fire in the back without the flames being seen. A task he set to once his father was settled, the many broken branches that were scattered around the tree they had climbed a welcome and easy source of wood.

"We'll wait for this fog to clear before we move on," said Jakob once he got a small fire going. "In the meantime, I'll see if the slavers had any food left. Then I want to try to do something about your ribs."

Dougal nodded, liking the plan, if for no other reason than the fact that he didn't have the energy to do anything other than stay right where he was. "You'll need to find some linen so you can wrap my ribs."

"That shouldn't be a problem," replied Jakob. He wasn't looking forward to going back to where the attack occurred.

Still, he couldn't avoid it. That was the only place to get the supplies that he needed. "Here."

Jakob reached out to his father, offering him the dagger hilt first.

"Keep it," said Dougal. "You have greater need of a weapon than I do."

What was left unsaid by his father but what Jakob couldn't fail to comprehend was that Dougal wasn't in a position to defend himself from anything that might attack him, not even a toddler with a stick, so the steel was wasted on him.

Jakob nodded. Without saying another word, he walked out of the cave, several rays of sunlight streaming through the gloom, and headed back up the path. When he got to the top of the ridge, he was pleased to see that the fog was still moving away from him.

After cresting the slope, he began walking toward where the creatures in the fog had attacked him and the others in his party. The whole time his hand never strayed very far from the hilt of the dagger in his belt, his eyes moving regularly from side to side in search of movement, listening for any sound that was out of the ordinary for this desolate wilderness, his steps light and slow, not rushed.

Every so often he stopped and listened just as he did when he was in the fog. A useful exercise that quickly became a habit for him.

Taking a moment to steel himself for what he knew that he was going to find, he looked out over the Highlands, the massive, snow-covered peaks rising up in every direction. It truly was a sight to behold.

Despite all that had befallen him and his father, nothing good having happened since they had entered the Highlands other than their escape from the slavers aided by the creatures in the fog who were also intent on killing them, he liked it here. For some unexplainable reason, it felt like the home he never had since his father had moved around so much as a soldier, never staying in the same place for more than a year or two until they reached the small farmstead just outside Hardholm in western Caledonia.

Maybe his father was right. Maybe the Highlands was where they were meant to be. Assuming, of course, that they could stay alive during the next few days, which would require remaining free from any other slavers who might be coming this way and avoiding the fog if it returned.

Pushing all those worries from his mind, he went to work, first looking for some herbs that would help with his father's pain and aid the healing process. Dougal had trained him to fight as soon as he could stand. He had also taught him much more, including how to track, how to evade pursuers, and how to heal a variety of injuries, and if he couldn't do that at least ease the pain.

He knew that the herbs that he was locating would help, at least for a time. But he feared that even with all that his father had taught him with respect to medicine, it wouldn't be enough for him to help with the internal injuries with which he had no experience.

Aloysius could have done it. The Magus had shown him several times how he used the Talent to heal an injury and clean the body of disease.

Much to his regret, however, Jakob hadn't gotten very far in that aspect of his training with the old Magus. His instructor instead wanted to first ensure that he could defend himself with the natural magic of the world and then fight with it before he picked up any other useful skills.

For the old Magus, healing with the Talent was a tertiary concern, and before Aloysius could go much farther with his instruction in that area, he and his father had left Caledonia abruptly, faster than they had desired. Jakob hoped that Aloysius' decision with respect to his training didn't come back to bite him and his father both in the ass.

That worry taunted Jakob as he walked among the bodies, slavers and prisoners both, looking for some very specific items that could be of use to him and his father. He was tempted to give it a try, to use the Talent in an attempt to heal his father. He had watched closely when Aloysius had done it.

He knew that he shouldn't, however. Seeing and doing were two different things, and he worried that if he made even the slightest of mistakes, he would kill his father. So he would keep that option in the back of his mind, employing it only if absolutely necessary. And in the meantime Jakob would do everything that he could to ensure that he didn't need to take the risk in the first place.

Wrapping the small bundle of supplies that he had gathered in the handful of linen shirts that he had taken from those unfortunate enough to be caught by the monsters in the mist, he headed back through the long grass toward the tree, the top of which could be seen just above the slope a few hundred yards away.

For just a few seconds, he allowed his thoughts to drift back to his lessons with the Magus. He had enjoyed spending time with Aloysius quite a bit. Learning something new always gave him a thrill, and the old Magus had been a constant source of captivating and useful knowledge.

That was quickly followed, just as it always was, by the loss and pain that had haunted him across the Burnt Ocean. Unconsciously his hand went to the necklace that he wore around his neck, a gift of a sort from Aloysius.

At least that's the way he liked to think of the amulet, though a small voice in the back of his brain warned him that it might be more of a curse than a boon, which one not yet having been determined. Regardless, he gained some small comfort, and admittedly a hint of unease, when he brushed with his fingers the gem hidden beneath his shirt.

He stopped abruptly, having come upon the body of the Sergeant. The man who had taken him and his father and put them in this dreadful situation. The man who had no compassion and viewed the prisoners he had led into the Highlands as no more than tools to be put to work and discarded when they were no longer of use.

Jakob stared down at the man, or rather what was left of him, feeling nothing at all. Not anger. Not remorse.

The Sergeant had been ripped apart, his limbs strewn about in the long grass even though it was his father who had put him out of his misery. The Sergeant had met a terrible end even in death. Still, Jakob felt no sympathy for the man.

Instead he felt sick, never having seen such barbarity before though knowing from his father's stories that it certainly was possible and all too frequent. Thankfully, there was nothing in his stomach to expel.

Rather than moving away, Jakob forced himself to stare at the Sergeant's remains. His father liked to tell him that everything in life was a lesson. The one that he was learning now was probably one of the most important.

Based on his experiences, first escaping Caledonia and then since coming to the Highlands, he understood that he needed to get used to this. To this savagery. Because he believed with all his heart that this was only the beginning.

The creatures would return with the fog. It was a given.

If he was going to have any chance against them, he needed to be willing to do what they did. To demonstrate a level of brutality that would make the monsters in the mist think twice about coming for him. To teach them that if they wanted his blood, he would take theirs as well.

A vain hope, perhaps. He didn't know if he had such

violence within him. But he had a strange feeling that he would be finding out soon.

About to move on, not wanting to leave his father alone for very long, a flash of light off to his left caught his eye. Reaching down into the long grass with his free hand, he picked up the Sergeant's sword.

It wasn't an expensive weapon, though it was well made, and as he swung it through the air a few times, his eyes focused on the metal. He could tell that the blade was crafted from good steel.

He knelt again, picking up the sheath. Putting down his bundle for just a moment, he looped the belt across his back, then practiced pulling the sword free several times, ensuring that he could do so quickly, getting faster each time he did it. Satisfied, he sheathed his sword and picked up his supplies, heading for the cave.

His dagger wouldn't do much against one of those creatures in the mist or the Stalkers that haunted these mountains when the fog wasn't smothering the land. The sword gave him more of a fighting chance.

Reaching the path that led down below the crest of the cliff, before he ducked down into their hiding place, Jakob looked back the way he had come.

The billowing fog was still there, though it continued to recede. Slowly. Very slowly. Almost as if it didn't want to go.

He could sense the malevolence within the grey mist. The hate. The hunger to kill.

Jakob was certain that the fog would catch up with him again soon. And when it did, with the sword across his back, he would be ready.

16

FOLLOWING IN THE WAKE

Declan stood at the bow of the *Freedom*, enjoying the soothing motion of the ship as it sliced through the water, the vessel navigating the fifteen- to twenty-foot waves as if they were nothing more than gentle swells. The warmth of the sun shone down on him, and every so often a taste of salty spray shot up over the prow. As he stared to the west, seeing nothing but the deep blue all the way to the horizon, he relished the quiet and the calm, having rarely experienced either during his time in the Colosseum.

Perhaps that's why he scarcely gave himself time to relax. In the Colosseum, if you relaxed, you died. Better to be ready for whatever might come whenever it might come.

In fact, taking his ease was almost a foreign concept to Declan, following him from his time in the Royal Guard. From even before that, he realized. But considering where he came from before reaching Caledonia, that only made sense.

He hadn't had a choice. Otherwise, he'd be dead. Kill or be killed.

Because of that, he preferred to stay busy. Always. He

needed to be doing something so that he didn't feel as if he were wasting his time.

It wasn't the most comfortable way to get through life. Still, he was who he was, and there was little that he could do to change that. Especially now when his way of looking at the world had been ingrained so deeply within him.

Due to his need to always be doing, during the passage across the Burnt Ocean, Declan spent most of his time working with the Company of Blood, continuing with their training, unable to break away from the habits formed after twenty years in the practice yard.

Today, however, he ceded that responsibility to the Corporals. Dorlan, Jenus, Asaia, and the other squad commanders were leading that morning's training session. It wasn't that he didn't want to be down by the practice circle he had painted on the deck near the main mast. It was that he needed to give his squad leaders more authority and freedom to act, and this was the best way to begin that process.

So today he would take some time for himself, even though he felt exceedingly uncomfortable doing that. As if he was doing something wrong, like when he was a child and evaded his chores, a failing for which his father had always taken him to task.

He would be the first to admit that he was a creature of habit. He would also be the first to admit that he was very much looking forward to reaching the Caledonian Territories.

Declan understood Bryen's desire for a fresh start. He wanted the same.

In Caledonia, he had been a soldier in the Royal Guard. A gladiator, then Master of the Gladiators. And now Sergeant of the Blood Company.

It was time to begin something new. He just wasn't sure what that should be. At least not yet. And he hoped, he believed, that he would find his way once they got settled in Fal

Carrach. Or perhaps the Highlands. Maybe Benewyn. It would depend on what Bryen and Aislinn decided. He wanted to stay close to them if at all possible.

"Are you done with the young ones, Magus Rafia?" asked Declan, referring to the daily training she conducted with Bryen and Aislinn on the application of the Talent.

Bryen had killed the Ghoule Overlord and then destroyed the Curse or contained it. Declan wasn't really sure which because when Bryen explained it to him it was all a bit too esoteric for him. He was simply pleased that Bryen had won those combats, revealing a depth of power in the Talent, thanks to the Seventh Stone and the Spear of the Magii, not seen in a thousand or more years. While throughout those challenges Aislinn had demonstrated a strength and precise skill rarely achieved by a Magus.

Yet still the Keeper of Haven and the Master of the Magii required that they continue with their education in how to use the natural magic of the world.

He agreed wholeheartedly with her requirement. No matter how skilled you might be, that didn't mean you couldn't learn something new.

That's what he liked about Rafia. Her rigor. Her exactness. The fact that she had expectations that she demanded be met, and she would do all that she could to help her students achieve those expectations, so long as they were willing to put in the required effort.

There was also her dry humor. Well, now that he thought about it, obviously there was quite a bit more that he liked about her. But better not to think about all that too often when confined to a ship for such a long period of time.

"How did you know I was there?" asked Rafia, slightly perturbed that Declan had found her out so easily.

She had crept up to the bow quietly, trying to take him by surprise, thinking that the pounding of the waves would hide her approach. She was more irritated about her failure than the fact that once again he had addressed her by her honorific.

Magus.

This time, she chose to ignore the gentle jab, not wanting to give him the satisfaction of knowing that he had gotten under her skin quite so easily.

"I have my ways."

"Very mysterious of you. Almost as mysterious as a Magus."

"No one can be as mysterious as a Magus," countered Declan.

"I'll give you that." Rafia smiled, enjoying the back and forth. "But you still haven't answered my question."

"I used to be a tracker," Declan replied with a grin, keeping his eyes on the empty sea that stretched out in front of him before dipping below the horizon. "You give me too much credit."

Rafia stared at him, once again trying to read him. Trying to grasp how his mind worked. It was one of her unique skills, her ability to get a sense of other people with just a glance.

Yet with Declan, she couldn't do it. That failure only served to frustrate her even more while also engaging her curiosity.

Why was Declan different from everyone else? Why couldn't she figure out what he was thinking?

Then a strange thought came to her. Maybe she was overanalyzing. The real meaning of his words wasn't hidden behind innuendo or insinuation like it was for so many others. Maybe she actually needed to accept that what Declan said was what he meant.

"No, not usually," she disagreed, knowing that he was referring to more than what she had just referenced. "Usually I don't give you enough."

For several minutes the two stood silently next to one another, eyes on the surging waves, watching as a pod of dolphins positioned themselves right beneath the prow, racing the ship. Every so often they glanced up at the clouds as the billowing white masses sped across the sky, pushed by a strong and constant wind.

Declan knew that Rafia had joined him for a reason. Whether to talk or to simply find some peace, he didn't know. So he kept quiet, waiting. She would get to whatever she wanted to discuss when she was ready.

Nevertheless, try as he might to control his natural urges, as the minutes passed, he became more restless, finding it more difficult to remain still, shifting from one foot to the other. Apparently, he had gotten enough peace and quiet for the day. His body was telling him that it was time to do rather than think.

"Am I making you uncomfortable?" asked Rafia, noticing his unease.

"Not at all," Declan replied, hoping that he hadn't insulted her. "I'm just not used to not doing anything."

Rafia chuckled, nodding. She could understand that. She had not known Declan for very long. However, she had come to learn swiftly that he was always on the move.

Standing still, staying in the same place for as long as he had been, was quite an accomplishment for him. She took his effort to remain with her as a sign of respect. Perhaps even affection, although she thought she was a fool to even hint at that possibility, afraid to allow her mind to wander down that road.

"I can tell you have a question," said Rafia. There was a topic that she wanted to discuss with him, but she wasn't ready to raise it. So better to start with him.

"Is it that obvious?"

"Only to me," replied Rafia.

"Really," nodded Declan, a small smile cracking his usually serious expression. "Very mysterious, indeed."

His comment made them both smile. "I have my ways as well, Master of the Gladiators. Now to your question."

"How do you fight a Magus with steel?"

"You don't, if you can avoid it," she replied in a tone that was both serious and joking at the same time.

"And if you can't? If the combat can't be avoided?"

"Steel obviously will kill a Magus," shrugged Rafia. "Unless you're good at throwing a dagger or with a bow, you need to get close, and that's the challenge. It's virtually impossible to kill a Magus with steel if that Magus is touching the Talent."

Declan considered what Rafia said. He wasn't surprised, the same thought passing through his mind. "So distraction. Better that they don't see you coming."

"Yes, buying time to get close is key. Subterfuge. Deception." Rafia gave Declan's question a bit more thought, then grinned. "Or arrows as I said. Though it will need to be a lot of arrows to occupy a Magus for a time. They were effective against the Elders and would be so against Magii as well."

Declan nodded, his mind already beginning to work out a strategy.

"Why are you asking? I'm the Master of the Magii, at least in name. You have nothing to fear from the Order, especially where we're going. There might be a handful of Magii in New Caledonia, no more than that."

"I wasn't worried about the Order. I was thinking about Tetric."

Rafia nodded, understanding. "You're concerned about coming up against another Dark Magus."

"I'm just thinking ahead. I like to be prepared. Have a plan in place for any eventuality with the understanding that any strategy likely will change based on the unique circumstances of each situation. Tetric was something of a surprise. I don't like surprises unless I'm the cause of the surprise."

"I've noticed that about you. And you believe there could be another Dark Magus in our future? Bryen eliminated the Ghoule Overlord and the Curse. We have little to fear in Caledonia. And as I said, there are very few Magii in the Territories, and I'm familiar with all of them. We have little to fear from them. None of them are like Tetric. None have taken the wrong path."

"I don't doubt you, Magus Rafia," Declan's use of her formal title bringing a twist of aggravation to her lips and a frown, which he ignored. "Still, why not? If one could turn to the Curse with none the wiser, why not others?"

It was a simple logic, she had to admit, and not something that she could argue against. Especially after what happened what seemed ages ago but was only half a decade. Thinking of that incident, the betrayal, still set her blood boiling. It also filled her with a sadness deeper than the Burnt Ocean. "You know, you really do keep me on my toes."

"I try my best," Declan replied with a grin, finally turning his gaze from the sea and looking at Rafia, catching her sharp eyes. As always, he was intrigued by the loose strands of curly hair that she continually had to twist behind her ears because of the gusts of wind. "Now why did you decide to join me, Magus Rafia? You appear to have something on your mind?"

Rafia hesitated for a moment. "I just needed some space, what with us being on this ship for so long."

Declan nodded, turning away from her, his eyes going back to the waves rolling toward them. "I can understand that. Close quarters can chafe after a while."

Now it was Rafia's turn to fidget. She hadn't been completely honest with him, and it didn't feel right. Keeping something back from Declan.

She needed to tell him the truth, yet she didn't understand why that was the case. What drove her to reveal parts of herself to him that she would never divulge to anyone else. That as well only served to aggravate her.

"And I miss Sirius," she continued.

"I can understand that. You knew him quite well and for a very long time."

"It felt like it was longer than I wanted it to be sometimes," said Rafia, trying to smile, realizing that her joke wasn't very funny. That she was trying to use humor to cover the swirl of emotions cascading through her and she wasn't doing a very good job of it.

Declan understood what Rafia was attempting to do, sympathizing with her. "I didn't know him well," he offered, "though Sirius seemed to be a good man."

Rafia smiled, thankful for Declan's understanding. "He was, especially if you did what he wanted you to do."

"That certainly makes sense." Declan nodded. "I had my doubts about him in the beginning. After I learned what he had done to Bryen."

"Those doubts were deserved," agreed Rafia.

"In the end, though, he did right by Bryen. That's all that mattered to me. That tells me all I need to know about him."

"He did. Keep in mind, however, that his helping Bryen served his own purposes as well."

"True," Declan admitted. "Although I think there was more to it than just that."

"Why do you say that?" asked Rafia. She didn't know if he knew the whole truth about Bryen's heritage and how he was connected to Sirius.

Declan turned to face her again. For quite some time he didn't say anything. Then he smiled. "It seemed that there was more between them than just the fact that Sirius was teaching Bryen how to use the Talent."

Rafia didn't say a word for quite some time, simply staring at Declan. Maybe he did know the truth, but he wasn't sure if she did and didn't feel as if it was his place to disclose it.

"For someone who comes across as having little interest in

the interactions between people unless there's a steel blade involved, you really are quite observant, aren't you?"

"Thank you," mumbled Declan, "I think."

He wasn't sure if the Magus' comment was a compliment. Nevertheless, he chose to interpret it as such.

"You know, Declan, there is a quality about you that I find both quite intriguing and unsettling."

"I'm afraid to ask why that might be," he replied hesitantly, displaying the first trace of discomfort that Rafia had ever seen from him. The fact that she was the cause of it pleased her more than she was willing to admit to herself.

"Because you're different from any other man I've met or known, Declan."

Declan nodded, thinking about what Rafia had just told him. "And I should view that as a good thing?"

"Most definitely," smiled Rafia.

Then, not wanting to think, just wanting to do, Rafia reached up, placed a hand against Declan's whiskered cheek, and lifted her lips to his. The heat that she felt at the kiss reached all the way down to her toes, and she believed that Declan experienced the same, noting how his stance shifted, how he seemed to be preparing to reach for her but he held himself back.

Rafia pulled away for just a second, looking up into Declan's eyes, which sparkled with mischief and some other emotion that she couldn't identify. She didn't care. She had more important matters to address.

She leaned back up toward Declan, seeking another kiss, when she felt Declan's iron grip on her arms, keeping her in place.

"What's the matter?" asked Rafia, not understanding what he was doing or why.

Declan didn't really understand it himself, his need to pull back, because he really wanted to kiss Rafia again. He hadn't kissed a woman in quite a long time. Years, in fact. And he understood that his desire for Rafia didn't come from his lack of attention from the fairer sex.

No, it came from the fact that he had felt a spark when their lips touched that he had never experienced before when he had been with any other woman. There was a connection between them, something that wasn't just physical.

He knew it. He felt it, that spark surging through his body. Still, he needed to control that feeling. At least for now.

"Perhaps we should take a step back," he suggested. He then did exactly that, releasing his hold on Rafia and moving a few feet farther away from her.

"You didn't like the kiss?" asked Rafia, her confusion quickly shifting to embarrassment, anger not too far off on the horizon.

"No, it wasn't ..."

"You don't like me in that way?" asked Rafia, the hurt plain in her eyes.

"I do, it's just that ..."

"I thought we had a connection," said Rafia, not allowing Declan to get a word in. "If you're concerned, the feeling is mutual. You have nothing to fear in that regard."

"No, it's that ..."

"Well what is it?" demanded Rafia, her voice rising just as the wind picked up.

Declan sighed, realizing that he had lost control of the situation, Rafia's temper coming to the forefront. After what had just happened, he couldn't fault her for it. Then he corrected himself. He never had control over the situation to begin with, a common occurrence when spending time with Rafia, whose personality and demeanor rivalled that of any queen.

"You can't tell me?" continued Rafia, her eyes blazing with fury now. "I took a risk showing you how I feel. Certainly you can share your feelings. I'm no schoolgirl. I can handle rejection."

"Rafia," said Declan, having lost patience with the Magus. He wanted to be sympathetic to her feelings, but he realized that such an approach now would cause more damage than good. "I do like you. That should be obvious to you."

"Nothing is ever obvious with you, Master of the Gladiators," countered Rafia.

"Look, I'm sorry that I tend to be aloof. The fact is, I can tell that you're still grieving. I just don't want to rush anything. I don't want you to feel as if you're making a mistake. I don't want to be there for you just because you feel the need to be with someone. I want to be there for you because you want *me* to be there for you."

Rafia stepped up just as close to Declan as she did when she gave him the kiss, though this time her eyes held little warmth. "You think too much, Declan."

"I do not," he protested. "I'm just trying to be sensitive to your feelings."

"You do think too much," she stated harshly. "You just did. It's exactly as you told your gladiators in the Pit. Sometimes it's better not to think. Better just to do. Better to let your instincts guide you."

"Rafia, I just …"

"No more excuses, Declan. You had your chance."

With that, Rafia turned on her heel and left, the sailors and gladiators close enough to hear the argument quickly averting their gaze, not wanting to be caught by Rafia's fiery eyes.

Cursing quietly, Declan moved away from the bow, the training circle near the center of the vessel calling to him. That beautiful, infuriating woman was right. It was time to do, not think. And she was also correct that he did that better when he had a steel blade in his hand.

～

RAFIA STALKED TOWARD THE STERN, ignoring the several greetings offered to her, keeping her head down as her simmering anger threatened to boil over. Reaching the back rail, she leaned over the side, drinking in the fresh sea air and the salty spray, hoping that it would calm her.

She was furious with Declan, yes, but she was even more furious with herself for being so brazen. For taking such a risk. For not thinking about what the likely result of her action would be.

She needed time to think. To recover what little dignity that she still had.

Pushing herself up from the rail, she spread her hands along the surface, taking several deep breaths as she stared at the vessel's wake.

She felt like a fool.

She had thrown herself at Declan, and he refused to have anything to do with her.

That insufferable, arrogant ...

Rafia stopped herself, realizing that she was thinking what she wanted and not about what had actually happened. She wasn't entirely correct, was she? a voice that she rarely listened to whispered in the back of her brain.

She hated when this happened. When she felt the need to analyze every single action and decision she made.

She had done it so frequently when she had been with Sirius that it had become second nature. Most often the exercise had proven to be incredibly frustrating, although she did admit reluctantly that on occasion the analysis had proven useful.

Consequently, she couldn't ignore the voice entirely, even though she wanted to, because the voice sounded very much like Declan's. That gravelly, certain voice was telling her that she had made a mistake. That she had read the situation incorrectly. That she had allowed her emotions to get in the way and, as a result, had interpreted Declan's response to her kiss the wrong way.

Growling in irritation, she reminded the voice that she didn't make mistakes like that. Then the voice admonished her that she had failed time after time to get a good read on Declan. That he was an enigma to her, so how could she assume that her first instinct was the right one. That perhaps she had over-reacted.

Wouldn't it have been better if she had stayed at the bow and spoken with Declan so that she could better understand his hesitation rather than setting a fire and running off? Just as she had done so many times when she was with Sirius? One time literally in fact.

She shook her head as if she were trying to get rid of the words running through her mind, but it was no use. No matter how much she wanted to, she couldn't disagree with the voice.

She had been thinking that very same thing before approaching him at the bow. That if she assumed anything when speaking with Declan, it very likely could be the wrong assumption, since he did such an excellent job of hiding his thoughts, beliefs, and feelings.

When, prompted by the voice, she made that admission, she realized that she indeed may have overreacted. She may not have given Declan the opportunity to explain, even though at the time she believed that there was little more for them to say to one another.

Finally, she let out a long breath. It certainly felt as if Declan had rejected her. Yet the more she thought about it, the more she listened to the voice of reason within her, the more she realized that it was a much more nuanced interaction than she had assumed, her roiling emotions getting in the way of a clear perspective.

Rafia closed her eyes, a new aggravation building within her.

She still wasn't happy. Even though Declan had not necessarily rejected her, he had embarrassed her.

She couldn't leave the situation between them as is. She needed to do something about it to ensure that they were both on a level playing field again.

Hearing the shouts coming from near the main mast, she pushed herself off the railing and strode purposefully down the deck, working her way through the three rows of sailors and gladiators who surrounded the training circle.

Admittedly, the voice in the back of her head was arguing against her decision, suggesting several other approaches that would be more effective for improving the communication between them. Now, however, she wasn't listening to the voice. She knew what she wanted to do, and she was going to do it.

She had assumed that as soon as their encounter ended, Declan would come here. She was right, so she felt more confident that her plan was the right one as well. She understood how training his gladiators was both a challenge and a soothing experience for him.

Her objective now was to make the training circle her space. By doing that, she could rectify any imbalance in their relationship.

The last training combat had just come to an end, Declan speaking privately with Chesin and Asaia first before offering a few suggestions to those watching that he thought they would want to incorporate into their own efforts in the ring. That done, Declan looked to move the proceedings along.

"Who wants to step into the circle next?" he asked.

Before anyone else could reply, a strong voice called out. "I do, but only if you're willing to join me."

Declan turned at the voice, his eyes narrowing. He should have expected as much. He had no desire to cross blades with her. He couldn't refuse, however. Not now.

He had sensed her embarrassment when she had left him

at the bow and to refuse her request would only shame her further. That was something that he was not willing to do.

"Are you certain, Magus Rafia?"

"More than certain, Master of the Gladiators," she replied, stepping across the line painted on the deck, pulling free her twin daggers from the sheaths on her hips.

"As you wish, Magus Rafia. Only daggers?"

Rafia chuckled at that. "No need to fear, Declan. Just steel today. Although if you don't give me a good fight, I might lose my patience with you and give you a spanking with the Talent."

That comment drew laughs from several of the onlookers, amused by the visual that Rafia had given them. Those laughs died quickly when Declan swept his gaze around the ring.

"As you say, Magus Rafia," replied Declan, knowing that using her honorific would irritate her. If he could get into her head, he might be able to end this practice combat before either of them got hurt, because the look in Rafia's eyes suggested that she wouldn't shed a tear if Declan came out of the session nursing an injury or two. "I will try not to disappoint you."

Declan stepped forward, pulling the dagger from the sheath on his belt, then reaching down and doing the same for the one strapped to his left boot.

"Shall we begin, Magus?"

Declan had barely gotten out his question before Rafia was on him with a tenacity that drew wide-eyed stares and several gasps from those around them. For the next several minutes, neither Declan nor Rafia said a word, the Magus slicing and slashing with a precision that many of those observing the bout had only seen when the Volkun fought in the Pit.

Yet Rafia's unabating assault didn't faze Declan in the least. He had eyes only for the Magus, often staring right into her sharp blue orbs, not needing to watch her movements, instead anticipating where her daggers would be and either parrying the strikes or curling out of the way so that the blades only cut through the air rather than across his flesh.

"Will you always be running away from me, Master of the Gladiators?" challenged Rafia, her question drawing a loud ooh from those watching that drowned out the cheers that had erupted for the two fighters as soon as the combat had started.

Declan smiled at the question. "No, Magus Rafia. I am not running away from you."

"Because it seems like you are," she replied, hoping to break through the calm that seemed to radiate off him, realizing after just a few minutes that if she was to have any chance at winning she needed to catch him in a mistake.

"No such luck, Magus Rafia. I will never run away from you."

Declan's last comment startled Rafia, her fluid attack faltering for just a heartbeat. That was all that Declan needed to seize the momentum.

Darting toward Rafia with a deceptive grace, he jabbed for her thigh with the dagger in his left hand, catching her responding slash with the dagger in his right, then pivoting on his right foot and gaining some space with a backward stab.

Rafia had no choice but to step back quickly, the speed of Declan's assault catching her by surprise. She stumbled, thankfully keeping her feet, though Declan was on her before she had even straightened to her full height.

For the next several minutes, Declan and Rafia glided around the circle, two dancers beating out a constant rhythm of steel striking steel. The cheers around them died away, the gladiators and sailors watching in awe, recognizing what could only be described as a virtuoso performance, two masters of the blade going against one another.

Then the ring of steel ended, Declan and Rafia poised in the very center of the circle. The dance had come to a satisfying end for the audience, a roar issuing from the crowd. Many of those privileged to watch the combat applauded, never having expected the Magus to put on such a show, demonstrating a precision with her daggers that they had rarely, if ever, seen and truly appreciated.

"I knew you wanted to get close to me," Rafia said, energized by the duel, her steel held firmly against Declan's groin.

"That was never in doubt," he replied, his dagger at her throat, the cold metal streaked with the sweat of her exertions. "As I said before, I do want to get close to you. I just don't want to move too fast. That's all."

"Who would have guessed that a man raised in blood and violence could be so sensitive?" Rafia finally smiled, the voice in the back of her head once again her own. "Thank you for dueling with me Declan."

Declan sheathed his daggers when Rafia did the same, reaching out to shake her offered hand. Yet when he tried to let go, she wouldn't allow it.

Rafia kept him there, making sure that their eyes locked together, both understanding that they had reached an agreement, perhaps even something more than an agreement, on what the future might hold.

Davin took a deep breath of the sea air, the wind whipping through his long red hair. From here, holding onto the rigging halfway up the main mast, he could see for leagues in all directions, although at the moment there was little to glimpse other than the rolling swells of the Burnt Ocean and what he believed was a pod of whales about a half mile off the starboard side. So he kept climbing, knowing that there was an even better view to come.

Some of the gladiators of the Blood Company had grown tired of being on the *Freedom*, feeling confined, seeing much the same thing every day. Doing much the same thing every day.

They often compared it to their experience in the Colosseum, how one day was much like the next, and that they never wanted to have to deal with that kind of repetitiveness again. As a result, they were very much looking forward to stepping off the ship in Ballinasloe.

Davin could understand that desire. He had lived it for more than five years. The uniformity and discipline required to survive in the Pit. However, he wasn't in as much of a rush as some of his friends to leave the *Freedom*.

He loved being on the ship. He was enthralled by everything going on around him because it was all new. He had never encountered any of it before. So he spent as much time as he could learning whatever the sailors were willing to teach him.

In a matter of weeks, he had proven more than competent at whatever task Captain Gregson gave him, although it was climbing the rigging and the yardarms that gave him a particular thrill. The Captain had even said that he was a natural sailor, that he should have been born on the coast rather than in Tintagel.

"Permission to come aboard?" asked Davin as he climbed into the crow's nest atop the mainmast.

"Granted," Bryen replied, his eyes never leaving the training circle far below.

"If you need some time to yourself, I can come back later."

Davin knew Bryen often disappeared for a few hours every day. He had done the same thing in the Pit, needing to get away from everyone else. He was a quiet person by nature, so spending most of his day with other people in a small space often became too much for him, draining him of his energy. On the *Freedom*, the three crow's nests were really the only option for getting away.

"No, you're welcome to join me."

For several minutes the two friends didn't say a word, focused on the training combat taking place below them. Of course, based on the intensity of the fight, neither was really certain that it was a training session.

It had the look and feel of a real duel, which really wasn't unexpected considering the two combatants involved. They were more similar than either cared to admit, and that was quite obvious as they glided around the ring.

"The Magus is just as accomplished with a blade as Declan is."

"She is indeed," agreed Bryen. "I guess I should have warned him."

"You know that wouldn't have mattered to Declan. She challenged him. There was no way that he was going to back down from that."

"True. Declan has never really demonstrated the ability to turn away from a fight."

"I don't think he wanted to turn away from this one. I think he was looking forward to this one."

"How can you be so sure?"

"The smile," Davin replied. "Before I came up here I watched the very beginning of the combat down on the deck. The whole time, even while the Magus pressed him, he was smiling."

A roar from below drew their gaze back to the training circle. The combat had reached its conclusion, Declan and Rafia having their blades in a position where a flick of the wrist guaranteed a slow death for both of them.

A draw. Just as Bryen had anticipated.

"He's never going to be able to get away from her," said Davin with a huge smile on his face, the gladiator pulling his eyes from the deck and gazing out over the sea as the *Freedom* cut through the waves for the Fal Carrach shore, still at least a month distant, although Captain Gregson believed that with this ship they might be able to make it there faster if no storms appeared to slow them down. A faint hope, he had said, because there were always storms or worse in the Burnt Ocean. "Do you think he knows that?"

"Probably," Bryen replied, "and I don't think he cares. I don't think that he wants to get away."

"You could be right about that," agreed Davin.

"Those two deserve each other. They have similar personalities. Similar viewpoints on the world. Similar ways of doing things."

"You mean that they both believe that they're usually right and can be cantankerous when you don't agree with them or don't do what they want you to do?"

"Just so," nodded Bryen. "Speaking of cantankerous."

Davin shook his head in frustration. "I know. I just don't have any ideas as to what to do about Lycia. Every time I'm with her she sucks the joy right out of me."

"Yes, it's hard to miss."

"She's been this way for a while now."

"Moody and more cantankerous than Declan and Rafia combined?"

"Exactly that," grumbled Davin, "which is saying something. She takes it to a whole new level."

"The last time I saw Lycia smile was when we were riding on the backs of the Griffons, escaping the Temple of the Ghoules."

"Whether because of the excitement of the flight or the fact that we were evading certain death, I couldn't tell you."

Bryen nodded, thinking about what Davin had said, an idea popping into his head. Maybe it would even work.

Davin turned to his friend, who was gazing off to the port side. He took a quick glance himself. Storm clouds were forming to the south. With this wind driving them to the west, that building front probably wouldn't be a problem.

Although as Captain Gregson liked to say about the weather in the Burnt Ocean, once you thought you knew what was going to happen, you would be proven wrong, the weather patterns changing in a heartbeat, particularly the farther south you traveled as cold water and a plethora of icebergs were added to the mix.

"You've talked to her? About the ..."

"I have," said Bryen, understanding to what Davin was referring and his friend's hesitation. This was a matter that didn't involve him, and Davin wanted to stay out of it, although doing so was proving difficult. "It wasn't an easy conversation. But we seemed to get past at least the primary issue between us. She didn't stab me, so at least there was that."

"A small victory right there," agreed Davin. "How did you avoid the blade?"

He was fairly certain that Lycia would never stab Bryen. Still, he couldn't be entirely sure. His sister did have a habit of becoming volatile when she got really angry.

"I was honest with her," explained Bryen. "I told her how I felt. I told her I didn't want to hurt her, that everything that had happened had taken me in a different direction. And I apologized."

"How did she take it?" Davin asked. Usually he knew everything that was going on with his sister, but with respect to her relationship with Bryen, he was flying blind, Lycia choosing to keep this part of her life to herself.

"As well as could be expected," Bryen replied. "I should have told her sooner, and my waiting made things more difficult for both of us."

"Don't beat yourself up about it," said Davin, clapping his friend on the shoulder. "And I know you still are, so stop it. We need to move on."

"Easier said than done."

Davin nodded, understanding. "For some, yes. The reality is that as soon as you left the Pit, you were moving in a different direction. She understood that, although I know it was exceedingly difficult for her to accept."

"You can't blame her for that."

"You're right. I can't and I don't." Davin shook his head as if to say that he wished he had an easy solution, but he didn't because there really wasn't one to be had. "You've found your path, or at least you're in the process of doing so. Lycia needs to find hers. That's the catch right there. That's why she is as she is. She feels a bit lost. Once she finds her way, her circumstances will improve."

"You're right, Davin." Bryen looked at his friend with a newfound respect. "Who knew that you would be a fount of such erudition."

"I have my moments," said Davin. "Now about the path for Lycia, perhaps we could help her find it."

"Why do you want to do that? Nothing good ever happens when you try to involve yourself in your sister's life more than she wants you to. You should know that by now."

"I'm well aware of that. That's why I said perhaps *we* could help her find it."

"Davin, this is a bad idea."

"It's not a bad idea," Davin countered. "It's the only idea I've got for trying to help her. She's driving me crazy. We need to do something."

"For her or for you?"

"For both of us."

Bryen believed that his initial hesitation was legitimate. Lycia never looked kindly on anyone pushing her in a certain direction, getting downright ornery if you tried to nudge her to do something that she didn't want to do.

Other than Declan, of course. Or Bryen. But that only had to do with fighting in the Pit or in the training circle.

What Davin suggested was a dangerous idea. Still, it was obvious that Lycia was struggling to find her way. If they could help her onto the right path ...

"What did you have in mind?" asked Bryen, regretting the question as soon as it left his mouth.

"Perhaps another conversation with her?" Davin suggested. "No more than that, of course." He knew that he needed to be careful. He understood how Lycia would react if she sensed anything suspicious going on. "I can help you with that. I know her better than anyone."

"Thanks, but no," replied Bryen. He had witnessed too many conversations between the brother and sister to have any faith that Davin and Lycia interacting for an extended period of time would be a positive thing. The only time the two didn't get on each other's nerves was when they were partnered together in the training circle. "I know how conversations between you and your sister tend to play out. You'll just make it worse."

"I will not," Davin protested.

"You will."

"I will not ..."

"You will," cut in Bryen. "Most of the conversations between you and Lycia end in an argument. It's been that way since you two first entered the Pit."

"People can change, you know." Even Davin realized that he had just offered a very weak argument.

"Yes, people can change," Bryen agreed. Then he turned his gaze back toward his friend, forcing Davin to pull his eyes from the ocean and look at him. "But can you?"

"What do you mean?" Davin stared at Bryen, his eyes sharpening. He realized that Bryen had just shifted their discussion toward him. That they were no longer speaking about Lycia. "You're not just talking about me and my sister now, are you?"

"You're right. I'm talking about you."

"Me? What about me? I'm not upset about you and Aislinn. I'm doing quite well, in fact."

Bryen stared at Davin for quite some time. He was impressed. Usually, Davin would have become uncomfortable beneath his gaze.

Not this time, however. Davin kept an irreproachable expression on his face the entire time Bryen held him with his deep, grey eyes.

"You haven't been doing anything differently the last few weeks?" Bryen prompted finally.

"I don't know what you're talking about," replied Davin, his expression of innocence still unbroken.

"You haven't been taking any wild chances?" Bryen offered. "When we were in the Lost Land, you said multiple times that you were tired of that adventure. That you needed to take a break."

"I was tired of it."

"Yes, you said as much, many times in fact, but you really weren't," challenged Bryen. "I could see it in your eyes the entire time. Despite the danger we faced, despite the multiple times that we almost died, you loved every second of it."

"I still don't know what you're talking about," countered Davin, although his countenance was shifting now, beginning to crack, as if he had just been found out.

"I could see it in your eyes, Davin. You can say whatever you want. But your eyes will never lie. They will always give you away."

Davin shrugged, realizing that there was little reason to try to keep up with the charade. "So, maybe I did enjoy that experience. What's wrong with that? Maybe I just like to complain from time to time."

"From time to time?"

"What are you suggesting?"

"You like to complain all the time," said Bryen. "Just like your sister prefers to keep all that inside and allow it all to simmer before all those emotions boil over."

"And you don't?"

Bryen opened his mouth to respond then held back. He gave Davin a sly smile, letting him know that he understood what he was trying to do. "We're not talking about me."

"I still don't understand what you're driving at."

Bryen kept what he was going to say next to himself, realizing it would only take them off onto a tangent and away from the reason he had climbed into the crow's nest to begin with. He had known that it was only a matter of time before Davin joined him.

"What I'm saying, Davin, is that you thrive on adventure and risk. The adrenaline when you take a chance, the more dangerous the better. You need it. If you don't get that rush, you get grumpy."

Davin shrugged again, beginning to see where his friend was taking the conversation and not in the mood to help him get there.

"So maybe I do," he replied defensively. "What's the matter with that?"

"Diving off the crow's nest to be towed behind the ship," challenged Bryen. "You think that's a good idea?"

Bryen waited for a response, Davin simply shrugging again. "I never really thought about it, I guess. I just decided to do it. Besides, it's not as dangerous as fighting in the Pit."

Bryen nodded, understanding. His friend was incredibly consistent with respect to his impetuousness.

"I'm assuming that's why you came up here. To have another go. It's about that time of the day for you."

"I just came up here for the view," Davin said defensively, not realizing that his friend had been watching him so closely, because Bryen was right. This was the time of the day when he usually had his fun.

"Then why the rope?"

Davin's hand went to the coiled length that he carried across one shoulder, having forgotten that it was there. Davin smiled then, as if he had been caught with his hand in the cookie jar. He pulled the long, twisted strand free and dropped it onto the deck of the lookout.

"All right, yes. You're right. I do need some excitement. I don't like it when things slow down. This is what I do to combat that."

"You need it, don't you?" asked Bryen. "If you're not doing something like this, you don't really feel alive, do you?"

"True," sighed Davin. "Once we defeated the Curse and then the Ghoule Legions, I started getting bored. Here on the *Freedom*, I've been doing everything I can to stay busy, and I really am enjoying this journey, but it's not enough. I still need that thrill. When I get bored, I get depressed. I need to do something to jolt me out of it. Happy? You finally got me to admit it."

Bryen could understand why that was the case for Davin. After living on the streets of Tintagel and then being in the Pit for so long, Davin had gotten used to the adrenaline that made you feel even more alive than you could possibly feel living a more common life, as if you were always balanced on the very edge of a steel blade. And when that rush faded, you felt empty inside.

The natural reaction was to find something else to fill that gaping hole. Davin had done that. It was just that simple.

He didn't feel truly alive if he wasn't doing something to achieve that rush. He didn't feel whole. And here, on the *Freedom*, Davin had found a solution.

A dangerous one. Probably not the best one. But a solution, nonetheless.

Bryen had to give his friend credit for his creativity, even if he didn't agree with the approach he had selected to address what was missing within him.

"Diving off the crow's nest will certainly do that for you."

"Exactly," agreed Davin, who bent down and began to tie the rope to the mast when he realized that Bryen wasn't going to try to stop him. "Did you want to have a go first? I don't mind. Maybe if you do it as well, Lycia will leave me alone."

Bryen clapped his friend on the shoulder and started to climb down the rigging. "No. You do realize that you need to deal with this, right? Before you do something that you'll regret? Or before you kill yourself by accident? If that happens, Lycia will never forgive you."

"I know," Davin called after Bryen, his expression serious now as he gave the rope a few tugs to make sure it was secured properly to the mast. "I just don't know how."

Bryen stopped his descent for a second, nodding, staring out across the waves. He wished he had a better solution for giving his friend what he needed. Unfortunately, he didn't.

"I know what you mean. One suggestion if I may, at least for this voyage."

"Sure."

"Spend more time down there," said Bryen, nodding toward the practice ring as he resumed his descent, "rather than up here."

Davin smiled, nodding himself. "Good advice." Then he grinned broadly, lifting his eyebrows, giving his friend a hopeful expression. "Just one more time?"

"One more time," Bryen agreed.

"ARE YOU STILL ANGRY WITH ME?"

Bryen had snuck up next to Lycia, who sat tucked into an

alcove where one of the decks at the stern of the vessel made specifically for the Griffons met the railing, one leg hanging off the side.

"Not as much as I was before," she grumbled.

She had cut her red hair just the other day, feeling the need for a change, although it didn't seem to have done anything for her. Her formerly long locks were now shorter than those of almost every gladiator in the Blood Company, except for those who had lost their hair, which actually was a fairly good number. Not really a surprise, considering the stress associated with surviving in the Pit.

"That's a good thing, I guess. I'll take it."

"It is," Lycia replied with a smile. "Rather than just killing you, I only want to hurt you badly."

"Progress indeed," joked Bryen, hoping that Lycia was joking as well.

Lycia pushed herself off the railing, jumping down to the deck and standing next to Bryen.

"Usually you make better decisions," said Lycia, giving him a nudge with her shoulder. "I just can't believe you selected the Lady Winborne instead of me."

After Bryen and Lycia talked about his feelings for Aislinn and the direction he was going in his life while they made their way to the Temple of the Ghoules, she had tried to hide it, but she had been depressed and angry. With Bryen at first, and then with herself for failing to move on as fast as she thought she should.

She couldn't fault Bryen for the choice that he had made. And she didn't have the right to hold him to a vision that she had created for them that had become obsolete as soon as he had been taken from the Colosseum.

Still, it didn't make the hurt go away any faster, a depression settling within her when she wasn't diverted by more pressing matters and she was forced to deal with her emotions.

"Sometimes neither can I," Bryen replied. "I do love you, Lycia."

"I know, I love you too," growled Lycia, shaking her head gently in frustration. "You know it's hard to be angry with you when you're like this."

"I do what I can," he replied with a grin.

"Well, what's done is done," said Lycia, giving him a companionable clap on his back that was a bit harder than it needed to be rather than the hug that he had expected. "You made your choice. Now you're going to have to live with it."

Bryen smiled, Lycia's message clear. She had moved on. Or at least she believed that she had. There was no need to have a repeat of the conversation they had already engaged in.

Taking Lycia at her word, in a flash of understanding, he realized what was holding her back. She was much like Davin, which really wasn't all that surprising.

Her brother had been searching for a way to experience the adrenaline that was so important to who he was. Lycia, on the other hand, thrived on being needed.

At the moment, she didn't have that, and Bryen being on the ship didn't help, because he was a constant reminder of what she had lost.

There was nothing he could do about the latter, at least not until they reached New Caledonia, but he could do something about the former, about Lycia needing to be needed.

A shout of excitement drew their gaze to the other side of the ship, turning just in time to watch Davin shoot right past them, splashing into the water and disappearing beneath the waves, the rope tied to the mainmast drifting back behind the ship. They waited a few seconds, both breathing a bit easier when his red hair popped to the surface, already a hundred yards behind the fast-moving vessel.

Davin waited until the rope he had tied off to the mast became taut before he pulled himself up to his bare feet, falling the first few times before he found his balance and then began surfing behind the ship.

Bryen and Lycia watched for a few minutes, Davin's broad smile visible even at this distance. Several times he tried to jump over the *Freedom's* wake, only to crash miserably in the water, getting dragged behind the ship until he was able to pull himself back up onto his feet and try it all again.

Bryen shook his head in amusement. Davin wasn't very good at what he was doing. He was having some fun, though, and that's what mattered for him now.

Moreover, Bryen had no doubt that eventually Davin would become quite skilled at surfing through the ocean. Once he put his mind toward learning a new skill, he always mastered it. What use this new skill might have beyond the purpose he was using it for now, Bryen wasn't sure, although a few ideas did come to mind.

"My brother is a fool."

"He is," Bryen agreed. "But he is who he is. Just as you are who you are."

"What do you mean by that?" asked Lycia. "Where are you going?"

Bryen had jumped up onto the stern deck, heading toward one of the Griffons, the large animal lying beneath the open-sided tent Captain Gregson had constructed to protect them from the elements.

"Come on. I've got a friend I'd like you to meet. And I'd like you to do something for me if you're up for it."

FOR THE FIRST time in a very long time, Lycia whooped with pleasure, Arabella diving down toward the waves, the Griffon tilting her wings to level out just ten feet above the water, every so often one of her paws breaking through a wave taller than the rest. In fact, she couldn't remember the last time she felt so happy, so at peace with herself.

If ever there had been such a time, it was before her father's death. Before she and Davin had been forced onto the streets of Tintagel.

Arabella squawked loudly, enjoying the rush just as much as Lycia was, pumping her wings to gain more height so that they could do it all again. A patch of black feathers beneath her beak the only blemish in her tawny fur and feathers.

Lycia had learned quickly that Arabella was the right Griffon for her, the animal swooping down out of the clouds at every opportunity, surging through the air at an incredible speed.

The first dive had frightened Lycia. The second not so much. The third she screamed almost as loud as Arabella shrieked, relishing the freedom and the excitement the maneuver generated.

When Bryen introduced her to Arabella just a few hours before, she had been uncertain about what he was asking her to do. He, Aislinn, and Rafia searched around the *Freedom* with the Talent regularly to ensure that no surprises came their way.

Even so, Bryen still preferred to send out scouts every day, just to get a feel for what was around them. Just to make sure that he wasn't missing anything. A characteristic of his that she had seen when she met him for the first time on the white sand.

At first, she thought he was just giving her something to do, a task that really didn't need to be done that would get her away from him for a little while. As soon as she met Arabella, she didn't care.

After Bryen taught Lycia how to approach Arabella and she ran her fingers through the Griffon's feathers for the first time, Lycia felt as if she had met a kindred spirit.

As soon as she hopped onto Arabella's back, Bryen showing

her where to grip her feathers so that it wouldn't be painful for the large animal and it would give her the best balance and control, she didn't care why Bryen wanted her to scout around the ship.

She just wanted to get into the air.

Arabella obliged, launching them into the sky. As soon as they left the deck and the massive vessel shrank in size with every beat of the Griffon's wings, she felt like she was exactly where she was supposed to be, thankful for the freedom that her assignment gave her.

Patting Arabella gently on her neck, Lycia smiled, seeing that the Griffon had attained the height that she wanted for her next dive. Rather than leaning in toward Arabella's neck, instead Lycia pulled back gently on her feathers, catching the Griffon's attention before she tucked in her wings and hurtled toward the ocean.

"What's that over there?" Lycia wondered, pointing to a spot in the ocean just to their east no more than a quarter mile away.

Arabella screeched in response, rather than diving just dipping her wing and curling in that direction, gradually flying lower until they were only a hundred feet above the waves.

When Lycia had first seen the shape that broke the surface of the Burnt Ocean, she thought it might be one of the blue whales that Captain Gregson said migrated through these waters during this time of the year. Yet as she and Arabella approached, her eyes widened, a bolt of concern sending her heart racing just a bit faster.

It wasn't a blue whale that followed the *Freedom*, the much larger shape now no more than a league behind the vessel.

And it wasn't just one.

There were three of the creatures swimming side by side, the angle at which Lycia first saw them making her think that it was a solitary animal. Every so often one of the beasts dove beneath the waves and disappeared for a few minutes, then rose back up to the surface, always in line with the others.

The creatures, trailing in the ship's wake, were closing fast. Whoever manned the crow's nest wouldn't see them until they were only a few hundred yards off the stern, and even then it would be the animals' wakes that they would see first, the blue and white coloring of their scales helping the creatures to blend into the waves.

"Let's head back, Arabella. As fast as we can."

In response, the Griffon dipped her wing toward the west, catching a gust of air, then pumping her wings furiously to get ahead of the creatures pursuing the *Freedom*.

Lycia hoped that they got back to the vessel in time, because each one of the beasts on its own appeared to be almost as long as the ship.

17

ALWAYS MOVING FORWARD

Talia stared out of the multipaned window that ran along the length of the back wall of the large warehouse her father had purchased when he first arrived in Ballinasloe. She loved standing here in her father's office, looking out onto the pier and watching his vision come to life.

She stopped herself, a tear coming to her eye as the weight of her father's death hit her again just as it did every time she thought of him. A daily occurrence. At least this time she didn't break down into a river of tears.

Turning away from the view, she took in the large space. A desk was placed in the very middle of the room, a large table with chairs by the door, the shelves beyond that filled with as many sea charts as books, all of these having a nautical theme. This had been her father's refuge, and now it had become hers as well.

An accident, most everyone had said. A tragedy that no one could have anticipated. Who could possibly know that fog would force them into Mermaid's Cove? Who could possibly think that Stalkers would emerge from that fog? Who could reasonably assume that those creatures terrorizing the country-side knew how to swim?

All good questions. And no good answers.

Captain Jennison and the sailors who had survived that terrible night had disagreed vociferously with the perspective that it had all been happenstance. They viewed it as a setup. Someone wanted them in Mermaid's Cove at exactly that day and time. Somehow they had made that happen.

It was preposterous to think that someone could control the fog or the Stalkers. It was almost insane, in fact. Yet Captain Jennison and his crew held to their beliefs more staunchly than a dog to a bone.

Talia believed them. Her father had told her a great deal about his suspicions regarding what was happening along the New Caledonian coast.

He couldn't prove anything. Still, he wasn't one to make up stories just to suit his purposes. He was smart and always logical. And as she talked through his ideas, that logic became readily apparent.

She had believed him then even though she had her doubts. Those doubts disappeared once Captain Jennison told her what happened as well as his own suspicions.

She didn't care about what other people said. She would prove the truth of what had occurred in Mermaid's Cove. She would identify who was responsible and make that person pay in blood. It was just a matter of when.

Pushing those thoughts aside until she had the resources to move forward with her plan, she directed her gaze back out of the third story window. From her perch, she gained a view of her family's pier extending out into the Ballinasloe harbor. Beyond that was the Sea of Mist, thin wisps of the ever-present fog just kissing the rough waves off to the east.

In that moment, she had more pressing matters to deal

with. The past could guide her decisions and her goals, but she needed to focus on the present and the future.

Talia and her mother had moved forward with their plans for expansion, not only wanting to build their business, but also wanting to ensure that they did everything possible to protect against the desires and demands of Governor Roosarian.

With that in mind, they had followed through with the agreements her father had put in place before his death, purchasing the warehouses on each side of the one housing her office. Renovations had already begun on both. They were being fitted out as lodging for her ships' crews and their families. The idea was to build a village within the city of Ballinasloe, one that could function independently from the larger metropolis.

Along with the warehouses, they had completed the acquisition of the two piers that were next to theirs, expanding their control over the southernmost section of the waterfront. They then began construction on a stone and timber wall that would separate the Carlomin property from the others on the docks.

They wanted more than just the concept of an enclave within the heart of Roosarian power. They wanted a visual reminder that the good Governor couldn't miss.

The workers had made a great deal of progress in just the last week, the wall reaching a height of thirty feet with a balustrade running along the top. It stretched around the pier and then curled out into the water to make it more difficult for anyone thinking to enter their property by going for a swim. The barrier resembled the palisades surrounding most of the larger towns in Caledonia and it actually was taller and sturdier than the wall surrounding the city proper.

Talia was quite pleased by the speed of their progress. There were many reasons for creating this private sanctuary directly opposite the fortress being built on the island in the center of the Ballinasloe harbor.

Safety, of course, Talia using the excuse of her father's death when the Governor pushed back upon learning what they were doing. Privacy. Efficiency in terms of meeting the needs of their business as well as the people working for them.

However, perhaps what most appealed to Talia was the fact that once Roosarian completed the fortress the townspeople had named the Rock, the Governor would have to stare out across the water at what would become a small redoubt of its own over which she exercised no authority.

And the way the work on her docks was proceeding, unlike the construction on the island a few thousand yards distant, her enclave would be completed years before Roosarian's. To reach the so-called Rock, all the equipment, supplies, and workers had to be transported over the water, which inevitably slowed the work.

Talia thought that was a foolish approach and incredibly inefficient. Better to think things through before settling on a strategy that was both costly and demonstrated a distinct lack of creativity.

There was a large sandbar running from the island directly to the coast just a quarter mile down the harbor on the northern side. Why not build a bridge across the shallow water there to make things easier both for the construction and to ensure that the Crag had a function other than dominating the harbor?

Talia castigated herself for allowing her thoughts to wander.

What Governor Roosarian did with respect to the island was of little import to her if it didn't affect her directly. The only thing that mattered to her was how that insufferable woman was attempting to harm her family and her business.

She and her mother had experienced much the same

before. That painful loss had pushed Talia and her family in a different direction. What they had received from their forced sale of the winery at least was enough to begin a new business -- one that they hoped would allow them to avoid the politics that captured their last one -- and led to the birth of Carlomin Trading Company.

A naïve hope, Talia knew now. Politics and business were based on the same scarce resource. Money. And the same thing that happened in Roo's Nest was occurring now.

Hakea Roosarian, Lady of Caledonia and Governor of Fal Carrach, wanted their business. Her claim of only seeking a partnership was nothing more than a convenient lie to get her foot in the door. Once the Governor did, she would give them the boot and take it all for herself.

That wasn't going to happen, Talia promised herself. This was her family's business, and it would stay her family's business no matter what a grasping, conniving woman who was responsible for her father's death wanted.

She couldn't prove it ... yet.

But she would. No matter how long it took, she would.

In the meantime, she would do everything within her power to hinder Roosarian's efforts to acquire the business her father had helped to build.

To do that required completion of the changes she was implementing. And as with the wall, some of those changes would allow them to better defend themselves in ways both exceedingly obvious and others less so.

Nodding to herself as she considered all the projects currently under development, Talia abruptly turned away from the window, walked through the open door, trotted down the steps two at a time to the bottom floor, and strode out into the fading sunlight. She wanted to check on what kind of progress had been made in several key areas before full night descended.

She greeted every worker she passed on the docks, stopping to talk whenever they didn't appear to be in too much of a rush. It meant that it took longer for her to get where she needed to be, but she knew that it was time well spent.

She had learned from her father that treating people with respect, demonstrating that you cared about them and their families, played a key role in gaining their trust. Because if the people working for you didn't trust you, then your business had little chance of succeeding.

As her father had liked to say, business was more than just supply and demand, resources and production, revenue and expense. It was the people. Without the people, you had no business.

"How goes it, Master Hari?" asked Talia as the master shipbuilder stepped out from behind the sails that kept prying eyes from the work he was doing on one of the Carlomins' fifteen frigates.

All of the Carlomin ships in the Territories except for those currently on runs were tied up along the pier and having several structural improvements completed. Almost all of the work resulted from Talia's ideas that Hari Hoohannen had built upon to create a final product that was even more innovative and, assuming all went well, advantageous.

"Like a salmon swimming upstream, Lady Carlomin," the large man replied, his eyes crinkling in delight, a very large hammer in one hand, blueprints in the other. He handed the hammer to an apprentice working beneath the sails, rolled up the blueprints, and joined Talia. "It's hard work, but we'll get there eventually."

"Of that I have no doubt, Master Hari."

Talia began walking along the pier toward where two vessels were currently in drydock, the enhancements being made to these cutters requiring that they be out of the water.

Stepping beneath the sails that hid the work being done, Hari followed.

"This latest idea of yours is particularly diabolical," said Hari as he guided her toward where several of his apprentices were fitting the addition in place.

"You say that as if it's a bad thing, Master Hari."

"That wasn't my intention, Lady Carlomin. Far from it." When Hari approached the side of the vessel, the apprentices stepped back, giving him and Talia a clear view. "This creation of yours is one of my favorites."

"Ours," corrected Talia as she stepped up next to the burly shipbuilder, running her hand along the wood and the metal. "Ours. A joint creation."

Yes, this was coming along nicely. Hopefully this would work as they envisioned. She had her doubts when she first proposed the concept. Yet as soon as Master Hari heard what she had in mind, he had spent a good number of sleepless nights thinking about how he could improve upon it, and what she was studying now made her feel much more confident that her suggestion could be employed as intended. Though of course the proof would be in the test, and she couldn't conduct the test until the labor was done and this ship was back in the water.

"Will it work as we hope it will?" Talia asked, her concern evident in her voice.

All of the innovations that she had been working on with Master Hari were designed to allow the crews to better defend themselves while not negatively affecting the speed of what were the fastest ships in the Burnt Ocean.

As her father had taught her, speed was the key. It was good for business. It was good for keeping them free from the pirates who were becoming more of a nuisance based on what the other merchants were experiencing.

"Have no fear of that, Lady Carlomin. These improvements will work better than we anticipated. I'm sure of it."

"I'm pleased to hear you say that, Master Hari," said Talia, stepping back and thanking the apprentices for their hard work before walking out from behind the sail. "Still, I worry."

"Just like every other inventor, Lady Carlomin," replied Hari with a deep laugh as he followed Talia back out onto the pier. "Have no fear. I have no doubt that it will not only work as we hope, but it will work better than we expected."

"You're being too kind, Master Hari. And please, as I've said many times, call me Talia. There's no need for formality. I am not a Lady of Caledonia. I am but a merchant trying to make her way in the world."

The master shipbuilder nodded at what she said, then chuckled, the squeaky laugh sounding out of place on the hulking man. He was amused that she would say something like that. Humble to a fault, in his opinion. He liked that about her.

Even more, he liked her drive. She had a goal in mind, and she wasn't afraid to try new ways of doing things to achieve that goal.

For someone who was always looking to create, to build on what had come before, to improve on the past, she was the perfect employer.

"You're more than just a merchant, Lady Carlomin. Say what you want, I know the truth. You're destined for great things. I'm sure of it."

"How can you be so certain?" Talia asked, half joking, though also intensely curious.

"My wife, Lady Carlomin. I told her what we were doing and why. She's never wrong. She believes in you just as I do."

"And if you believe that she is wrong, you'll never tell her. Isn't that right, Master Hari?"

"Indeed it is, Lady Carlomin," Hari replied with a grin. "The secret to a happy marriage."

"I'll keep that in mind," Talia replied, smiling herself, "for when I find someone worthy of my attention." She didn't think that the master shipbuilder would ever be able to drop the formality between them. It just wasn't his way. "Do you think we will gain the advantages we seek when all this work is complete, Master Hari?"

Hari took some time before responding. He never rushed to answer a question. Ever. He liked to consider all the possibilities from every angle before doing so.

That's one of the reasons Talia liked the usually gruff old man so much. He told her what she needed to hear. Not what she wanted to hear.

She could understand why that had proven to be a problem with his former employer. It wasn't with her.

Talia only wanted the truth. Always. Good or bad, it didn't matter, so long as it was the truth.

"With the proper training, yes," Hari replied finally, nodding as if he were agreeing with himself. "These and the other enhancements you've ordered will work. They will allow us to do what we've discussed."

"Excellent. Once the first ship is ready, I would ask that you accompany me as we train the crews. I hope that won't slow your work."

"I wouldn't have it any other way, Lady Carlomin. My apprentices know what they're about. While we're testing, they'll keep building. Based on how our work is progressing, we're ahead of schedule, so we should be putting this wonderful lady," motioning to the vessel hidden beneath the sail that they had just inspected, "back in the water sooner than we thought originally."

"That's good news, Master Hari. I'm both impressed and pleased. How soon?"

"The end of the week at the latest, Lady Carlomin. I'll know by tomorrow morning for sure. I'll keep you apprised."

"Thank you, Master Hari," Talia replied with a satisfied nod. "I'll get the training schedule in place so that we'll be ready."

"Of course, Lady Carlomin. Now if you wouldn't mind my stepping away for a moment, I need to supervise this next step. It's tricky, and I don't want the lads and lasses to make a mistake. If they do, what I just told you with respect to timing will be incorrect, and I don't like to be wrong."

"I never knew that about you," murmured Talia with a straight face, the apprentices' efforts beneath the sail knocking it out of the way for a few seconds to reveal them maneuvering a large, curved piece of steel that resembled a bird's wing against the side of the ship.

Hari looked at Talia for a moment, not sure how to take what she had just said, then smiling when her dry humor hit him. "You remind me of my daughter, Lady Carlomin. That's probably why we get along so well."

"That's very kind of you to say, Master Hari. I'm honored. Now off with you. I've taken up too much of your time as it is. I'll check with you tomorrow to confirm the arrangements."

Hari nodded, tipped his head in respect, then ran off to where his apprentices were struggling to place the piece of metal, immediately giving instructions once he was back beneath the sail as he helped to manhandle the steel into the position he wanted.

"Master Hari certainly was a good find," said Isana, coming up behind her daughter. "How did you manage to spring him free from under the grips of Governor Roosarian. That woman rarely lets anything go once she gets her claws into it. Higher salary?"

"We're paying him exactly the same as Roosarian did," Talia replied.

"And he still decided to come work for us?" asked Isana, believing that they would have had to pay a great deal more to acquire the services of the most accomplished shipbuilder in the Territories.

"He did, and from what he told me when we reached an agreement, his decision wasn't based on money. Although he does appreciate the bonus schedule that he initially refused but I included in his contract anyway."

"Is that so?" replied Isana, having a difficult time believing her daughter.

Noticing her mother's skepticism, Talia expanded on her response. "He didn't like having his employer looking over his shoulder all the time, checking on his work, nitpicking what he was doing. He also didn't hide his dislike for Roosarian's approach to doing business in Fal Carrach and Ballinasloe in particular. So he was open to my proposal. Money was the very last item we discussed, actually. It was more an afterthought than anything else."

"There must have been more to it than that," suggested Isana.

"There was," Talia agreed. "Primarily he was intrigued by the work we wanted him to do. Master Hari likes a challenge, and we gave him one. More than one, in fact."

"You certainly have," Isana replied, watching as Master Hari and his apprentices continued their work beneath the sail, several curses erupting from the master shipbuilder as his assistants didn't do as he required as quickly as he wanted.

Talia grinned upon hearing Hari's colorful language. He was only this animated when things were working as he wanted them to. When she turned away, her mother followed as they walked farther down the pier.

"And, of course, it helped that Master Hari dislikes Lady Roosarian more than you might expect. She forced his sister out of business, taxing her to the point where she couldn't make ends meet. She ran the most well-respected smithy in town, taking it over when her husband passed away. Apparently, Roosarian wanted to become a partner with her just as she does with us. When Master Hari's sister refused, he believes Roosarian was responsible for burning down the forge, although he couldn't prove it, his sister barely escaping the blaze herself."

"So the Governor has a standard practice for dealing with people who choose not to obey her."

"It certainly seems that way," agreed Talia. "Master Hari's not one to forgive and forget. He also has a very strong desire for revenge."

"That's a motivation I can understand."

"Indeed it is. He believes that everything we're trying to do will weaken Roosarian's hold on Fal Carrach, so he's all for it."

"You found all this out how?"

"My eyes and ears in the city," Talia replied. "Or rather father's eyes and ears. It didn't take me long to connect with them after he passed."

"What else have they learned?" asked Isana, pleased at how rapidly her daughter had taken over the reins of the business.

"That Governor Roosarian is quite unhappy with us. Father did not accept her proposal, nor did we. Our business is expanding as is our presence on the docks. Our profits are rising. And, of course, our stealing Master Hari away from her has put her in a particularly foul mood."

"She likely doesn't approve of our making our own little enclave on the docks."

"That as well, yes. From what our sources are telling me, she sees that as the most egregious of our crimes. A direct challenge to her authority in the city. Apparently, she was raging about it just last night when she hosted a banquet at the Rock seeking to expand her influence with a few key merchants in the city."

"Good," said Isana, her face set, eyes blazing. "Her anger can only help us. Strong emotions lead to bad decisions."

"Desperate decisions," added Talia. "Still, we'll need to be careful as we discussed."

"Of course, Talia. You're correct. We must be ready for whatever she might have in mind for us."

"Which brings me to the next matter that has displeased the good Governor Roosarian. I was speaking with our captains this morning. There's no lack of sailors who are interested in working for us now that they know that those who do obtain free lodging here with their families as well as access to several other benefits and services."

"You still plan on hiring them?"

"I do. We'll have four more ships complete in the next few weeks so we need skilled sailors. These new hires can finish the work on them and fit them out for their maiden voyages."

"They're all being vetted?" asked Isana. If they had spies working for them, she was certain that Roosarian did as well. It was only smart business, after all.

"Of course. I'm overseeing the process myself."

"Good, we don't want any Roosarian agents working their way in."

"We'll do our best to prevent that. But you know as well as I that no vetting is ever perfect, or it shouldn't be if you want to keep your rivals on their toes. So I'll allow one or two to get through."

"What then?"

"We'll make use of them, of course. We'll feed Roosarian the information we want her to have."

Isana nodded her approval, pleased by her daughter's strategic approach. "By the way, we received another summons today requesting that we appear at the Rock."

"Governor Roosarian wants to speak with us again. This is what, the third time?"

"Yes, she's quite insistent," replied Isana, "and very predictable. We can use that against her as well."

"Has she changed her offer in any way?"

"No, not in any substantial way. Her entreaties are simply becoming shriller and more demanding, like a spoiled child whose toy has been taken away."

"She can yell all she wants. I wouldn't sell her our business even if she offered ten times what it was worth."

"Nor would I. Even so, as we have discussed, we need to be careful, Talia."

"I know. If she's behind what happened to father …"

"There's nothing to prevent her from doing the same to us. And just as you believe, so do I. Somehow, she was responsible for your father's death."

"So another variable we need to deal with."

"Yes, even with the guarded compound and the improvements to the ships that you've been implementing, we need protection. Maybe even some soldiers on each vessel."

"Remember, speed is our greatest weapon," replied Talia. "But I'll give it some thought. There's nothing to stop her from trying to get at us when our cutters are docked."

"Exactly," replied Isana. "Now let's move on to the last few of our issues. The convoy system that we were pondering."

"What are the captains' thoughts?"

Talia had suggested the approach as a way to offer more security when their ships were out on the ocean, giving them safety in numbers from the pirates who already were seeking to seize them. Although it would take some work to coordinate, because they couldn't always guarantee that more than one of their ships would be going to the same port at the same time, and they didn't want that to be the deciding factor in the contracts they accepted.

As Talia had noted, speed was the key to their business. If

they didn't maintain that competitive advantage, they would be out of business in short order.

"They all agreed that it was a good idea, but they noted that there would be times when moving in a convoy wouldn't make sense based on cargo or port of call."

"Did they offer any suggestions for solving the issue?"

"They did. They agreed to always have two ships sailing in the same direction whenever possible if a convoy didn't make sense. That shouldn't be a problem for us based on how the business is growing. Right now we're sending more than one ship to the same port more than half the time as it is, and that will only increase when the contracts with the spice guild and the lumber consortium are finalized later this month."

"Who made that suggestion?"

"Captain Aaronson. I'm assuming you're all right with it?"

"I am," replied Talia. She was already thinking that she needed to keep an eye on Captain Aaronson. If he continued to make suggestions like that, he could prove to be an even more valuable resource than he already was. And with their fleet expanding, she was thinking that she could rely on him to play a larger role when the time was right. "Are you?"

"By all means."

"You'll let the captains know?"

"I will." Isana nodded, glad to get that issue out of the way because there were several more that required their attention. "And how is progress on the wall going?"

"It should be complete by the end of the week."

"Excellent. That leads to three other matters that we need to discuss that have come to my attention because of what we're doing."

"What's the first?" asked Talia.

"Because so many sailors want to move onto our docks with their families, we've been approached by a woman who runs one of the schools in Ballinasloe. She can't afford her rent anymore. She wanted to discuss moving her school into our enclave."

"That's an intriguing thought," said Talia. Without giving it much consideration, the idea appealed to her. "When do we speak with her?"

"Tomorrow." Isana smiled, knowing that her daughter had seen the value of the proposal just as quickly as she did. "And we've been approached by a tavern owner as well."

"The rent is too expensive?"

"That's what she said."

"Let me guess. Governor Roosarian owns their buildings."

"Indeed she does. Shocking, isn't it?"

"When do we speak to the tavern owner?" asked Talia.

"Right after we talk with the maester," Isana replied. "And one more request. Arellia Hoohannen."

"Master Hari's sister?" asked Talia, not really surprised to hear that name.

"She would like to rebuild her blacksmith business on our docks, but she doesn't have the funds for the equipment, losing much of what she owned in the fire. She said that she would give us twenty five percent of the net revenue for three years if we funded her efforts to get back on her feet."

Talia smiled at that. The best blacksmith in the town wanting to work on their docks? Who wouldn't agree to that? "What did you tell her?"

"I told her we would do it at twenty percent for the first two years. With the quality of her work and her customer base, we'll recoup our expenses in the first six months."

"Arellia was all right with that?"

Isana laughed. "More than all right. Thrilled."

"When does she start?"

"Next week. I've got a crew scheduled to begin construction of the forge tomorrow."

Talia nodded, pleased by her mother's news. They had just

gained another advantage over Roosarian, and best of all Master Hari would be delighted. A happy master shipbuilder was exactly what she wanted considering all the challenges she was throwing his way.

"There's one other topic I wanted to raise with you?"

"What would that be?" asked Isana, looking closely at her daughter, hearing the tone in her voice that suggested that she might not like the topic Talia was about to raise.

"Many families in Ballinasloe and the surrounding villages have lost someone to the pirates," said Talia. "I think that we should start crewing our ships with those family members or at least give them the opportunity to work on our docks or in our shipyard. Have them become a part of our larger family."

Isana stared at her daughter for quite a long time. However, unlike when she was younger, Talia did not wilt under her mother's gaze. Instead, she stared right back at her with confidence, most of it real.

"I take it that some of these other family members are soldiers?" asked Isana.

"Unavoidably so," replied Talia. "You know that many of the settlers coming over from Caledonia used to serve in the Royal Guard or one of the Duchy Guards."

"And these individuals could then employ those skills for the benefit of our company?"

"If they so choose," replied Talia. "We certainly wouldn't force them. Although these men and women obviously would be a good place to start if we're going to include trained fighters on all of our ships and ensure that our company's enclave is well defended. There's no point in building a wall, after all, if we don't have anyone to guard it."

"You understand where this could take us, Talia, don't you?"

Talia nodded, knowing that her mother was referring to more than just their desire to better protect their sailors and their vessels.

"Rumors of who's leading the pirates are running rampant," said Talia. "You know that as well as I do. And if the rumors prove true, which I believe they will, then having a large number of people, many of whom are skilled in the use of a blade, wanting revenge against the cause of their family's misfortunes ... well, that's a powerful tool to be wielded. A necessary tool. If there ever proves to be a time that we need to challenge Roosarian openly, it would be good to have our own fighters at our backs."

"You've given this a great deal of thought, haven't you?"

"I have," Talia confirmed.

Isana nodded. "You've considered all the risks ..."

"As well as all of the rewards," finished Talia. "Exactly as you and father taught me to do."

"You still mean to take a more direct role in all this? Despite how the Governor might perceive it?"

"I do," Talia nodded.

"If there are soldiers on our ships, it would be a waste of their time and our money to just have them standing guard when the ship is in port."

"I agree," nodded Talia, smiling, knowing that she had won her mother over.

"We would want them doing what they do best while our ships were on the water."

"That we would."

Isana stared at her daughter for quite a long time, her gaze unwavering, as sharp as a hawk's, her strong nose actually giving her a passing resemblance.

Just like her mother, Talia was desperate for revenge. Their vessels were fast. Faster than any ship on the water. If they had a chance to go after the pirates themselves since Roosarian either didn't care or was in league with them, why not do it?

In the early days of Caledonia, privateers played a critical role in protecting the Kingdom's coast and allowing commerce to thrive. Why shouldn't the same approach be utilized here in the Territories regardless of whatever the Governor of Fal Carrach might want or say?

Roosarian cared about Roosarian. She had no interest in anyone who couldn't be of use to her.

Besides, everything that Talia and her mother were discussing and deciding was based on one guiding principle beyond that of building the Carlomin Trading Company.

To avenge her father.

Her thoughts shifted back to the topic that had consumed her in her father's office.

They would make those who murdered him pay. Stalkers may have been the ones to do the deed, but Talia found it hard to believe that they simply appeared there at the wrong time.

Someone put those monsters there. That someone needed to answer for their crimes.

She didn't know why she thought that. She had no proof beyond her father's suspicions. It was just a feeling, a belief, that refused to go away.

Just a hunch, really. But she had learned to trust her hunches.

She did know that if she was going to stop the pirates and get the proof she wanted, then she would need to employ some unique, possibly dangerous strategies. That was fine with her, so long as she had men and women trained to fight ready to put those strategies into practice.

"Just be careful," Isana said finally.

"I'm always careful," Talia replied.

Isana snorted at that. "I think we have different definitions of what being careful actually means."

18

HUNTED

"Do you see anything?"

"No, nothing yet," replied Declan, his expression grim as he searched for the tell-tale humps of the beasts that were pursuing them.

Declan and Rafia stood near the stern of the *Freedom*, their eyes sweeping across the rough swells that had been whipped up into a hard chop during the last few hours. The reason for that was quite obvious. Dark clouds that signaled a coming storm rushed toward them from the west.

They were in for a rough time of it, Declan knew, the waves likely doubling in height by the time the storm hit. His only hope was that perhaps the gale would allow them to escape whatever was tracking them from the east.

Of course, because of his predilection for the truth, he doubted that would be the case. He wasn't one to rely on what could be, instead preparing himself for the likelihood of what would be.

Battling a sea creature known for sinking vessels in the Burnt Ocean while caught in a tempest.

Declan grinned as he thought about that possibility. Life was one challenge after the next, but at least it wasn't boring.

He and Rafia had maintained their position ever since Lycia had reported what she had discovered upon returning on her Griffon. She had said that whatever was pursuing them had been no more than a league distant. Yet they had seen neither hide nor hair, and they should have by now.

Had the beasts slowed? Had they given up? Or was there a more concerning reason for why these monsters hadn't made their appearance?

In the meantime, Captain Gregson had called every hand to the main deck, getting his sailors into the rigging and working the sails. With the winds intensifying, Gregson was searching for any gusts that would give them just a little more speed. Even if just a knot or two. If it gave them a chance of staying ahead of the sea dragons, the Captain wanted it.

Despite his efforts, much like Declan, Gregson was realistic about their chances, understanding from experience that if the creatures behind them were intent on catching up to them, they would. With that depressing thought playing through his mind, he was thankful for his passengers.

His sailors stood little chance of fending off the monsters on their own. Perhaps with the Volkun and the Blood Company on board they would have better odds of staying afloat.

Although he refused to get his hopes up. Nothing as yet had proven effective at preventing a Bakunawa, much less three of the monsters, from taking a ship to the bottom.

"Will they attack from below?" asked Rafia, thinking much the same as Declan. The beasts should have been visible by now. Since they weren't, that suggested a cunning that she didn't really want to contemplate.

"Your guess is as good as mine. Although I really hope not. That would make this fight even more difficult than it likely already will be. There's little that we'll be able to do if they come at us from below."

"Always so positive?" wondered Rafia.

"No, always realistic."

"Yes, that does tend to be how you look at the world, isn't it? Always focusing on what is, not on what you want it to be."

"Exactly so."

"And you never seem to be too high or too low. Always on an even keel."

"Yes, I do prefer it that way," agreed Declan. "No reason to get excited if there's little cause for doing so."

"Have you always been this way? Stoic? Always under control? Often annoyingly so?"

"I can't recall a time that I wasn't," Declan replied, ignoring Rafia's dig, his eyes focused on a swell larger than all the others just a hundred yards off the starboard side.

For a moment, he thought that it might be what they were looking for. It turned out to be nothing, the water surging toward the ship and then crashing back down. It was just a much larger wave, this one at least twenty feet from trough to crest. Likely the first of many with the storm brewing not too far away and headed straight for them.

"Why is that?" asked Rafia, intensely curious.

"Why is what?"

"Why do you think that you're always calm, always matter of fact, never getting too worked up about anything?"

"I do get worked up about certain things, you've just never been around when it's happened."

"I'll believe that when I see it," said Rafia, her gaze suggesting that she really did want to have a look at what Declan was like when he lost his temper.

Breaking away from the Magus' distracting eyes, Declan considered the question for a time before finally answering.

"Probably because of my father. He was much the same way as I am."

"That certainly makes sense," nodded Rafia. With Declan more talkative than usual, her previous efforts to get him to reveal more about himself largely unsuccessful, she decided to take advantage of this brief moment in time when he seemed to be willing to speak more freely. "Who was your father?"

"Dennys Blackgard."

"Blackgard?" pondered Rafia. "Why is that name familiar?"

"It's a fairly common name," offered Declan, his eyes continuing to scan the ocean behind them.

He shook his head in irritation. He should have kept his mouth shut. But he hadn't, his thoughts on the yet to be seen Bakunawa. Instead, he had given a piece of himself away to the one person aboard this vessel who likely knew the significance of his name.

"No, it's not. Blackgard means something in the north. You're from Skaffa Falls and the Valley of the Dead," said Rafia, taking her eyes from the waves for just a flash so that she could gauge Declan's reaction when she offered him that piece of information. She wasn't surprised when his stoic expression didn't change, the Master of the Gladiators giving her no other response other than a barely visible nod, as if to congratulate her for figuring that out.

"I am," he replied.

"You were a Sentinel," exclaimed Rafia, shocked. In all her time as a Magus, she had never met a Sentinel before. They rarely, if ever, left their homeland. And for good reason.

Rafia knew the history well from her time studying at the Aeyrie. The Blackgards were an ancient family, the Lords of Skaffa Falls since the city in the cliffs was first built. Because of where they governed, they were the first to battle against the Ancient One, a creature of immense evil bent on conquering the world.

In fact, some of the texts that she had read while serving as the Keeper of Haven had insinuated that the Curse and all the evil in the various realms began with the Ancient One, but she had yet to find any evidence to support that theory. Of course, that didn't mean the theory wasn't correct. It just meant that she hadn't proven it yet.

Regardless, the Ancient One had conquered what was now named the Valley of the Dead, an island just off that desolate coast and linked to the mainland by an archipelago of smaller islands connected by bridges. From there, the Ancient One planned on invading all the other realms, only the Blackgards and their retainers in a position to stand in the monster's way.

The ruling Blackgard at the time -- Henry, if Rafia remembered correctly, as it was centuries since she had read the history -- had been put in the position of having to betray the early Sentinels, those men and women pledged to the cause of keeping the Ancient One from conquering all the lands of man. Henry didn't want to sell out those fighting with him.

Unfortunately, he didn't have much of a choice. The Ancient One had Henry's family in his grasp, believing that his hostages would force the first Lord of Skaffa Falls to allow him to get his Army of the Dead across the eight bridges connecting the island to the mainland before the Sentinels could mount an effective defense.

It didn't play out as the Ancient One wanted and expected. Despite the cost to his family, Henry refused to accede to the Ancient One's demands.

At the last second, Henry sprang the trap set for the Sentinels on the Ancient One instead. That gave the Sentinels the victory, but in the process Henry lost his wife and two of his sons to the deadly Skath, the disciples of the Ancient One.

After the battle was won, Henry, distraught at the deaths of his loved ones, confessed to what he had almost done, what in his mind was the ultimate betrayal of his fighting brothers and sisters. Rather than sentencing him to death or banishment for the almost betrayal, his comrades charged him and his surviving family with commanding the Sentinels in perpetuity, forever guarding the Valley of the Dead against the return of the Ancient One.

They couldn't fault Henry for what he had considered doing. They could honor him for having the courage to make such a sacrifice, placing the larger cause above those he so dearly loved and had lost.

Henry accepted the punishment willingly, the Blackgard family carrying that heavy responsibility ever since through the millennia. If the stories were accurate, and Rafia had no cause to distrust their validity, Henry never found a way to forgive himself for what happened, for repenting his sins despite all that he did to ensure that the Ancient One didn't escape the island and instead was imprisoned in the Spirit World.

The price Henry Blackgard paid to achieve that objective haunted him for the rest of his days. A tortured soul, to the say the least. But an honorable one.

Knowing what Declan had suffered through in the Royal Guard and then in Tintagel, much of that information provided by Bryen and unsurprisingly not Declan himself, it seemed like struggle, pain, and sacrifice ran in the family.

"I was a Sentinel, yes. Before I came to Caledonia."

"Why aren't you one now? What happened?"

Declan glanced at her quickly, her expression demonstrating a keen interest in his response. "You really have no trouble delving into a person's private life, do you?"

Rafia gave Declan a bright smile and nod, confirming her guilt. "No, I don't. It's the best way to learn about someone."

Declan could only shake his head in disbelief. "Some would call that prying."

"I would call it digging for useful information."

"Talking with you, Magus, can be quite taxing."

"You don't believe that, Declan," Rafia replied. "Otherwise you wouldn't be speaking with me at all. And you're using my formal title and saying that just to try to knock me off the scent. You do it every time you don't want to continue a conversation."

"As you say, Magus."

"As I know," challenged Rafia. "Declan, don't be more difficult than you usually are. I've been enjoying my time here with you. There's no reason for this to be any more of a struggle than it already is."

"As you wish, Magus."

"Declan ..."

Declan laughed. "Sorry, Rafia. I couldn't resist."

"You're getting to be just as bad as Bryen."

"I'll take that as a compliment."

"You would, wouldn't you?"

"I would, indeed."

"Enough of this, Declan," said Rafia, finally revealing a touch of exasperation. "You still haven't answered my questions. Why aren't you a Sentinel? What happened? I thought that once you became a Sentinel you are always a Sentinel."

"You are," confirmed Declan.

"Then how could you be ..."

"Rafia, if you give me a chance to answer, I'll tell you." His promise gained Declan the brief space that he needed to gather his thoughts, Rafia motioning with her hand for him to please hurry up and continue. He could tell that her curiosity was getting the better of her, so he waited just a bit longer than necessary before he started explaining. "You're right. Once a Sentinel always a Sentinel. In fact, I was bound by the Talent upon birth to serve as a Sentinel."

"Then how could you be here and not at the Valley of the Dead? A bond like that ..."

"The bond can be broken at the discretion of the Lord of Skaffa Falls," interrupted Declan right when Rafia figured out how it was possible to be released from such an obligation. "My father was the youngest brother. There was a falling out. What occurred isn't important. Because of what happened, my Uncle Gregor – he was the Lord Commander of the Sentinels then, I don't know if he's still alive – had a decision to make. Execute my father or exile him."

"That sounds like more than just a falling out," suggested Rafia.

"It was, you're right, but the details really aren't important."

"I disagree. The details usually are an integral part to any story."

"That may be, but you're going to need to learn to be disappointed," said Declan, ignoring Rafia's prodding. The Magus stuck her tongue out at him. Declan refused to acknowledge such childish behavior, as he kept to a barebones retelling of what had occurred. "My Uncle Gregor liked my father, so he chose exile."

"And your uncle didn't want you around either."

"No, my brother and I were exiled with him. I can't fault my uncle for what he did. He was concerned that the bad blood generated by what had happened would create more problems for him if my brother and I continued to serve as Sentinels."

"So the Magus who bonded you as a Sentinel undid that bond."

"Just so. My father, my brother, and I ended up in Caledonia after that. My brother and I joined the Royal Guard. My father was just getting his feet back under him when he died of the pneumonia he had caught on the voyage south but could never seem to get rid of."

"There is so much more that I want to ask you."

"I can tell. Don't get your hopes up," said Declan. "Be happy with what I shared with you."

"Why have you never told anyone any of this?" asked Rafia.

"The Blackgard name is well respected by those who pay attention to their history."

"There are many names that are well respected throughout history," countered Declan.

"Maybe so, but you didn't use the power of your name when you came to Caledonia, did you?"

"No, I didn't."

"If those in the Royal Guard had known, you could have been Captain eventually."

"Maybe. Keep in mind as well that my brother and I were former Sentinels. That's a rare thing, and it would have led to many questions that we didn't want to or couldn't answer. We didn't really want to draw any attention to that fact."

"Which explains why you didn't tell them," said Rafia.

"Yes, that and the fact that I never thought that my family name was relevant when I was serving in the army and certainly not in the Pit. Besides, when we got to Caledonia, my brother and I wanted to make our way on our own. The only names that matter are the ones that you earn. Not the ones that are given to you by birth."

Rafia pulled her eyes from the ship's wake, staring at Declan for almost a minute, lost in thought. Why wasn't she surprised? Most everyone else would have made use of a name like Blackgard, especially upon coming to a new Kingdom to start a new life.

But no, not Declan. He needed to earn his way. He needed to prove not so much to others but more to himself that he could make a new name for himself.

And he was well on his way to doing that until that incident in the Royal Guard involving that obnoxious lord as Bryen had told her. She had to give Declan credit. There was a certain way that he wanted to live his life, standards that he wanted to adhere to, and he certainly had done that despite the many obstacles placed in his path.

Then why did she feel as if she was only hearing part of a larger story? That was a question to mull when there was more time.

"Declan, you truly have a unique way of looking at the world," said Rafia, not knowing what else to say.

"I'll take that as a compliment."

"You should, yes."

Just then there was a shout from above them. Davin stood in the crow's nest atop the mizzenmast, flapping his arms to get their attention and yelling at the top of his lungs, although they had a difficult time hearing what he was saying because of the strength of the wind, those threatening storm clouds rushing toward them.

"He's not going to jump again and get dragged behind the ship, is he?" asked Rafia.

"The boy is a fool," growled Declan, "but no, I don't think so. Not with those beasts behind us."

"He's having a hard time adjusting to life outside of the Colosseum," said Rafia as she reached for the Talent so that she could search beyond the stern.

"Yes, and I can understand why," said Declan. "The Pit can do strange things to you."

"I can only imagine. Would you care to share?" asked Rafia.

"I think I've shared enough today," responded Declan.

"Probably so," agreed Rafia, her posture stiffening, her eyes tightening. "Another time perhaps. We've got a larger problem. Problems I should say."

Declan looked to where Rafia pointed just a few hundred yards behind them. Davin joined them just a few seconds later, having slid down a rope from the crow's nest to get to the deck as quickly as he could, sending a sailor to warn Captain Gregson as soon as his boots hit the deck.

"You see them?" Davin asked.

"They're hard to miss," said Declan. Three wakes larger

than the waves surging around them plowed through the ocean right behind them, those wakes growing bigger by the second, blue and silver scales along the monsters' backs glittering even in the deepening gloom caused by the oncoming storm.

"Truly impressive," said Bryen, who came to stand next to his friend, the Spear of the Magii in his hands. Aislinn's father had commissioned not only a very large ship, but also a very fast one. Even so, the beasts chasing them were closing the distance with a scary ease. "Bakunawa as Captain Gregson suspected?"

"Yes, unfortunately the Captain was correct," confirmed Declan.

They all realized right then that the sailor had reached the Captain because a controlled chaos erupted on the deck of the *Freedom*, sailors scrambling about in the rigging, preparing for the fight that they knew was coming. Only seconds later, the ship turned hard to starboard, seeking to milk another knot or two from the gusting wind and perhaps gain a little more space on the monsters.

But no such luck. With a gracefulness unexpected for such large creatures, the Bakunawa turned with the vessel. Because of that turn, Declan and the others were able to get a sense of their actual size. What they saw chilled their blood.

"So these Bakunawa are dragons, right?" asked Davin.

"Sea dragons," replied Rafia.

"I know they're bigger, but how do they compare to black dragons?" asked Davin. "Perhaps we can use our experience in the Trench to our advantage now."

"A good thought, lad," said Declan. "Keep in mind that fighting on land is a lot different than fighting on sea. Still, of all the lessons we learned there, I think it'd be fair to say that we have a chance if we maintain our discipline and focus. And as with the black dragons, try for their vulnerable parts. Their eyes, perhaps."

Davin wasn't convinced by Declan's suggestion, trying to figure out how he was supposed to get close enough to an eye when there was such a large, gaping maw filled with teeth half as long as he was tall to get past first.

"Having a few Magii on board won't hurt," Davin suggested.

"Yes, everything that Declan said will be important," said Rafia. "Just remember that distinct from the black dragons, in addition to being a whole lot bigger, they're also more aggressive, meaner, and faster. If one of those nasties is given the chance to climb onto this ship, it will flood us in a matter of minutes. We can't let that happen."

"Wonderful," murmured Bryen. "I never thought I'd face a beast worse than a black dragon." Bryen turned away from the stern, judging that they only had a few minutes before the Bakunawa would be upon them, one of the sea dragons having disappeared completely beneath the waves. "Declan, let's call the Blood Company to the stern deck and the side railings. You know what to do."

"That I do lad." Declan followed Bryen, shouting orders. The gladiators who had been waiting near the mainmast responded immediately, those not already on deck sprinting out of the hatches with weapons in hand.

Not one of the gladiators who made up the Blood Company knew how to sail. But they did know how to fight.

19

CAT AND MOUSE

Talia stood at the helm of the *Vengeance*, relishing the warm sun on her face and the rush of the chilled breeze blowing back her hair. It was a beautiful late afternoon, the temperature beginning to drop, the sun slowly sliding toward the coast and the western horizon. There wasn't a cloud in the sky, which was more than rare for the Sea of Mist, a fogbank usually somewhere off in the distance.

The three-masted frigate ran with the wind, tracking the coast north toward Ballinasloe. Just yesterday they had dropped a large shipment at the port town of Rosecrea, a special delivery for Governor Sakarin. Thanks to the unique design of the *Vengeance* and the excellent training given to her sailors, they were able to unload the armor and weapons and load the cargo -- spices, cotton, and silks -- for the return trip in less than four hours.

Talia was more than pleased. She was ecstatic.

Although she kept her pleasure well hidden. She wanted to present a particular image as one of the owners of Carlomin Trading Company and walking around the deck with a huge smile on her face like a giddy schoolgirl would be going against the persona she sought to display.

Still, she couldn't prevent a small smile from breaking out. No one else in the Territories or Caledonia could unload and then load a ship this size so swiftly. In the past, it would have taken a day or more to complete both tasks.

She'd have to congratulate Master Hari for this latest innovation of his. She had been skeptical at first, not believing that it could be done. But the master shipbuilder had proven her wrong, and she had learned something important along the way.

Design was critical to innovation, but that didn't mean all innovations needed to be new creations. Innovation could mean building upon or refining the old, such as just a few adjustments to a traditional process as had been the case for speeding up the loading and unloading of the *Vengeance*, and still the resulting changes, though not earth-shaking, could be quite powerful.

A bigger innovation was the *Vengeance* itself. This was one of their newest ships. Its maiden voyage in fact, its construction completed just a few weeks before in Ballinasloe.

Talia ran her hand along the smooth wood of the portside rail, loving the texture beneath her fingers. She could feel the strength and grace in the ship.

The cutter sliced beautifully through the sea, the ten-foot waves barely affecting her. Talia already knew that this ship was even faster than all the others sailing for her company. What for most other vessels would be a trip of two weeks from Ballinasloe to Rosecrea, the southern port located in the Benewyn Territory just around the eastern cape and touching the Endless Ocean, was going to take her a week at most.

A remarkable feat. Even more important, that meant even higher profits because of the bonuses she'd earn that were included in the contracts with the merchants making use of her services for this run.

"Captain Carlomin," called down the lookout in the crow's nest. Rather than describing what he saw, the sailor simply pointed toward the stern.

Talia turned and using the spyglass Master Hari had given to her as a gift located what had caught the lookout's attention. Three ships were sailing toward them from the southwest. Judging by their angle of pursuit, they hoped to cut off the *Vengeance* before she made port.

Talia wasn't overly concerned. She took her time studying the vessels, wanting to make sure that she was correct in what she saw.

She didn't recognize any of the ships. No flags. No markings. Except for the black sails. Just as she assumed would be the case.

Pirates.

A rapacious smile graced her usually serious countenance.

Good. Even better, it appeared that the timing would be exactly right.

Except for one key factor.

The *Vengeance* was too fast. If they continued to the north at their current speed, she would outpace her pursuers with ease.

Talia didn't want that. She had something else in mind than winning the race.

Nodding to herself, pleased that the strategy that she had discussed with her mother was coming into play, Talia turned toward the helmswoman, her eyes sparking with malice.

"You know what to do, Ariel."

The helmswoman nodded, then spun the wheel hard to port. The *Vengeance* curled through the waves and headed in closer to the coast, seeking one of the many small coves that dotted this section of the shoreline.

Let her pursuers think that she was trying to escape them, Talia thought. Let them believe that she was an easy target. That would only help her achieve the goal that she had in mind.

Talia nodded to herself once again, even more pleased now. The ships following turned sharply after her, maintaining their pursuit.

Good. The pirates chasing her probably thought that she was the mouse and they were the cats. They would learn their mistake fast enough, and not long after they came to that realization, they would regret their error in a way that they never thought possible.

Talia stood just beneath the helm, examining closely the fifteen pirates who strode across the plank connecting the *Vengeance* to the unnamed vessel that had chased them down.

With their mismatched coats and hats they looked like pirates, or at least what she assumed pirates should look like. Talia wasn't entirely sure, as she had never really come across a pirate until now. Each of the grim-faced men gripped a cutlass, a dagger or two also in their belts.

Their expressions were hard, serious. But not murderous. That didn't surprise her.

There was something off about these marauders. Talia couldn't put her finger on it right away. Anyone could look like a pirate if they wore the right clothes and carried the right weapons. And she acknowledged that these men certainly dressed the part.

But they didn't move like pirates. No, she assumed that pirates moved with a looseness that matched their temperament, their lack of discipline, and these men didn't have that.

These men were focused, and they walked on their toes as if

they were always ready for a fight. These men moved like soldiers.

It was just as she had suspected. Filing that knowledge away for later use, she was intensely curious as to how the next few minutes were going to play out.

The three ships had chased them into the small cove Ariel had sailed into at Talia's instruction. Two of the frigates remained near the entrance, dropping their anchors and blocking the way out. The third had come up alongside the *Vengeance*, the pirates tying the two ships together, several dozen more armed men waiting at the rails to jump across if their captain called for them.

Just a few sailors stood on the deck with Talia, so when the captain of the unflagged vessel ordered them to drop anchor and prepare to be boarded, Talia had acquiesced without a fight, making the captain and his men believe that she had taken the easy course, deciding that she had no choice but to surrender against such overwhelming odds.

"I'm Captain Blackbeard," said the large man, his imposing form towering over Talia. He wore his shirt open almost to his belt, a dozen or more chains of silver and gold around his neck. His black, three-pointed hat was pushed up off of his forehead. "A woman captains this ship? What fools would dare sail with a woman?"

Talia stared at the captain, almost allowing a smirk to crack her stern visage. She stopped herself just in time. She was finding it difficult to take her captor's appearance seriously.

He wore the clothes of a pirate, yes, though it appeared to her as if he had gone a bit overboard trying to get into the role that he was expected to play. Besides, the clothes couldn't hide his bearing. He wasn't that good an actor. He held himself like a soldier just like the men lined up behind him.

She did have to give him credit for the name that he had

selected. He did, indeed, have a very long beard, and it was black.

"What's your real name, Blackbeard?" asked Talia, finally releasing her smirk and earning several chuckles from her crew standing behind her. They seemed to be just as amused with the Captain's appearance as she was.

For just a second, Talia thought that the Captain actually was going to respond to her question honestly, his real name on the tip of his tongue. He caught himself just in time, however.

"Don't try to play with me, missy, unless we're going into your cabin to have a little fun. I don't have the patience for a girl trying to play at being a sailor. If you give me any problems at all, it'll be a watery grave for you."

Captain Blackbeard stared at Talia, expecting to see something other than what he saw now. She should have been afraid, terrified actually, worried for herself and her ship.

He didn't sense any of that. The woman continued to stare at him as if she didn't have a care in the world, more amused than anything else.

Did she not understand the dire nature of her circumstances?

Where was the fear that was so common when he captured a ship? Where were the tears that he had assumed he would observe as soon as this woman caught sight of him and his men? Where was the begging for him to spare her life?

Feeling distinctly uncomfortable because the scene wasn't playing out as it had so many times in the past, Captain Blackbeard decided that he needed to cow the woman standing before him so that he could get on with his work.

"You'll wipe that grin from your face this instant, little missy. I don't have the time or the patience for this. I was feeling beneficent today when I saw you coming up the coast, but no more. I rule the Sea of Mist, and my name strikes fear into the heart of every sailor who hears of me. You need to ..."

Talia quickly tuned out Captain Blackbeard's bluster. She wasn't in a rush. Even so, she really didn't feel the need to listen to this blowhard. The man certainly was full of himself, and clearly he was in his element as he tried to lord it over her.

"I'm sorry, what was that?" Talia asked, her thoughts having drifted as Captain Blackbeard's diatribe began to bore her.

"Were you not listening to me, little missy?" asked Captain Blackbeard, his tone revealing his incredulity. "Are you daft?" Who was this woman? Did she not know who he was? Did she not understand that he was in charge now? That he controlled her fate and that of her crew and ship? Not knowing what else to say, he repeated his question. "What's in the cargo?"

Talia responded immediately, not seeing the need to be any more difficult than she already was. Captain Blackbeard was playing a role. She needed to play her role as well if she wanted to gain the result that she had in mind.

"Spices, silks, and cotton."

Captain Blackbeard nodded. Maybe this woman was finally coming to her senses and beginning to understand the situation she found herself in, the shock of her capture finally wearing off. "How many more sailors are on board?"

"Just a handful belowdecks. No more than that."

Captain Blackbeard nodded again. This was more like it. This was what he was used to. "Where are you headed?"

"Ballinasloe."

"Then we'll be happy to lighten your load so you can get to Ballinasloe all the faster."

Captain Blackbeard's joke drew laughter from the pirates standing around him. Talia and her sailors just stared at him, failing to see the humor. His visage then scrunched up as if he was constipated when he heard what the woman asked him next.

"Are you sure you want to do that, Captain Blackbeard?"

"You must be daft, woman! You dare to challenge me?"

"I asked you whether you really wanted to do this," said Talia. "Once you go down this road, you can never go back. There's only one penalty for piracy, after all."

"Are you threatening me?" demanded Captain Blackbeard. "You can't be serious?"

Talia shook her head. "No, I just want to make sure you understand what you're doing. Because if you plan on going forward with what you have in mind, you're not going to like the consequences."

Captain Blackbeard stared at Talia for several seconds. Who was this woman? Was she right in the head?

He was beginning to think that his first take on this woman had been the correct one. Clearly, she didn't understand the severity of the situation in which she found herself. And if she did, which he found hard to believe, she didn't appear to care.

Just as he had thought to himself initially, there was no place on the high seas for a woman. They didn't know what they were doing. They belonged in the home.

Or better yet in the tavern if they were pretty. And he had to admit that this woman was quite pretty, if only she had a brain to go with her beauty.

What was he to make of her? On all the other ships he had taken, the captains and crews had been pissing their pants in fright, one captain even blubbering like a baby while he begged for his life.

Yet this woman wasn't frightened of him in the least. She actually seemed to be enjoying herself even though she was surrounded by armed men.

She appeared confident, almost as if she believed that she was in control of what was happening on deck. If he wasn't so put out by the woman he'd be impressed.

Maybe that's why she unsettled him so.

He shook his head in frustration. He didn't need this aggravation. He would deal with her just as he did all the others who had failed to obey him quickly enough.

"Listen here, little missy. This ship isn't yours anymore. It belongs to me now. If you don't like it, too bad. And if you can't seem to understand that and you don't start to behave, then I'll throw you overboard to the sharks. Do you understand what I'm telling you?"

Talia stared at Captain Blackbeard for quite a long time, her eyes hardening with each passing second. Clearly, she was less than impressed, and she was beginning to tire of this scene. Still, she stayed within her role, at least for the few minutes more that was necessary.

"Yes, Captain Blackbeard. As you command." She had to work hard to keep the scorn that she was feeling from coming out in her voice, struggling to add a hint of meekness to her words.

"That's better," he replied, hearing what he wanted to hear in her tone. "I'm glad you've come to your senses." Although he really didn't think that she had, in fact, come to realize the precarious nature of her current situation, he didn't know what else to do but carry on with what had worked for him in the past.

Captain Blackbeard nodded to his men, who moved without a word toward the hatches that led belowdecks in search of the sailors likely hiding from them. Once they found the rest of the crew, they would check and confirm the cargo.

The pirates doubted that they would need to transfer the cargo to their ship. They could tell that this vessel that they had taken likely would be going with them. It had sleek lines, and they had watched it cut through the Sea of Mist with an impressive agility.

Without having to say a word, the men were all thinking the same thing. This was too nice a ship to leave in the hands of a woman.

As the minutes passed, the pirates still below, Captain Blackbeard and the men waiting with him started to get restless. Taking this ship had begun just as all the other seizures had, but as soon as they had set foot on board the vessel, how things had played out had been anything but normal.

It was quiet. Too quiet. There were no shouts of indignation or screams of terror from beneath their feet, or even the occasional sound of steel striking steel because some sailor decided to be a brave fool, paying for that one brief moment of stupidity with his life.

No, there was nothing but a strange, unsettling silence that had settled over the ship, and that silence was making Captain Blackbeard distinctly uncomfortable. He tried to maintain a demeanor of authority, back straight, gaze focused on Talia and her sailors.

Yet as the silence continued, he began to lift himself up onto his toes, then back down to his heels. Then he moved from side to side, struggling to hide his increasing nervousness.

Thankfully, it wasn't much longer before he heard it. Finally. Footsteps on the stairs. His men must have found all the other sailors and were herding them back up to the deck.

Captain Blackbeard stumbled back in shock, almost falling to the deck, when dozens of sailors burst out of the holds and up through the hatches, not a word said by the men and women rushing out into the open. The pirates with Blackbeard were too astounded to do anything more than stare as they were quickly surrounded and relieved of their weapons.

The sailors who had been hiding below didn't stop there. Several squads scrambled across the railing and charged into the pirates who had backed away in confusion, blood visible on several of their cutlasses, confirming what Captain Blackbeard suspected had happened to the men he had sent below.

Taken by surprise and not expecting such a rapid assault, a quick, brutal fight erupted on the deck of his vessel.

He knew in an instant how it was going to end. The clash, short but sharp, was over in a matter of minutes, his men overwhelmed quickly by the sheer number of their skilled attackers.

Captain Blackbeard could only watch in disbelief as his few surviving men were rounded up quickly and imprisoned in the hold of their own vessel. Yet even as he had a difficult time making sense of what was happening around him, a small part of his mind continued to work normally, and it was this part that helped him to understand that he had just been played the fool.

The sailors who had just boarded his vessel weren't sailors. They were soldiers. Their movements were too precise and choreographed to be anything but.

Why would this woman be transporting soldiers? That was a question for another time. The situation had turned against him, and he needed to find a way to extricate himself and his crew.

So he turned to a tactic that had worked for him in the past. Bluster.

"I order you to release us now! This instant! If you don't, I'll feed every one of you to the sharks!" yelled Captain Blackbeard, the man already disarmed and his hands tied behind his back along with those of his men. "You don't stand a chance against my other ships!"

Blackbeard nodded to the two ships that continued to block the entrance to the small cove. Combined, he had enough men on both to give these soldiers who had just taken his own ship a good fight. They had experience in that area, after all. They all did.

Talia looked at Captain Blackbeard for several seconds, a trace of sympathy actually appearing on her face before it just as quickly disappeared. She shook her head in amusement. Then she stepped up close to the hulking Captain Blackbeard, completely at her ease even though she came up to no higher than the man's chest.

"You don't seem to understand, Captain Blackbeard. You thought you were trying to capture me?" Talia chuckled at that thought, the men with her who were guarding the Captain and the other pirates doing so as well. Captain Blackbeard clearly didn't understand what was happening, and that made Talia's men laugh even harder. "No, no, you don't seem to comprehend what is happening here. But you'll get it. You see, you weren't trying to capture me at all."

"What are you talking about?" demanded Captain Blackbeard. "I did capture you. You've only succeeded because of your miserable, cowardly deception, and that will only aid you for so long once the men on my other two ships realize what you've done. You and your crew can count the time you have left alive in minutes. That's a promise!"

"I'll speak in small words and slowly so you can understand," the venom in Talia's voice as potent as a viper's. "You were my target. We're here because I wanted to be here. We're here because I wanted to capture you. Because we need to have a conversation, you and me. You didn't capture me. I captured you."

Captain Blackbeard's eyes finally widened in fear as her words began to work their way through the confusion fogging his brain. He was about to start in again about how even with the number of sailors that this dreadful woman could command, there was no way she could take his other two vessels.

He never got the words out, his throat constricting, his rising shock and fear making it difficult to breathe.

Talia didn't even bother to look, needing to only gaze upon Captain Blackbeard's crestfallen expression to confirm that he was watching two ships that were the mirror images of the *Vengeance* streak through the entrance into the cove, their steel battering rams slicing through the water like a dagger through the chest.

Right on time.

~

"It won't be long now, boys," said Captain Redding. The small man with just a few strands of wispy hair hanging down from his almost completely bald head stood at the helm of the southernmost ship blocking the entrance to the cove.

"What's the take going to be, you think? The boys are getting antsy."

Captain Redding glanced briefly at Hedley with a greedy grin, the large man having served as his first mate since this entire scheme had been put in place more than a year before. The first mate was a good man. He knew the ship inside and out.

More importantly, he knew how to keep the men in line. The boys tended to get a bit rambunctious now and then, particularly when there were slim pickings.

He didn't think that Hedley would have to worry about that for a while as he stared across the sheltered bay at the sleek vessel Captain Blackbeard had lashed to his own.

Redding chuckled softly to himself. Blackbeard. The man thought the name inspired fear in all who heard it. Maybe it did when his sailors were at his back and they had taken a ship, but for him the only thing the man inspired when he saw his beard was the desire to laugh.

After all, he knew Blackbeard's real name. Engelbert. No one would be frightened by someone named George Engelbert.

Because of that, Captain Redding understood the need for a new name, but couldn't the man have been more creative? Why did he feel the need to name himself after his whiskers?

Redding shrugged his useless thoughts away, returning his

attention to the prize they had just taken. He had heard of the *Vengeance*. Another of the new ships built by the Carlomin Trading Company, and everyone knew how successful the Carlomin Trading Company had been since they had set up shop in Ballinasloe.

The family was smart. They focused on high-end products and had cornered the market for shipping luxury and high-margin goods. He and his crew could expect to earn a greater payout by taking just one of their vessels than they had in the past six months, during which time they had captured eight of the larger trading vessels owned by the other merchants doing business in the Sea of Mist.

Fifty percent of what they pulled out of their prize's hold would go to their benefactor. The remainder would be split equally among the pirates, and he, as the captain, would get ten shares compared to the one for each member of his crew.

Even better, if they decided to take the ship itself as a prize, which he fully believed that they would because it would aid them in their efforts to constrict the shipping along the eastern coast of New Caledonia, then they'd enjoy an even bigger haul that would exceed by a large margin what they had taken during all of the last year. So this particular seizure could prove to be a gold mine for all of them.

"It's going to be a big one, Hedley. Have no fear. The boys are going to be quite happy when we're done here. Quite happy, indeed."

"That's what I thought," nodded Hedley. He knew just as well as Captain Redding how momentous what they had just accomplished was. No one had succeeded in snaring a Carlomin vessel until now. Knowing that, they were all anxious to see what they'd find on board, stories of the riches carried by the Carlomin Trading Company circulating through every tavern in every port. "The boys will need a break after this. They haven't been ashore for more than a month. They're going to want to spend their take as soon as we're done here."

"Girls and ale," replied Captain Redding with a laugh. "Don't worry, Hedley. I'm just as interested as you and the men are in getting to a port where we can have some fun."

"The boys will appreciate that, Captain."

"I have no doubt of that, Hedley." Captain Redding squinted, trying to get a better look at what was happening on board the *Vengeance*. The ship was only a few hundred yards away, but everything he looked at was blurry.

His vision was getting worse, so he promised himself that part of his take today would go toward a pair of spectacles. They were expensive and rare in the Territories, but he knew someone who might be able to provide a pair down in Newry.

He could make out with a good bit of squinting that the gangplank had been removed and that Blackbeard's ship was now lashed firmly to the *Vengeance*. Yet there was little going on atop the main deck.

He had seen several fuzzy shapes go belowdecks, so he had assumed that Engelbert's crew was checking the hold so that they could see what the cargo might be. They had done this more than a dozen times, as had the men with them, so it was old hat to them now.

Yet as the minutes passed it seemed that Blackbeard and his men were taking far too long at what should have been a commonplace task for them.

Finally, Redding caught a flash of movement, blurry shapes rushing out of the hatches.

Wait. What was going on?

There were far more shapes coming up onto the *Vengeance's* deck than had gone below. Even with his bad vision, he realized that many of those shapes now were jumping across onto Engelbert's ship.

What was that fool of a Captain doing? The man spent more time grooming his beard than doing his job.

Captain Redding motioned toward the two ships that were fastened together. "Hedley, what the blazes is going on over ..."

He never got the rest of his words out, a massive crash knocking Captain Redding and Hedley to the deck as the ship heeled over, the far railing that they had fallen against almost touching the water before the ship righted itself again, though not without the sound of cracking and breaking timber. One mast crashed onto the deck, another broke right through it, ending its descent in the crew's quarters. With the masts came the sails, which fluttered down to cover the wreckage.

It took Redding and Hedley quite some time to get their bearings. When they finally regained their feet, both unstable after the hard knocks they had suffered, the captain and his first mate stumbled to the railing and looked over the side. Just below the waterline a steel battering ram had pierced the hull, a massive hole at least twenty feet wide allowing the water to rush in, his ship already beginning to list dangerously on that side.

Catching a quick flicker of motion on his other side, Captain Redding turned just in time to see another ship with a long, retractable ram, now fully extended, smash amidships into the vessel moored right next to his.

What in blazes was happening?

But he realized just as he thought it that he was asking himself a foolish question. Because even as his ship began to sink below the surface, dozens of blurry shapes were leaping across the bow onto his main deck.

As one of those blurry shapes ran toward him, a cutlass in his hand, he knew exactly what was happening.

He was being boarded.

Somehow the tables had been turned on them.

Captain Redding reached for the cutlass at his hip,

desperate to defend himself, a tremor of fear shooting through him when his hand came away empty. He realized too late that he had lost his steel during the crash.

Before he could retrieve his weapon, which lay only a few feet away from him against the side of the helm, he felt the first touch of cold steel slide through his chest.

He only had a moment to stare into the remorseless eyes of the soldier who had just killed him before his vision, failing him for quite some time, faded to darkness.

"How goes it, Sirena?"

Talia had returned to the helm of the *Vengeance*. Captain Blackbeard and the pirates who were still alive had been locked away in one of the smaller holds. She had never thought that she would be so lucky on her ship's maiden voyage, first in terms of actually finding some of the pirates, or rather the pirates finding them, and second, with respect to the success of the plan she and her crews had carried out to perfection.

The two pirate ships assigned to prevent her escape were sinking, one with its stern already below the water, the other listing so badly that she thought it was going to capsize before slipping beneath the waves. After taking off those pirates who had surrendered once they realized they didn't stand a chance against the very grim soldiers who had boarded their ships, her two vessels had pulled back, freeing their steel rams, which despite their quite effective use were still in excellent shape.

She and her mother had decided that they would not allow the pirates along the coast to dictate their decisions. With that in mind, they put in place a more aggressive strategy. One that might allow them to prove the validity of her late father's claims.

As a part of that strategy, they had sought to turn the tables on the pirates. And as had just been demonstrated, their tactics had worked exactly as they hoped they would.

Carlomin ships never sailed alone anymore. Because of the profits they were making off their now fifteen frigates, she had modified several cutters to serve as escorts and be ready to close the trap if they were lucky enough to find any pirates during their runs.

The *Resolve* and the *Reckoning*, which had just been outfitted with battering rams as well as several other improvements under Master Hari's close supervision, had sailed just at the edge of the horizon when they left Rosecrea, tracking the *Vengeance* and keeping an eye out for any ships foolish enough to pursue the vessel.

Much to Talia's delight, Captain Blackbeard and his compatriots had taken the bait. Hook, line, and sinker.

"Better than expected, Captain Carlomin," replied the Captain of the Carlomin Trading Company's Guard. "We suffered no deaths and just ten casualties that the physicks are already seeing to. For most just a few slices from a pirate who got lucky."

"And the pirates?"

"Fifty-two dead, twenty wounded," replied Sirena. "I expect three or four more to die from their wounds, but that's no great loss."

"I won't argue with that," nodded Talia. "And your thoughts on Captain Blackbeard's ship?"

"A couple sailors from the *Vengeance* went over to take a look. They say that the ship is well maintained. But as you saw during the chase, it's not fast enough to be a part of the Carlomin fleet."

"Can it be improved in any way?" asked Talia, thinking of Master Hari's unique expertise and how much he loved a challenge. They had no shortage of customers seeking their services, so another ship in the Carlomin fleet certainly wouldn't hurt.

"I don't believe so, though I would leave that determination to Master Hari."

"That's disappointing," murmured Talia.

"But, even if this ship doesn't meet Master Hari's standards, I was thinking we might still find a use for it."

Talia smiled, already knowing what Sirena had in mind. "Bait."

"Exactly so, Captain Carlomin."

"I like how your mind works, Sirena," Talia said, a smile breaking out on her stern visage. "You'll take care of things?"

"Yes, Captain Carlomin. I'll see to it. We'll refit the ship in Benewyn before bringing it up to Ballinasloe so that no one will be able to identify it."

"Perfect," said Talia. "And the infamous Captain Blackbeard? How is he faring?"

"Ranting from the hold that he's going to gain revenge upon us as soon as he escapes."

"A confident man," said Talia. "Perhaps we should test his resolve."

"A good idea, Captain Carlomin. Shall I bring him to you?"

Talia's smile turned feral, already having determined how to gain the information that she needed from the leader of this small pirate fleet.

"Yes, Sirena. Please do. And in chains. I want him to understand his position as soon as he steps out onto the deck."

"Do you want him handled gently, Captain Carlomin?"

"No, Sirena," Talia replied, her voice cold. "There's no need to be gentle with him. If he becomes a problem, deal with him as you see fit. Make him start to realize that he's no longer the captain of anything. Now, he's just a man who deserves a noose around his neck."

"With pleasure, Captain Carlomin."

Talia watched Sirena climb down the ladder from the helm and then stride across the deck toward the stern hatch, picking up several soldiers waiting to assist her along the way.

Sirena, a former soldier in the Royal Guard, had lost her husband to the pirates less than a year ago. Today's success would help her in some small way to deal with that loss.

Nevertheless, Talia knew from experience that this and any other victories against the men who had slaughtered innocents would never be enough. No matter how many pirate ships they took, no matter how many pirates they killed, it would never be enough. Because no matter what they did, their actions would never be able to bring back the people they loved.

All they could do was seek to gain some measure of revenge. To do that, they would cut away at the pirates one ship at a time. They would reduce their number until they were no longer a threat. And they would not stop until they had wiped the Sea of Mist clean of their corrosive presence.

That would have to be enough for now.

Even so, Talia wasn't just interested in the pirates themselves. She wanted to know who was backing them.

Because she believed in her father's theory, that someone with a great deal of power in the Territories was using the pirates as their own private navy, expanding their wealth and their reach at others' expense, not caring who was harmed, not caring who was killed.

Talia believed that she could confirm who that person might be with the help of the pirates, and she would start with Captain Blackbeard.

Because she had recognized him the second that he had stepped aboard the *Vengeance*. The last time she had seen him was right after her father's death, accompanying Hakea Roosarian when the Governor of Fal Carrach approached her once again with the goal of stealing her company out from under her.

20

INCREASING RESISTANCE

"You must be careful, my love. What was is not what is."

"I'm sorry, Ursina. What you just said sounds like something that a Magus would say. What does that mean exactly?"

"Speaking plainly, he does not trust you."

"Of course he trusts me," retorted Kendric, harrumphing at his wife's notion that his own brother didn't have any confidence or faith in him. "He wouldn't have given me the Northern Territory if he didn't trust me."

"Think about what you just said, my love," replied Ursina. "You said that he gave you the Northern Territory. You did not say that you had earned it." Ursina lifted her eyebrows, nodding slightly, her expression subtly challenging. "And we both know that what's given can be just as easily taken away."

"Yes, but there is no possible way that ..."

Before Kendric could continue with his protest, he felt the light touch of his wife's warm hand on his arm. In a flash, that warmth infused his entire body. He reveled in the sensation, even as that warmth began to infuse him with a drowsiness that both appealed to him and repelled him at the same time. His focus, which had been razor sharp just moments before, began to flit this way and that, making it almost impossible for him to concentrate.

"Perhaps he wasn't entirely truthful with you when he gave you the Northern Territory, my love," suggested Ursina, leaning in close to her husband so that she could whisper in his ear while still rubbing her hand on his arm. "Perhaps he gave you the Northern Territory because he didn't want you in Caledonia or perhaps you were just to begin the hard work needed to make this Territory what it could be and then step back beneath his shadow. Who knows the workings of your brother's mind other than your brother? We've talked of this before. It is a distinct possibility and would certainly explain a great many things."

"Yes, we have discussed it," he murmured, although his slightly confused expression suggested that maybe he really didn't recall those conversations. "I remember ..."

There was more that Kendric wanted to say, but he was finding it difficult to locate the right words. The clarity that he had been enjoying just a few minutes earlier had disappeared in an instant.

This had happened before, he knew. Many times. Too many times. And it was happening with increasing frequency.

He needed to talk with Ursina about this. It was the strangest thing, his mind fogging up like the dreaded mist that came down from the north with no warning and no good cause. It seemed to be similar to a concussion, this inability to think, remembering when he had been training with Kevan in the practice yard, a hard whack to his head sending Kendric to the ground in a daze.

He hadn't been able to think straight for days. Similar, yes, but not the same. What he was experiencing now wasn't the result of a whack on the head.

Kendric shook his head in frustration, his brief memory of

being with his brother slipping from his grasp. Ursina had some skill as a healer. Perhaps she could aid him with this.

Had she tried to help with respect to this ailment? He could never remember whether he had requested her assistance in the past.

"Perhaps what your brother said isn't what he really meant, my love. Perhaps he sent you here to Shadow's Reach so that he wouldn't have to worry about you anymore."

"Why would he have to worry about me?" Kendric wondered, barely able to get the question out before the fog crept back up on him, clouding his thoughts once again.

Pieces of his past began to flicker through the mist, his mind retrieving various memories of his time growing up with his older brother. Kevan teaching him how to ride the waves along the beach near Battersea all the way to the shore. Kevan teaching him how to sail, the two of them braving the Silent Sea against the wishes of their parents. Kevan sparring with him in the practice ring and usually getting the better of him. He and Kevan traveling through the Duchy so that they would better understand the needs of the people who looked to them for their protection and success.

He loved his older brother, and he knew that Kevan loved him. Kendric did feel just a bit jealous, as if he resided in Kevan's shadow. Thus, his decision to travel to the Territories when the opportunity was presented to him.

But wasn't that only natural after all? His brother was the firstborn and Duke of the Southern Marches.

There was nothing wrong with Kendric deciding to come to the Territories. It had been his own decision. And it was to be expected, wasn't it? He was ambitious after all, and there was only so much that he could expect if he had stayed in the Southern Marches.

Better that he make his way somewhere else. Both he and

Kevan had agreed on that. Yet then why did it seem to bother him more now than it did when he was in Caledonia?

He had been looking forward to coming to Shadow's Reach. To assuming responsibility for the Northern Territory. Hadn't he?

Those were the other questions that he wanted to ask Ursina. Perhaps she could help him better understand these feelings. How thoughts of his brother were taking him down a darker path. Then just as quickly as Kendric decided that he needed to raise these issues with his wife, the thoughts faded away into the mist that billowed around in his mind like the Murk that draped itself around Shadow's Reach like a widow's shawl.

"Because he knows what you can do, my love," replied Ursina, continuing to slowly rub his arm with her hand, comforting him, then moving it to his chest, earning a sigh of pleasure from her husband for her efforts. "He knows that you possess certain qualities that he does not. He worries about that. About you. It's the only explanation that makes sense."

She stepped even closer to him, leaning in and kissing him lightly on the lips. Her eyes caught his own. Then she kissed him softly again, staying with him longer.

His wife truly was a beautiful woman, Kendric thought. Also intelligent. Fun. Competent, dangerously so at times. Always looking out for him.

He still couldn't believe his luck, never thinking that he would find someone to love like her. Yet as soon as he had seen her, their eyes locking when she came to introduce herself in the framework of the Shadow Keep, he knew that she would be his and he would be hers.

Within days they had been married, and since then she had joined him as a partner in his quest to make the Northern Territory into what he dreamed it could be. A Duchy just like any other in Caledonia. And perhaps something more.

Kendric contemplated his good fortune every day, made even more aware of what she offered to him as his partner when he thought of Ursina's knack for solving problems. A critical skill, since the only thing more common in the Northern Territory besides the steady influx of settlers from across the Burnt Ocean was problems.

Ursina had proven to be incredibly skilled at addressing several of the challenges that frustrated him as Governor of Shadow's Reach and the surrounding lands.

Farmers unhappy because of the taxes charged on the sale of their produce and goods in the markets of the city? Ursina dealt with the matter expeditiously. He hadn't received a complaint since. In fact, the farmers had agreed to a slight increase in the tax in order to continue to peddle their products and wares within the city walls.

Miners in the Northern Peaks unhappy because their terms of service were extended unilaterally beyond their original commitment based on the need of the Territory? Ursina took care of the issue in just a few days. Not a word from the miners since.

Some of the tradespeople and merchants in Shadow's Reach seeking to form a council to petition for changes in how the Governor oversaw business in the Territory, arguing that Kendric exercised too much influence? Ursina convinced them that there was no need to follow through on their proposal. Not even a whisper since then.

Complaints by the traders that the roads weren't safe enough, bandits and monsters lurking not too far away from Shadow's Reach? Ursina removed their fears in just a single conversation.

He really didn't know what he would have done without his wife. Ursina had taken every task he had given to her with a will, leaving him with the time that he needed to focus on the most important project that needed to be completed in the

Territory's capital. Building the citadel of Shadow's Reach, what would be a testament to his power and a reminder to all, both in New Caledonia and on the other side of the Burnt Ocean, of who ruled the Northern Territory.

The Shadow Keep, the center of what would be a much larger castle, was well on its way to completion. All the towers were finished, two of the four walls almost done, the other two starting to rise. Construction had just begun on the open dome that would serve as the roof, the hole in the center to be closed with stained glass ordered from a well-known artisan in Ironhill.

"But he's my brother," protested Kendric. "Kevan has nothing to fear from me. He knows that, or at least he should. We grew up together. We were always looking out for one another. He knew quite well that I wanted to come here. We discussed it many times. That's why he purchased the grant, at my request. We both agreed that it was the right thing to do. He wasn't trying to get rid of me. He was trying to help me."

Ursina nodded in understanding, her eyes tinged with purple still holding her husband's as her gaze narrowed. Usually, at times like these, when they discussed important matters, he had trouble tracking the conversation, having no choice but to leave the important decisions to her, so her husband's brief moment of lucidity was unexpected.

"That may be, my love. Perhaps I was wrong. Perhaps it's not your brother who fears you. Who fears what you've accomplished. Who fears what you will accomplish."

"Exactly," agreed Kendric, his confusion slowly returning once again. "Wait, what do you mean by that?"

"I'm simply suggesting that perhaps it's not your brother who's afraid of what you might do here in the Northern Territory," shrugged Ursina, as if the matter was of little import. "Perhaps it's your niece who's afraid."

"Aislinn?"

"Yes, Aislinn. Perhaps she fears you."

"Why would she fear me? I'm her uncle. I'm not even in Caledonia, and I have no plans of returning there. She'll follow her father and rule the Southern Marches."

Ursina stepped in close to Kendric once again, rubbing her hand against his chest gently, soothingly, then moving her motions slowly to his abdomen, pulling his eyes to hers in the process. Kendric lost himself in Ursina's gaze, his thoughts beginning to wander once again.

"Because of your work here in the Northern Territory, my love. It is quite obvious, is it not?"

"Quite obvious? What is quite obvious?"

"Your love for your niece does you credit. Nevertheless, we must put that aside for now. I know you see it, my love. You are just too good a person to actually say it."

"Well of course I see it," said Kendric, although his bewildered air suggested that maybe he didn't.

"I knew you did," said Ursina. "You just care for your niece a little too much. You know just as well as I do that there is really only one reason for Aislinn to come here."

"Only one reason?" asked Kendric. "Yes, it's just as my brother said. She is coming here to see the Northern Territory since he can't. That's what makes the most sense. For her to see all that we've accomplished here."

"And to confirm with her own eyes whether she needs to view you as a threat." Ursina shook her head sadly. "I'm sorry, my love. Your niece is coming here to check up on you. You know it just as well as I do. As I said, you're just too good a person to say it."

"Why would Aislinn view me as a threat? I've done nothing but focus my attention on Shadow's Reach. On making the Northern Territory a Duchy in its own right. Something comparable to the Southern Reaches. That's what I told Kevan I was going to do and that's what we're doing."

"Exactly so," nodded Ursina. "You just confirmed my suspicions with your own words. You see it, don't you?"

"Yes, but do we really think that ..."

"She will worry about what you have done here, my love. The success that we have had. She will worry that you will eclipse her in the eyes of her father."

"Why would she worry ..."

"She will worry that you would take what you have done here and bring it back with you to the Southern Marches."

"But I have no desire to return to the Southern Marches. This is my home now. Our home. I ..."

"All that you say is true, my love. Still, it won't matter to her. She is your brother's daughter, raised by him, raised by the Duke. She will look at you, at what you have accomplished, and view you as a threat to her interests."

"I appreciate your concern, Ursina, I really just don't ..."

"Your concern for your niece does you credit, my love," interrupted Ursina. "But as you told me just the other day, we must put that aside. We must forget for a moment that she is family. We must focus on what's best for us, my love. We must be ready for when your niece arrives. We must ensure that she cannot do anything to prevent us from achieving the goals that we have set for ourselves. For the Territory."

What Ursina left unsaid was the thought that perhaps Aislinn Winborne might not make it to Shadow's Reach at all, though better to keep that possibility to herself, as she wanted to avoid agitating her husband even more than he already was. He was in a fragile state right now, and she didn't fancy making their current conversation more difficult.

The thought of Aislinn not making it across the sea did give Ursina a few ideas that might be of use if there proved to be a need. Crossing the treacherous and unpredictable Burnt Ocean could be exceedingly dangerous. Many ships were never seen again, and the number of ships disappearing was increasing every month because of a fog much like the one that drifted down from the north becoming a more common occurrence in the southern quadrant of that expansive sea.

Yet there was no certainty in relying on something that she couldn't control. She craved that above all else. Certainty.

At the moment the only thing certain was that if Aislinn reached Ballinasloe despite the dangers of the Burnt Ocean, it was a long way from Fal Carrach to Shadow's Reach. And as everyone who had crossed the Burnt Ocean and made port had come to learn, unexpected threats abounded in the wilds of New Caledonia. Hazards that sometimes couldn't be avoided, if they were managed the right way.

"Of course, my love," sighed Kendric, seemingly having tired of the struggle to compose his own thoughts. "I agree with you entirely."

"I know you do, Kendric," replied Ursina with a satisfied smile. "That's why we must move faster. Much faster."

"As always, you're right. I agree wholeheartedly, Ursina."

"Good. I knew that you would, my love. I will see what I can do to speed things along. If we do this the right way, your niece appearing in Shadow's Reach will have little impact upon us. It might even give us some opportunities."

Kendric nodded, not really listening to Ursina, stuck within the fog clouding his mind. Every time he thought he had found a way to break free from his confusion, the grey mist smothered him once again, cutting off any moment of fleeting clarity that he had enjoyed.

"Could you remind me of what those next steps will be, my love?" asked Kendric, wanting to understand, angry with himself that he couldn't, fearing that his wife would look poorly on him for not recalling what they had already discussed.

"Oh, my love," chuckled Ursina, "that sense of humor of yours that first attracted me to you remains as sharp as ever."

She reached up again, pulling Kendric's lips down to hers

for a lingering soft kiss. When she let him go, her eyes sparkled in delight. She still couldn't believe how easy it had been. Then again, she should have assumed as much. Playing off of someone's desires always made it so much easier to attain what she wanted.

"As you explained, my love," began Ursina, "we shall create more than just a Duchy here in New Caledonia. We will build a Kingdom of our own. To make that happen we will need to put in play some tactics that we might not like but are absolutely essential to our success."

"Are you sure that's what we discussed, Ursina?" asked Kendric, having difficulty recalling any of that. "A Kingdom?"

"We did, Kendric." Her voice had taken on a hint of exasperation, tiring of her husband's struggles and frequent interruptions, though if she was honest with herself her frustration wasn't with her husband. Rather, it was with herself for not being more thorough in her work. She would correct those mistakes when she had time. "Your loyalty to your brother is admirable. Unfortunately, we can't allow that to get in the way of what we must do, particularly with your niece on the way here."

"I understand, Ursina. You're right. I'm sorry. I just forgot."

"I am right, Kendric. Remember that." Her eyes blazed more brightly now, her gaze harder, as if she was close to losing patience with her husband. As if her true self was about to emerge. "We must think of ourselves now. We can't allow the gains that we have made to be taken from us. I know that you want to do right by your brother, but we must remember that your brother is an ocean away. There is nothing that he can do for us from there. There is nothing that he would want to do for us. We must do what is necessary on our own. We must make sure that your brother and your niece understand that the Northern Territory, that New Caledonia, is ours. It will always be ours."

"Of course, Ursina. We will do just as you say. Have no fear of that."

"I fear nothing, my love," replied Ursina sweetly, having regained control of her emotions, "other than losing you."

"That is a wasted fear, Ursina. You know that I will always be with you. I will always be at your side."

"I know, my love. Still, I worry, what with all these other challenges that we face that are not of our own making. I fear that they will take you away from me, even if only briefly."

"What new challenges are these?" asked Kendric, concern lacing his voice.

"Our friends are attempting to deal with some unanticipated issues, and from what I can tell they're not dealing with them very well."

"What issues are these?" wondered Kendric. "Beyond that of the fog that encroaches from the north?"

"Yes, unfortunately our partners are not as skilled as we are at ensuring that potential problems are addressed before they become real problems," said Ursina. "The one who views herself as the Queen of the Seas is struggling to build the fleet that she needs to actually take the name as her own and extend her power to the south. The one who fancies himself the Lord of the Mountains is not finding the going easy, as he seems to have alienated a good number of his people. His progress is much slower than any of us would prefer."

"They need our assistance?" asked Kendric, although his words grew softer with each one he spoke. That warmth that he had felt at Ursina's touch was slowly building within him. He was getting tired again, as if he had worked a full day, yet judging by the play of the shadows across the floor of the room, it wasn't yet noon.

"They may," replied Ursina. "They may not. I will continue to monitor their situations. If there is a need for us to take action, we can discuss what that action might be."

"Thank you, Ursina. You make my life so much easier."

"That is why I'm here, my love," she replied with a broad smile, although the smile came from her thoughts of how she could wrest the Territories from their two apparently incompetent partners and claim those provinces as their own. Doing that would give them control over most of the eastern coast of New Caledonia. From there, taking the rest of the continent would be much easier. "Although there is one more issue that we need to discuss before I leave you for a few hours."

"Another problem?" growled Kendric, his irritation plain. "It seems that's all that we deal with these days."

Ursina ignored her husband's pouting, knowing that it would work in her favor during the next few minutes.

"We received a letter on the last ship across the Burnt Ocean, my love," Ursina began to explain, "the letter arriving late because the ship required some repairs at Roo's Nest before making the journey."

"A letter from whom? My brother?"

"No, my love. From Marden Beleron. He sent it to you since you are the head of the King's Council in New Caledonia."

"What did he want?"

"Nothing to worry us now, my love, though perhaps in the future."

"What do you mean, Ursina?"

Ursina waved the letter in front of her husband, although she made no move to give it to him. "Marden was rethinking his approach to New Caledonia."

"How so?"

"In his correspondence he requests that you work with the Governors to make certain changes to the charters that were given to you and the others by his father, Corinthus Beleron. Let me rephrase. He doesn't request. He orders."

"What kind of changes?" asked Kendric softly, his voice a mix of worry, fear, and anger.

"The kind of changes that greatly narrow some of the privileges and powers you and the other Governors currently enjoy. The kind of changes that make New Caledonia nothing more than new provinces to Old Caledonia. The kind of changes that give Marden supremacy here as well as across the sea."

"He can't do that!" protested Kendric. "He can't change something that his father did."

"He can," replied Ursina. "It's within the authority of the Caledonian monarch to do just that. In fact, it's within the authority of any monarch to do pretty much whatever the monarch wants to do."

"I know that," he replied testily. "I'm well aware of what a king can do. I'm saying he can't do that because he's dead. The Volkun killed him."

"Quite right, my love," nodded Ursina, knowing that this was exactly the right time to plant the seed. The seed that would help take her husband down the road that would give them both what they truly wanted. "I'm saying that the Caledonian monarch can do whatever he or she likes with the Territories. And I wouldn't be surprised if the person who takes Marden's place entertains a similar view of the Territories as he did." Ursina shrugged, as if to say that there was really nothing that they could do. "We won't know what might happen until a new monarch assumes the throne. Though, of course, that might be delayed what with the Ghoules still a threat."

"Right, sorry, I let my temper get the better of me." Kendric shook his head in frustration. He had come to New Caledonia because of the rights granted to him in the charter his brother purchased for him. They couldn't let those rights be taken away. "You're right, of course, Ursina. But what can we do about it? I am not a King. I am a Governor. Perhaps we will achieve what we want, but I will always be answerable to a King or a Queen of Caledonia, even if that ruler is a thousand leagues distant."

"We do what we've been doing," said Ursina. "We just do it faster, so that if at some point in the coming months we get another edict from whomever assumes the Caledonian throne it won't matter."

"Why wouldn't it matter if ..."

"Because in new lands, my love, kings and queens often are not born. They are made. Just as we are making a new Duchy. So perhaps we need to broaden our perspective and our goals. Perhaps here, in New Caledonia, we need to think about what we can do to ensure that if ever another edict comes from Caledonia, it will mean nothing to us because by then no one will be able to take anything away from us. We will have made New Caledonia and ourselves into something more. We will answer to no one but ourselves."

Kendric stared at his wife for several seconds, appearing slightly confused until everything that his wife had just suggested finally became clear to him. Beautiful, intelligent, and clever. That was the best way to describe his wife. What would he do without her?

"To think of all that we have had to deal with today. When we began, I thought there was only one issue that required our attention."

"What issue would that be, my love?" asked Ursina, feeling the need to bring their conversation to a close. There was much that she needed to do, and she had taken longer with Kendric than she had intended, so she walked a few steps toward the door.

"Work on the Shadow Keep has slowed," said Kendric, suddenly gaining one of those brief moments of coherence that were becoming fewer and farther between. He planned to make the most of it. "The foreman came to see me early this morning. He's having a difficult time getting the stonemasons to go down into the tunnels we excavated and finish the work on the foundation so that we can ensure the fortress itself can maintain the weight of the dome."

"Why are they balking at doing the work, my love?" asked Ursina, her interest piqued.

"They claim that they're hearing growls and hisses. Seeing spirits. Shadowy shapes in the dark staring at them. Then when they search for what they thought they saw, there's nothing to be seen. Can you believe that?"

"It sounds to me like they're just trying to get out of doing the work required of them."

"That was my feeling as well, Ursina. I will deal with it. You have enough to manage as it is."

Ursina returned to her husband, gliding across the floor seductively. She touched his cheek warmly with her hand, her eyes with those hints of irresistible purple never failing to capture Kendric's attention. However, for just a flash, Kendric thought he glimpsed Ursina's eyes turn completely black in color, even the scleras.

He shrugged it off. He had to have been mistaken, because all he saw right now were those wonderful streaks of violet.

"Leave it to me, my love. I will manage it." Ursina turned away again, heading for the door, Kendric watching her go, his moment of clarity gone, replaced by the fog that frustrated him so much. "I will see you in a few hours," she called over her shoulder. "By then, I'm certain the stonemasons will be back at work."

As Ursina stalked down the completed hallways of the Shadow Keep, her anger radiated off her. She and her husband had much to oversee. This latest irritation, although it didn't compare to their other challenges in terms of scope, infuriated her because it was simply one more thing that she needed to address.

Yet once she began making her way down the circular stairs to the floors beneath the fortress, taking the time to think about it a bit more, her anger fizzled out as she realized that this problem actually was an opportunity that might help her deal with some of the other issues currently plaguing her and Kendric's efforts to make the Northern Territory more than just a province of Caledonia.

"Why are the stonemasons balking?" demanded Ursina. She stopped right behind the foreman, forcing him to turn, the three men he had been conversing with now standing behind him.

"They can tell you for themselves, Lady Winborne," said Gower. "These three speak for the others."

Ursina turned her sharp gaze onto the three men, her eyes flashing dangerously. All of the stonemasons, broad at the shoulder and muscular due to the nature of their work, actually took a step back then. They wouldn't admit it openly, but this woman frightened them. The fear was instinctual. It was as if she was the lion and they the lambs.

"You don't want to do the work?" demanded Ursina, her voice soft and cold, sending a shiver through Gower and the other three men. "You are being paid well. There is no good cause for this delay."

"It's not that we don't want to do the work," said the stonemason standing closest to Gower, the man apparently the spokesman for the group. "It's that the men are afraid. There's something down here that shouldn't be."

Ursina laughed at that, although the sound wasn't one of humor. "You are all large men. You have little to fear down here."

The stonemason ignored Ursina's taunt. "We thought so as well, my Lady. We've never had to deal with this on jobs before."

"Deal with what?" asked Ursina. "Unexplained noises? Sightings of spirits? That's all quite ridiculous."

"If that were only the half of it," said the stonemason.

"There's something terrible down here, my Lady, I tell you truly. We've all seen it. Large. Hides in the shadows. Growls. No one will go much farther beyond this room now. It's like it's stalking us, but why it hasn't attacked yet none of us know."

"How do you know that it's real? How do you know it's not just something made of your imagination?"

"The eyes, my Lady. We've all seen the eyes staring at us out of the darkness. Blood-red eyes."

Ursina stared at the man for quite some time. Now she was glad that Kendric had brought this issue to her attention. Because this wasn't a problem as she suspected originally. Instead, this indeed was an opportunity. One that would allow her to address several other problems all at the same time.

"There is nothing down here that you need fear," said Ursina. "But I do understand your concerns. So I will try to help you."

Ursina raised her right hand, a mist of dark black spinning out of her palm. Rather than being afraid, Gower and the three stonemasons were transfixed, unable to look away as the wispy threads started to spin faster, the pulsing black beginning to reach out toward them.

"When I'm done with you," said Ursina, "you will fear nothing at all and everyone will fear you. I promise you that."

21

LOCKING UP

"How long do you think it will be this time?" asked Tommie, the archer actually wearing her spectacles as she stood at the very edge of the parapet, watching as the Murk crept in from the north, the massive wall of greyish white blocking out the sun as it swept down over the mountains to consume them once again.

"Does it matter?" muttered Duff. He tended to be in a good mood, although never at this very moment. Not when he was about to lock himself away from the world for however long it proved necessary. "It's always too long."

"Better alive than dead," murmured Tommie, pushing away from the wall that reached chest-high on her petite frame and surrounded the top of the broch. She headed toward the trap door that led down into the tower.

"True," Duff admitted softly, "although this isn't how I want to live."

He hated this. Running away. Hiding.

Every time the fog came. Every time the Wraiths came.

The hazy tendrils were reaching for them rapidly, already beginning to touch the green that surrounded the broch.

The hunters were anxious this time.

Duff already could see a few hazy shapes right at the edge of the fog.

Tall. Thin. Hungry.

"Are you coming, Duff?" asked Tommie.

Duff waited until the fog began to crawl up the sides of the tower before turning away and making for the entrance to the redoubt. When he saw the first faint wisp curl around the top of the wall, he stepped inside and pulled the trap door closed behind him, locking it.

He was safe. His people were safe.

That's what mattered.

But if that was the case, then why was he so angry?

They were safe so long as they hid from the Wraiths.

They were safe so long as they gave up their homes and their lands to the monsters in the mist.

He hated that. He hated the position that he and the other Highlanders found themselves in.

Not even able to stand against the Wraiths. Not even able to fight for themselves.

He needed to find a solution to this challenge.

He needed to figure out some way for the Highlanders to not have to cower in their brochs when the fog drifted down from the north.

He needed to find some way to fight the Wraiths in the Murk.

THE END OF BOOK I.

I HOPE you enjoyed Book I of *The Tales of the Territories*. Keep reading for the first three chapters of Book 2, *Monsters in the Mist*.

BONUS MATERIAL

If you really enjoyed this story, I need you to do me a HUGE favor – please follow me on Amazon and BookBub. And if you have a few minutes, consider writing a review.

Keep reading for the first three chapters of *Monsters in the Mist,* Book 2 of my series *The Tales of the Territories.* Order Book 2 on Amazon or from my author website PeterWachtBooks.com.

PETER WACHT

MONSTERS IN THE MIST

THE TALES OF THE TERRITORIES
2

Monsters in the Mist
By Peter Wacht

Book 2 of The Tales of the Territories

This book is a work of fiction. Names, characters, places, and incidents are the product of the author's imagination or are used fictitiously. Any resemblance to actual events, locales, or persons, living or dead, is coincidental.

Cover design by Ebooklaunch.com

Published in the United States by Kestrel Media Group LLC.
    ISBN: 978-1-950236-34-3
    eBook ISBN: 978-1-950236-35-0
    Library of Congress Control Number: 2023903641

1. A FORTUITOUS MEETING

The small fire crackled softly, the ragged flames doing just enough to warm him on a chilly night. He had selected this spot with care, having used several similar locations much like this one during his travels through the Highlands.

A small notch in the mountain that gave him a view of the peaks to the east. It guaranteed him a beautiful view when the sun rose in the morning.

Just as important, the boulders and trees at his back helped to shield his fire from any prying eyes.

Although apparently not as well as he would have liked this evening.

He remained sitting -- calm, confident -- despite the movement he detected in the darkness. They were trying to be quiet. They probably believed that they were doing a good job of sneaking up on him. But they weren't as skilled at skulking through the night as they thought they were.

Rusty most likely. Probably a bit complacent as well.

He could use that against them when the opportunity presented itself.

He didn't know who they were, but he could guess.

He had to give them credit though. They were taking their time and demonstrating a surprising caution for just a single target.

Probably because they didn't know what to make of him. Hence their unease.

Good. He could use that as well when the time came.

The hardest part now was the waiting, and that's what began to gnaw at him. He took a few deep breaths to calm himself.

He wasn't going anywhere, so there was no point in feeling anxious. To calm his nerves, he worked out in his mind how he believed the next few minutes were going to play out.

He was prepared for what he anticipated would happen. He had placed his sword against the cracked stump so that the hilt rested right next to his hand.

And a small part of him was actually looking forward to it.

It had been an uneventful journey through the Highlands since he had exited the portal right in front of the Crag, having no cause to think of using his steel.

Until now, of course.

He had made it with little trouble into the northwest of the Territory. Probably no more than ten leagues away from the Northern Steppes now. Once he reached the grassland, it would be just a few more days until he came upon the Northern Peaks. From there, just a few days more to Shadow's Reach.

He hoped that Aislinn, Bryen, Declan, and the rest of the Blood Company were doing well aboard the *Freedom*. That it wouldn't take them too long to complete the passage across the Burnt Ocean and join him. Having been in the Highlands for only a short time, there was already a great deal that he needed to relay to them.

Although he missed his friends, he had been enjoying his travels through the snow-capped spires. He stopped in every village he came across, almost every single one of them centered around a broch that had been built or was well on its way to being completed.

After talking with so many of the Highlanders struggling to make their way in this rugged land, he could understand the need for such fortifications. Why the towers were so essential to their survival.

He hadn't yet come up against the many perils threatening the people living among these peaks. Although he had a feeling that was about to change.

Only a few more minutes passed before a stout fellow with a large axe in his hand and the hilt of a sword peeking above his shoulder ambled out of the darkness, seemingly without a care in the world. The visitor stopped on the other side of the fire, giving him a cocky grin. There was a confidence to his stride that told the man sitting by the fire exactly what his visitor had been. Or perhaps what he still was.

"Hello there, friend."

"That remains to be seen," he replied, his grey eyes flashing in the dim glow of the flames.

"Remains to be seen?" asked the visitor, clearly confused. "What do you mean by that?"

Studying the visitor with a keen eye, he took a moment before responding. Clearly, the axe-wielding fellow had put a great deal of work into finding him. The location he had selected for his campsite was well off the beaten trail and well hidden unless you had come this way before. Or unless you knew exactly what you were looking for.

His visitor was a soldier.

Or rather the visitor had been.

Or maybe the visitor still was.

Depending on the need.

He was certain of it. He could tell by the man's bearing even though he was trying to hide it.

Regardless, at that moment the man was more than just a soldier. The whip coiled on his belt gave him away.

"I mean I don't know yet if you're my friend. That still needs to be determined. Of course, I won't be holding my breath on the answer."

He watched the man on the other side of the fire nod. The soldier gave him a half smile and then a wink, as if they both already knew how the game they were engaged in was going to end, yet both still felt the need to play it.

Then the soldier rested the haft of his axe against his shoulder, his smile shifting into a smirk.

He knew what his visitor was thinking. The sometime soldier wasn't quite sure what to make of him. Few people traveled in the Highlands by themselves anymore.

That suggested to the soldier that he wasn't aware of the dangers haunting these peaks or he simply didn't care.

The first possibility didn't bother the soldier. Many people having just arrived in the Highlands learned of the perils hidden within these mountains too late to help themselves.

The second possibility obviously did. And with good reason.

He should have been frightened by the soldier's appearance. Or at least nervous.

But he wasn't.

That made the soldier uncomfortable. That and the fact that his annoyance at the soldier for interrupting the quiet of the evening radiated from him, almost as if it were a physical thing.

"You know, it's not safe to be out here on your own."

"That's what I've been told," he replied in a disinterested tone.

The soldier with the axe waited for him to say more. When he didn't reply, the soldier scrunched up his face, not realizing that with his drawn features and his unkempt whiskers he made himself look like a ferret when doing so.

He enjoyed his visitor's growing discomfort. The soldier really didn't know what to make of him. And that annoyed the soldier.

Good. Something else that he could use against him when the time was right.

He also could tell that the soldier was losing patience. The soldier had come up here for a reason and time was a wasting. He wanted to get this done so that he could enjoy the fire for the night and then move on. So best for him to just push ahead despite his feeling that there was something not quite right about him.

"Looks like you could use some company," said the soldier as he gripped the hilt of his axe tightly, finding some comfort in the steel as he took a step closer to the flames. "You look a bit lonely."

"I prefer to be on my own," he replied quietly.

The soldier stopped for just a second, then shrugged, ignoring the comment that had been infused with the hint of an order. In an attempt to demonstrate that he was in charge, the soldier sat down on a rock across the fire from him.

"What are you doing out here in the Highlands all on your own, friend?"

"Just passing through ... friend." He said the last as if it left a bitter taste in his mouth.

The soldier ignored him, intent on his task and looking forward to the fun he believed that he was going to have when this was over. "Shadow's Reach, I take it?"

"Thinking about it."

"What would you do in Shadow's Reach?"

"I have a few things in mind."

"Shadow's Reach is still a long way off," said the ferret-faced fellow, dropping the blade of his axe to the ground, then leaning forward, elbows pressed to his knees as his fingers reached for the warmth of the fire.

"I've been enjoying the hike. I'm not in a rush."

"Have you now?"

"I have."

"You're not the easiest person to talk with, friend."

"I'm not your friend, friend." He stared hard at the much too confident soldier sitting across from him. His eyes cold. He was less than impressed by what he saw. Less a soldier now and more a thug.

He was getting tired of this conversation. He was getting tired of his unwanted guest. He hoped that his visitor would move things along at a faster pace.

"No reason to get angry, friend." The soldier emphasized the last word, wanting to make sure he understood that he was losing patience as well. "I'm just trying to have a conversation with you. I'm trying to help you actually. I wouldn't want you to lose your way in these mountains."

"You're trying to buy time so that the men with you get to their assigned positions in the wood behind you."

"You don't say," the soldier replied, grinning. Clearly, the soldier didn't care about his revelation. Actually, the soldier seemed pleased that the cat was out of the bag.

"I do. The problem, though, is that you wanted your men to surround the campsite. They've realized that they can't because we're on a ledge. If I were you I'd be a little concerned because it took them a bit longer than it should have to figure that out and then reorganize themselves. Definitely not a good sign. Doesn't say much for their grasp of tactics or their decision making. Although it seems that they've finally worked things out and now believe that I won't be able to make a break for it."

"You're quite sure of yourself." With the light of the fire, the soldier took a closer look at the old man. He was glad that finally he could drop the pretense. After a time it became exhausting. "You look familiar, friend."

"I've been told that before."

"Very familiar, friend." For some strange reason, the soldier believed that he knew this old man, or at least he had seen him before, but for the life of him he couldn't recall when or where.

"I have a fairly common face."

The soldier grunted. "Where have you served?"

He smiled thinly then. Finally, they were getting to the meat of it. The fellow across from him must have concluded that his men had been given plenty of time to find their places.

Even so, the visitor with the axe waited a little longer. Probably still worried that he was going to try to escape.

His visitor had nothing to fear. He wasn't going anywhere. He was invested now. Besides, he already knew how this was going to end.

"Caledonia."

"That's not a very helpful response, friend," the soldier said through gritted teeth, struggling to reign in his rising anger. Talking with this old man was like talking to the child of the woman he had taken up with. Getting a useful response for the simplest of questions was like pulling teeth. The doomed old man's arrogance was both impressive and aggravating.

"I'm not here to help you ... friend. Now are we going to get to the reason you're really here. I've had a long day and I'd like to get some sleep."

The soldier snorted in laughter. Arrogant indeed. It wouldn't take him long to whip that trait out of the old man. And he'd enjoy doing it. "You know how to use that, friend?" He pointed to the sword leaning against the cracked stump.

"I wouldn't have it with me otherwise."

"It looks like it's a nice blade. Well made."

"It is. It's served me well over the years."

"You're not going to need it where you're going, friend.

You'll be trading it in for a pick axe or shovel. So I think I'll take it for my own."

"You can try," he replied. His smile became more menacing as he sensed that the next stage of the combat was about to begin. Finally they were getting to the heart of the engagement rather than dancing around the edges. This entire exchange had grown more than tiresome.

"I'll do more than try, old man. I'll carry it with pride."

"You can dream, but I can guarantee you that you'll never touch the hilt of this blade."

"Promises, promises."

"I keep my promises, friend," he said, biting off the last word. "You'll find that out soon enough."

"As do I, friend." The soldier pushed himself up from his seat, having enjoyed the warmth for a time, now feeling the need to end this little charade. "Are you ready to go? Clearly you know what's going on. There's no need for you to make this any more difficult than you already have."

"And where is it that you think I'm going?"

"To the mines, of course." The man motioned for him to come around the fire. "Come on, friend. As I said, no reason to make this difficult. Hand over the sword and then we can enjoy a quiet night before moving on tomorrow morning."

"And if I don't want to work in the mines?" he asked.

"You don't have a choice, friend. You're surrounded. You're outnumbered. Just count yourself lucky that we didn't treat you the way we've treated some of the others who've proven obstinate."

"You don't want to hurt me too badly because you get paid more if you deliver healthy prisoners who can work."

"Now we're understanding one another," the soldier said with a bright smile as he hefted his axe. "That wasn't so difficult after all, now was it?"

"So that's the way of it. Into the mines. I get worked to death. You take the golds for me."

"It is, indeed. Sorry, friend, but that's the way of the world here in New Caledonia. The strong survive. The weak don't. And as I said, I'll take your sword as well. You're not going to need it where you're going and I've got a use for it."

The slaver whistled sharply, three men stepping out of the darkness. All three held their whips loosely in their hands, swords sheathed across their backs.

It was exactly as he thought. They wanted him as healthy and whole as possible. It would be easier for him to recover from a slash from a whip than one inflicted by a sword.

"You sure you want to do this. I'll give you one chance for you and your men to leave here unharmed."

The soldier turned slaver stared at him, and then he and his men broke out into laughter.

"You really are annoying," the slaver said, "but you're funny as well. We'll have a good time getting to know one another as we head to the mine."

The leader of the slavers nodded. His men stepped around the fire in response. They pulled the grips on their whips back toward their shoulders, allowing the steel tips to trail along the ground.

They were experienced in their work. They knew how to use their weapons.

He believed that the one coming at him from his left would aim for his left leg. The two coming at him from his right would aim for his right leg and his right arm, assuming by where his sword was placed that he was right handed.

Easy. No fuss. A quick capture.

He could see it in their eyes. These slavers had done it before many times. They assumed that they would do it many more times in the future in just the same manner.

One old man, even an old man with a sword, would offer them little in the way of a challenge.

That was their mistake. The slavers were ready for what they assumed would be a simple takedown.

And, he had to admit, it did prove to be a simple takedown. Just not for them.

He moved faster than the shadows playing across the fire, the three slavers barely seeing him pull his sword from its sheath. The slaver to his left didn't know what had happened until he looked down and saw the steel sticking out of his gut. The man whimpered softly in pain, an acknowledgment of his own end clear as his eyes glazed over. The dying slaver dropped to the ground with a heavy sigh when he pulled the blade free.

The eyes of the two slavers coming at him from the other direction widened in shock. They had never seen anyone move so rapidly or with such lethality.

The two slavers pulled back their whips, preparing to send the spiked tips streaking through the air.

They were too slow. Much, much too slow.

He glided around the fire as if he were a part of the gloom, slashing with an economical motion across the throat of the closest slaver.

The man released his whip, his hands pawing frantically at the blood gushing from his throat. He dropped to his knees, sagging, unable to stop the flow of red as his life poured out onto the rocky ground.

With the last slaver distracted by his dying friend, he cut down with his steel, slicing through the whip that was streaking toward his neck, the sharp tip whistling off into the darkness. Reversing his motion, he brought his steel up in an arc that sliced from groin to gut.

Satisfied with the efficiency of his work, he stepped back and returned to where he had been sitting, staring across the fire at the man with the axe who had felt the need to converse with him instead of just sending all of his men at him at once.

"You should have accepted my offer when you could have," the slaver hissed through clenched teeth, still trying to come to grips with the slaughter he had just witnessed.

It was at that moment that the third slaver, hands pressing futilely to the horrific wound across his midsection, ribs and organs exposed, dropped face first into the fire, sending up a shower of sparks.

Clearly, the leader of this band of slavers was not happy. His right eye was twitching. A nervous tic he assumed, probably brought on by stress or anger or a combination of both.

He smiled as he reached that conclusion. The slaver hadn't expected this to happen. His men were all experienced in their work.

Yet, he had made the three who came for him look like fools. That meant the lead slaver looked like a fool as well, and the man with the axe couldn't have that.

"Are you lucky or good?" the soldier turned slaver asked, playing for time as he tried to work out a new strategy as quickly as he could.

"Probably a little of both," he admitted.

The slaver nodded. He had decided what he was going to do next. The old man had killed three of his friends in just a few seconds. The old man would have a harder time against his entire gang. "Let's see how you do against the rest of my men."

Once again, the slaver whistled. His remaining men walked out from the darkness. Only a few of them still grasped their whips. The rest had opted for their swords.

They didn't want to meet the same fate as their comrades. Whips were of little use against a man who knew how to use a blade with such practiced efficiency.

"You sure you want to do this?" he asked from across the fire. His tone suggested that he wasn't worried about the number of slavers standing against him. Rather, he sounded more resigned to what was going to be required of him.

"Oh, I do. I really, really do. Forget the mines. I'm just going to cut you into little pieces."

"Mind if we join the fun?"

The leader of the slavers was so startled by this new voice that he jumped an inch off the ground. He turned around swiftly, almost tripping over the rock behind him as he took in the four newcomers who stood at the edge of the shadows.

The petite woman carried a nocked bow. Two of the men held swords. They radiated a competence that suggested that they knew what they were doing with their steel.

The last was the largest of the three, a long, thin scar running across his bald head. He carried what looked like an overlarge blacksmith's hammer, a weapon that most men probably couldn't carry, much less swing.

"Who are you?" demanded the slaver.

Several of his men had turned to face these new arrivals. They still held the advantage in numbers. But that didn't make them feel any better.

The slavers' unease was made plain by how they gripped the hilts of their swords nervously and shuffled from side to side. The confidence that they normally enjoyed when taking captives, which had begun to drain away when they observed the old man kill their friends so swiftly, spiraled down even faster upon seeing these four new arrivals.

"Just some concerned Highlanders," the bald man replied pleasantly.

"Concerned Highlanders?" the slaver repeated, still trying to understand what was going on. Who in their right mind would take on a full contingent of slavers? Well, an almost full contingent, he admitted to himself. He didn't want to think about the men who he had lost just moments before, although he was finding it difficult because Rolf, who had collapsed into the fire, was beginning to burn and the stench that he was giving off was horrendous. "You're going to try to help the old man? Are you serious?"

The scarred man chuckled softly. "From what we saw, the old man as you call him doesn't need our help. But we do need some exercise, so we thought that we would join in the fun. Tommie!"

The arrow streaked from the woman's bow, slamming into the chest of the lead slaver. The stout fellow stood there for just a few more heartbeats, not quite comprehending what had happened, before dropping his axe and falling into the fire on his back, joining his already burning comrade.

The shock of that attack set the tone, the fight that followed short and swift. The Highlanders, aided by the swordsman, made quick work of the slavers.

Forcing them up against the fire, the slavers had nowhere to go. With Tommie staying on the outside and picking her targets, she took down three more men on her own.

After that, it was just a matter of finishing off the rest. All of whom lost interest in the fight before it really even began. All of them desperate to escape. Yet none of them had the skill or wherewithal to get past the old man with the sword or the scarred fellow with the hammer.

"Thank you for your help, Sergeant Westgard." He raised his blade, already wiped clean of blood, to his forehead. He gave the scarred man a nod of respect. "As always, your timing is excellent."

"Thank you, Blademaster," the man with the hammer replied. He raised the head of his weapon to his forehead as well, returning the gesture to his former commander and mentor.

"A pleasure to come across you here. And I see that many of your friends from the Royal Guard are still with you."

"It's that sense of loyalty I instill in others, Blademaster. Once they get to know me, they can't get enough of me."

Tommie snorted in amusement. "It's something all right, though likely not that."

"And just as respectful as I remember them," the Blademaster replied with a grin.

That earned a few quiet laughs from the two Highlanders standing with Tommie.

"We'll check the woods around us, just to make sure," said Martin.

Bertie followed him beyond the fire and in among the trees. Tommie remained where she was, bow on her string. Ready. Just in case.

"So this is what you're doing here in the Highlands, Duff?" asked the Blademaster, having sheathed his sword in the scabbard he held in his hand.

"What do you mean?"

"Helping people in need."

Duff shrugged sheepishly. "Just doing what I can. Slavers, Stalkers, Wraiths. They have no place here."

The Blademaster smiled. "A leopard can't change his spots."

Duff smiled, having heard the Blademaster tell him that many times in the past. Hearing one of the slavers groan, he stepped over to the man.

Duff studied the wound across the slaver's chest. It was only a matter of time. He nodded, relaying to the man what he was intending to do. He saw in the slaver's eyes that the fellow understood and appreciated his kindness.

Duff reached down and picked up the man's sword. With a quick stab, the point of the sword cut into the slaver's throat, speeding the dying man on his way.

Duff's action didn't faze the Blademaster in the least. Especially since he had been the one to teach his former Sergeant that he should never leave a dying man to his misery, even when he deserved it.

"It's been a while, Sergeant."

"It has, Blademaster."

"I take it that these are the slavers that are such a problem in these peaks."

"They are. Or at least these were. And they're not even the worst of the lot."

"I've heard of these men. Of the Stalkers and Wraiths as well."

"It seems like we need to have a conversation, Blademaster, if you're going to be traveling through the Highlands."

"That we do, Sergeant."

2. DISAPPOINTING NEWS

"What was the take, Farkan?"

"Not as good as we would have liked, my Lady," replied the soldier as he paged through the manifest he had acquired from the ship's captain.

Instead of the leather armor so common to the provincial Guards in the Territories, the man wore a pair of loose-fitting trousers and a worn, dirty shirt over his broad shoulders with the sleeves rolled up. He also had a cutlass thrust into his belt along with several daggers. He was used to the daggers.

Instead of the cutlass, he would have preferred the long sword with which he was so familiar. But that weapon wouldn't fit with what he was playing at now.

He could bear it, nonetheless. A job was a job, and this job paid well. So he could do without his favored blade for a while longer.

"Explain," the woman demanded sharply. "This ship carried everything we needed. Nothing that we really wanted appears to be in the hold."

"Yes, my Lady, I understand. And my apologies, my Lady."

"I don't need your apologies," cut in the woman. "I want an answer, Farkan."

"Of course, my Lady. I was getting to that." He sighed. This was going to be a difficult conversation. He didn't need this so early in the morning. "When we seized this ship, it had already made several stops. The only thing left in the hold when we got to her was some grain and a few crates and pallets with some pottery and furniture. And the grain was going bad, which explained why whoever ordered it refused to accept it. Weevils." He shrugged his shoulders and gave her a look that said that what was done was done. No sense in getting angry about bad luck.

"Why did it take so long for you to find this ship, Farkan?" asked the woman, her hands clenched into fists.

This was supposed to be an easy seizure. She had been assured that it would be. Apparently not.

Maybe Farkan was incompetent. Maybe she trusted him too much. If that proved to be the case, then she would deal with him in a way that would ensure the other captains working for her understood what the cost of failure was.

"The particulars that I gave you were from the best sources that I have," she growled. "They are never wrong. You should have taken the ship before it reached its first port of call."

"Yes, my Lady," agreed Farkan, beginning to feel distinctly uncomfortable. His employer had a very short and sharp temper, and he had no desire to feel the brunt of her anger. Not after the stories he had heard. "We would have, and we were about to do so in fact. We caught up to her three days out from Ballinasloe. Right before we were about to attack, three cutters came out of the sun. I didn't believe it would be wise to try to take on three ships all at one time. Doing so would have put our larger mission at risk. We withdrew and caught up to her again farther along on her journey."

"You made the decision to withdraw?" demanded the

woman. "You didn't withdraw! You ran! I thought you were a man of character, Farkan. A man of courage. Yet you sailed away like a dog with his tail between his legs. A neutered dog, in fact."

The woman's eyes blazed fiercely. She began flexing her fingers and then making and unmaking a fist with her right hand, like she was preparing to strike him. Or reach for the sword at her left hip.

The grizzled veteran began to stammer, his discomfort growing. He knew how good she was with a blade.

"We had no choice, my Lady. I swear. It was three of the Carlomin cutters, the ones with the rams on the prows. If it wasn't them, we would have taken them on. But we couldn't take the risk of one of those ship killers slicing into us. And those cutters were fast. We barely got away. If not for the fog that we found, we wouldn't have. I swear it, my Lady. We wouldn't have withdrawn if we didn't have any other choice."

"The Carlomins," spat out Farkan's employer as if the name was a curse.

That young woman and her mother were becoming an increasingly bigger irritant. An irritant that needed to be removed as swiftly as possible. Yet how to do that?

Hakea Roosarian contemplated that question, lost in thought as she stood atop the floating pier built within the hidden cove, her men continuing to bring out of the hold of the seized ship anything that might be of use to them. Which was very little.

It was going to be slim pickings, which Hakea didn't find surprising. Obviously, the merchant who owned the vessel had instructed his captain to get the most valuable items off first, understanding the risk of sailing along the New Caledonian coast these days.

What the merchant was losing now, other than his ship if she chose to take it – which she would because she needed to get something of value out of this missed opportunity, would have little impact upon him. Because he still had a dozen vessels sailing back and forth across the Burnt Ocean.

He'd recoup the loss of the ship in a matter of months. She'd need to try again to gain the leverage she needed on him.

Worse, those two upstart women were enjoying the success that she so richly deserved. The success that she would have been reaping by now if they hadn't refused to bring her into their company as she had proposed.

Talia and Isana Carlomin had stood up to her, the Governor of Fal Carrach, treating her like someone who didn't deserve their respect. Like someone who didn't need to be obeyed.

That was bad enough all on its own. But now they were taking a more aggressive role against the pirates working along the coast. And that meant that they were interfering directly in her business.

Hakea couldn't allow that to continue. Too much was at stake.

She would deal with the two Carlomin women just as she did the father. And soon.

Because not only were their efforts hindering her men working in the Sea of Mist, but also because they were giving the other merchants the idea that they could protect themselves if they worked together. That they didn't need to listen to her entreaties. That they didn't need her.

She had to put a stop to that. Swiftly.

She had come to Fal Carrach to make a name for herself, to make her fortune and to achieve the position in life that she had no chance of achieving in Caledonia. She had had little choice.

Hakea Roosarian was the daughter of one of the lesser lords of Roo's Nest, the youngest brother of the Duke, Wencilius Roosarian.

She found herself in the Territories because of the mistakes her father had made. Even so, that didn't mean that she couldn't make the most of her circumstances.

Her father and uncle had a falling out, and she really couldn't blame her uncle for what he did as a result. She could place the full weight of blame on her father for that, and she did.

Wittan Roosarian stupidly had tried to remove his brother as Duke of Roo's Nest, thinking that he could steal the seat right out from under him. It didn't work out as he had hoped.

Her father had forgotten one key lesson. Well, many important lessons actually, but in her opinion, this indeed was the most important.

It didn't really matter who ruled in a Duchy so long as you had the Guard behind you. And that's where her father had badly misjudged.

Wittan had thought that he could bring the Guard to his side after just a few conversations and vague promises to its commanding officers that likely would not be kept unless absolutely necessary. The Guard of Roo's Nest had ignored him, hearing the falsehoods in her father's words, and remained loyal to her uncle.

Her father had sealed his fate as soon as that happened.

Hakea had watched when her father was taken to the chopping block. The once proud and very foolish man had been blubbering like a child and pissing his pants when they placed his neck against the wood. The headsman hadn't wasted any time. With one swing of that very large axe, Hakea had become the last of her father's line.

She both loved and hated her father for what he had done. She wasn't upset that he had tried to take the throne for himself. She was upset that he had failed.

She meant to take what her father couldn't here in New Caledonia. Once she did, she would rebuild the line.

And even though Uncle Wencilius had killed his own

brother, regrettably so he had told her and she had believed him, she was still thankful for what he had given her.

A chance.

He had gifted her a grant to the Territory of Fal Carrach. Probably out of a mixture of regret and guilt, as she had been his favorite niece.

He chose not to kill her for her father's treachery, an act of mercy, but he didn't want her in Caledonia where she could cause trouble. Sending her to New Caledonia was the best solution for everyone.

Yet though she had Fal Carrach, which was more than she could have ever expected to gain in Caledonia, still she wasn't satisfied.

She wanted more. So much more.

And she would do whatever was necessary to get what she wanted.

She was about to rip into Farkan and tell him exactly what he deserved for his failure, desperate to release the anger boiling within her.

Instead, she held her tongue when she saw the handful of men with their hands tied behind their backs who were brought stumbling out of the hatch and made to walk toward the gangplank that led down to the dock.

"Why are they here?" Hakea asked, distracted by the sailors who had survived the assault.

Farkan jumped at the chance to redirect his employer's attention. "They hid during the attack. We didn't find them until we'd come into the cove and were doing a final search for hidden holds."

Hakea nodded, understanding. Most merchants had a storage area or two secreted about their vessels. There were times when they didn't want certain cargo to be found.

"How did you find the holds?"

"It wasn't easy," replied Farkan, hoping that this might be a chance to impress Governor Roosarian and perhaps place himself in a better light. "Whenever we take a ship, I assign a squad of men to work their way through the vessel, knocking on the walls and the decks to see if they can identify any hollow spaces that shouldn't be there. On this ship, there was only one." He motioned toward the sailors who were just now stepping down onto the dock. "They're what we found rather than what we were hoping for."

Hakea nodded. She was surprised and also disappointed. She would have much preferred finding a secret cargo rather than a handful of sailors hiding away like rats.

"You know what to do," she said, her voice cold.

"Yes, my Lady. It will be done as you've ordered."

She allowed her captains the discretion to decide whether to leave alive those captured when a ship was seized, unless she gave express orders that an example needed to be made. Having a few survivors often was useful to her purposes. They helped to spread stories about the pirates ravaging the eastern coast of New Caledonia. Stoking the fear that was already prevalent.

She couldn't do that this time.

These sailors had seen her men at work. They had seen the cove and likely could locate it if they were of such a mind.

Worst of all, they had seen her.

She couldn't permit that.

3. CREATURES FROM THE DEEP

"Majdi, what do you think you're doing?" demanded Declan.

The largest member of the Blood Company stood with the archers positioned at the stern deck, another row of archers just above them on the helm. Rather than holding a bow with a quiver of arrows across his back, the gladiator hefted a harpoon with several more right next to him stuck point first into the deck.

"I was hoping to do a little fishing," he replied with a straight face, although the comment drew several guffaws of laughter from the men and women standing with him.

Declan stared at Majdi for quite a long time, his grim expression not changing, the gladiators around Majdi beginning to get nervous, before he too burst out laughing. That got many of the gladiators around them laughing even more, the humor helping to break the tension that had been building as the three Bakunawa chasing them through the increasingly rougher water drew steadily closer.

"If you catch anything, I get first cut," said Declan.

Majdi grinned at that. "You have a deal."

Declan glanced quickly behind the *Freedom*. He had been

tracking the three huge wakes surging toward them for the last hour. They were close now. No more than a few hundred yards behind them. Approaching at a remarkable speed, because the *Freedom* was flying through the water, the hull barely touching the ocean as the tempestuous blasts of wind filled her sails.

He thought that he could see the sharp blue of the animals' eyes breaking through the water that surged around the sea dragons as their terrifyingly long bodies slithered through the waves.

At this distance, he couldn't be certain. He was certain that the Bakunawa had just picked up their pace.

It was time. The next battle was about to begin.

The Bakunawa were done hunting. They were ready to feast.

"Archers, prepare to fire!" Declan shouted.

"I can't believe those sea dragons are staying with us." Bryen stood at the helm right next to Captain Gregson, impressed by the Bakunawa's speed and tenacity.

"This is nothing," he replied. "I've heard of those beasts outswimming a typhoon because they had a pod of blue whales in their sights."

"And no blue whales near us to distract these monsters?" Bryen asked.

"Unfortunately not."

"You're not making me feel any better about our chances of escaping."

"I'm not trying to."

But that was the question, wasn't it, thought Captain Gregson. Could they escape the Bakunawa?

When he had first taken the helm of the *Freedom*, he had

thought that perhaps they could. This was the fastest ship he had ever been given the privilege of commanding.

Now, he knew better. Their sails were stretched to the breaking point by the gales surging across the Burnt Ocean from east to west, and even then the sea dragons had no trouble at all staying with them.

The Bakunawa had been pursuing them for several hours now, and they showed no signs of flagging. Even worse, they were swimming faster. Narrowing the gap, slowly but steadily.

He could try to evade the beasts, swerving in different directions.

He discarded that idea as soon as it came to him. That would only slow them down.

He wasn't trying to avoid a drift of icebergs. He was trying to elude the fastest predator in the ocean.

The only way to do that was to make sure that the *Freedom's* sails stayed full with the wind, just as they were now. He could try to tack to find stronger gusts, but he didn't think that he would find much success doing that.

The sails were bursting with air, the masts creaking and cracking as they strained against the powerful rush of wind. Besides, if he shifted off their present course, it would only make it that much easier for the Bakunawa to catch them.

Looking over his shoulder, Gregson cursed quietly. In just the last few seconds, the Bakunawa had swum even closer. They were gaining on the *Freedom* faster than he would have liked.

He was running out of options. At this pace, the monsters would be on them in a matter of minutes.

There was only one choice now. Stay on their current track.

"How long can you keep this up?" asked Bryen, having reached the same conclusion as Captain Gregson.

"We shouldn't have to worry about the wind," replied Gregson, who turned back toward the bow, studying the sails, understanding from his decades on the open ocean that he had little hope of getting even one more knot out of the vessel. Something that he desperately wanted to do although he understood that even if they somehow did that, it would do them little good and it would only increase the risk of them losing a mast. "It will stay with us for at least the next few hours. The problem is that we might not have a few more hours left with those beasts in pursuit."

There was little that he could do to stop what was about to happen. The Bakunawa were going to catch them. They had made a good run of it, but it wasn't going to be enough.

Unless …

"Emelina," Gregson said. "Hard to port, please."

"Hard to port?" his wife replied, seeking confirmation. "Piotr, if we …"

"I know, Emelina. Hard to port."

Going against her better judgment, Emelina did as her husband ordered, turning the wheel sharply toward the south. She understood his thinking, and although his decision worried her, she didn't disagree with him. At least not enough to argue with him, and she would never do that when they both stood on the helm.

The Bakunawa were about to catch them. There was no denying that reality.

But turning into the fast-approaching storm, the bank of dark clouds blotting out the horizon for as far as they could see, might give them a chance to escape, assuming those animals didn't sink the ship before they reached the tempest.

"You're a brave man," said Bryen, understanding what Captain Gregson had in mind. "Not many others would have made the decision that you just did."

"Not brave," answered Captain Gregson. "Just desperate. I'd prefer taking my chances against the storm rather than against the Bakunawa. The storm will be much more forgiving than those monsters."

Bryen wasn't in a position to argue with him.

"The question now is, are we going to get into that storm before those beasts attack?" asked Captain Gregson.

Bryen turned back toward the stern. "No, we're not. We're going to have to fight."

The Bakunawa in the center had increased its speed even more, pushing in front of the other two, the animal's powerful tail propelling it through the water and creating a wake at least thirty feet in height. He wasn't too worried about that animal. At least he could see it.

He was more concerned about the other two Bakunawa. Those monsters had disappeared beneath the waves.

That could mean only one thing.

The Bakunawa were about to attack.

~

THE END OF CHAPTER 3.

To keep reading *Monsters in the Mist*, visit my author website at PeterWachtBooks.com or Amazon to get your copy.

LOOKING FOR MORE …

This short story is a prelude to the events in *The Tales of the Territories* and is FREE to readers who receive my newsletter. Learn more at PeterWachtBooks.com.

www.ingramcontent.com/pod-product-compliance
Lightning Source LLC
Chambersburg PA
CBHW070231200726
48293CB00005B/1573